COUNT ZERO

COUNT ZERO

William Gibson

The right of William Gibson to be identified as the author of this
work has been asserted by him in accordance with the
Copyright, Designs and Patents Act 1988.

First published in Great Britain in 1986
by Gollancz
An imprint of the Orion Publishing Group
Carmelite House, 50 Victoria Embankment,
London EC4Y 0DZ
An Hachette UK Company

This edition published in Great Britain in 2016 by Gollancz

5 7 9 10 8 6 4

A CIP catalogue record for this book
is available from the British Library

ISBN 978 1 473 21740 9

Typeset by Deltatype Ltd, Birkenhead, Merseyside

Printed in Great Britain by CPI Group (UK) Ltd,
Croydon, CR0 4YY

www.williamgibsonbooks.com
www.orionbooks.co.uk
www.gollancz.co.uk

FOR MY D
Quiero hacer contigo
lo que la primavera
hace con los cerezos
– Neruda

COUNT ZERO INTERRUPT
– On receiving an interrupt,
decrement the counter to zero.

1

Smooth-Running Gun

They set a slamhound on Turner's trail in New Delhi, slotted it to his pheromones and the colour of his hair. It caught up with him on a street called Chandni Chawk and came scrambling for his rented BMW through a forest of bare brown legs and pedicab tyres. Its core was a kilogram of recrystallised hexogene and flaked TNT.

He didn't see it coming. The last he saw of India was the pink stucco façade of a place called the Khush-Oil Hotel.

Because he had a good agent, he had a good contract. Because he had a good contract, he was in Singapore an hour after the explosion. Most of him, anyway. The Dutch surgeon liked to joke about that, how an unspecified percentage of Turner hadn't made it out of Palam International on that first flight, and had to spend the night there in a shed, in a support vat.

It took the Dutchman and his team three months to put Turner together again. They cloned a square metre of skin for him, grew it on slabs of collagen and shark-cartilage polysaccharides. They bought eyes and genitals on the open market. The eyes were green.

He spent most of those three months in a ROM-generated simstim construct of an idealised New England boyhood of the previous century. The Dutchman's visits were grey dawn dreams, nightmares that faded as the sky lightened beyond his second-floor bedroom window. You could smell the lilacs, late at night. He read Conan Doyle by the light of a sixty-watt bulb behind a parchment shade printed with clipper ships. He masturbated in the smell of clean cotton sheets and thought about cheerleaders. The Dutchman opened a door in his back brain and came strolling in to ask questions, but in the morning his mother called him down to Wheaties, eggs and bacon, coffee with milk and sugar.

And one morning he woke in a strange bed, the Dutchman standing beside a window spilling tropical green and a sunlight that hurt his eyes.

'You can go home now, Turner. We're done with you. You're good as new.'

He was good as new. How good was that? He didn't know. He took the things the Dutchman gave him and flew out of Singapore. Home was the next airport Hyatt.

And the next. And ever was.

He flew on. His credit chip was a rectangle of black mirror, edged with gold. People behind counters smiled when they saw it, nodded. Doors opened, closed behind him. Wheels left ferroconcrete, drinks arrived, dinner was served.

In Heathrow a vast chunk of memory detached itself from a blank bowl of airport sky and fell on him. He vomited into a blue plastic canister without breaking stride. When he arrived at the counter at the end of the corridor, he changed his ticket.

He flew to Mexico.

And woke to the rattle of steel buckets on tile, wet swish of brooms, a woman's body warm against his own.

The room was a tall cave. Bare white plaster reflected

sound with too much clarity; somewhere beyond the clatter of the maids in the morning courtyard was the pounding of surf. The sheets bunched between his fingers were coarse chambray, softened by countless washings.

He remembered sunlight through a broad expanse of tinted window. An airport bar, Puerto Vallarta. He'd had to walk twenty metres from the plane, eyes screwed shut against the sun. He remembered a dead bat pressed flat as a dry leaf on runway concrete.

He remembered riding a bus, a mountain road, and the reek of internal combustion, the borders of the windshield plastered with postcard holograms of blue and pink saints. He'd ignored the steep scenery in favour of a sphere of pink Lucite and the jittery dance of mercury at its core. The knob crowned the bent steel stem of the transmission lever, slightly larger than a baseball. It had been cast around a crouching spider blown from clear glass, hollow, half filled with quicksilver. Mercury jumped and slid when the driver slapped the bus through switchback curves, swayed and shivered in the straight-aways. The knob was ridiculous, handmade, baleful; it was there to welcome him back to Mexico.

Among the dozen-odd microsofts the Dutchman had given him was one that would allow a limited fluency in Spanish, but in Vallarta he'd fumbled behind his left ear and inserted a dustplug instead, hiding the socket and plug beneath a square of flesh-tone micropore. A passenger near the back of the bus had a radio. A voice had periodically interrupted the brassy pop to recite a kind of litany, strings of ten-digit figures, the day's winning numbers in the national lottery.

The woman beside him stirred in her sleep.

He raised himself on one elbow to look at her. A stranger's face, but not the one his life in hotels had taught him to expect. He would have expected a routine beauty, bred out

3

of cheap elective surgery and the relentless Darwinism of fashion, an archetype cooked down from the major media faces of the previous five years.

Something Midwestern in the bone of the jaw, archaic and American. The blue sheets were rucked across her hips, the sunlight angling in through hardwood louvres to stripe her long thighs with diagonals of gold. The faces he woke with in the world's hotels were like God's own hood ornaments. Women's sleeping faces, identical and alone, naked, aimed straight out to the void. But this one was different. Already, somehow, there was meaning attached to it. Meaning and a name.

He sat up, swinging his legs off the bed. His soles registered the grit of beach-sand on cool tile. There was a faint, pervasive smell of insecticide. Naked, head throbbing, he stood. He made his legs move. Walked, tried the first of two doors, finding white tile, more white plaster, a bulbous chrome shower head hung from rust-spotted iron pipe. The sink's taps offered identical trickles of blood-warm water. An antique wristwatch lay beside a plastic tumbler, a mechanical Rolex on a pale leather strap.

The bathroom's shuttered windows were unglazed, strung with a fine green mesh of plastic. He peered out between hardwood slats, wincing at the hot clean sun, and saw a dry fountain of flower-painted tiles and the rusted carcass of a VW Rabbit.

Allison. That was her name.

She wore frayed khaki shorts and one of his white t-shirts. Her legs were very brown. The clockwork Rolex, with its dull stainless case, went around her left wrist on its pigskin strap. They went walking, down the curve of beach, towards Barre de Navidad. They kept to the narrow strip of firm wet sand above the line of surf.

Already they had a history together; he remembered her at a stall that morning in the little town's iron-roofed mercado, how she'd held the huge clay mug of boiled coffee in both hands. Mopping eggs and salsa from the cracked white plate with a tortilla, he'd watched flies circling fingers of sunlight that found their way through a patchwork of palm frond and corrugated siding. Some talk about her job with some legal firm in LA, how she lived alone in one of the ramshackle pontoon towns tethered off Redondo. He'd told her he was in personnel. Or had been, anyway. 'Maybe I'm looking for a new line of work …'

But talk seemed secondary to what there was between them, and now a frigate bird hung overhead, tacking against the breeze, slid sideways, wheeled, and was gone. They both shivered with the freedom of it, the mindless glide of the thing. She squeezed his hand.

A blue figure came marching up the beach towards them, a military policeman headed for town, spit-shined black boots unreal against the soft bright beach. As the man passed, his face dark and immobile beneath mirrored glasses, Turner noted the carbine-format Steiner-Optic laser with Fabrique Nationale sights. The blue fatigues were spotless, creased like knives.

Turner had been a soldier in his own right for most of his adult life, although he'd never worn a uniform. A mercenary, his employers vast corporations warring covertly for the control of entire economies. He was a specialist in the extraction of top executives and research people. The multinationals he worked for would never admit that men like Turner existed …

'You worked your way through most of a bottle of Herradura last night,' she said.

He nodded. Her hand, in his, was warm and dry. He was watching the spread of her toes with each step, the nails painted with chipped pink gloss.

The breakers rolled in, their edges transparent as green glass.

The spray beaded on her tan.

After their first days together, life fell into a simple pattern. They had breakfast in the mercado at a stall with a concrete counter worn smooth as polished marble. They spent the morning swimming, until the sun drove them back into the shuttered coolness of the hotel, where they made love under the slow wooden blades of the ceiling fan, then slept. In the afternoons they explored the maze of narrow streets behind the Avenida, or went hiking in the hills. They dined in beach-front restaurants and drank on the patios of the white hotels. Moonlight curled in the edge of the surf.

And gradually, without words, she taught him a new style of passion. He was accustomed to being served, serviced anonymously by skilled professionals. Now, in the white cave, he knelt on tile. He lowered his head, licking her, salt Pacific mixed with her own wet, her inner thighs cool against his cheeks. Palms cradling her hips, he held her, raised her like a chalice, lips pressing tight, while his tongue sought the locus, the point, the frequency that would bring her home. Then, grinning, he'd mount, enter, and find his own way there.

Sometimes, then, he'd talk, long spirals of unfocused narrative that spun out to join the sound of the sea. She said very little, but he'd learned to value what little she did say, and, always, she held him. And listened.

A week passed, then another. He woke to their final day together in that same cool room, finding her beside him. Over breakfast he imagined he felt a change in her, a tension.

They sunbathed, swam, and in the familiar bed he forgot the faint edge of anxiety.

In the afternoon, she suggested they walk down the beach, towards Barre, the way they'd gone that first morning.

Turner extracted the dustplug from the socket behind his ear and inserted a sliver of microsoft. The structure of Spanish settled through him like a tower of glass, invisible gates hinged on present and future, conditional, preterite perfect. Leaving her in the room, he crossed the Avenida and entered the market. He bought a straw basket, cans of cold beer, sandwiches, and fruit. On his way back, he bought a pair of sunglasses from the vendor in the Avenida.

His tan was dark and even. The angular patchwork left by the Dutchman's grafts was gone, and she had taught him the unity of his body. Mornings, when he met the green eyes in the bathroom mirror, they were his own, and the Dutchman no longer troubled his dreams with bad jokes and a dry cough. Sometimes, still, he dreamed fragments of India, a country he barely knew, bright splinters, Chandni Chawk, the smell of dust and fried breads …

The walls of the ruined hotel stood a quarter of the way down the bay's arc. The surf here was stronger, each wave a detonation.

Now she tugged him towards it, something new at the corners of her eyes, a tightness. Gulls scattered as they came hand in hand up the beach to gaze into shadow beyond empty doorways. The sand had subsided, allowing the structure's facade to cave in, walls gone, leaving the floors of the three levels hung like huge shingles from bent, rusted tendons of finger-thick steel, each one faced with a different colour and pattern of tile.

7

HOTEL PLAYA DEL M was worked in childlike seashell capitals above one concrete arch.

'Mar,' he said, completing it, though he'd removed the microsoft.

'It's over,' she said, stepping beneath the arch, into shadow.

'What's over?' He followed, the straw basket rubbing against his hip. The sand here was cold, dry, loose between his toes.

'Over. Done with. This place. No time here, no future.'

He stared at her, glanced past her to where rusted bedsprings were tangled at the junction of two crumbling walls.

'It smells like piss,' he said. 'Let's swim.'

The sea took the chill away, but a distance hung between them now. They sat on a blanket from Turner's room and ate, silently. The shadow of the ruin lengthened. The wind moved her sun-streaked hair.

'You make me think about horses,' he said finally.

'Well,' she said, as though she spoke from the depths of exhaustion, 'they've only been extinct for thirty years.'

'No,' he said, 'their hair. The hair on their necks, when they ran.'

'Manes,' she said, and there were tears in her eyes. 'Fuck it.' Her shoulders began to heave. She took a deep breath. She tossed her empty Carta Blanca can down the beach. 'It, me, what's it matter?' Her arms around him again. 'Oh, come on, Turner. Come on.'

And as she lay back, pulling him with her, he noticed something, a boat, reduced by distance to a white hyphen, where the water met the sky. When he sat up, pulling on his cut-off jeans, he saw the yacht. It was much closer now, a graceful sweep of white riding low in the water. Deep water. The beach must fall away almost vertically here, judging by

8

the strength of the surf. That would be why the line of hotels ended where it did, back along the beach, and why the ruin hadn't survived. The waves had licked away its foundation.

'Give me the basket.'

She was buttoning her blouse. He'd bought it for her in one of the tired little shops along the Avenida. Electric blue Mexican cotton, badly made. The clothing they bought in the shops seldom lasted more than a day or two.

'I said give me the basket.'

She did. He dug through the remains of their afternoon, finding his binoculars beneath a plastic bag of pineapple slices drenched in lime and dusted with cayenne. He pulled them out, a compact pair of 6 × 30 combat glasses. He snapped the integral covers from the objectives and the padded eyepieces, and studied the streamlined ideograms of the Hosaka logo. A yellow inflatable rounded the stern and swung towards the beach.

'Turner, I—'

'Get up.' Bundling the blanket and her towel into the basket. He took a last warm can of Carta Blanca from the basket and put it beside the binoculars. He stood, pulling her quickly to her feet, and forced the basket into her hands.

'Maybe I'm wrong,' he said. 'If I am, get out of here. Cut for that second stand of palms.' He pointed. 'Don't go back to the hotel. Get on a bus, Manzanillo or Vallarta. Go home.' He could hear the purr of the outboard now.

He saw the tears start, but she made no sound at all as she turned and ran, up past the ruin, clutching the basket, stumbling in a drift of sand. She didn't look back.

He turned, then, and looked towards the yacht. The inflatable was bouncing through the surf. The yacht was named *Tsushima*, and he'd last seen her in Hiroshima Bay. He'd seen the red Shinto gate at Itsukushima from her deck.

He didn't need the glasses to know that the inflatable's passenger would be Conroy, the pilot one of Hosaka's ninjas. He sat down cross-legged in the cooling sand and opened his last can of Mexican beer.

He looked back at the line of white hotels, his hands inert on one of *Tsushima*'s teak railings. Behind the hotels, the little town's three holograms glowed: Banamex, Aeronaves, and the cathedral's six-metre Virgin.

Conroy stood beside him. 'Crash job,' Conroy said. 'You know how it is.' Conroy's voice was flat and uninflected, as though he'd modelled it after a cheap voice-chip. His face was broad and white, dead white. His eyes were dark-ringed and hooded, beneath a peroxide thatch combed back from a wide forehead. He wore a black polo shirt and black slacks. 'In-side,' he said, turning. Turner followed, ducking to enter the cabin door. White screens, pale flawless pine; Tokyo's austere corporate chic.

Conroy settled himself on a low, rectangular cushion of slate-grey ultrasuede. Turner stood, his hands slack at his sides. Conroy took a knurled silver inhaler from the low enamel table between them. 'Choline enhancer?'

'No.'

Conroy jammed the inhaler into one nostril and snorted. 'You want some sushi?' He put the inhaler back on the table. 'We caught a couple of red snapper about an hour ago.'

Turner stood where he was, staring at Conroy.

'Christopher Mitchell,' Conroy said. 'Maas Biolabs. Their head hybridoma man. He's coming over to Hosaka.'

'Never heard of him.'

'Bullshit. How about a drink?'

Turner shook his head.

'Silicon's on the way out, Turner. Mitchell's the man who

made biochips work, and Maas is sitting on the major patents. You know that. He's the man for monoclonals. He wants out. You and me, Turner, we're going to shift him.'

'I think I'm retired, Conroy. I was having a good time, back there.'

'That's what the psych team in Tokyo say. I mean, it's not exactly your first time out of the box, is it? She's a field psychologist, on retainer to Hosaka.'

A muscle in Turner's thigh began to jump.

'They say you're ready, Turner. They were a little worried, after New Delhi, so they wanted to check it out. Little therapy on the side. Never hurts, does it?'

2

Marly

She'd worn her best for the interview, but it was raining in Brussels and she had no money for a cab. She walked from the Eurotrans station.

Her hand, in the pocket of her good jacket – a Sally Stanley but almost a year old – was a white knot around the crumpled telefax. She no longer needed it, having memorised the address, but it seemed she could no more release it than break the trance that held her here now, staring into the window of an expensive shop that sold menswear, her focus phasing between sedate flannel dress shirts and the reflection of her own dark eyes.

Surely the eyes alone would be enough to cost her the job. No need for the wet hair she now wished she'd let Andrea cut. The eyes displayed a pain and an inertia that anyone could read, and most certainly these things would soon be revealed to Herr Josef Virek, least likely of potential employers.

When the telefax had been delivered, she'd insisted on regarding it as some cruel prank, another nuisance call. She'd had enough of those, thanks to the media, so many that Andrea had ordered a special program for the apartment's phone, one that filtered out incoming calls from any number that wasn't listed in her permanent directory. But that, Andrea had insisted, must have been the reason for the telefax. How else could anyone reach her?

But Marly had shaken her head and huddled deeper into Andrea's old terry robe. Why would Virek, enormously wealthy, collector and patron, wish to hire the disgraced former operator of a tiny Paris gallery?

Then it had been Andrea's time for head-shaking, in her impatience with the new, the *disgraced* Marly Krushkhova, who spent entire days in the apartment now, who sometimes didn't bother to dress. The attempted sale, in Paris, of a single forgery, was hardly the novelty Marly imagined it to have been, she said. If the press hadn't been quite so anxious to show up the disgusting Gnass for the fool he most assuredly was, she continued, the business would hardly have been news. Gnass was wealthy enough, gross enough, to make for a weekend's scandal.

Andrea smiled. 'If you had been less attractive, you would have got far less attention.' Marly shook her head. 'And the forgery was Alain's. You were innocent. Have you forgotten that?' Marly went into the bathroom, still huddled in the threadbare robe, without answering.

Beneath her friend's wish to comfort, to help, Marly could already sense the impatience of someone forced to share a very small space with an unhappy, non-paying guest.

And Andrea had had to loan her the fare for the Eurotrans.

With a conscious, painful effort of will, she broke from the circle of her thoughts and merged with the dense but sedate flow of serious Belgian shoppers.

A girl in bright tights and a boyfriend's oversized loden jacket brushed past, scrubbed and smiling. At the next intersection, Marly noticed an outlet for a fashion line she'd favoured in her own student days. The clothes looked impossibly young.

In her white and secret fist, the telefax.

Galerie Duperey, 14 Rue au Beurre, Bruxelles.

Josef Virek.

The receptionist in the cool grey anteroom of the Galerie Duperey might well have grown there, a lovely and likely poisonous plant, rooted behind a slab of polished marble inlaid with an enamelled keyboard. She raised lustrous eyes as Marly approached. Marly imagined the click and whirr of shutters, her bedraggled image whisked away to some far corner of Josef Virek's empire.

'Marly Krushkhova,' she said, fighting the urge to produce the compacted wad of telefax, smooth it pathetically on the cool and flawless marble. 'For Herr Virek.'

'Fraulein Krushkhova,' the receptionist said, 'Herr Virek is unable to be in Brussels today.'

Marly stared at the perfect lips, simultaneously aware of the pain the words caused her and the sharp pleasure she was learning to take in disappointment. 'I see.'

'However, he has chosen to conduct the interview via a sensory link. If you will please enter the third door on your left ...'

The room was bare and white. On two walls hung un-framed sheets of what looked like rain-stained cardboard, stabbed through repeatedly with a variety of instruments. *Katatonenkunst*. Conservative. The sort of work one sold to committees sent round by the boards of Dutch commercial banks.

She sat down on a low bench covered in leather and finally allowed herself to release the telefax. She was alone, but as-sumed that she was being observed somehow.

'Fraulein Krushkhova.' A young man in a technician's dark green smock stood in the doorway opposite the one through which she'd entered. 'In a moment, please, you will cross the room and step through this door. Please grasp the

14

knob slowly, firmly, and in a manner that affords maximum contact with the flesh of your palm. Step through carefully. There should be a minimum of spatial disorientation.'

She blinked at him 'I beg—'

'The sensory link,' he said, and withdrew, the door closing behind him.

She rose, tried to tug some shape into the damp lapels of her jacket, touched her hair, thought better of it, took a deep breath, and crossed to the door. The receptionist's phrase had prepared her for the only kind of link she knew, a simstim signal routed via Bell Europa. She'd assumed she'd wear a helmet studded with dermatrodes, that Virek would use a passive viewer as a human camera.

But Virek's wealth was on another scale of magnitude entirely.

As her fingers closed around the cool brass knob, it seemed to squirm, sliding along a touch-spectrum of texture and temperature in the first second of contact.

Then it became metal again, green-painted iron, sweeping out and down, along a line of perspective, an old railing she grasped now in wonder.

A few drops of rain blew into her face.

Smell of rain and wet earth.

A confusion of small details, her own memory of a drunken art school picnic warring with the perfection of Virek's illusion.

Below her lay the unmistakable panorama of Barcelona, smoke hazing the strange spires of the Church of the Sagrada Familia. She caught the railing with her other hand as well, fighting vertigo. She knew this place. She was in Park Güell, Antonio Gaudí's tatty fairyland, on its barren rise behind the centre of the city. To her left, a giant lizard of crazy-quilt

15

ceramic was frozen in mid-slide down a ramp of rough stone. Its fountain-grin watered a bed of tired flowers.

'You are disoriented. Please forgive me.'

Josef Virek was perched below her on one of the park's serpentine benches, his wide shoulders hunched in a soft topcoat.

His features had been vaguely familiar to her all her life. Now she remembered, for some reason, a photograph of Virek and the king of England. He smiled at her. His head was large and beautifully shaped beneath a brush of stiff dark grey hair. His nostrils were permanently flared, as though he sniffed invisible winds of art and commerce. His eyes, very large behind the round, rimless glasses that were a trademark, were pale blue and strangely soft.

'Please.' He patted the bench's random mosaic of shattered pottery with a narrow hand. 'You must forgive my reliance on technology. I have been confined for over a decade to a vat. In some hideous industrial suburb of Stockholm. Or perhaps of hell. I am not a well man, Marly. Sit beside me.'

Taking a deep breath, she descended the stone steps and crossed the cobbles.

'Herr Virek,' she said, 'I saw you lecture in Munich, two years ago. A critique of Faessler and his *Autistiches Theater*. You seemed well then …'

'Faessler?' Virek's tanned forehead wrinkled. 'You saw a double. A hologram perhaps. Many things, Marly, are perpetrated in my name. Aspects of my wealth have become autonomous, by degrees; at times they even war with one another. Rebellion in the fiscal extremities. However, for reasons so complex as to be entirely occult, the fact of my illness has never been made public …'

She took her place beside him and peered down at the dirty pavement between the scuffed toes of her black Paris boots.

She saw a chip of pale gravel, a rusted paper clip, the small dusty corpse of a bee or hornet. 'It's amazingly detailed ...'

'Yes,' he said, 'the new Maas biochips. You should know,' he continued, 'that what I know of your private life is very nearly as detailed. More than you yourself do, in some instances.'

'You do?' It was easiest, she found, to focus on the city, picking out landmarks remembered from a half-dozen student holidays. There, just there, would be the Ramblas, parrots and flowers, the taverns serving dark beer and squid.

'Yes. I know that it was your lover who convinced you that you had found a lost Cornell original ...'

Marly shut her eyes.

'He commissioned the forgery, hiring two talented student-artisans and an established historian who found himself in certain personal difficulties ... He paid them with money he'd already extracted from your gallery, as you have no doubt guessed. You are crying ...'

Marly nodded. A cool forefinger tapped her wrist.

'I bought Gnass. I bought the police off the case. The press weren't worth buying; they rarely are. And now, perhaps, your slight notoriety may work to your advantage.'

'Herr Virek, I ...'

'A moment, please. Paco! Come here, child.'

Marly opened her eyes and saw a child of perhaps six years, tightly got up in dark suit coat and knickers, pale stockings, high-buttoned black patent boots. Brown hair fell across his forehead in a smooth wing. He held something in his hands, a box of some kind.

'Gaudí began the park in 1900,' Virek said. 'Paco wears the period costume. Come here, child. Show us your marvel.'

'Señor,' Paco lisped, bowing, and stepped forward to exhibit the thing he held.

Marly stared. Box of plain wood, glass-fronted. Objects ...

'Cornell,' she said, her tears forgotten. 'Cornell?' She turned to Virek.

'Of course not. The object set into that length of bone is a Braun biomonitor. This is the work of a living artist.'

'There are more? More boxes?'

'I have found seven. Over a period of three years. The Virek Collection, you see, is a sort of black hole. The unnatural density of my wealth drags irresistibly at the rarest works of the human spirit. An autonomous process, and one I ordinarily take little interest in …'

But Marly was lost in the box, in its evocation of impossible distances, of loss and yearning. It was sombre, gentle, and somehow childlike. It contained seven objects.

The slender fluted bone, surely formed for flight, surely from the wing of some large bird. Three archaic circuit boards, faced with mazes of gold A smooth white sphere of baked clay. An age-blackened fragment of lace. A finger-length segment of what she assumed was bone from a human wrist, greyish white, inset smoothly with the silicon shaft of a small instrument that must once have ridden flush with the surface of the skin – but the thing's face was seared and blackened.

The box was a universe, a poem, frozen on the boundaries of human experience.

'*Gracias*, Paco …'

Box and boy were gone.

She gaped.

'Ah. Forgive me, I have forgotten that these transitions are too abrupt for you. Now, however, we must discuss your assignment …'

'Herr Virek,' she said, 'what is "Paco"?'

'A subprogram.'

'I see.'

'I have hired you to find the maker of the box.'

'But, Herr Virek, with your resources ...'

'Of which you are now one, child. Do you not wish to be employed? When the business of Gnass having been stung with a forged Cornell came to my attention, I saw that you might be of use in this matter.' He shrugged. 'Credit me with a certain talent for obtaining desired results.'

'Certainly, Herr Virek! And, yes, I do wish to work!'

'Very well, You will be paid a salary. You will be given access to certain lines of credit, although, should you need to purchase, let us say, substantial amounts of real estate ...'

'Real estate?'

'Or a corporation, or spacecraft. In that event, you will require my indirect authorisation. Which you will almost certainly be given. Otherwise, you will have a free hand. I suggest, however, that you work on a scale with which you yourself are comfortable. Otherwise, you run the risk of losing touch with your intuition, and intuition, in a case such as this, is of crucial importance.' The famous smile glittered for her once more.

She took a deep breath. 'Herr Virek, what if I fail? How long do I have to locate this artist?'

'The rest of your life,' he said.

'Forgive me,' she found herself saying, to her horror, 'but I understood you to say that you live in a – a vat?'

'Yes, Marly. And from that rather terminal perspective, I should advise you to strive to live hourly in your own flesh. Not in the past, if you understand me. I speak as one who can no longer tolerate that simple state, the cells of my body having opted for the quixotic pursuit of individual careers. I imagine that a more fortunate man, or a poorer one, would have been allowed to die at last, or be coded at the core of some bit of hardware. But I seem constrained, by a byzantine net of circumstance that requires, I understand, something

19

like a tenth of my annual income. Making me, I suppose, the world's most expensive invalid. I was touched, Marly, at your affairs of the heart. I envy you the ordered flesh from which they unfold.'

And, for an instant, she stared directly into those soft blue eyes and knew, with an instinctive mammalian certainty, that the exceedingly rich were no longer even remotely human.

A wing of night swept Barcelona's sky, like the twitch of a vast slow shutter, and Virek and Güdell were gone, and she found herself seated again on the low leather bench, staring at torn sheets of stained cardboard.

3

Bobby Pulls a Wilson

It was such an easy thing, death. He saw that now: it just happened. You screwed up by a fraction and there it was, something chill and odourless, ballooning out from the four stupid corners of the room, your mother's Barrytown living room.

Shit, he thought, *Two-a-Day'll laugh his ass off, first time out and I pull a wilson.*

The only sound in the room was the faint steady burr of his teeth vibrating, supersonic palsy as the feedback ate into his nervous system. He watched his frozen hand as it trembled delicately, centimetres from the red plastic stud that could break the connection that was killing him

Shit.

He'd come home and got right down to it, slotted the ice-breaker he'd rented from Two-a-Day and jacked in. punching for the base he'd chosen as his first live target. Figured that was the way to do it; you wanna do it, then *do* it. He'd only had the little Ono-Sendai deck for a month, but he already knew he wanted to be more than just some Barrytown hot-dogger. Bobby Newmark, aka Count Zero, but it was already over. Shows never ended this way, not right at the beginning. In a show, the cowboy hero's girl or maybe his partner would run in, slap the trodes off, hit that little red OFF stud. So you'd make it, make it through.

But Bobby was alone now, his autonomic nervous system overridden by the defences of a database three thousand kilometres from Barrytown, and he knew it. There was some magic chemistry in that impending darkness, something that let him glimpse the infinite desirability of that room, with its carpet-coloured carpet and curtain-coloured curtains, its dingy foam sofa-suite, the angular chrome frame supporting the components of a six-year-old Hitachi entertainment module.

He'd carefully closed those curtains in preparation for his run, but now, somehow, he seemed to see out anyway, where the condos of Barrytown crested back in their concrete wave to break against the darker towers of the Projects. That condo-wave bristled with a fine insect fur of antennas and chicken-wired dishes, strung with lines of drying clothes. His mother liked to bitch about that; she had a dryer. He remembered her knuckles white on the imitation bronze of the balcony railing, dry wrinkles where her wrist was bent. He remembered a dead boy carried out of Big Playground on an alloy stretcher, bundled in plastic the same colour as a cop car. Fell and hit his head. Fell. Head. Wilson.

His heart stopped. It seemed to him that it fell sideways, kicked like an animal in a cartoon.

Sixteenth second of Bobby Newmark's death. His hot-dogger's death.

And something *leaned in*, vastness unutterable, from beyond the most distant edge of anything he'd ever known or imagined, and touched him.

::: WHAT ARE YOU DOING? WHY ARE THEY DOING THAT TO YOU?

Girlvoice, brownhair, darkeyes—

: KILLING ME KILLING ME GET IT OFF GET IT OFF.

22

Darkeyes, desertstar, tanshirt, girlhair –

::: BUT IT'S A TRICK, SEE? YOU ONLY THINK IT'S GOT YOU. LOOK. NOW I FIT HERE AND YOU AREN'T CARRYING THE LOOP ...

And his heart rolled right over, on its back, and kicked his lunch up with its red cartoon legs, galvanic frog-leg spasm hurling him from the chair and tearing the trodes from his forehead. His bladder let go when his head clipped the corner of the Hitachi, and someone was saying fuck fuck fuck into the dust smell of carpet. Girlvoice gone, no desertstar, flash impression of cool wind and water-worn stone ...

Then his head exploded. He saw it very clearly, from somewhere far away. Like a phosphorus grenade.

White.

Light.

4

Clocking In

The black Honda hovered twenty metres above the octagonal deck of the derelict oil rig. It was nearing dawn, and Turner could make out the faded outline of a biohazard trefoil marking the helicopter pad.

'You got a biohazard down there, Conroy?'

'None you aren't used to,' Conroy said.

A figure in a red jumpsuit made brisk arm signals to the Honda's pilot. Propwash flung scraps of packing waste into the sea as they landed. Conroy slapped the release plate on his harness and leaned across Turner to unseal the hatch. The roar of the engines battered them as the hatch slid open. Conroy was jabbing him in the shoulder, making urgent lifting motions with an upturned palm. He pointed to the pilot.

Turner scrambled out and dropped, the prop a blur of thunder, then Conroy was crouching beside him. They cleared the faded trefoil with the bent-legged crab scuttle common to helicopter pads, the Honda's wind snapping their pants legs around their ankles. Turner carried a plain grey suitcase moulded from ballistic ABS, his only piece of luggage; someone had packed it for him, at the hotel, and it had been waiting on *Tsushima*. A sudden change in pitch told him the Honda was rising. It went whining away towards the coast, showing no lights. As the sound faded, Turner heard the cries of gulls and the slap and slide of the Pacific.

'Someone tried to set up a data haven here once,' Conroy said. 'International waters. Back then nobody lived in orbit, so it made sense for a few years . . .' He started for a rusted forest of beams supporting the rig's superstructure. 'One scenario Hosaka showed me, we'd get Mitchell out here, clean him up, stick him on *Tsushima*, and full steam for old Japan. I told 'em, forget *that* shit. Maas gets on to it and they can come down on this thing with anything they want. I told 'em, that compound they got down in the DF, that's the ticket, right? Plenty of shit Maas wouldn't pull there, not in the fucking middle of Mexico City . . .'

A figure stepped from the shadows, head distorted by the bulbous goggles of an image-amplification rig. It waved them on with the blunt, clustered muzzles of a Lansing flechette gun.

'Biohazard,' Conroy said as they edged past. 'Duck your head here. And watch it, the stairs get slippery.'

The rig smelled of rust and disuse and brine. There were no windows. The discoloured cream walls were blotched with spreading scabs of rust. Battery-powered fluorescent lanterns were slung, every few metres, from beams overhead, casting a hideous green-tinged light, at once intense and naggingly uneven. At least a dozen figures were at work, in this central room; they moved with the relaxed precision of good technicians. *Professionals*, Turner thought; their eyes seldom met and there was little talking. It was cold, very cold, and Conroy had given him a huge parka covered with tabs and zippers.

A bearded man in a sheepskin bomber jacket was securing bundled lengths of fibre-optic line to a dented bulkhead with silver tape. Conroy was locked in a whispered argument with a black woman who wore a parka like Turner's. The bearded tech looked up from his work and saw Turner.

'Shee-it,' he said, still on his knees, 'I figured it was a big one, but I guess it's gonna be a rough one, too.' He stood, wiping his palms automatically on his jeans. Like the rest of the techs, he wore micropore surgical gloves. 'You're Turner.' He grinned, glanced quickly in Conroy's direction, and pulled a black plastic flask from a jacket pocket. 'Take some chill off. You remember me. Worked on that job in Marrakesh. IBM boy went over to Mitsu-G. Wired the charges on that bus you 'n' the Frenchman drove into that hotel lobby.'

Turner took the flask, snapped its lid, and tipped it. Bourbon. It stung deep and sour, warmth spreading from the region of his sternum. 'Thanks.' He returned the flask and the man pocketed it.

'Oakey,' the man said. 'Name's Oakey? You remember?'

'Sure,' Turner lied, 'Marrakesh.'

'Wild Turkey,' Oakey said. 'Flew in through Schiphol, I hit the duty-free. Your partner there,' another glance at Conroy, 'he's none too relaxed, is he? I mean, not like Marrakesh, right?'

Turner nodded.

'You need anything,' Oakey said, 'lemme know.'

'Like what?'

''Nother drink, or I got some Peruvian flake, the kind that's real yellow.' Oakey grinned again.

'Thanks,' Turner said, seeing Conroy turn from the black woman. Oakey saw, too, kneeling quickly and tearing off a fresh length of silver tape.

'Who was that?' Conroy asked, after leading Turner through a narrow door with decayed black gasket seals at its edges. Conroy spun the wheel that dogged the door shut; someone had oiled it recently.

'Name's Oakey,' Turner said, taking in the new room. Smaller. Two of the lanterns, folding tables, chairs, all new.

26

On the tables, instrumentation of some kind, under black plastic dust covers.

'Friend of yours?'

'No,' Turner said. 'He worked for me once.' He went to the nearest table and flipped back a dust cover. 'What's this?' The console had the blank, half-finished look of a factory prototype.

'Maas-Neotek cyberspace deck.'

Turner raised his eyebrows. 'Yours?'

'We got two. One's on site. From Hosaka. Fastest thing in the matrix, evidently, and Hosaka can't even de-engineer the chips to copy them. Whole other technology.'

'They got them from Mitchell?'

'They aren't saying. The fact they'd let go of 'em just to give our jockeys an edge is some indication of how badly they want the man.'

'Who's on console, Conroy?'

'Jaylene Slide. I was talking to her just now.' He jerked his head in the direction of the door. 'The site man's out of LA, kid called Ramirez.'

'They any good?' Turner replaced the dust cover.

'Better be, for what they'll cost. Jaylene's got herself a hot rep the past two years, and Ramirez is her understudy. Shit,' Conroy shrugged, 'you know these cowboys. Fucking crazy ...'

'Where'd you get them? Where'd you get Oakey, for that matter?'

Conroy smiled. 'From *your* agent, Turner.'

Turner stared at Conroy, then nodded. Turning, he lifted the edge of the next dust cover. Cases, plastic and styrofoam, stacked neatly on the cold metal of the table. He touched a blue plastic rectangle stamped with a silver monogram: S & W.

27

'Your agent,' Conroy said, as Turner snapped the case open. The pistol lay there in its moulded bed of pale blue foam, a massive revolver with an ugly housing that bulged beneath the squat barrel. 'S & W Tactical, .408, with a xenon projector,' Conroy said. 'What he said you'd want.'

Turner took the gun in his hand and thumbed the battery-test stud for the projector. A red LED in the walnut grip pulsed twice. He swung the cylinder out. 'Ammunition?'

'On the table. Handloads, explosive tips.'

Turner found a transparent cube of amber plastic, opened it with his left hand, and extracted a cartridge. 'Why did they pick me for this, Conroy?' He examined the cartridge, then inserted it carefully into one of the cylinder's six chambers.

'I don't know,' Conroy said. 'Felt like they had you slotted from go, whenever they heard from Mitchell ...'

Turner spun the cylinder rapidly and snapped it back into the frame. 'I said, "Why did they pick me for this, Conroy?"' He raised the pistol with both hands and extended his arms, pointing it directly at Conroy's face. 'Gun like this, sometimes you can see right down the bore, if the light's right, see if there's a bullet there.'

Conroy shook his head, very slightly.

'Or maybe you can see it in one of the other chambers ...'

'No,' Conroy said, very softly, 'no way.'

'Maybe the shrinks screwed up, Conroy. How about that?'

'No,' Conroy said, his face blank. 'They didn't, and you won't.'

Turner pulled the trigger. The hammer clicked on an empty chamber. Conroy blinked once, opened his mouth, closed it, watched as Turner lowered the Smith & Wesson. A single bead of sweat rolled down from Conroy's hairline and lost itself in an eyebrow.

'Well?' Turner asked, the gun at his side.

Conroy shrugged. 'Don't do that shit,' he said.

'They want me that bad?'

Conroy nodded. 'It's your show, Turner.'

'Where's Mitchell?' He opened the cylinder again and began to load the five remaining chambers.

'Arizona. About fifty kilos from the Sonora line, in a mesa-top research arcology. Maas Biolabs North America. They own everything around there, right down to the border, and the mesa's smack in the middle of the footprints of four recon satellites. Mucho tight.'

'And how are we supposed to get in?'

'We aren't. Mitchell's coming out, on his own. We wait for him, pick him up, get his ass to Hosaka intact.' Conroy hooked a forefinger behind the open collar of his black shirt and drew out a length of black nylon cord, then a small black nylon envelope with a Velcro fastener. He opened it carefully and extracted an object, which he offered to Turner on his open palm. 'Here. This is what he sent.'

Turner put the gun down on the nearest table and took the thing from Conroy. It was like a swollen grey microsoft, one end routine neurojack, the other a strange, rounded formation unlike anything he'd seen. 'What is it?'

'It's biosoft. Jaylene jacked it and said she thought it was output from an AI. It's sort of a dossier on Mitchell, with a message to Hosaka tacked on the end. You better jack it yourself; you wanna get the picture fast …'

Turner glanced up from the grey thing. 'How'd it grab Jaylene?'

'She said you better be lying down when you do it. She didn't seem to like it much.'

Machine dreams hold a special vertigo. Turner lay down on a virgin slab of green temperfoam in the makeshift dorm and jacked Mitchell's dossier. It came on slow; he had time to close his eyes.

Ten seconds later, his eyes were open. He clutched the green foam and fought his nausea. Again, he closed his eyes ... It came on, again, gradually, a flickering, non-linear flood of fact and sensory data, a kind of narrative conveyed in surreal jump-cuts and juxtapositions. It was vaguely like riding a rollercoaster that phased in and out of existence at random, impossibly rapid intervals, changing altitude, attack, and direction with each pulse of nothingness, except that the shifts had nothing to do with any physical orientation, but rather with lightning alternations in paradigm and symbol-system. The data had never been intended for human input.

Eyes open, he pulled the thing from his socket and held it, his palm slick with sweat. It was like waking from a nightmare. Not a screamer, where impacted fears took on simple, terrible shapes, but the sort of dream, infinitely more disturbing, where everything is perfectly and horribly normal, and where everything is utterly *wrong* ...

The *intimacy* of the thing was hideous. He fought down waves of raw transference, bringing all his will to bear on crushing a feeling that was akin to love, the obsessive tenderness a watcher comes to feel for the subject of prolonged surveillance. Days or hours later, he knew, the most minute details of Mitchell's academic record might bob to the surface of his mind, or the name of a mistress, the scent of her heavy red hair in the sunlight through—

He sat up quickly, the plastic soles of his shoes smacking the rusted deck. He still wore the parka, and the Smith & Wesson, in a side pocket, swung painfully against his hip.

It would pass. Mitchell's psychic odour would fade, as surely as the Spanish grammar in the lexicon evaporated after each use. What he had experienced was a Maas security

30

dossier compiled by a sentient computer, nothing more. He replaced the biosoft in Conroy's little black wallet, smoothed the Velcro seal with his thumb, and put the cord around his neck.

He became aware of the sound of waves lapping the flanks of the rig.

'Hey, boss,' someone said, from beyond the brown military blanket that screened the entrance to the dorm area, 'Conroy says it's time for you to inspect the troops, then you and him depart for other parts.' Oakey's bearded face slid from behind the blanket. 'Otherwise, I wouldn't wake you up, right?'

'I wasn't sleeping,' Turner said, and stood, fingers reflexively kneading the skin around the implanted socket.

'Too bad,' Oakey said. 'I got derms'll put you under all the way, one hour on the button, then kick in some kind of righteous upper, get you up and on the case, no lie ...'

Turner shook his head. 'Take me to Conroy.'

5

The Job

Marly checked into a small hotel with green plants in heavy brass pots, the corridors tiled like worn marble chessboards. The elevator was a scrolled gilt cage with rosewood panels smelling of lemon oil and small cigars.

Her room was on the fifth floor. A single tall window overlooked the avenue, the kind of window you could actually open. When the smiling bellman had gone, she collapsed into an armchair whose plush fabric contrasted comfortably with the muted Belgian carpet. She undid the zips on her old Paris boots for the last time, kicked them off, and stared at the dozen glossy carrier bags the bellman had arranged on the bed. *Tomorrow*, she thought, *she'd buy luggage. And a toothbrush.*

'I'm in shock,' she said to the bags on the bed. 'I must take care. Nothing seems real now.' She looked down and saw that her hose were both out at the toe. She shook her head. Her new purse lay on the white marble table beside the bed; it was black, cut from cowhide tanned thick and soft as Flemish butter. It had cost more than she would have owed Andrea for her share of a month's rent, but that was also true of a single night's stay in this hotel. The purse contained her passport and the credit chip she'd been issued in the Galerie Duperey, drawn on an account held in her name by an orbital branch of the Nederlandse Algemeen Bank.

She went into the bathroom and worked the smooth brass levers of the big white tub. Hot, aerated water hissed out through a Japanese filtration device. The hotel provided packets of bath salts, tubes of creams and scented oils. She emptied a tube of oil into the filling tub and began to remove her clothes, feeling a pang of loss when she tossed the Sally Stanley behind her. Until an hour before, the year-old jacket had been her favourite garment and perhaps the single most expensive thing she'd ever owned. Now it was something for the cleaners to take away; perhaps it would find its way to one of the city's flea markets, the sort of place where she'd hunted bargains as an art school girl ...

The mirrors misted and ran, as the room filled with scented steam, blurring the reflection of her nakedness. Was it really this easy? Had Virek's slim gold credit chip checked her out of her misery and into this hotel, where the towels were white and thick and scratchy? She was aware of a certain spiritual vertigo, as though she trembled at the edge of some precipice. She wondered how powerful money could actually be, if one had enough of it, really enough. She supposed that only the Vireks of the world could really know, and very likely they were functionally incapable of *knowing*; asking Virek would be like interrogating a fish in order to learn more about water. Yes, my dear, it's wet; yes, my child, it's certainly warm, scented, scratchy-towelled. She stepped into the tub and lay down.

Tomorrow she would have her hair cut. In Paris.

Andrea's phone rang sixteen times before Marly remembered the special program. It would still be in place, and this expensive little Brussels hotel would not be listed. She leaned out to replace the handset on the marble-topped table and it chimed once, softly.

33

'A courier has delivered a parcel, from the Galerie Duperey.'

When the bellman – a younger man this time, dark and possibly Spanish – had gone, she took the package to the window and turned it over in her hands. It was wrapped in a single sheet of handmade paper, dark grey, folded and tucked in that mysterious Japanese way that required neither glue nor string, but she knew that once she'd opened it, she'd never get it folded again. The name and address of the Galerie were embossed in one corner, and her name and the name of her hotel were handwritten across the centre in perfect italic script.

She unfolded the paper and found herself holding a new Braun holoprojector and a flat envelope of clear plastic. The envelope contained seven numbered tabs of holofiche. Beyond the miniature iron balcony, the sun was going down, painting the Old Town gold. She heard car horns and the cries of children. She closed the window and crossed to a writing desk. The Braun was a smooth black rectangle powered by solar cells. She checked the charge, then took the first holofiche from the envelope and slotted it.

The box she'd seen in Virek's simulation of Park Güell blossomed above the Braun, glowing with the crystal resolution of the finest museum-grade holograms. Bone and circuit-gold, dead lace, and a dull white marble rolled from clay. Marly shook her head. How could anyone have arranged these bits, this garbage, in such a way that it caught at the heart, snagged in the soul like a fish hook? But then she nodded. It could be done, she knew, it had been done many years ago by a man named Cornell, who'd also made boxes.

Then she glanced to the left, where the elegant grey paper lay on the desktop. She'd chosen this hotel at random, when she'd grown tired of shopping. She'd told no one she was here, and certainly no one from the Galerie Duperey.

6

Barrytown

He stayed out for something like eight hours, by the clock on his mother's Hitachi. Came to staring at its dusty face, some hard thing wedged under his thigh. The Ono-Sendai. He rolled over. Stale puke smell.

Then he was in the shower, not sure quite how he'd got there, spinning the taps with his clothes still on. He clawed and dug and pulled at his face. It felt like a rubber mask.

'Something happened.' Something bad, big, he wasn't sure what.

His wet clothes gradually mounded up on the tile floor of the shower. Finally he stepped out, went to the sink and flicked wet hair back from his eyes, peered at the face in the mirror. Bobby Newmark, no problem.

'No, Bobby, problem. Gotta problem ...'

Towel around his shoulders, dripping water, he followed the narrow hallway to his bedroom, a tiny, wedge-shaped space at the very back of the condo. His holoporn unit lit as he stepped in, half a dozen girls grinning, eyeing him with evident delight. They seemed to be standing beyond the walls of the room, in hazy vistas of powder-blue space, their white smiles and taut young bodies bright as neon. Two of them edged forward and began to touch themselves.

'Stop it,' he said.

The projection unit shut itself down at his command; the

dreamgirls vanished. The thing had originally belonged to Ling Warren's older brother; the girls' hair and clothes were dated and vaguely ridiculous. You could talk with them and get them to do things with themselves and each other. Bobby remembered being thirteen and in love with Brandi, the one with the blue rubber pants. Now he valued the projections mainly for the illusion of space they could provide in the makeshift bedroom.

'Something fucking happened,' he said, pulling on black jeans and an almost clean shirt. He shook his head. 'What? Fucking *what*?' Some kind of power surge on the line? Some flukey action down at the Fission Authority? Maybe the base he'd tried to invade had suffered some strange breakdown, or been attacked from another quarter ... But he was left with the sense of having *met* someone, someone who ... He'd unconsciously extended his right hand, fingers spread, beseechingly. 'Fuck,' he said. The fingers balled into a fist. Then it came back: first, the sense of the big thing, the *really* big thing, reaching for him across cyberspace, and then the girl-impression. Someone brown, slender, crouching somewhere in a strange bright dark full of stars and wind. But it slid away as his mind went for it.

Hungry, he got into sandals and headed back towards the kitchen, rubbing at his hair with a damp towel. On his way through the living room, he noticed the ON telltale of the Ono-Sendai glaring at him from the carpet. 'Oh shit.' He stood there and sucked at his teeth. It was still jacked in. Was it possible that it was still linked with the base he'd tried to run? Could they tell he wasn't dead? He had no idea. One thing he did know, though, was that they'd have his number and good. He hadn't bothered with the cut-outs and frills that would've kept them from running a backtrack.

They had his address.

36

Hunger forgotten, he spun into the bathroom and rooted through the soggy clothing until he found his credit chip.

He had two hundred and ten New Yen stashed in the hollow plastic handle of a multi-bit screwdriver. Screwdriver and credit chip secure in his jeans, he pulled on his oldest, heaviest pair of boots, then clawed unwashed clothing from beneath the bed. He came up with a black canvas jacket with at least a dozen pockets, one of them a single huge pouch across the small of the back, a kind of integral rucksack. There was a Japanese gravity knife with orange handles beneath his pillow; that went into a narrow pocket on the jacket's left sleeve, near the cuff.

The dreamgirls clicked in as he was leaving: 'Bobby, Bobb-y, come back and play ...'

In his living room, he yanked the Ono-Sendai's jack from the face of the Hitachi, coiling the fibre-optic lead and tucking it into a pocket. He did the same with the trode-set, then slid the Ono-Sendai into the jacket's pack-pocket.

The curtains were still drawn. He felt a surge of some new exhilaration. He was leaving. He *had* to leave. Already he'd forgotten the pathetic fondness that his brush with death had generated. He parted the curtains carefully, a thumb-wide gap, and peered out.

It was late afternoon. In a few hours, the first lights would start blinking on in the dark bulks of the Projects. Big Playground swept away like a concrete sea; the Projects rose beyond the opposite shore, vast rectilinear structures softened by a random overlay of retrofitted greenhouse balconies, cat-fish tanks, solar heating systems, and the ubiquitous chicken wire dishes.

Two-a-Day would be up there now, sleeping, in a world Bobby had never seen, the world of a mincome arcology.

Two-a-Day came down to do business, mostly with the hot-doggers in Barrytown, and then he climbed back up. It had always looked good to Bobby, up there, so much happening on the balconies at night, amid red smudges of charcoal, little kids in their underwear swarming like monkeys, so small you could barely see them. Sometimes the wind would shift, and the smell of cooking would settle over Big Playground, and sometimes you'd see an ultralight glide out from some secret country of rooftop so high up there. And always the mingled beat from a million speakers, waves of music that pulsed and faded in and out of the wind.

Two-a-Day never talked about his life, where he lived. Two-a-Day talked biz, or, to be more social, women. What Two-a-Day said about women made Bobby want to get out of Barrytown worse than ever, and Bobby knew that biz would be his only ticket out. But now he needed the dealer in a different way, because now he was entirely out of his depth.

Maybe Two-a-Day could tell him what was happening. There wasn't supposed to be any lethal stuff around that base. Two-a-Day had picked it out for him, then rented him the software he'd need to get in. And Two-a-Day was ready to fence anything he could've got out with. So Two-a-Day had to know. Know *something*, anyway.

'I don't even have your number, man,' he said to the Projects, letting the curtains fall shut. Should he leave something for his mother? A note? 'My ass,' he said to the room behind him, '*out* of here,' and then he was out the door and down the hall, headed for the stairs. 'For*ever*,' he added, kicking open an exit-door.

Big Playground looked safe enough, except for a lone shirtless duster deep in some furious conversation with God. Bobby cut the duster a wide circle; he was shouting and jumping and karate-chopping the air. The duster had dried

38

blood on his bare feet and the remnants of what had probably been a Lobe haircut.

Big Playground was neutral territory, at least in theory, and the Lobes were loosely confederated with the Gothicks; Bobby had fairly solid affiliations with the Gothicks, but retained his indie status. Barrytown was a dicey place to be an indie. *At least*, he thought, as the duster's angry gibberish faded behind him, *the gangs gave you some structure.* If you were Gothick and the Kasuals chopped you out, it made sense. Maybe the ultimate reasons behind it were crazy, but there were rules. But indies got chopped out by dusters running on brainstem, by roaming predatory loonies from as far away as New York – like that Penis Collector character last summer, kept the goods in his pocket in a plastic bag ...

Bobby had been trying to chart a way out of this landscape since the day he was born, or anyway it felt that way. Now, as he walked, the cyberspace deck in the pack-pocket banged against his spine. Like it, too, was urging him to get out. 'Come on, Two-a-Day,' he said to the looming Projects, 'get your ass down outta there and be in Leon's when I get there, okay?'

Two-a-Day wasn't in Leon's.

Nobody was, unless you wanted to count Leon, who was probing the inner mysteries of a wallscreen converter with a bent paper clip.

'Why don't you just get a hammer and pound the fucker 'til it works?' Bobby asked. 'Do you about as much good.'

Leon looked up from the converter. He was probably in his forties, but it was hard to say. He seemed to be of no particular race, or, in certain lights, to belong to some race that nobody else belonged to. Lots of hypertrophied facial bone and a mane of curly, non-reflective black hair. His basement pirate club had been a fixture in Bobby's life for the past two years.

Leon stared dully at Bobby with his unnerving eyes, pupils of nacreous grey overlaid with a hint of translucent olive. Leon's eyes made Bobby think of oysters and nail polish, two things he didn't particularly like to think about in connection with eyes. The colour was like something they'd use to upholster bar stools.

'I just mean you can't fix shit like that by poking at it,' Bobby added uncomfortably. Leon shook his head slowly and went back to his exploration. People paid to get into the place because Leon pirated kino and simstim off cable and ran a lot of stuff that Barrytowners couldn't otherwise afford to access. There was dealing in the back and you could make 'donations' for drinks, mostly clean Ohio hooch cut with some synthetic orange drink Leon scored in industrial quantities.

'Say, uh, Leon,' Bobby began again, 'you seen Two-a-Day in here lately?'

The horrible eyes came up again and regarded Bobby for entirely too long. 'No.'

'Maybe last night?'

'No.'

'Night before?'

'No.'

'Oh. Okay. Thanks.' There was no point in giving Leon a hard time. Lots of reasons not to, actually. Bobby looked around at the wide dim room, at the simstim units and the unlit kino screens. The club was a series of nearly identical rooms in the basement of a semi-residential rack zoned for singles and a sprinkling of light industry. Good soundproofing: you hardly ever heard the music, not from outside. Plenty of nights he'd popped out of Leon's with a head full of noise and pills, into what seemed a magic vacuum of silence, his ears ringing all the way home across Big Playground.

Now he had an hour, probably, before the first Gothicks started to arrive. The dealers, mostly black guys from the Projects or whites from the city or some other 'burb, wouldn't turn up until there was a patch of Gothicks for them to work on. Nothing made a dealer look worse than just sitting there, waiting, because that would mean you weren't getting any action, and there was no way a genuinely hot dealer would be hanging out in Leon's just for the pleasure of it. It was all hotdog shit, in Leon's, weekenders with cheap decks who watched Japanese icebreaker kinos ...

But Two-a-Day wasn't like that, he told himself, on his way up the concrete stairs. Two-a-Day was on his way. Out of the Projects, out of Barrytown, out of Leon's. On his way to the City. To Paris, maybe, or Chiba. The Ono-Sendai bumped against his spine. He remembered that Two-a-Day's icebreaker cassette was still in it. He didn't want to have to explain that to anyone. He passed a news kiosk. A yellow fax of the New York edition of the *Asahi Shimbun* was reeling past a plastic window in the mirrored siding, some government going down in Africa, Russian stuff from Mars ...

It was that time of day when you could see things very clear, see every little thing so far down the streets, fresh green just starting from the black branches of the trees in their holes in the concrete, and the flash of steel on a girl's boot a block away, like looking through a special kind of water that made seeing easier, even though it was nearly dark. He turned and stared up at the Projects. Whole floors there were forever unlit, either derelict or the windows blacked out. What did they do in there? Maybe he'd ask Two-a-Day sometime.

He checked the time on the kiosk's Coke clock. His mother would be back from Boston by now, had to be, or else she'd miss one of her favourite soaps. New hole in her head. She

41

was crazy anyway, nothing wrong with the socket she'd had since before he was born, but she'd been whining for years about static and resolution and sensory bleed-over, so she'd finally swung the credit to go to Boston for some cheap-ass replacement. Kind of place where you don't even get an appointment for an operation. Walk in and they just slap it in your head ... He knew her, yeah, how she'd come through the door with a wrapped bottle under her arm, not even take her coat off, just go straight over and jack into the Hitachi, soap her brains out good for six solid hours. Her eyes would unfocus, and sometimes, if it was a really good episode, she'd drool a little. About every twenty minutes she'd manage to remember to take a ladylike nip out of the bottle.

She'd always been that way, as long as he could remember, gradually sliding deeper into her half-dozen synthetic lives, sequential simstim fantasies Bobby had had to hear about all his life. He still harboured creepy feelings that some of the characters she talked about were relatives of his, rich and beautiful aunts and uncles who might turn up one day, if only he weren't such a little shit. *Maybe*, he thought now, *it had been true, in a way*; she'd jacked that shit straight through the pregnancy, because she'd told him she had, so he, foetus Newmark, curled up in there, had reverberated to about a thousand hours of *People of Importance* and *Atlanta*. But he didn't like to think about being curled up in Marsha Newmark's belly. It made him feel sweaty and kind of sick.

Marsha-momma. Only in the past year or so had Bobby come to understand the world well enough – as he now saw it – to wonder exactly how she still managed to make her way in it, marginal as that way had become, with her bottle and the socket ghosts to keep her company. Sometimes, when she was in a certain mood and had had the right number of nips, she still tried to tell him stories about his father. He'd known

42

since age four that these were bullshit, because the details changed from time to time, but for years he'd allowed himself a certain pleasure in them anyway.

He found a loading bay a few blocks west of Leon's, screened from the street by a freshly painted blue dumpster, the new paint gleaming over pocked, dented steel. There was a single halogen tube slung above the bay. He found a comfortable ledge of concrete and sat down there, careful not to jar the Ono-Sendai. Sometimes you just had to wait. That was one of the things Two-a-Day had taught him.

The dumpster was overflowing with a varied hash of industrial scrap. Barrytown had its share of grey-legal manufacturers, part of the 'shadow economy' the news faces liked to talk about, but Bobby never paid much attention to news faces. Biz. It was all just biz ...

Moths strobed crooked orbits around the halogen tube. Bobby watched blankly as three kids, maybe ten at the oldest, scaled the blue wall of the dumpster with a length of dirty white nylon line and a makeshift grapple that might once have been part of a coatrack. When the last one made it over the top, into the mess of plastic scrap, the line was drawn swiftly up. The scrap began to creak and rustle.

Just like me, Bobby thought, *I used to do that shit, fill my room up with weird garbage I'd find.* One time Ling Warren's sister found most of somebody's arm, all wrapped in green plastic and done up with rubber bands.

Marsha-momma'd get these two-hour fits of religion sometimes, come into Bobby's room and sweep all his best garbage out and gum some god-awful self-adhesive hologram up over his bed. Maybe Jesus, maybe Hubbard, maybe Virgin Mary, it didn't much matter to her when the mood was on her. It used to piss Bobby off real good, until one day he was big enough to walk into the front room with a ballpeen

43

hammer and cock it over the Hitachi; you touch my stuff again and I'll kill your friends, Mom, all of 'em. She never tried it again. But the stick-on holograms had actually had some effect on Bobby, because religion was now something he felt he'd considered and put aside. Basically, the way he figured it, there were just some people around who needed that shit, and he guessed there always had been, but he wasn't one of them, so he didn't.

Now one of the dumpster kids popped up and conducted a slit-eyed survey of the immediate area, then ducked out of sight again. There was a clunking, scraping sound. Small white hands tipped a dented alloy canister up and over the edge, lowering it on the nylon line. *Good score*, Bobby thought; you could take the thing to a metal dealer and get a little for it. They lowered the thing to the pavement, about a metre from the soles of Bobby's boots; as it touched down, it happened to twist around, showing him the six-horned symbol that stood for biohazard. 'Hey, fuck,' he said, drawing his feet up reflexively.

One of them slid down the rope and steadied the canister. The other two followed. He saw that they were younger than he'd thought.

'Hey,' Bobby said, 'you know that could be some real bad shit? Give you cancer and stuff.'

'Go lick a dog's ass 'til it bleeds,' the first kid down the rope advised him, as they flicked their grapple loose, coiled their line, and dragged the canister around the corner of the dumpster and out of sight.

He gave it an hour and a half. Time enough; Leon's was starting to cook.

At least twenty Gothicks postured in the main room, like a herd of baby dinosaurs, their crests of lacquered hair bobbing and twitching. The majority approached the Gothick ideal: tall, lean, muscular, but touched by a certain gaunt restlessness, young athletes in the early stages of consumption. The graveyard pallor was mandatory, and Gothick hair was by definition black. Bobby knew that the few who couldn't warp their bodies to fit the subcultural template were best avoided; a short Gothick was trouble, a fat Gothick homicidal.

Now he watched them flexing and glittering in Leon's like a composite creature, slime mould with a jigsaw surface of dark leather and stainless spikes. Most of them had nearly identical faces, features reworked to match ancient archetypes culled from kino banks. He chose a particularly artful Dean whose hair swayed like the mating display of a nocturnal lizard.

'Bro,' Bobby began, uncertain if he'd met this one before.

'My man,' the Dean responded languidly, his left cheek distended by a cud of resin. 'The Count, baby,' as an aside to his girl, 'Count Zero Interrupt.' Long pale hand with a fresh scab across the back grabbing ass through the girl's leather skirt. 'Count, this is my squeeze.' The Gothick girl regarded Bobby with mild interest but no flash of human recognition whatever, as though she were seeing an ad for a product she'd heard of but had no intention of buying.

Bobby scanned the crowd. A few blank faces, but none he knew. No Two-a-Day. 'Say, hey,' he confided, 'how you know how it is 'n' all, I'm lookin' for this close personal friend, business friend,' and at this the Gothick sagely bobbed his crest, 'goes by Two-a-Day ...' He paused. The Gothick looked blank, snapping his resin. The girl looked bored, restless. ''Wareman,' Bobby added, raising his eyebrows, 'black 'wareman.'

'Two-a-Day,' the Gothick said. 'Sure. Two-a-Day. Right, babe?' His girl tossed her head and looked away.

'You know 'im?'

'Sure.'

'He here tonight?'

'No,' the Gothick said, and smiled meaninglessly.

Bobby opened his mouth, closed it, forced himself to nod. 'Thanks, bro.'

'Anything for my man,' the Gothick said.

Another hour, more of the same. Too much white, chalk-pale Gothick white. Flat bright eyes of their girls, their bootheels like ebony needles. He tried to stay out of the simstim room, where Leon was running some kind of weird jungle fuck tape phased you in and out of these different kinda animals, lotta crazed arboreal action up in the trees, which Bobby found a little disorienting. He was hungry enough now to feel a little spaced, or maybe it was afterburn from whatever it was had happened to him before, but he was starting to have a hard time concentrating, and his thoughts drifted in odd directions. Like who, for instance, had climbed up into those trees full of snakes and wired a pair of those rat-things for simstim?

The Gothicks were into it, whoever. They were thrashing and stomping and generally into major tree-rat identification. Leon's new hit tape, Bobby decided.

Just to his left, but well out of range of the stim, two Project girls stood, their baroque finery in sharp contrast with Gothick monochrome. Long black frock coats opened over tight red vests in silk brocade, the tails of enormous white shirts hanging well beneath their knees. Their dark features were concealed beneath the brims of fedoras pinned and hung with fragments of antique gold: stickpins, charms, teeth, mechanical watches. Bobby watched them covertly; the clothes said they had money, but that someone would make it worth your ass if you tried to go for it. One time Two-a-Day had come down from the Projects in this ice-blue

46

shaved-velour number with diamond buckles at the knees, like maybe he hadn't had time to change, but Bobby had acted like the 'wareman was dressed in his usual leathers, because he figured a cosmopolitan attitude was crucial in biz.

He tried to imagine going up to them so smooth. just putting it to them: Hey, you ladies surely must know my good friend Mr Two-a-Day? But they were older than he was, taller, and moved with a dignity he found intimidating. Probably they'd just laugh, but somehow he didn't want that at all.

What he did want now, and very badly, was food. He touched his credit chip through the denim of his jeans. He'd go across the street and get a sandwich ... Then he remembered why he was here, and suddenly it didn't seem very smart to use his chip. If he'd been sussed, after his attempted run, they'd have his chip number by now; using it would spotlight him for anyone tracking him in cyberspace, pick him out in the Barrytown grid like a highway flare in a dark football stadium. He had his cash money, but you couldn't pay for food with that. It wasn't actually illegal to have the stuff, it was just that nobody ever did anything legitimate with it. He'd have to find a Gothick with a chip, buy a New Yen's worth of credit, probably at a vicious discount, then have the Gothick pay for the food. And what the hell was he supposed to take his change in?

Maybe you're just spooked, he told himself. He didn't know for sure that he was being backtracked, and the base he'd tried to crack was legit, or was supposed to be legit. That was why Two-a-Day had told him he didn't have to worry about black ice. Who'd put lethal feedback programs around a place that leased soft kino porn? The idea had been that he'd bleep out a few hours of digitalised kino, new stuff that hadn't made it to the bootleg market. It wasn't the kind of score anybody was liable to kill you for ...

47

But somebody had tried. And something else had happened. Something entirely else. He trudged back up the stairs again, out of Leon's. He knew there was a lot he didn't know about the matrix, but he'd never heard of anything that weird … You got ghost stories, sure, and hotdoggers who swore they'd seen things in cyberspace, but he had them figured for wilsons who jacked in dusted; you could hallucinate in the matrix as easily as anywhere else …

Maybe that's what happened, he thought. The voice was just part of dying, being flatlined, some crazy bullshit your brain threw up to make you feel better, and something had happened back at the source, maybe a brownout in their part of the grid, so the ice had lost its hold on his nervous system.

Maybe. But he didn't know. Didn't know the turf. His ignorance had started to dig into him recently, because it kept him from making the moves he needed to make. He hadn't ever much thought about it before, but he didn't really know that much about anything in particular. In fact, up until he'd started hotdogging, he'd felt like he knew about as much as he needed to. And that was what the Gothicks were like, and that was why the Gothicks would stay here and burn themselves down on dust, or get chopped out by Kasuals, and the process of attrition would produce the percentage of them who'd somehow become the next wave of childbearing, condo-buying Barrytowners, and the whole thing could go round again …

He was like a kid who'd grown up beside an ocean, taking it as much for granted as he took the sky, but knowing nothing of currents, shipping routes, or the ins and outs of weather. He'd used decks in school, toys that shuttled you through the infinite reaches of that space that wasn't space, mankind's unthinkably complex consensual hallucination, the matrix, cyberspace, where the great corporate hotcores burned like neon novas, data so dense you suffered sensory overload if you tried to apprehend more than the merest outline.

But since he'd started hotdogging, he had some idea of how precious little he knew about how anything worked, and not just in the matrix. It spilled over, somehow, and he'd started to wonder, wonder and think. How Barrytown worked, what kept his mother going, why Gothicks and Kasuals invested all that energy in trying to kill each other off. Or why Two-a-Day was black and lived up in the Projects, and what made that different.

As he walked, he kept up his search for the dealer. White faces, more white faces. His stomach had started to make a certain amount of noise; he thought about the fresh package of wheat cutlets in the fridge at home, fry 'em up with some soy and crack a pack of krill wafers ...

Passing the kiosk again, he checked the Coke clock. Marsha was home for sure, deep in the labyrinthine complexities of *People of Importance*, whose female protagonist's life she'd shared through a socket for almost twenty years. The *Asahi Shimbun* fax was still rolling down behind its little window, and he stepped closer in time to see the first report of the bombing of A Block, Level 3, Covina Concourse Courts, Barrytown, New Jersey ...

Then it was gone, past, and there was a story about the formal funeral of the Cleveland Yakuza boss. Strictly trad. They all carried black umbrellas.

He'd lived all his life in 503, A Block.

That enormous thing, leaning in, to stomp Marsha Newmark and her Hitachi flat. And of course it had been meant for him.

'There's somebody doesn't mess around,' he heard himself say.

'Hey! My man! Count! You dusted, bro? Hey! Where you headin'!'

The eyes of two Deans twisting to follow him in the course of his headlong panic.

7

The Mall

Conroy swung the blue Fokker off the eroded ribbon of pre-war highway and throttled down. The long rooster tail of pale dust that had followed them from Needles began to settle; the hovercraft sank into its inflated apron-bag as they came to a halt.

'Here's the venue, Turner.'

'What hit it?' Rectangular expanse of concrete spreading to uneven walls of weathered cinder block.

'Economics,' Conroy said. 'Before the war. They never finished it. Ten klicks west of here and there's whole sub-divisions, just pavement grids, no houses, nothing.'

'How big a site team?'

'Nine, not counting you. And the medics.'

'What medics?'

'Hosaka's. Maas is biologicals, right? No telling how they might have our boy kinked. So Hosaka's built a regular little neurosurgery and staffed it with three hotshots. Two of them are company men, the third's a Korean who knows black medicine from both ends. The medical pod's in that long one there' – he pointed – 'gotta partial section of roof.'

'How'd you get it on site?'

'Brought it from Tucson inside a tanker. Faked a break-down. Got it out, rolled it in. Took all hands. Maybe three minutes.'

'Maas,' Turner said.

'Sure.' Conroy killed the engines. 'Chance you take,' he said, in the abrupt silence. 'Maybe they missed it. Our guy in the tanker sat there and bitched to his dispatcher in Tucson on the CB, all about his shit-eating heat-exchanger and how long it was going to take to fix it. Figure they picked that up. You think of a better way to do it?'

'No. Given that the client wants the thing on the site. But we're sitting here now in the middle of their recon footprint ...'

'Sweetheart' – and Conroy snorted – 'maybe we just stopped for a screw. Break up our trip to Tucson, right? It's that kind of place. People stop here to piss, you know?' He checked his black Porsche watch. 'I'm due there in an hour, get a copter back to the coast.'

'The rig?'

'No. Your fucking jet. Figured I handle that myself.'

'Good.'

'I'd go for a Dornier Systems ground-effect plane myself. Have it wait down the road until we see Mitchell heading in. It could get here by the time the medics clean him up; we toss him in and take off for the Sonora border ...'

'At subsonic speeds,' Turner said. 'No way. You're on your way to California to buy me that jump jet. Our boy's going out of here in a multi-mission combat aircraft that's barely even obsolete.'

'You got a pilot in mind?'

'Me,' Turner said, and tapped the socket behind his ear. 'It's a fully integrated interactive system. They'll sell you the interface software and I'll jack straight in.'

'Didn't know you could fly.'

'I can't. You don't need hands-on to haul ass for Mexico City.'

'Still the wild boy, Turner? You know the rumour's that somebody blew your dick off, back there in New Delhi?' Conroy swung around to face him, his grin cold and clean.

Turner dug the parka from behind the seat and took out the pistol and the box of ammunition. He was stuffing the parka back again when Conroy said, 'Keep it. It gets cold as hell here, at night.'

Turner reached for the canopy-latch, and Conroy revved the engines. The hovercraft rose a few centimetres, swaying slightly as Turner popped the canopy and climbed out. White-out sun and air like hot velvet. He took his Mexican sunglasses from the pocket of the blue work shirt and put them on. He wore white deck shoes and a pair of tropical combat fatigues. The box of explosive shells went into one of the thigh pockets on the fatigues. He kept the gun in his right hand, the parka bundled under his left arm.

'Head for the long building,' Conroy said, over the engine. 'They're expecting you.'

He jumped down into the furnace glow of desert noon as Conroy revved the Fokker again and edged it back to the highway. He watched as it sped east, its receding image distorted through wrinkles of rising heat.

When it was gone, there was no sound at all, no movement. He turned, facing the ruin. Something small and stone-grey darted between two rocks.

Perhaps eighty metres from the highway the jagged walls began. The expanse between had once been a parking lot.

Five steps forward and he stopped. He heard the sea, surf pounding, soft explosions as breakers fell. The gun was in his hand, too large, too real, its metal warming in the sun.

No sea, no sea, he told himself, can't hear it. He walked on, the deck shoes slipping in drifts of ancient window glass seasoned with brown and green shards of bottle. There were rusted discs that had been bottle-caps, flattened rectangles that had been aluminium cans. Insects whirred up from low clumps of dry brush.

Over. Done with. This place. No time ...

He stopped again, straining forward, as though he sought something that would help him name the thing that was rising in him. Something hollow ...

The mall was doubly dead. The beach hotel in Mexico had lived once, at least for a season ...

Beyond the parking lot, the sunlit cinder block, cheap and soulless, waiting.

He found them crouched in the narrow strip of shade provided by a length of grey wall. Three of them; he smelled the coffee before he saw them, the fire-blackened enamel pot balanced precariously on the tiny Primus cooker. He was meant to smell it, of course; they were expecting him. Otherwise, he'd have found the ruin empty, and then, somehow, very quietly and almost naturally, he would have died.

Two men, a woman; cracked, dusty boots out of Texas, denim so shiny with grease that it would probably be waterproof. The men were bearded, their uncut hair bound up in sun-bleached topknots with lengths of rawhide, the woman's hair centre-parted and pulled back tight from a seamed, windburned face. An ancient BMW motorcycle was propped against the wall, flecked chrome and battered paintwork daubed with airbrush blobs of tan and grey desert camo.

He released the Smith & Wesson's grip, letting it pivot around his index finger, so that the barrel pointed up and back.

'Turner,' one of the men said, rising, cheap metal flashing from his teeth. 'Sutcliffe.' Trace of an accent, probably Australian.

'Point team?' He looked at the other two.

'Point,' Sutcliffe said, and probed his mouth with a tanned thumb and forefinger, coming away with a yellowed, steel-capped prostho. His own teeth were white and perfectly even. 'You took Chauvet from IBM for Mitsu,' he said, 'and they say you took Semenov out of Tomsk.'

'Is that a question?'

'I was security for IBM Marrakesh when you blew the hotel.'

Turner met the man's eyes. They were blue, calm, very bright. 'Is that a problem for you?'

'No fear,' Sutcliffe said. 'Just to say I've seen you work.' He snapped the prostho back in place. 'Lynch' – nodding towards the other man – 'and Webber' – towards the woman.

'Run it down to me,' Turner said, and lowered himself into the scrap of shade. He squatted on his haunches, still holding the gun.

'We came in three days ago,' Webber said, 'on two bikes. We arranged for one of them to snap its crankshaft, in case we had to make an excuse for camping here. There's a sparse transient population, gypsy bikers and cultists. Lynch walked an optics spool six kilos east and tapped into a phone ...'

'Private?'

'Pay,' Lynch said.

'We sent out a test squirt,' the woman continued. 'If it hadn't worked, you'd know it.'

Turner nodded. 'Incoming traffic?'

'Nothing. It's strictly for the big show, whatever that is ...' She raised her eyebrows.

'It's a defection.'

'Bit obvious, that,' Sutcliffe said, settling himself beside Webber, his back to the wall. 'Though the general tone of the operation so far suggests that we hirelings aren't likely to even know who we're extracting. True, Mr Turner? Or will we be able to read about it in the fax?'

Turner ignored him. 'Go on, Webber.'

'After our landline was in place, the rest of the crew filtered in, one or two at a time. The last one in primed us for the tankful of Japs.'

'That was raw,' Sutcliffe said, 'bit too far up front.'

'You think it might have blown us?' Turner asked.

Sutcliffe shrugged. 'Could be, could be no. We hopped it pretty quick. Damned lucky we'd the roof to tuck it under.'

'What about the passengers?'

'They only come out at night,' Webber said. 'And they know we'll kill them if they try to get more than five metres away from the thing.'

Turner glanced at Sutcliffe. 'Conroy's orders,' the man said.

'Conroy's orders don't count now,' Turner said. 'But that one holds. What are these people like?'

'Medicals,' Lynch said, 'bent medicals.'

'You got it,' Turner said. 'What about the rest of the crew?'

'We rigged some shade with mimetic tarps. They sleep in shifts. There's not enough water and we can't risk much in the way of cooking.' Sutcliffe reached for the coffee pot. 'We have sentries in place and we run periodic checks on the integrity of the landline.' He splashed black coffee into a plastic mug that looked as though it had been chewed by a dog. 'So when do we do our dance, Mr Turner?'

'I want to see your tank of pet medics. I want to see a command post. You haven't said anything about a command post.'

'All set,' Lynch said.

'Fine. Here.' Turner passed Webber the revolver. 'See if you can find me some sort of rig for this. Now I want Lynch to show me these medics.'

'He thought it would be you,' Lynch said, scrambling effort-lessly up a low incline of rubble. Turner followed. 'You've got quite a rep.' The younger man glanced back at him from beneath a fringe of dirty, sun-streaked hair.

'Too much of one,' Turner said. 'Any is too much. You worked with him before? Marrakesh?' Lynch ducked side-ways through a gap in the cinder block, and Turner was close behind. The desert plants smelled of tar; they stung and grabbed if you brushed them. Through a vacant, rectangu-lar opening intended for a window, Turner glimpsed pink mountain-tops; then Lynch was loping down a slope of gravel.

'Sure, I worked for him before,' Lynch said, pausing at the base of the slide. An ancient-looking leather belt rode low on his hips, its heavy buckle a tarnished silver death's head with a dorsal crest of blunt, pyramidal spikes. 'Marrakesh – that was before my time.'

'Connie, too, Lynch?'

'How's that?'

'Conroy. You work for him before? More to the point, are you working for him now?' Turner came slowly, deliberately down the gravel as he spoke; it crunched and slid beneath his deck shoes, uneasy footing. He could see the delicate little fletcher holstered beneath Lynch's denim vest.

Lynch licked dry lips, held his ground. 'That's Sut's contact. I haven't met him.'

'Conroy has this problem, Lynch. Can't delegate responsi-bility. He likes to have his own man from the start, someone to watch the watchers. Always. You the one, Lynch?'

Lynch shook his head, the absolute minimum of movement required to convey the negative. Turner was close enough to smell his sweat above the tarry odoor of the desert plants.

'I've seen Conroy blow two extractions that way,' Turner

57

said. 'Lizards and broken glass, Lynch? You feel like dying here?' Turner raised his fist in front of Lynch's face and slowly extended the index finger, pointing straight up. 'We're in their footprint. If a plant of Conroy's bleeps the least fucking pulse out of here, they'll be on to us.'

'If they aren't already.'

'That's right.'

'Sut's your man,' Lynch said. 'Not me, and I can't see it being Webber.' Black-rimmed, broken nails came up to scratch abstractedly at his beard. 'Now, did you get me back here exclusively for this little talk, or do you still wanna see our canful of Japs?'

'Let's see it.'

Lynch. Lynch was the one.

Once, in Mexico, years before, Turner had chartered a portable vacation module, solar-powered and French-built, its seven-metre body like a wingless housefly sculpted in polished alloy, its eyes twin hemispheres of tinted, photo-sensitive plastic; he sat behind them as an aged twin-prop Russian cargo-lifter lumbered down the coast with the module in its jaws, barely clearing the crowns of the tallest palms. Deposited on a remote beach of black sand, Turner spent three days of pampered solitude in the narrow, teak-lined cabin, microwaving food from the freezer and shower-ing, frugally but regularly, in cool fresh water. The module's rectangular banks of cells would swivel, tracking the sun, and he'd learned to tell time by their position.

Hosaka's portable neurosurgery resembled an eyeless ver-sion of that French module, perhaps two metres longer and painted a dull brown. Sections of perforated angle iron had been freshly brazed at intervals along the lower half of the hull, and supported simple spring suspensions for ten fat, heavily nubbed red rubber bicycle tyres.

'They're asleep,' Lynch said. 'It bobs around when they move, so you can tell. We'll have the wheels off when the time comes, but for now we like being able to keep track of them.'

Turner walked slowly around the brown pod, noting the glossy black sewage tube that ran to a small rectangular tank nearby.

'Had to dump that, last night. Jesus.' Lynch shook his head. 'They got food and some water.'

Turner put his ear to the hull.

'It's proofed,' Lynch said.

Turner glanced up at the steel roof above them. The surgery was screened from above by a good ten metres of rusting roof. Sheet steel, and hot enough now to fry an egg. He nodded. That hot rectangle would be a permanent factor in the Maas infrared scan.

'Bats,' Webber said, handing him the Smith & Wesson in a black nylon shoulder rig. The dusk was full of sounds that seemed to come from inner space, metallic squeaks and the cackling of bugs, cries of unseen birds. Turner shoved gun and holster into a pocket on the parka. 'You wanna piss, go up by that mesquite. But watch out for the thorns.'

'Where are you from?'

'New Mexico,' the woman said, her face like carved wood in the remaining light. She turned and walked away, heading for the angle of walls that sheltered the tarps. He could make out Sutcliffe and a young black man there. They were eating from dull foil envelopes. Ramirez, the on-site console jockey, Jaylene Slide's partner. Out of Los Angeles.

Turner looked up at the bowl of sky, limitless, the map of

stars. *Strange how it's bigger this way,* he thought, *and from orbit it's just a gulf, formless, and scale lost all meaning.* And tonight he wouldn't sleep, he knew, and the Big Dipper would whirl round for him and dive for the horizon, pulling its tail with it.

A wave of nausea and dislocation hit him as images from the biosoft dossier swam unbidden through his mind.

8

Paris

Andrea lived in the Quartier des Ternes, where her ancient building, like the others in her street, awaited sandblasting by the city's relentless renovators. Beyond the dark entrance, one of Fuji Electric's biofluorescent strips glowed dimly above a dilapidated wall of small wooden hutches, some with their slotted doors still intact. Marly knew that postmen had once made daily deposits of mail through those slots; there was something romantic about the idea, although the hutches, with their yellowing business cards announcing the occupations of long-vanished tenants, had always depressed her. The walls of the hallway were stapled with bulging loops of cable and fibre-optics, each strand a potential nightmare for some hapless utilities repairman. At the far end, through an open door panelled with dusty pebble-glass, was a disused courtyard, its cobbles shiny with damp.

The concierge was sitting in the courtyard as Marly entered the building, on a white plastic crate that had once held bottles of Evian water. He was patiently oiling each link of an old bicycle's black chain. He glanced up as she began to climb the first flight of stairs, but registered no particular interest.

The stairs were made of marble, worn dull and concave by generations of tenants. Andrea's apartment was on the fourth floor. Two rooms, kitchen, and bath. Marly had come here when she'd closed her gallery for the last time, when it was no longer possible to sleep in the makeshift bedroom she'd shared with Alain, the little room behind the storeroom. Now the building brought her depression circling in again, but the feel of her new outfit and the tidy click of her bootheels on marble kept it at a distance. She wore an oversized leather coat a few shades lighter than her handbag, a wool skirt, and a silk blouse from Paris Isetan. She'd had her hair cut that morning on Faubourg St.-Honoré, by a Burmese girl with a West German laser-pencil; an expensive cut, subtle without being too conservative.

She touched the round plate bolted in the centre of Andrea's door, heard it peep once, softly, as it read the whorls and ridges of her fingertips. 'It's me, Andrea,' she said to the tiny microphone. A series of clanks and tickings as her friend unbolted the door.

Andrea stood there, dripping wet, in the old terry robe. She took in Marly's new look, then smiled. 'Did you get your job, or have you robbed a bank?' Marly stepped in, kissing her friend's wet cheek.

'It feels a bit of both,' she said, and laughed.

'Coffee,' said Andrea, 'make us coffee. Grands crèmes. I must rinse my hair. And yours is beautiful ...' She went into the bathroom and Marly heard a spray of water across porcelain.

'I've brought you a present,' Marly said, but Andrea couldn't hear her. She went into the kitchen and filled the kettle, lit the stove with the old-fashioned spark gun, and began to search the crowded shelves for coffee.

'Yes,' Andrea was saying, 'I do see it.' She was peering into the hologram of the box Marly had first seen in Virek's construct of Gaudí's park. 'It's your sort of thing.' She touched a stud and the Braun's illusion winked out. Beyond the room's single window, the sky was stippled with a few wisps of cirrus. 'Too grim for me, too serious. Like the things you showed at your gallery. But that can only mean that Herr Virek has chosen well; you will solve his mystery for him. If I were you, considering the wage, I might take my own good time about it.' Andrea wore Marly's gift, an expensive, beautifully detailed man's dress shirt, in grey Flemish flannel. It was the sort of thing she liked most, and her delight in it was obvious. It set off her pale hair, and was very nearly the colour of her eyes.

'He's quite horrible, Virek, I think ...' Marly hesitated.

'Quite likely,' Andrea said, taking another sip of coffee. 'Do you expect anyone that wealthy to be a nice, normal sort?'

'I felt, at one point, that he wasn't quite human. Felt that very strongly.'

'But he isn't, Marly. You were talking with a projection, a special effect ...'

'Still ...' She made a gesture of helplessness, which immediately made her feel annoyed with herself.

'Still, he is very, very wealthy, and he's paying you a great deal to do something that you may be uniquely suited to do.' Andrea smiled and readjusted a finely turned charcoal cuff. 'You don't have a great deal of choice, do you?'

'I know. I suppose that's what's making me uneasy.'

'Well,' Andrea said, 'I thought I might put off telling you a bit longer, but I have something else that may make you feel uneasy. If "uneasy" is the word.'

'Yes?'

'I considered not telling you at all, but I'm sure he'll get to you eventually. He smells money, I suppose.'

Marly put her empty cup down carefully on the cluttered little rattan table.

'He's quite acute that way,' Andrea said.

'When?'

'Yesterday. It began, I think, about an hour after you would have had your interview with Virek. He called me at work. He left a message here, with the concierge. If I were to remove the screen-program,' and she gestured toward the phone, 'I think he'd ring within thirty minutes.'

Remembering the concierge's eyes, the ticking of the bicycle chain.

'He wants to talk, he said,' Andrea said. 'Only to talk. Do you want to talk with him, Marly?'

'No,' she said, and her voice was a little girl's voice, high and ridiculous. Then: 'Did he leave a number?'

Andrea sighed, slowly shook her head, and then said, 'Yes, of course he did.'

9

Up the Projects

The dark was full of honeycomb patterns the colour of blood. Everything was warm. And soft, too, mostly soft,

'What a mess,' one of the angels said, her voice far off, but low and rich and very clear.

'We should've clipped him out of Leon's,' the other angel said. 'They aren't gonna like this upstairs.'

'Must've had something in this big pocket here, see? They slashed it for him, getting it out.'

'Not all they slashed, sister. Jesus. Here.'

The patterns swung and swam as something moved his head. Cool palm against his cheek.

'Don't get any on your shirt,' the first angel said.

'Two-a-Day ain't gonna like this. Why you figure he freaked like that and ran?'

It pissed him off, because he wanted to sleep. He was asleep, for sure, but somehow Marsha's jack-dreams were bleeding into his head, so that he tumbled through broken sequences of *People of Importance*. The soap had been running continuously since before he was born, the plot a multi-headed narrative tapeworm that coiled back in to devour itself every few months, then sprouted new heads hungry for tension and thrust. He could see it writhing in its totality, the way Marsha could never see it, an elongated spiral of Sense/Net

DNA, cheap brittle ectoplasm spun out to uncounted hungry dreamers. Marsha, now, she had it from the POV of Michele Morgan Magnum, the female lead, hereditary corporate head of Magnum AG. But today's episode kept veering weirdly away from Michele's frantically complex romantic entanglements, which Bobby had anyway never bothered to keep track of, and jerking itself into detailed socioarchitectural descriptions of Soleri-style mincome arcologies. Some of the detail, even to Bobby, seemed suspect; he doubted, for instance, that there really were entire levels devoted to the sale of ice-blue shaved-velour lounge suits with diamond-buckled knees, or that there were other levels, perpetually dark, inhabited exclusively by starving babies. This last, he seemed to recall, had been an article of faith to Marsha, who regarded the Projects with superstitious horror, as though they were some looming vertical hell to which she might one day be forced to ascend. Other segments of the jack-dream reminded him of the Knowledge channel Sense/Net piped in free with every stim subscription; there were elaborate animated diagrams of the Projects' interior structure, and droning lectures in voice-over on the lifestyles of various types of residents. These, when he was able to focus on them, seemed even less convincing than the flashes of ice-blue velour and feral babies creeping silently through the dark. He watched a cheerful young mother slice pizza with a huge industrial waterknife in the kitchen corner of a spotless one-room. An entire wall opened onto a shallow balcony and a rectangle of cartoon-blue sky. The woman was black without being black, it seemed to Bobby, like a very, very dark and youthfully maternal version of one of the porno dolls on the unit in his bedroom. And had, it looked like, the identical small but cartoon-perfect breasts. (At this point, to add to his dull confusion, an astonishingly loud and very unNet voice said, 'Now I call *that* a definite sign of life,

Jackie. If the prognosis ain't lookin' up yet, at least somethin' is ...') And then went spinning back into the all-glitz universe of Michele Morgan Magnum, who was desperately struggling to prevent Magnum AG's takeover by the sinister Shikoku-based Nakamura industrial clan, represented in this case by (plot complication) Michele's main squeeze for the season, wealthy (but somehow grindingly in need of additional billions) New Soviet boy-politician Vasily Suslov, who looked and dressed remarkably like the Gothicks in Leon's.

The episode seemed to be reaching some sort of climax – an antique BMW fuel-cell conversion had just been strafed by servo-piloted miniature West German helicopters on the street below Covina Concourse Courts, Michele Morgan Magnum was pistol-whipping her treacherous personal secretary with a nickel-plated Nambu, and Suslov, whom Bobby was coming increasingly to identify with, was casually preparing to get his ass out of town with a gorgeous female bodyguard who was Japanese but reminded Bobby intensely of another one of the dreamgirls on his holoporn unit – when someone screamed.

Bobby had never heard anyone scream that way, and there was something horribly familiar about the voice. But before he could start to worry about it, those blood-red honeycombs came swirling in again and made him miss the end of *People of Importance. Still*, some part of him thought, as red went to black, *he could always ask Marsha how it came out.*

'Open your eyes, man. That's it. Light too bright for you?'

It was, but it didn't change. White, white, he remembered his head exploding years away, pure white grenade in that cool-wind desert dark. His eyes were open, but he couldn't see. Just white.

'Now, I'd leave you down, ordinarily, boy in your condition, but the people payin' me for this say get a jump on, so I'm wakin' you up before I'm done. You wonderin' why you can't see shit, right? Just light, that's all you can see, that's right. What we got here is a neural cut-out. Now, between you and me, this thing come out of a sex shop, but there's no reason not to use it in medicine if we want to. And we do want to, because you're still hurtin' bad, and anyway, it keeps you still while I get on with it.' The voice was calm and methodical. 'Now, your big problem, that was your back, but I took care of that with a stapler and a few feet of claw. You don't get any plastic work here, you understand, but the honeys'll think those scars are real interestin'. What I'm doin' now is I'm cleanin' this one on your chest, then I'll zip a little claw down *that* and we're all done, except you better move easy for a couple of days or you'll pull a staple. I got a couple of derms on you, and I'll stick on a few more. Meantime, I'm going to click your sensorium up to audio and full visual so you can get into bein' here. Don't mind the blood; it's all yours but there isn't any more comin'.'

White curdled to grey cloud, objects taking form with the slow deliberation of a dust vision. He was flat against a padded ceiling, staring straight down at a bloodstained white doll that had no head at all, only a greenish-blue surgical lamp that seemed to sprout from its shoulders. A black man in a stained green smock was spraying something yellow into a shallow gash that ran diagonally from just above the doll's pelvic bone to just below its left nipple. He knew the man was black because his head was bare, bare and shaved, slick with sweat; his hands were covered in tight green gloves and all that Bobby could see of him was the gleaming crown of his head. There were pink and blue dermadiscs stuck to the skin on either side of the doll's neck. The edges of the wound seemed to have been painted with something that looked like chocolate syrup, and the yellow spray made a hissing sound as it escaped from its little silver tube.

Then Bobby got the picture, and the universe reversed itself sickeningly. The lamp was suspended from the ceiling, the ceiling was mirrored, and he was the doll. He seemed to snap back on a long elastic cord, back through the red honeycombs, to the dreamroom where the black girl sliced pizza for her children. The waterknife made no sound at all, microscopic grit suspended in a needle-stream of high-speed water. The thing was intended to cut glass and alloy, Bobby knew, not to slice microwaved pizza, and he wanted to scream at her because he was terrified she'd take off her thumb without even feeling it.

But he couldn't scream, couldn't move or make a sound at all. She lovingly sliced the last piece, toed the kickplate that shut the knife down, transferred the sliced pizza to a plain white ceramic platter, then turned towards the rectangle of blue beyond the balcony, where her children were – no, Bobby said, way down in himself, *no* way. Because the things that wheeled and plunged for her weren't hang-gliding kids, but babies, the monstrous babies of Marsha's dream, and the tattered wings a confusion of pink bone, metal, patched taut membranes of scrap plastic ... He saw their teeth ...

'Whoa,' said the black man, 'lost you for a second. Not for long, you understand, just maybe a New York minute ...' His hand, in the mirrors overhead, took a flat spool of blue transparent plastic from the bloody cloth beside Bobby's ribs. Delicately, with thumb and forefinger, he drew out a length of some sort of brown, beaded plastic. Minute points of light flashed along its edges and seemed to quiver and shift. 'Claw,' he said, and with his other hand thumbed some sort of integral cutter in the sealed blue spool. Now the length of beaded stuff swung free and began to writhe. 'Good shit,' he said, bringing the thing into Bobby's line of sight. 'New. What they use in Chiba now.' It was brown, headless, each bead a body segment, each segment edged with pale shining legs. Then, with a conjurer's flick of his green-gloved wrists, he lay the centipede down the length of the open wound and pinched delicately at the final segment, the one nearest Bobby's face. As the segment came away, it withdrew a glittering black thread that had served the thing as a nervous system, and as that went, each set of claws locked shut in turn, zipping the slash tight as a new leather jacket.

'Now, you see,' said the black man, mopping the last of the brown syrup away with a wet white pad, 'that wasn't so bad, was it?'

His entrance to Two-a-Day's apartment wasn't anything like the way he'd so often imagined it. To begin with, he'd never imagined being wheeled in in a wheelchair that someone had appropriated from St Mary's Maternity – the name and a serial number neatly laser-etched on the dull chrome of the left armrest. The woman who was wheeling him would have fitted neatly enough into one of his fantasies; her name was Jackie, one of the two Project girls he'd seen at Leon's, and, he'd come to understand, one of his two angels. The wheelchair was silent as it glided across the scabrous grey wall-to-wall of the apartment's narrow entranceway, but the gold bangles on Jackie's fedora tinkled cheerfully as she pushed him along.

And he'd never imagined that Two-a-Day's place would be quite this large, or that it would be full of trees.

Pye, the doctor, who'd been careful to explain that he *wasn't* a doctor, just someone who 'helped out sometimes', had settled back on a torn bar stool in his makeshift surgery, peeled off his bloody green gloves, lit a menthol cigarette, and solemnly advised Bobby to take it real easy for the next week or so. Minutes later, Jackie and Rhea, the other angel, had wrestled him into a pair of wrinkled black pyjamas that looked like something out of a very cheap ninja kino, deposited him in the wheelchair, and set out for the central stem of elevators at the arcology's core. Thanks to an additional three derms from Pye's store of drugs, one of them charged with a good two thousand mikes of endorphin analogue, Bobby was alert and feeling no pain.

'Where's my stuff?' he protested, as they rolled him out into a corridor grown perilously narrow with decades of retrofitted ducts and plumbing. 'Where's my clothes and my deck and everything?'

'Your clothes, hon, such as they were, are taped up in a plastic bag waiting for Pye to shitcan 'em. Pye had to cut 'em off you on the slab, and they weren't but bloody rags to begin with. If your deck was in your jacket, down the back, I'd say the boys who chopped you out got it. Damn near got you in the process. And you *ruined* my Sally Stanley shirt, you little shithead.' Angel Rhea didn't seem too friendly.

'Oh,' Bobby said, as they rounded a corner, 'right. Well, did you happen to find a screwdriver in there? Or a credit chip?'

'No chip, baby. But if the screwdriver's the one with the two hundred and ten New ones screwed into the handle, that's the price of my new shirt ...'

Two-a-Day didn't look as though he was particularly glad to see Bobby. In fact, it almost seemed as if he didn't see him at all. Looked straight through him to Jackie and Rhea, and showed his teeth in a smile that was all nerves and sleep-lack. They wheeled Bobby close enough that he saw how yellow Two-a-Day's eyeballs looked, almost orange in the pinky-purple glow of the gro-light tubes that seemed to dangle at random from the ceiling.

'What took you bitches?' the 'wareman asked, but there was no anger in his voice, only bone weariness and something else, something Bobby couldn't identify at first.

'Pye,' Jackie said, swaggering past the wheelchair to take a package of Chinese cigarettes from the enormous wooden slab that served Two-a-Day as a coffee table. 'He's a perfectionist, ol' Pye.'

'Learned that in vet school,' Rhea added, for Bobby's benefit, "cept usually he's too wasted, nobody'd let him work on a dog ...'

'So,' Two-a-Day said, and finally let his eyes rest on Bobby, 'you gonna make it.' And his eyes were so cold, so tired and clinical, so far removed from the hustling manic bullshitter's act that Bobby had taken for the man's personality, that Bobby could only lower his own eyes, face burning, and lock his gaze on the table. Nearly three metres long and slightly over a metre wide, it was strapped together from timbers thicker than Bobby's thigh. *It must have been in the water once*, he thought; sections still retained the bleached silvery patina of driftwood, like the log he remembered playing beside a long time ago in Atlantic City. But it hadn't seen water for a long time, and the top was a dense mosaic of candle drippings, wine stains, oddly shaped overspray marks in matte black enamel, and the dark burns left by hundreds of cigarettes. It was so crowded with food, garbage, and gadgets that it looked as though some street vendor had set up to unload hardware, then decided to have dinner. There were half-eaten pizzas – krill balls in red sauce, and Bobby's stomach began to churn – beside cascading stacks of software, smudged glasses with cigarettes crushed out in purple wine-dregs, a pink styrene tray with neat rows of stale-looking canapés, open and unopened cans of beer, an antique Gerber combat dagger that lay unsheathed on a flat block of polished marble, at least three pistols, and perhaps two dozen pieces of cryptic-looking console gear, the kind of cowboy equipment that ordinarily would have made Bobby's mouth water.

Now his mouth was watering for a slice of cold krill pizza, but his hunger was nothing in the face of his abrupt humiliation at seeing that Two-a-Day just didn't care. Not that Bobby had thought of him as a friend, exactly, but he'd definitely had something invested in the idea that Two-a-Day saw him as *someone*, somebody with talent and initiative and a chance of getting out of Barrytown. But Two-a-Day's eyes told him he was nobody in particular, and a wilson at that ...

'Look here, my man,' someone said, not Two-a-Day, and Bobby looked up. Two other men flanked Two-a-Day on the fat chrome and leather couch, both of them black. The one who'd spoken wore a grey robe of some kind and antique plastic-framed glasses. The frames were square and oversized and seemed to lack lenses. The other man's shoulders were twice as wide as Two-a-Day's, but he wore the kind of plain black two-piece suit you saw on Japanese businessmen in kinos. His spotless white French cuffs were closed with bright rectangles of gold microcircuitry.

'It's a shame we can't let you have some downtime to heal up,' the first man said, 'but we have a bad problem here.' He paused, removed his glasses, and massaged the bridge of his nose. 'We require your help.'

'Shit,' Two-a-Day said. He leaned forward, took a Chinese cigarette from the pack on the table, lit it with a dull pewter skull the size of a large lemon, then reached for a glass of wine. The man with the glasses extended a lean brown forefinger and touched Two-a-Day's wrist. Two-a-Day released the glass and sat back, his face carefully blank. The man smiled at Bobby.

'Count Zero,' he said, 'they tell us that's your handle.'

'That's right,' Bobby managed, though it came out as a kind of croak.

'We need to know about the Virgin, Count.' The man waited.

Bobby blinked at him.

'Vyèj Mirak,' and the glassless glasses went back on. 'Our Lady, Virgin of Miracles. We know her' – and he made a sign with his left hand – 'as Ezili Freda ...'

Bobby became aware of the fact that his mouth was open, so he closed it. The three dark faces waited. Jackie and Rhea were gone, but he hadn't seen them leave. A kind of panic took him then, and he glanced frantically around at the strange forest of stunted trees that surrounded them. The gro-light tubes slanted at every angle, in any direction, pink-purple jackstraws suspended in a green space of leaves. No walls. You couldn't see a wall at all. The couch and the battered table sat in a sort of clearing, with a floor of raw concrete.

'We know she came to you,' the big man said, crossing his legs carefully. He adjusted a perfect trouser-crease, and a gold cufflink winked at Bobby. 'We know, you understand?'

'Two-a-Day tells me it was your first run,' the other man said. 'That the truth?'

Bobby nodded.

'Then you are chosen of Legba,' the man said, again removing the empty frames, 'to have met Vyèj Mirak.' He smiled.

Bobby's mouth was open again.

'Legba,' the man said, 'master of roads and pathways, the loa of communication ...'

Two-a-Day ground his cigarette out on the scarred wood, and Bobby saw that his hand was shaking.

10

Alain

They agreed to meet in the brasserie on the fifth sublevel of the Napoleon Court complex, beneath the Louvre's glass pyramid. It was a place they both knew, although it had had no particular meaning for them. Alain had suggested it, and she suspected him of having chosen it carefully, It was neutral emotional ground; a familiar setting, yet one that was free of memories. It was decorated in a style that dated from the turn of the century: granite counters, black floor-to-ceiling beams, wall-to-wall mirror, and the sort of Italian restaurant furniture, in dark welded steel, that might have belonged to any decade of the past hundred years. The tables were covered in grey linen with a fine black stripe, a pattern picked up and repeated on the menu-covers and matchbooks and the aprons of the waiters.

She wore the leather coat she'd bought in Brussels, a red linen blouse, and new black cotton jeans. Andrea had pretended not to notice the extreme care with which she'd dressed for the meeting, and then had loaned her a simple single strand of pearls, which set off the red blouse perfectly.

He'd come early, she saw as she entered, and already the table was littered with his things. He wore his favourite scarf, the one they'd found together at the flea market the year before, and looked, as he usually did, dishevelled but perfectly at ease. The tattered leather attaché case had disgorged its contents across the little square of polished granite: spiral notebooks, an unread copy of the month's controversial novel, Gauloise nonfilters, a box of wooden matches, the leather-bound agenda she'd bought for him at Browns.

'I thought you might not come,' he said, smiling up at her.

'Why would you have thought that?' she asked, a random response – *pathetic*, she thought – masking the terror she now felt, that she allowed herself at last to feel, which was fear of some loss of self, of will and direction, fear of the love she still felt. She took the other chair and seated herself as the young waiter arrived, a Spanish boy in a striped apron, to take her order. She asked for Vichy water.

'Nothing else?' Alain asked. The waiter hovered.

'No, thank you.'

'I've been trying to reach you for weeks,' he said, and she knew that that was a lie, and yet, as she often had before, she wondered if he was entirely conscious of the fact that he was lying. Andrea maintained that men like Alain lied so constantly, so passionately, that some basic distinction had been lost. They were artists in their own right, Andrea said, intent on restructuring reality, and the New Jerusalem was a fine place indeed, free of overdrafts and disgruntled landlords and the need to find someone to cover the evening's bill.

'I didn't notice you trying to reach me when Gnass came with the police,' she said, hoping at least that he would wince, but the boyish face was calm as ever, beneath clean brown hair he habitually combed back with his fingers.

'I'm sorry,' he said, crushing out his Gauloise. Because she'd come to associate the smell of the dark French tobacco with him, Paris had seemed full of his scent, his ghost, his trail. 'I was certain he'd never detect the – the nature of the piece. You must understand: once I had admitted to myself how badly we needed the money, I knew that I must act. You,

I knew, were far too idealistic. The gallery would have folded in any case. If things had gone as planned, with Gnass, we would be there now, and you would be happy. Happy,' he repeated, taking another cigarette from the pack.

She could only stare at him, feeling a kind of wonder, and a sick revulsion at her desire to believe him.

'You know,' he said, taking a match from the red and yellow box, 'I've had difficulties with the police before. When I was a student. Politics, of course.' He struck the match, tossed the box down, and lit the cigarette.

'Politics,' she said, and suddenly felt like laughing. 'I was unaware that there was a party for people like you. I can't imagine what it might be called.'

'Marly,' he said, lowering his voice, as he always did when he wished to indicate intensity of feeling, 'you know, you must know, that I acted for you. For us, if you will. But surely you know, you can *feel*, Marly, that I would never deliberately hurt you, or place you in jeopardy.' There was no room on the crowded little table for her purse, so she'd held it in her lap; now she was aware of her nails buried deep in the soft thick leather.

'Never hurt me ...' The voice was her own, lost and amazed, the voice of a child, and suddenly she was free, free of need, desire, free of fear, and all that she felt for the handsome face across the table was simple revulsion, and she could only stare at him, this stranger she'd slept beside for one year, in a tiny room behind a very small gallery in the rue Mauconseil. The waiter put her glass of Vichy down in front of her.

He must have taken her silence for the beginning of acceptance, the utter blankness of her expression for openness. 'What you don't understand,' and this, she remembered, was a favourite opening, 'is that men like Gnass exist, in some sense, to support the arts. To support *us*, Marly.' He smiled

77

then, as though he laughed at himself, a jaunty, conspiratorial smile that chilled her now. 'I suppose, though, that I should have credited the man with having at least the requisite sense to hire his own Cornell expert, although *my* Cornell expert, I assure you, was by far the more erudite of the two ...'

How was she to get away? *Stand*, she told herself. *Turn.* Walk calmly back to the entrance. Step through the door. Out into the subdued glitter of Napoleon Court, where polished marble overlay the rue du Champ Fleuri, a fourteenth-century street said to have been reserved primarily for prostitution. Anything, anything, only go, only leave, now, and be away, away from him, walking blind, to lose herself in the guidebook Paris she'd learned when she'd first come here.

'But now,' he was saying, 'you can see that things have worked out for the best. It's often like that, isn't it?' Again, the smile, but this time it was boyish, slightly wistful, and somehow, horribly, more intimate. 'We've lost the gallery, but you've found employment, Marly. You have a job to do, an interesting one, and I have the connections you'll need, Marly. I know the people you'll need to meet, in order to find your artist.'

'My artist?' Covering her abrupt confusion with a sip of Vichy.

He opened his scarred attaché and removed something flat, a simple reflection hologram. She took it, grateful to have something to do with her hands, and saw that it was a casual shot of the box she'd seen in Virek's construct of Barcelona. Someone was holding it forward. A man's hands, not Alain's, and on one of them, a signet ring of some dark metal. The background was lost. Only the box, and the hands.

'Alain,' she said, 'where did you get this?' Looking up to meet brown eyes filled with a terrible childlike triumph.

'It's going to cost someone a very great deal to find out.' He ground out his cigarette and stood. 'Excuse me.' He walked away, headed in the direction of the restrooms. As he vanished, behind mirrors and black steel beams, she dropped the hologram, reached across the table, and flipped back the lid of his attaché. There was nothing there, only a blue elastic band and some crumbs of tobacco.

'May I bring you something else? More Vichy, perhaps?' The waiter stood beside her.

She looked up at him, struck suddenly by a sense of familiarity. The lean dark face ...

'He's wearing a broadcast unit,' the waiter said. 'He's armed as well. I was the bellman in Brussels. Give him what he wants. Remember that the money means nothing to you.' He took her glass and placed it carefully on his tray. 'And, very likely, it will destroy him.'

When Alain returned, he was smiling.

'Now, darling,' he said, reaching for his cigarettes, 'we can do business.'

Marly smiled back and nodded.

11

On Site

He allowed himself three hours of sleep, finally, in the windowless bunker where the point team had established the command post. He'd met the rest of the site team. Ramirez was slight, nervous, perpetually wired on his own skill as a console jockey; they were depending on him, along with Jaylene Slide on the offshore rig, to monitor cyberspace around the grid sector that held the heavily iced banks of Maas Biolabs; if Maas became aware of them, at the last moment, he might be able to provide some warning. He was also charged with relaying the medical data from the surgery to the offshore rig, a complex procedure if they were to keep it from Maas. The line out ran to a phone booth in the middle of nowhere. Once past that booth, he and Jaylene were on their own in the matrix. If they blew it, Maas could backtrack and pinpoint the site. And then there was Nathan, the repairman, whose real job consisted of watching over the gear in the bunker. If some part of their system went down, there was at least a chance he could fix it. Nathan belonged to the species that had produced Oakey and a thousand others Turner had worked with over the years, maverick techs who liked earning danger money and had proven they could keep their mouths shut. The others, Compton, Teddy, Costa, and Davis, were just expensive muscle, mercs, the sort of men you hired for a job like this. For their benefit, he'd taken particular care in questioning Sutcliffe about the arrangements for clear-out. He'd explained where the copters would come in, the order of pick-up, and precisely how and when they would be paid.

Then he'd told them to leave him alone in the bunker, and ordered Webber to wake him in three hours.

The place had been either a pump house or some sort of nexus for electrical wiring. The stumps of plastic tubing that protruded from the walls might have been conduit or sewage line; the room provided no evidence that any of them had ever been connected to anything. The ceiling, a single slab of poured concrete, was too low to allow him to stand, and there was a dry, dusty smell that wasn't entirely unpleasant. The team had swept the place before they brought in the tables and the equipment, but there were still a few yellow flakes of newsprint on the floor, that crumbled when he touched them. He made out letters, sometimes an entire word.

Folding metal camp tables had been set up along a wall, forming an L, each arm supporting an array of extraordinarily sophisticated communications gear. *The best*, he thought, *that Hosaka had been able to obtain.*

He hunched his way carefully along the length of each table, tapping each console, each black box, lightly as he went There was a heavily modified military sideband transceiver rigged for squirt transmission. This would be their link in case Ramirez and Jaylene flubbed the data transfer. The squirts were prerecorded, elaborate technical fictions encoded by Hosaka's cryptographers. The content of a given squirt was meaningless, but the sequence in which they were broadcast would convey simple messages. Sequence B/C/A would inform Hosaka of Mitchell's arrival; D/F would indicate his departure from the site, while F/G would signal his death and the concurrent closure of the operation. Turner tapped the sideband rig again, frowning. He wasn't pleased with Sutcliffe's arrangements there. If the extraction was blown, it wasn't likely they'd get out, let alone get out clean, and Webber had quietly informed him that, in the event of trouble, she'd been ordered to use a hand-held anti-tank rocket on the medicals in their miniature surgery.

'They know,' she said. 'You can bet they're getting paid for it, too.'

The rest of them were depending on the helicopters, which were based near Tucson. Turner assumed that Maas, if alerted, would easily take them out as they came in.

When he'd objected to Sutcliffe, the Australian had only shrugged: 'It isn't the way I'd set it up under the best circumstances, mate, but we're all in here on short notice, aren't we?'

Beside the transceiver was an elaborate Sony biomonitor, linked directly with the surgical pod and charged with the medical history recorded in Mitchell's biosoft dossier. The medicals, when the time came, would access the defector's history; simultaneously, the procedures they carried out in the pod would be fed back to the Sony and collated, ready for Ramirez to ice them and shift them out into cyberspace, where Jaylene Slide would be riding shotgun from her seat in the oil rig. If it all went smoothly, the medical update would be waiting in Hosaka's Mexico City compound when Turner brought him in in the jet. Turner had never seen anything quite like the Sony, but he supposed the Dutchman would have had something very similar in his Singapore clinic. The thought brought his hand to his bare chest, where he unconsciously traced the vanished line of a graft-scar.

The second table supported the cyberspace gear. The deck was identical with the one he'd seen on the oil rig, a Maas-Neotek prototype. The deck configuration was standard, but Conroy had said that it was built up from the new biochips. There was a fist-sized lump of pale pink plastique squashed on top of the console; someone, perhaps Ramirez, had thumbed in twin depressions for eyes and a crude curve of idiot grin. Two wires, one blue, the other yellow, ran from the thing's pink forehead to one of the black, gaping tubes that protruded from the wall behind the console. Another of Webber's chores, if there seemed any danger of the site being overrun. Turner eyed the wires, frowning; a charge that size, in that small, enclosed space, guaranteed death for anyone in the bunker.

His shoulders aching, the back of his head brushing the rough concrete of the ceiling, he continued his inspection. The rest of the table was taken up with the deck's peripherals, a series of black boxes positioned with obsessive precision. He suspected that each unit was a certain specific distance from its neighbour, and they were perfectly aligned. Ramirez himself would have set them out, and Turner was certain that if he touched one, moved it the least fraction, the jockey would know. He'd seen that same neurotic touch before, in other console men, and it told him nothing about Ramirez. He'd watched other jockeys who reversed the trait, deliberately tangling their gear in a rat's nest of leads and cables, who were terrified of tidiness and plastered their consoles with decals of dice and screaming skulls. *There was no way to tell*, he thought; either Ramirez was good, or else they all might be dead soon.

At the far end of the table were five Telefunken ear-bead transceivers with adhesive throat-mikes, still sealed in individual bubble packs. During the crucial phase of the defection, which Turner took to be the twenty minutes on either side of Mitchell's arrival, he, Ramirez, Sutcliffe, Webber, and Lynch would be linked, although use of the transceivers was to be kept to an absolute minimum.

Behind the Telefunkens was an unmarked plastic carton

that contained twenty Swedish catalytic handwarmers, smooth flat oblongs of stainless steel, each in its own drawstring bag of Christmas-red flannelette.

'You're a clever bastard,' he said to the carton. 'I might have thought that one up myself ...'

He slept on a corrugated foam hiker's pad on the floor of the command post, using the parka as a blanket. Conroy had been right about the desert night, but the concrete seemed to hold the day's heat. He left his fatigues and shoes on; Webber had advised him to shake his shoes and clothing out whenever he dressed. 'Scorpions,' she'd said, 'they like sweat, any kind of moisture ...' He removed the Smith & Wesson from the nylon holster before he lay down, carefully positioning it beside the foam pad. He left the two battery lanterns on, and closed his eyes ...

And slid into a shallow sea of dream, images tossing past, fragments of Mitchell's dossier melding with bits of his own life ... He and Mitchell drove a bus through a cascade of plate glass, into the lobby of a Marrakesh hotel. The scientist whooped as he pressed the button that detonated the two dozen canisters of CN taped along the flanks of the vehicle, and Oakey was there, too, offering him whisky from a bottle, and yellow Peruvian cocaine on a round, plastic-rimmed mirror he'd last seen in Allison's purse. He thought he saw Allison somewhere beyond the windows of the bus, choking in the clouds of gas, and he tried to tell Oakey, tried to point her out, but the glass was plastered with Mexican holograms of saints, postcards of the Virgin, and Oakey was holding up something smooth and round, a globe of pink crystal, and he saw a spider crouched at its core, a spider made of quicksilver, but Mitchell was laughing, his teeth full of blood, and extending his open palm to offer Turner the grey biosoft. Turner saw

84

that the dossier was a brain, greyish-pink and alive beneath a wet clear membrane, pulsing softly in Mitchell's hand, and then he tumbled over some submarine ledge of dream and settled smoothly down into a night with no stars at all.

Webber woke him, her hard features framed in the square doorway, her shoulders draped in the heavy military blanket taped across the entrance.

'Got your three hours. The medicals are up, if you want to talk to 'em ...' She withdrew, her boots crunching gravel.

Hosaka's medics were waiting beside the self-contained neurosurgery. Under a desert dawn they looked as though they'd just stepped from some kind of matter transmitter in their fashionably rumpled Ginza casuals. One of the men was bundled in an oversized Mexican handknit, the sort of belted cardigan Turner had seen tourists wear in Mexico City. The other two wore expensive-looking insulated ski jackets against the desert cold. The men were a head shorter than the Korean, a slender woman with strong, archaic features and a birdlike ruff of red-tinged hair that made Turner think of raptors. Conroy had said that the two were company men, and Turner could see it easily; only the woman had the attitude, the stance that belonged to Turner's world, and she was an outlaw, a black medic. *She'd be right at home with the Dutchman*, he thought.

'I'm Turner,' he said. 'I'm in charge here.'

'You don't need our names,' the woman said, as the two Hosaka men bowed automatically. They exchanged glances, looked at Turner, then looked back to the Korean.

'No,' Turner said, 'it isn't necessary.'

'Why are we still denied access to the patient's medical data?' the Korean asked.

'Security,' Turner said, the answer very nearly an automatic response. In fact, he could see no reason to prevent them from studying Mitchell's records.

The woman shrugged, turned away, her face hidden by the upturned collar of her insulated jacket.

'Would you like to inspect the surgery?' the man in the bulky cardigan asked, his face polite and alert, a perfect corporate mask.

'No,' Turner said. 'We'll be moving you out to the lot twenty minutes prior to his arrival. We'll take the wheels off, level you with jacks. The sewage link will be disconnected. I want you fully operational five minutes after we set you down.'

'There will be no problem,' the other man said, smiling.

'Now I want you to tell me what you're going to be doing in there, what you'll do to him and how it might affect him.'

'You don't *know?*' the woman asked, sharply, turning back to face him.

'I said that I wanted you to tell me,' Turner said.

'We'll conduct an immediate scan for lethal implants,' the man in the cardigan said.

'Cortex charges, that sort of thing?'

'I doubt,' said the other man, 'that we will encounter anything so crude, but yes, we will be scanning for the full range of lethal devices. Simultaneously, we'll run a full blood screen. We understand that his current employers deal in extremely sophisticated biochemical systems. It would seem possible that the greatest danger would lie in that direction ...'

'It's currently quite fashionable to equip top employees with modified insulin-pump subdermals,' his partner broke in. 'The subject's system can be tricked into an artificial reliance on certain synthetic enzyme analogues. Unless the subdermal is recharged at regular intervals, withdrawal from the source – the employer – can result in trauma ...'

'We are prepared to deal with that as well,' said the other.

'Neither of you are even remotely prepared to deal with what I suspect we will encounter,' the black medic said, her voice cold as the wind that blew out of the east now. Turner heard sand hissing across the rusted sheet of steel above them.

'You,' Turner said to her, 'come with me.' Then he turned, without looking back, and walked away. It was possible that she might not obey his command, in which case he'd lose face with the other two, but it seemed the right move. When he was ten metres from the surgery pod, he halted. He heard her feet on the gravel.

'What do you know?' he asked, without turning.

'Perhaps no more than you do,' she said, 'perhaps more.'

'More than your colleagues, obviously.'

'They are extremely talented men. They are also ... servants.'

'And you are not.'

'Neither are you, mercenary. I was hired out of the finest unlicensed clinic in Chiba for this. I was given a great deal of material to study in preparation for my meeting with this illustrious patient. The black clinics of Chiba are the cutting edge of medicine; not even Hosaka could know that my position in black medicine would allow me to guess what it is that your defector carries in his head. The street tries to find its own uses for things, Mr Turner. Already, several times, I've been hired to attempt the removal of these new implants. A certain amount of advanced Maas biocircuitry has found its way into the market. These attempts at implanting are a logical step. I suspect Maas may leak these things deliberately ...'

'Then explain it to me.'

'I don't think I could,' she said, and there was a strange hint of resignation in her voice. 'I told you, I've seen it. I didn't say that I understood it.' Fingertips suddenly brushed the skin

87

beside his skull jack. 'This, compared with biochip implants, is like a wooden staff beside a myoelectric limb.'

'But will it be life-threatening, in his case?'

'Oh, no,' she said, withdrawing her hand, 'not for *him* ...' And then he heard her trudging back towards the surgery.

Conroy sent a runner in with the software package that would allow Turner to pilot the jet that would carry Mitchell to Hosaka's Mexico City compound. The runner was a wild-eyed, sun-blackened man Lynch called Harry, a rope-muscled apparition who came cycling in from the direction of Tucson on a sand-scoured bike with balding lug tyres and bone-yellow rawhide laced around its handlebars. Lynch led Harry across the parking lot. Harry was singing to himself, a strange sound in the enforced quiet of the site, and his song, if you could call it that, was like someone randomly tuning a broken radio up and down midnight miles of dial, bringing in gospel shouts and snatches of twenty years of international pop. Harry had his bike slung across one burnt, bird-thin shoulder.

'Harry's got something for you from Tucson,' Lynch said.

'You two know each other?' Turner asked, looking at Lynch. 'Maybe have a friend in common?'

'What's that supposed to mean?' Lynch asked.

Turner held his stare. 'You know his name.'

'He told me his fucking name, Turner.'

'Name's Harry,' the burnt man said. He tossed the bicycle down on a clump of brush. He smiled vacantly, exposing badly spaced, eroded teeth. His bare chest was filmed with sweat and dust, and hung with loops of fine steel chain, rawhide, bits of animal horn and fur, brass cartridge casings, copper coins worn smooth and faceless with use, and a small pouch made of soft brown leather.

Turner looked at the assortment of things strung across the skinny chest and reached out, flipping a crooked bit of bent gristle suspended from a length of braided string.

'What the hell is that, Harry?'

'That's a coon's pecker,' Harry said. 'Coon's got him a jointed bone in his pecker. Not many as know that.'

'You ever meet my friend Lynch before, Harry?'

Harry blinked.

'He had the passwords,' Lynch said. 'There's an urgency-hierarchy. He knew the top. He told me his name. Do you need me here, or can I get back to work?'

'Go,' Turner said.

When Lynch was out of earshot, Harry began to work at the thongs that sealed the leather pouch. 'You shouldn't be harsh with the boy,' he said. 'He's really very good. I actually didn't see him until he had that fletcher up against my neck.' He opened the pouch and fished delicately inside.

'Tell Conroy I've got him pegged.'

'Sorry,' Harry said, extracting a folded sheet of yellow notebook paper from his pouch. 'You've got who pegged?' He handed it to Turner; there was something inside.

'Lynch. He's Conroy's bumboy on the site. Tell him.' He unfolded the paper and removed the fat military microsoft.

There was a note in blue capitals: BREAK A LEG, ASSHOLE. SEE YOU IN THE DF.

'Do you really want me to tell him that?'

'Tell him.'

'You're the boss.'

'You fucking know it,' Turner said, crumpling the paper and thrusting it into Harry's left armpit. Harry smiled, sweetly and vacantly, and the intelligence that had risen in him settled again, like some aquatic beast sinking effortlessly down into a smooth sea of sun-addled vapidity. Turner stared into his eyes, cracked yellow opal, and saw nothing there but sun and the broken highway. A hand with missing joints came up to scratch absently at a week's growth of beard. 'Now,' Turner said. Harry turned, pulled his bike up from the tangle of brush, shouldered it with a grunt, and began to make his way back across the ruined parking lot. His oversized, tattered khaki shorts flapped as he went, and his collection of chains rattled softly.

Sutcliffe whistled from a rise twenty metres away, held up a roll of orange surveyor's tape. It was time to start laying out Mitchell's landing strip. They'd have to work quickly, before the sun was too high, and still it was going to be hot.

'So,' Webber said, 'he's coming in by air.' She spat brown juice on a yellowed cactus. Her cheek was packed with Copenhagen snuff.

'You got it,' Turner said. He sat beside her on a ledge of buff shale. They were watching Lynch and Nathan clear the strip he and Sutcliffe had laid out with the orange tape. The tape marked out a rectangle four metres wide and twenty long. Lynch carried a length of rusted I-beam to the tape and heaved it over. Something scurried away through the brush as the beam rang on concrete.

'They can see that tape, if they want to,' Webber said, wiping her lips with the back of her hand. 'Read the head-lines on your morning fax, if they want to.'

'I know,' Turner said, 'but if they don't know we're here already, I don't think they're going to. And you couldn't see it from the highway.' He adjusted the black nylon cap Ramirez had given him, pulling the long bill down until it touched his sunglasses. 'Anyway, we're just moving the heavy stuff, the things that could tear a leg off. It isn't going to look like anything, not from orbit.'

'No,' Webber agreed, her seamed face impassive beneath her sunglasses. He could smell her sweat from where she sat, sharp and animal.

'What the hell do you do, Webber, when you aren't doing this?' He looked at her.

'Probably a hell of a lot more than you do,' she said. 'Part of the time I breed dogs.' She took a knife from her boot and began to strop it patiently on her sole, flipping it smoothly with each stroke, like a Mexican barber sharpening a razor. 'And I fish. Trout.'

'You have people, in New Mexico?'

'Probably more than you've got,' she said flatly. 'I figure the ones like you and Sutcliffe, you aren't from any place at all. This is where you live, isn't it, Turner? On the site, today, the day your boy comes out. Right?' She tested the blade against the ball of her thumb, then slid it back into its sheath.

'But you have people? You got a man to go back to?'

'A woman, you want to know,' she said. 'Know anything about breeding dogs?'

'No,' he said.

'I didn't think so.' She squinted at him. 'We got a kid, too. Ours. She carried it.'

'DNA splice?'

She nodded.

'That's expensive,' he said.

'You know it; wouldn't be here if we didn't need to pay it off. But she's beautiful.'

'Your woman?'

'Our kid.'

12

Café Blanc

As she walked from the Louvre, she seemed to sense some articulated structure shifting to accommodate her course through the city. The waiter would be merely a part of the thing, one limb, a delicate probe or palp. The whole would be larger, much larger. How could she have imagined that it would be possible to live, to move, in the unnatural field of Virek's wealth without suffering distortion? Virek had taken her up, in all her misery, and had rotated her through the monstrous, invisible stresses of his money, and she had been changed. *Of course*, she thought, *of course*; it moves around me constantly, watchful and invisible, the vast and subtle mechanism of Herr Virek's surveillance.

Eventually she found herself on the pavement below the terrace of the Blanc. It seemed as good a place as any. A month before, she would have avoided it; she'd spent too many evenings with Alain there. Now, feeling that she had been freed, she decided to begin the process of rediscovering her own Paris by choosing a table at the Blanc. She took one near a side-screen. She asked a waiter for a cognac, and shivered, watching the Paris traffic flow past, perpetual river of steel and glass, while all around her, at other tables, strangers ate and smiled, drank and argued, said bitter goodbyes or swore private fealties to an afternoon's feeling.

But – she smiled – she was a part of it all. Something in

her was waking from a long and stifled sleep, brought back into the light in the instant she'd fully opened her eyes to Alain's viciousness and her own desperate need to continue loving him. But that need was fading, even as she sat here. The shabbiness of his lies, somehow, had broken the chains of her depression. She could see no logic to it, because she had known, in some part of herself, and long before the business with Gnass, exactly what it was that Alain did in the world, and that had made no difference to her love. In the face of this new feeling, however, she would forgo logic. It was enough, to be here, alive, at a table in the Blanc, and to imagine all around her the intricate machine that she now knew Virek had deployed.

Ironies, she thought, seeing the young waiter from Napoleon Court step up onto the terrace. He wore the dark trousers he had worked in, but the apron had been replaced with a blue windbreaker. Dark hair fell across his forehead in a smooth wing. He came towards her, smiling, confident, knowing that she wouldn't run. There was something in her then that wanted very badly to run, but she knew that she wouldn't. Irony, she told herself: as I luxuriate in the discovery that I am no special sponge for sorrow, but merely another fallible animal in this stone maze of a city, I come simultaneously to see that I am the focus of some vast device fuelled by an obscure desire.

'My name is Paco,' he said, pulling out the white-painted iron chair opposite her own.

'You were the child, the boy, in the park ...'

'A long time ago, yes.' He sat. 'Señor has preserved the image of my childhood.'

'I have been thinking, about your Señor.' She didn't look at him, but at the passing cars, cooling her eyes in the flow of traffic, the colours of polycarbon and painted steel. 'A man

93

like Virek is incapable of divesting himself of his wealth. His money has a life of its own. Perhaps a will of its own. He implied as much when we met.'

'You are a philosopher.'

'I'm a tool, Paco. I'm the most recent tip for a very old machine in the hands of a very old man, who wishes to penetrate something and has so far failed to do so. Your employer fumbles through a thousand tools and somehow chooses me ...'

'You are a poet as well!'

She laughed, taking her eyes from the traffic; he was grinning, his mouth bracketed in deep vertical grooves. 'While I walked here, I imagined a structure, a machine so large that I am incapable of seeing it. A machine that surrounds me, anticipating my every step.'

'And you are an egotist as well?'

'Am I?'

'Perhaps not. Certainly, you are observed. We watch, and it is well that we do. Your friend in the brasserie, we watch him as well. Unfortunately, we've been unable to determine where he obtained the hologram he showed you. Very likely, he already had it when he began to phone your friend's number. Someone got to him, do you understand? Someone has put him in your way. Don't you think that this is most intriguing? Doesn't it pique the philosopher in you?'

'Yes, I suppose it does. I took the advice you gave me, in the brasserie, and agreed to his price.'

'Then he will double it.' Paco smiled.

'Which is of no importance to me, as you pointed out. He has agreed to contact me tomorrow. I assume that you can arrange the delivery of the money. He asked for cash.'

'Cash' – he rolled his eyes – 'how risqué! But, yes, I can. And I know the details as well. We were monitoring the conversation. Not difficult, as he was helpful enough to broadcast it himself, from a bead microphone. We were anxious to learn who that broadcast was intended for, but we doubt he knows that himself ...'

'It was unlike him,' she said, frowning, 'to excuse himself, to break off that way, before he had made his demands. He fancies he has a flair for the dramatic moment.'

'He had no choice,' Paco said. 'We engineered what he took to be a failure of the bead's power source. It required a trip to the hommes, then. He said very nasty things about you, alone in the cubicle.'

She gestured to her empty glass as a waiter passed. 'I still find it difficult to see my part in this, my value. To Virek, I mean.'

'Don't ask me. You are the philosopher, here. I merely execute Señor's orders, to the best of my ability.'

'Would you like a brandy, Paco? Or perhaps some coffee?'

'The French,' he said, with great conviction, 'know nothing about coffee.'

13

With Both Hands

'Maybe you can run that one by me again,' Bobby said, around a mouthful of rice and eggs. 'I thought you already said it's not a religion.'

Beauvoir removed his eyeglass-frames and sighted down one of the earpieces. 'That wasn't what I said. I said you didn't have to worry about it, is all, whether it's a religion or not. It's just a *structure*. Lets you an' me discuss some things that are happening, otherwise we might not have words for it, concepts ...'

'But you talk like these, whatchacallem, *lows*, are—'

'Loa,' Beauvoir corrected, tossing his glasses down on the table. He sighed, dug one of the Chinese cigarettes from Two-a-Day's pack, and lit it with the pewter skull. 'Plural's same as the singular.' He inhaled deeply, blew out twin streams of smoke through arched nostrils. 'You think religion, what are you thinking about, exactly?'

'Well, my mother's sister, she's a Scientologist, real orthodox, you know? And there's this woman across the hall, she's Catholic. My old lady,' and he paused, the food gone tasteless in his mouth, 'she'd put these holograms up in my room sometimes, Jesus or Hubbard or some shit. I guess I think about that.'

'Vodou isn't like that,' Beauvoir said. 'It isn't concerned with notions of salvation and transcendence. What it's about is getting things *done*. You follow me? In our system, there are *many* gods, spirits. Part of one big family, with all the virtues, all the vices. There's a ritual tradition of communal manifestation, understand? Vodou says, there's God, sure, Gran Mèt, but He's big, too big and too far away to worry Himself if your ass is poor, or you can't get laid. Come on, man, you know how this works, it's *street* religion, came out of a dirt-poor place a million years ago. Vodou's like the street. Some duster chops out your sister, you don't go camp on the Yakuza's doorstep, do you? No way. You go to somebody, though, who can get the thing *done*. Right?'

Bobby nodded, chewing thoughtfully. Another derm and two glasses of the red wine had helped a lot, and the big man had taken Two-a-Day for a walk through the trees and the fluorescent jackstraws, leaving Bobby with Beauvoir. Then Jackie had shown up all cheerful, with a big bowl of this eggs-and-rice stuff, which wasn't bad at all, and as she'd put it down on the table in front of him, she'd pressed one of her tits against his shoulder.

'So,' Beauvoir said, 'we are concerned with getting things done. If you want, we're concerned with systems. And so are you, or at least you want to be, or else you wouldn't be a cowboy and you wouldn't have a handle, right?' He dunked what was left of the cigarette in a fingerprinted glass half full of red wine. 'Looks like Two-a-Day was about to get down to serious partying, about the time the shit hit the fan.'

'What shit's that?' Bobby asked, wiping his mouth with the back of his hand.

'You,' Beauvoir said, frowning. 'Not that any of it is your fault. As much as Two-a-Day wants to make out that's the case.'

'He does? He seems pretty tense now. Real bitchy, too.'

'Exactly. You got it. Tense. Scared shitless is more like it.'

'So how come?'

'Well, you see, things aren't exactly what they seem, with Two-a-Day. I mean, yeah, he actually does the kind of shit you've known him to, hustles hot software to the caspers, pardon me' – and he grinned – 'down in Barrytown, but his main shot, I mean the man's real ambitions, you understand, lie elsewhere.' Beauvoir picked up a wilted canapé, regarded it with evident suspicion, and flicked it over the table, into the trees. 'His thing, you understand, is dicking around for a couple of bigtime Sprawl oungans.'

Bobby nodded blankly.

'Dudes who serve with both hands.'

'You lost me there.'

'We're talking a professional priesthood here, you want to call it that. Otherwise, just imagine a couple of major dudes – console cowboys, among other things – who make it their business to get things done for people. "To serve with both hands" is an expression we have, sort of means they work both ends. White and black, got me?'

Bobby swallowed, then shook his head.

'Sorcerers,' Beauvoir said. 'Never mind. Bad dudes, big money, that's all you need to know. Two-a-Day, he acts like an upline joeboy for these people. Sometimes he finds something they might be interested in, he downloads it on 'em, collects a few favours later. Maybe he collects a dozen too many favours, they download something on *him*. Not quite the same proposition, you follow? Say they get something they think has potential, but it scares them. These characters tend to a certain conservatism, you see? No? Well, you'll learn.'

Bobby nodded.

'The kind of software someone like you would rent from Two-a-Day, that's nothin'. I mean, it'll *work*, but it's nothin' anybody heavy would ever bother with. You've seen a lot of

98

cowboy kinos, right? Well, the stuff they make up for those things isn't much, compared with the kind of shit a real heavy operator can front. Particularly when it comes to icebreakers. Heavy icebreakers are kind of funny to deal in, even for the big boys. You know why? Because ice, all the really hard stuff, the walls around every major store of data in the matrix, is always the product of an AI, an artificial intelligence. Nothing else is fast enough to weave good ice and constantly alter and upgrade it. So when a really powerful icebreaker shows up on the black market, there are already a couple of very dicey factors in play. Like, for starts, where did the product come from? Nine times out of ten, it came from an AI, and AIs are constantly screened, mainly by the Turing people, to make sure they don't get too smart. So maybe you'll get the Turing machine after your ass, because maybe an AI somewhere wants to augment its private cashflow. Some AI's have citizenship, right? Another thing you have to watch out for, maybe it's a *military* icebreaker, and that's bad heat, too, or maybe it's taken a walk out of some zaibatsu's industrial espionage arm, and you don't want that either. You takin' this shit in, Bobby?'

Bobby nodded. He felt like he'd been waiting all his life to hear Beauvoir explain the workings of a world whose existence he'd only guessed at before.

'Still, an icebreaker that'll really cut is worth mega, I mean *beaucoup*. So maybe you're Mr Big in the market, someone offers you this thing, and you don't want to just tell 'em to take a walk. So you buy it. You buy it, real quiet, but you don't *slot* it, no. What do you do with it? You take it home, have your tech fix it up so that it looks real average. Like you have it set up in a format like this,' and he tapped a stack of software in front of him, 'and you take it to your joeboy, who owes you some favours, as usual ...'

'Wait a sec,' Bobby said. 'I don't think I like—'

'Good. That means you're getting smart, or anyway smarter. Because that's what they did. They brought it out here to your friendly 'wareman, Mr Two-a-Day, and they told him their problem. "Ace," they say, "we want to check this shit out, test-drive it, but no way we gonna do it ourselves. It's down to you, boy." So, in the way of things, what's Two-a-Day gonna do with it? Is *he* gonna slot it? No way at all. He just does the same damn thing the big boys did to him, 'cept he isn't even going to bother telling the guy he's going to do it to. What he does, he picks a base out in the Midwest that's full of tax-dodge programs and yen-laundry flowcharts for some whorehouse in Kansas City, and everybody who didn't just fall off a tree *knows* that the motherfucker is eyeball-deep in ice, *black* ice, totally lethal feedback programs. There isn't a cowboy in the Sprawl or out who'd mess with that base, first because it's dripping with defences, second, because the stuff inside isn't worth anything to anybody but the IRS, and they're probably already on the owner's take.'

'Hey,' Bobby said, 'lemme get this straight—'

'I'm *giving* it to you straight, white boy! He picked out that base, then he ran down his list of hotdoggers, ambitious punks from over in Barrytown, wilsons dumb enough to run a program they'd never seen before against a base that some joker like Two-a-Day fingered for them and told them was an easy make. And who's he pick? He picks somebody new to the game, natch, somebody who doesn't even know where he *lives*, doesn't even have his *number*, and he says, here, my man, you take this home and make yourself some money. You get anything good, I'll fence it for you!' Beauvoir's eyes were wide; he wasn't smiling. 'Sound like anybody you know, man, or maybe you try not to hang out with losers?'

'You mean he knew I was going to get killed if I plugged into that base?'

'No, Bobby, but he knew it was a possibility if the package didn't work. What he mainly wanted was to watch you try. Which he didn't bother to do himself, just put a couple of cowboys on it. It could've gone a couple different ways. Say, if that icebreaker had done its number on the black ice, you'd have got in, found a bunch of figures that meant dick to you, you'd have got back out, maybe without leaving any trace at all. Well, you'd have come back to Leon's and told Two-a-Day that he'd fingered the wrong data. Oh, he'd have been real apologetic, for sure, and you'd have got a new target and a new icebreaker, and he'd have taken the first one back to the Sprawl and said it looked okay. Meanwhile, he'd have an eye cocked in your direction, just to monitor your health, make sure nobody came looking for the icebreaker they might've heard you'd used. Another way it might have gone, the way it nearly did go, something could've been funny with the icebreaker, the ice could've fried you dead, and one of those cowboys would've had to break into your momma's place and get that software back before anybody found your body.'

'I dunno, Beauvoir, that's pretty fucking hard to—'

'Hard my ass. *Life* is hard. I mean, we're talkin' *biz*, you know?' Beauvoir regarded him with some severity, the plastic frames far down his slender nose. He was lighter than either Two-a-Day or the big man, the colour of coffee with only a little whitener, his forehead high and smooth beneath close-cropped black frizz. He looked skinny, under his grey shark-skin robe, and Bobby didn't really find him threatening at all. 'But our problem, the reason we're here, the reason you're here, is to figure out what *did* happen. And that's something else.'

'But you mean he set me up. Two-a-Day set me up so I'd

101

get my ass killed?' Bobby was still in the St Mary's Maternity wheelchair, although he no longer felt like he needed it. 'And he's in deep shit with these guys, these heavies from the Sprawl?'

'You got it now.'

'And that's why he was acting that way, like he doesn't give a shit, or maybe hates my guts, right? And he's real scared?'

Beauvoir nodded.

'And,' Bobby said, suddenly seeing what Two-a-Day was really pissed about, and why he was scared, 'it's because I got my ass jumped, down by Big Playground, and those Lobe fucks ripped me for my deck! And their software, it was still in my deck!' He leaned forward, excited at having put it together. 'And these guys, it's like they'll kill him or something, unless he gets it back for them, right?'

'I can tell you watch a lot of kino,' Beauvoir said, 'but that's about the size of it, definitely.'

'Right,' Bobby said, settling back in the wheelchair and putting his bare feet up on the edge of the table. 'Well, Beauvoir, who *are* these guys? Whatchacallem, hoonguns? Sorcerers, you said? What the fuck's that supposed to mean?'

'Well, Bobby,' Beauvoir said, 'I'm one, and the big fella – you can call him Lucas – he's the other.'

'You've probably seen one of these before,' Beauvoir said, as the man he called Lucas put the projection tank down on the table, having methodically cleared a space for it.

'In school,' Bobby said.

'You go to school, man?' Two-a-Day snapped. 'Why the fuck didn't you stay there?' He'd been chain-smoking since he came back with Lucas, and seemed in worse shape than he'd been in before.

'Shut up, Two-a-Day,' Beauvoir said. 'Little education

might do you some good.'

'They used one to teach us our way around in the matrix, how to access stuff from the print library, like that ...'

'Well, then,' Lucas said, straightening up and brushing non-existent dust from his big pink palms, 'did you ever use it for that, to access print books?' He'd removed his immaculate black suit coat; his spotless white shirt was traversed by a pair of slender maroon suspenders, and he'd loosened the knot of his plain black tie.

'I don't read too well,' Bobby said. 'I mean, I can, but it's work. But yeah, I did. I looked at some real old books on the matrix and stuff.'

'I thought you had,' Lucas said, jacking some kind of small deck into the console that formed the base of the tank. 'Count Zero. *Count zero interrupt*. Old programmer talk.' He passed the deck to Beauvoir, who began to tap commands into it.

Complex geometric forms began to click into place in the tank, aligned with the nearly invisible planes of a three-dimensional grid. Beauvoir was sketching in the cyberspace co-ordinates for Barrytown, Bobby saw.

'We'll call you this blue pyramid, Bobby. There you are.' A blue pyramid began to pulse softly at the very centre of the tank. 'Now we'll show you what Two-a-Day's cowboys saw, the ones who were watching you. From now on, you're seeing a recording.' An interrupted line of blue light extruded from the pyramid, following a grid line. Bobby watched, seeing himself alone in his mother's living room, the Ono-Sendai on his lap, the curtains drawn, his fingers moving across the deck.

'Icebreaker on its way,' Beauvoir said. The line of blue dots reached the wall of the tank. Beauvoir tapped the deck, and the co-ordinates changed. A new set of geometrics replaced the first arrangement. Bobby recognised the cluster of orange rectangles centred in the grid. 'That's it,' he said.

The blue line progressed from the edge of the tank, headed for the orange base. Faint planes of ghost-orange flickered around the rectangles, shifting and strobing, as the line grew closer.

'You can see something's wrong right there,' Lucas said. 'That's their ice, and it was already hip to you. Rumbled you before you even got a lock.'

As the line of blue dots touched the shifting orange plane, it was surrounded by a translucent orange tube of slightly greater diameter. The tube began to lengthen, travelling back, along the line, until it reached the wall of the tank ...

'Meanwhile,' Beauvoir said, 'back home in Barrytown ...' He tapped the deck again and now Bobby's blue pyramid was in the centre. Bobby watched as the orange tube emerged from the wall of the projection tank, still following the blue line, and smoothly approached the pyramid. 'Now at this point, you were due to start doing some serious dying, cowboy.' The tube reached the pyramid; triangular orange planes snapped up, walling it in. Beauvoir froze the projection.

'Now,' Lucas said, 'when Two-a-Day's hired help, who are all in all a pair of tough and experienced console jockeys, when they saw what you are about to see, my man, they decided that their deck was due for that big overhaul in the sky. Being pros, they had a backup deck. When they brought it on line, they saw the same thing. It was at that point that they decided to phone their employer, Mr Two-a-Day, who, as we can see from this mess, was about to throw himself a party ...'

'Man,' Two-a-Day said, his voice tight with hysteria, 'I *told* you. I had some clients up here needed entertaining. I paid those boys to watch, they were watching, and they phoned me. I phoned you. What the hell you *want*, anyway?'

'Our property,' Beauvoir said softly. 'Now watch this, real close. This motherfucker is what we call an anomalous phenomenon, no shit ...' He tapped the deck again, starting the recording.

Liquid flowers of milky white blossomed from the floor of the tank; Bobby, craning forward, saw that they seemed to consist of thousands of tiny spheres or bubbles, and then they aligned perfectly with the cubical grid and coalesced, forming a top-heavy, asymmetrical structure, a thing like a rectilinear mushroom. The surfaces, facets, were white, perfectly blank. The image in the tank was no longer than Bobby's open hand. but to anyone jacked into a deck it would have been enormous. The thing unfolded a pair of horns; these lengthened, curved, became pincers that arced out to grasp the pyramid. He saw the tips sink smoothly through the flickering orange planes of the enemy ice.

'She said, "What are you doing?"' he heard himself say. 'Then she asked me why they were doing that, doing it to me, killing me ...'

'Ah,' Beauvoir said, quietly, 'now we are getting somewhere.'

He didn't know where they were going, but he was glad to be out of that chair. Beauvoir ducked to avoid a slanting gro-light that dangled from twin lengths of curly-cord; Bobby followed, almost slipping in a green-filmed puddle of water. Away from Two-a-Day's couch-clearing, the air seemed thicker. There was a greenhouse smell of damp and growing things.

'So that's how it was,' Beauvoir said. 'Two-a-Day sent some friends round to Covina Concourse Courts, but you were gone. Your deck was gone, too.'

'Well,' Bobby said, 'I don't see it's exactly his fault, then. I mean, if I hadn't split for Leon's – and I was *lookin'* for

Two-a-Day, even lookin' to try to get up here – then he'd have found me, right?'

Beauvoir paused to admire a leafy stand of flowering hemp, extending a thin brown forefinger to lightly brush the pale, colourless flowers.

'True,' he said, 'but this is a *business* matter. He should have detailed someone to watch your place for the duration of the run, to ensure that neither you nor the software took any unscheduled walks.'

'Well, he sent Rhea 'n' Jackie over to Leon's, because I saw 'em there.' Bobby reached into the neck of his black pyjamas and scratched at the sealed wound that crossed his chest and stomach. Then he remembered the centipede thing Pye had used as a suture, and quickly withdrew his hand. It itched, a straight line of itch, but he didn't want to touch it.

'No, Jackie and Rhea are ours. Jackie is a mambo, a priestess, the horse of Danbala ...' Beauvoir continued on his way, picking out what Bobby presumed was some existing track or path through the jumbled forest of hydroponics, although it seemed to progress in no particular direction. Some of the larger shrubs were rooted in bulbous green plastic trash bags filled with dark humus. Many of these had burst, and pale roots sought fresh nourishment in the shadows between the gro-lights, where time and the gradual fall of leaves conspired to produce a thin compost. Bobby wore a pair of black nylon thongs Jackie had found for him, but there was already damp earth between his toes.

'A horse?' he asked Beauvoir, dodging past a prickly-looking thing that suggested an inside-out palm tree.

'Danbala rides her, Danbala Wedo, the snake. Other times, she is the horse of Aida Wedo, his wife.'

Bobby decided not to pursue it. He tried to change the subject: 'How come Two-a-Day's got such a motherhuge place? What are all these trees 'n' things for?' He knew that Jackie and Rhea had wheeled him through a doorway, in the St Mary's chair, but he hadn't seen a wall since. He also knew that the arcology covered x-number of hectares, so that it was possible that Two-a-Day's place was very large indeed, but it hardly seemed likely that a 'wareman, even a very sharp one, could afford this much space. *Nobody* could afford this much space, and why would anybody want to live in a leaky hydroponic forest?

The last derm was wearing off, and his back and chest were beginning to burn and ache.

'Ficus trees, mapou trees ... This whole level of the Projects is a *lieu saint*, holy place.' Beauvoir tapped Bobby on the shoulder and pointed out twisted, bicoloured strings dangling from the limbs of a nearby tree. 'The trees are consecrated to different loa. That one is for Ougou, Ougou Feray, god of war. There's a lot of other things grown up here, herbs the leaf-doctors need, and some just for fun. But this isn't Two-a-Day's place, this is communal.'

'You mean the whole Project's into this? All like voodoo and stuff?' It was worse than Marsha's darkest fantasies.

'No, man,' and Beauvoir laughed. 'There's a *mosque* up top, and a couple or ten thousand holy roller Baptists scattered around, some Church o' Sci ... All the usual stuff. Still' – he grinned – '*we* are the ones with the tradition of getting shit *done* ... But how this got started, this level, that goes way back. The people who designed these places, maybe eighty, a hundred years ago, they had the idea they'd make 'em as self-sufficient as possible. Make 'em grow food. Make 'em heat themselves, generate power, whatever. Now this one, you drill far enough down, is sitting on top of a lot of geothermal water. It's real hot down there, but not hot enough to run an engine, so it wasn't gonna give 'em any power. They made a stab at power, up on the roof, with about a hundred Darrieus rotors, what they call eggbeaters. Had themselves a wind farm, see? Today they get most of their watts off the Fission Authority, like anybody else. But that geothermal water, they pump that up to a heat exchanger. It's too salty to drink, so in the exchanger it just heats up your standard Jersey tap water, which a lot of people figure isn't worth drinking anyway ...'

Finally, they were approaching a wall of some kind. Bobby looked back. Shallow pools on the muddy concrete floor caught and reflected the limbs of the dwarf trees, the bare pale roots straggling down into makeshift tanks of hydroponic fluid. 'Then they pump that into shrimp tanks, and grow a lot of shrimp. Shrimp grow real fast in warm water. Then they pump it through pipes in the concrete, up here, to keep this place warm. That's what this level was for, to grow 'ponic amaranth, lettuce, things like that. Then they pump it out into the catfish tanks, and algae eat the shrimp shit. Catfish eat the algae, and it all goes around again. Or anyway, that was the idea. Chances are they didn't figure anybody'd go up on the roof and kick those Darrieus rotors over to make room for a mosque, and they didn't figure a lot of other changes either. So we wound up with this space. But you can still get you some damned good shrimp in the Projects ... Catfish, too.'

They had arrived at the wall. It was made of glass, beaded heavily with condensation. A few centimetres beyond it was another wall, that one made of what looked like rusty sheet steel. Beauvoir fished a key of some kind from a pocket in his sharkskin robe and slid it into an opening in a bare alloy beam dividing two expanses of window. Somewhere nearby, an engine whined into life; the broad steel shutter rotated up and out, moving jerkily, to reveal a view that Bobby had often imagined.

They must be near the top, high up in the Projects, because Big Playground was something he could cover with two hands. The condos of Barrytown looked like some grey-white fungus, spreading to the horizon. It was nearly dark, and he could make out a pink glow, beyond the last range of condo-racks.

'That's the Sprawl, over there, isn't it? That pink.'

'That's right, but the closer you get, the less pretty it looks. How'd you like to go there, Bobby? Count Zero ready to make the Sprawl?'

'Oh, yeah,' Bobby said, his palms against the sweating glass, 'you got no idea ...' The derm had worn off entirely now, and his back and chest hurt like hell.

14

Night Flight

As the night came on, Turner found the edge again.

It seemed like a long time since he'd been there, but when it clicked in, it was like he'd never left. It was that superhuman synchromesh flow that stimulants only approximated. He could only score for it on the site of a major defection, one where he was in command, and then only in the final hours before the actual move.

But it had been a long time; in New Delhi, he'd only been checking out possible escape routes for an executive who wasn't entirely certain that relocation was what he wanted. If he had been working the edge, that night in Chandni Chawk, maybe he'd have been able to dodge the thing. Probably not, but the edge would've told him to try.

Now the edge let him collate the factors he had to deal with at the site, balancing clusters of small problems against single, larger ones. So far there were a lot of little ones, but no real ball-breakers. Lynch and Webber were starting to get in each other's hair, so he arranged to keep them apart. His conviction that Lynch was Conroy's plant, instinctive from the beginning, was stronger now. Instincts sharpened, on the edge; things got witchy. Nathan was having trouble with the low-tech Swedish handwarmers; anything short of an electronic circuit baffled him. Turner put Lynch to work on the handwarmers, fuelling and priming them, and let Nathan carry them out, two at a time, and bury them shallowly, at metre intervals, along the two long lines of orange tape.

The microsoft Conroy had sent filled his head with its own universe of constantly shifting factors: airspeed, altitude, attitude, angle of attack, g-forces, headings. The plane's weapon delivery information was a constant subliminal litany of target designators, bomb fall lines, search circles, range and release cues, weapons counts. Conroy had tagged the microsoft with a simple message outlining the plane's time of arrival and confirming the arrangement for space for a single passenger.

He wondered what Mitchell was doing, feeling. The Maas Biolabs North America facility was carved into the heart of a sheer mesa, a table of rock thrusting from the desert floor. The biosoft dossier had shown Turner the mesa's face, cut with bright evening windows; it rode above the uplifted arms of a sea of saguaros like the wheelhouse of a giant ship. To Mitchell, it had been prison and fortress, his home for nine years. Somewhere near its core he had perfected the hybridoma techniques that had eluded other researchers for almost a century; working with human cancer cells and a neglected, nearly forgotten model of DNA synthesis, he had produced the immortal hybrid cells that were the basic production tools of the new technology, minute biochemical factories endlessly reproducing the engineered molecules that were linked and built up into biochips. Somewhere in the Maas arcology, Mitchell would be moving through his last hours as their star researcher.

Turner tried to imagine Mitchell leading a very different sort of life following his defection to Hosaka, but found it difficult. Was a research arcology in Arizona very different from one on Honshu?

*

111

There had been times, during that long day, when Mitchell's coded memories had risen in him, filling him with a strange dread that seemed to have nothing to do with the operation at hand.

It was the intimacy of the thing that still disturbed him, and perhaps the feeling of fear sprang from that. Certain fragments seemed to have an emotional power entirely out of proportion to their content. Why should a memory of a plain hallway in some dingy Cambridge graduate dormitory fill him with a sense of guilt and self-loathing? Other images, which logically should have carried a degree of feeling, were strangely lacking in affect: Mitchell playing with his baby daughter on an expanse of pale woollen broadloom in a rented house in Geneva, the child laughing, tugging at his hand. Nothing. The man's life, from Turner's vantage, seemed marked out by a certain inevitability; he was brilliant, a brilliance that had been detected early on, highly motivated, gifted at the kind of blandly ruthless in-company manipulation required by someone who aspired to become a top research scientist. If anyone was destined to rise through laboratory-corporate hierarchies, Turner decided, it would be Mitchell.

Turner himself was incapable of meshing with the intensely tribal world of the zaibatsumen, the lifers. He was a perpetual outsider, a rogue factor adrift on the secret seas of inter-corporate politics. No company man would have been capable of taking the initiatives Turner was required to take in the course of an extraction. No company man was capable of Turner's professionally casual ability to realign his loyalties to fit a change in employers. Or, perhaps, of his unyielding commitment once a contract had been agreed upon. He had drifted into security work in his late teens, when the grim doldrums of the postwar economy were giving way to the impetus of new technologies. He had done well in security,

112

considering his general lack of ambition. He had a ropy, muscular poise that impressed his employer's clients, and he was bright, very bright. He wore clothes well. He had a way with technology.

Conroy had found him in Mexico, where Turner's employer had contracted to provide security for a Sense/Net simstim team who were recording a series of thirty-minute segments in an ongoing jungle adventure series. When Conroy arrived, Turner was finishing his arrangements. He'd set up a liaison between Sense/Net and the local government, bribed the town's top police official, analysed the hotel's security system, met the local guides and drivers and had their histories double-checked, arranged for digital voice protection on the simstim team's transceivers, established a crisis-management team, and planted seismic sensors around the Sense/Net suite-cluster.

He entered the hotel's bar, a jungle-garden extension of the lobby, and found a seat by himself at one of the glass-topped tables. A pale man with a shock of white, bleached hair crossed the bar with a drink in each hand. The pale skin was drawn tight across angular features and a high forehead; he wore a neatly pressed military shirt over jeans, and leather sandals.

'You're the security for those simstim kids,' the pale man said, putting one of the drinks down on Turner's table. 'Alfredo told me.' Alfredo was one of the hotel bartenders. Turner looked up at the man, who was evidently sober and seemed to have all the confidence in the world.

'I don't think we've been introduced,' Turner said, making no move to accept the proffered drink.

'It doesn't matter,' Conroy said, seating himself, 'we're in the same ball game.'

Turner stared. He had a bodyguard's presence, something

113

restless and watchful written in the lines of his body, and few strangers would so casually violate his private space.

'You know,' the man said, the way someone might comment on a team that wasn't doing particularly well in a given season, 'those seismics you're using really don't make it. I've met people who could walk in there, eat your kids for breakfast, stack the bones in the shower, and stroll out whistling. Those seismics would say it never happened.' He took a sip of his drink. 'You get A for effort, though. You know how to do a job.'

The phrase *stack the bones in the shower* was enough. Turner decided to take the pale man out.

'Look, Turner, here's your leading lady.' The man smiled up at Jane Hamilton, who smiled back, her wide blue eyes clear and perfect, each iris ringed with the minute gold lettering of the Zeiss Ikon logo. Turner froze, caught in a split-second lock of indecision. The star was close, too close, and the pale man was rising—

'Nice meeting you, Turner,' he said. 'We'll get together sooner or later. Take my advice about those seismics; back 'em up with a perimeter of screamers.' And then he turned and walked away, muscles rolling easily beneath the crisp fabric of his tan shirt.

'That's nice, Turner,' Hamilton said, taking the stranger's place.

'Yeah?' Turner watched as the man was lost in the confusion of the crowded lobby, amid pink-fleshed tourists.

'You don't ever seem to talk to people. You always look like you're running a make on them, filing a report. It's nice to see you making friends for a change.'

Turner looked at her. She was twenty, four years his junior, and earned roughly nine times his annual salary in a given week. She was blonde, her hair cropped short for the series

114

role, deeply tanned, and looked as if she was illuminated from within by sunlamps. The blue eyes were inhumanly perfect optical instruments, grown in vats in Japan. She was both actress and camera, her eyes worth several million New Yen, and in the hierarchy of Sense/Net stars, she barely rated.

He sat with her, in the bar, until she'd finished two drinks, then walked her back to the suite-cluster.

'You wouldn't feel like coming in for another, would you, Turner?'

'No.' he said. This was the second evening she'd made the offer, and he sensed that it would be the last. 'I have to check the seismics.'

Later that night, he phoned New York for the number of a firm in Mexico City that could supply him with screamers for the perimeter of the suite-cluster.

But a week later, Jane and three others, half the series cast, were dead.

'We're ready to roll the medics,' Webber said. Turner saw that she was wearing fingerless brown leather gloves. She'd replaced her sunglasses with clear glass shooting glasses, and there was a pistol on her hip. 'Sutcliffe's monitoring the perimeter with the remotes. We'll need everybody else to get the fucker through the brush.'

'Need me?'

'Ramirez says he can't do anything too strenuous this close to jacking in. You ask me, he's just a lazy little LA shit.'

'No,' Turner said, getting up from his seat on the ledge, 'he's right. If he sprained his wrist, we'd be screwed. Even something so minor that he couldn't feel it could affect his speed ...'

Webber shrugged. 'Yeah. Well, he's back in the bunker, bathing his hands in the last of our water and humming to himself, so we should be just fine.'

When they reached the surgery, Turner automatically counted heads. Seven. Ramirez was in the bunker; Sutcliffe was somewhere in the cinder block maze, monitoring the sentry-remotes. Lynch had a Steiner-Optic laser slung over his right shoulder, a compact model with a folding alloy skeleton stock, integral batteries forming a fat handgrip below the grey titanium housing that served the thing as a barrel. Nathan was wearing a black jumpsuit, black paratrooper boots filmed with pale dust, and had the bulbous ant-eye goggles of an image-amplification rig dangling below his chin on a head strap.

Turner removed his Mexican sunglasses, tucked them into a breast pocket in the blue work shirt, and buttoned the flap.

'How's it going, Teddy?' he asked a beefy six-footer with close-cropped brown hair.

'Jus' fine,' Teddy said, with a toothy smile.

Turner surveyed the other three members of the site team, nodding to each man in turn: Compton, Costa, Davis.

'Getting down to the wire, huh?' Costa asked. He had a round, moist face and a thin, carefully trimmed beard. Like Nathan and the others, he wore black.

'Pretty close,' Turner said. 'All smooth so far.'

Costa nodded.

'We're an estimated thirty minutes from arrival,' Turner said.

'Nathan, Davis,' Webber said, 'disconnect the sewage line.' She handed Turner one of the Telefunken ear-bead sets. She'd already removed it from its bubble pack. She put one on herself, peeling the plastic backing from the self-adhesive throat-microphone and smoothing it into place on her sunburned neck.

Nathan and Davis were moving in the shadows behind the module. Turner heard Davis curse softly.

'Shit,' Nathan said, 'there's no cap for the end of the tube.'
The others laughed.

'Leave it,' Webber said. 'Get to work on the wheels. Lynch and Compton, unlimber the jacks.'

Lynch drew a pistol-shaped power driver from his belt and ducked beneath the surgery. It was swaying now, the suspension creaking softly; the medics were moving inside. Turner heard a brief, high-pitched whine from some piece of internal machinery, and then the chatter of Lynch's driver as he readied the jacks.

He put his ear-bead in and stuck the throat-mike beside his larynx. 'Sutcliffe? Check?'

'Fine,' the Australian said, a tiny voice that seemed to come from the base of his skull.

'Ramirez?'

'Loud and clear ...'

Eight minutes. They were rolling the module out on its ten fat tyres. Turner and Nathan were on the front pair, steering; Nathan had his goggles on. Mitchell was coming out in the dark of the moon. The module was heavy, absurdly heavy, and very nearly impossible to steer.

'Like balancing a truck on a couple of shopping carts,' Nathan said to himself. Turner's lower back was giving him trouble. It hadn't been quite right since New Delhi.

'Hold it,' Webber said, from the third wheel on the left. 'I'm stuck on a fucking rock ...'

Turner released his wheel and straightened up. The bats were out in force tonight, flickering things against the bowl of desert starlight. There were bats in Mexico, in the jungle, fruit bats that slept in the trees that overhung the suite-cluster where the Sense/Net crew slept. Turner had climbed those trees, had strung the overhanging limbs with taut lengths of molecular monofilament, metres of invisible razor waiting for an unwary intruder. But Jane and the others had died anyway, blown away on a hillside in the mountains near Acapulco. Trouble with a labour union, someone said later, but nothing was ever determined, really, other than the fact of the primitive claymore charge, its placement and the position from which it had been detonated. Turner had climbed the hill himself, his clothes filmed with blood, and seen the nest of crushed undergrowth where the killers had waited, the knife-switch and the corroded automobile battery. He found the butts of hand-rolled cigarettes and the cap from a bottle of Bohemia beer, bright and new.

The series had to be cancelled, and the crisis-management team did yeoman duty, arranging the removal of bodies and the repatriation of the surviving members of the cast and crew. Turner was on the last plane out, and after eight Scotches in the lounge of the Acapulco airport, he'd wandered blindly out into the central ticketing area and encountered a man named Buschel, an executive tech from Sense/Net's Los Angeles complex. Buschel was pale beneath an LA tan, his seersucker suit limp with sweat. He was carrying a plain aluminium case, like a camera case, its sides dull with condensation. Turner stared at the man, stared at the sweating case, with its red and white warning decals and lengthy labels explaining the precautions required in the transportation of materials in cryogenic storage.

'Christ,' Buschel said, noticing him. 'Turner. I'm sorry, man. Came down this morning. Ugly fucking business.' He took a sodden handkerchief from his jacket pocket and wiped his face. 'Ugly job. I've never had to do one of these, before ...'

'What's in the case, Buschel?' He was much closer now, although he didn't remember stepping forward. He could see the pores in Buschel's tanned face.

'You okay, man?' Buschel taking a step back. 'You look bad.'

'What's in the case, Buschel?' Seersucker bunched in his fist, knuckles white and shaking.

'Damn it, Turner,' the man jerking free, the handle of the case clutched in both hands now. 'They weren't damaged. Only some minor abrasion on one of the corneas. *They belong to the Net. It was in her contract, Turner.*'

And he'd turned away, his guts knotted tight around eight glasses of straight Scotch, and fought the nausea. And he'd continued to fight it, held it off for nine years, until, in his flight from the Dutchman, all the memory of it had come down on him, had fallen on him in London, in Heathrow, and he'd leaned forward, without pausing in his progress down yet another corridor, and vomited into a blue plastic waste canister.

'Come on, Turner,' Webber said, 'put some back in it. Show us how it's done.' The module began to strain forward again, through the tarry smell of the desert plants.

'Ready here,' Ramirez said, his voice remote and calm.

Turner touched the throat-mike. 'I'm sending you some company.' He removed his finger from the mike. 'Nathan, it's time. You and Davis, back to the bunker.'

Davis was in charge of the squirt gear, their sole nonmatrix link with Hosaka. Nathan was Mr Fix-it. Lynch was rolling the last of the bicycle wheels away into the brush beyond the parking lot. Webber and Compton were kneeling beside the module, attaching the line that linked the Hosaka surgeons with the Sony biomonitor in the command post. With the wheels removed, lowered and levelled on four jacks, the portable neurosurgery reminded Turner once again of the French vacation module. That had been a much later trip, four years after Conroy had recruited him in Los Angeles.

'How's it going?' Sutcliffe asked, over the link.

'Fine,' Turner said, touching the mike.

'Lonely out here,' Sutcliffe said.

'Compton,' Turner said, 'Sutcliffe needs you to help him cover the perimeter. You too, Lynch.'

'Too bad,' Lynch said, from the dark. 'I was hoping I'd get to see the action.'

Turner's hand was on the grip of the holstered Smith & Wesson, under the open flap of the parka. 'Now, Lynch.' If Lynch was Connie's plant, he'd want to be here. Or in the bunker.

'Fuck it,' Lynch said. 'There's nobody out there and you know it. You don't want me here, I'll go in there and watch Ramirez ...'

'Right,' Turner said, and drew the gun, depressing the stud that activated the xenon projector. The first tight-beam flash of noon-bright xenon light found a twisted saguaro, its needles like tufts of grey fur in the pitiless illumination. The second lit up the spiked skull on Lynch's belt, framed it in a sharp-edged circle. The sound of the shot and the sound of he bullet detonating on impact were indistinguishable, waves of concussion rolling out in invisible, ever-widening rings, out into the flat land like thunder.

In the first few seconds after, there was no sound at all, even the bats and bugs silenced, waiting. Webber had thrown herself flat in the scrub, and somehow he sensed her there, now, knew that her gun would be out, held dead steady in those brown, capable hands. He had no idea where Compton was.

Then Sutcliffe's voice, over the ear-bead, scratching at him from his brainpan: 'Turner. What was that?'

120

There was enough starlight now to make out Webber. She was sitting up, gun in her hands, ready, her elbows braced on her knees.

'He was Conroy's plant,' Turner said, lowering the Smith & Wesson.

'Jesus Christ,' she said. 'I'm Conroy's plant.'

'He had a line out. I've seen it before.'

She had to say it twice.

Sutcliffe's voice in his head, and then Ramirez: 'We got your transportation. Eighty klicks and closing … Everything else looks clear. There's a blimp twenty klicks south-southwest, Jaylene says, unmanned cargo and it's right on schedule. Nothing else. What the fuck's Sut yelling about? Nathan says he heard a shot.' Ramirez was jacked in, most of his sensorium taken up with the input from the Maas-Neotek deck. 'Nathan's ready with the first squirt …'

Turner could hear the jet banking now, braking for the landing on the highway. Webber was up and walking towards him, her gun in her hand. Sutcliffe was asking the same question, over and over.

He reached up and touched the throat-mike. 'Lynch. He's dead. The jet's here. This is it.'

And then the jet was on them, black shadow, incredibly low, coming in without lights. There was a flare of blow-back jets as the thing executed a landing that would have killed a human pilot, and then a weird creaking as it readjusted its articulated carbon fibre airframe. Turner could make out the green reflected glow of instrumentation in the curve of the plastic canopy.

'You fucked up,' Webber said.

Behind her, the hatch in the side of the surgery module popped open, framing a masked figure in a green paper contamination suit. The light from inside was blue-white, brilliant; it threw a distorted shadow of the suited medic out through the thin cloud of dust that hung above the lot in the wake of the jet's landing.

'Close it!' Webber shouted.

'Not yet!'

As the door swung down, shutting out the light, they both heard the ultralight's engine. After the roar of the jet, it seemed no more than the hum of a dragonfly, a drone that stuttered and faded as they listened.

'He's out of fuel,' Webber said. 'But he's close ...'

'He's here,' Turner said, pressing the throat-mike. 'First squirt.'

The tiny plane whispered past them, a dark delta against the stars. They could hear something flapping in the wind of its silent passage, perhaps one of Mitchell's pants legs. *You're up there*, Turner thought, *all alone, in the warmest clothes you own, wearing a pair of infrared goggles you built for yourself, and you're looking for a pair of dotted lines picked out for you in handwarmers.*

'You crazy fucker,' he said, his heart filling with a strange admiration, 'you really wanted out bad.'

Then the first flare went up, with a festive little pop, and the magnesium glare began its slow white parachute ride to the desert floor. Almost immediately, there were two more, and the long rattle of automatic fire from the west end of the mall. He was peripherally aware of Webber stumbling through the brush, in the direction of the bunker, but his eyes were fixed on the wheeling ultralight, on its gay orange and blue fabric wings, and the goggled figure hunched there in the open metal framework above the fragile tripod landing gear.

Mitchell.

The lot was bright as a football field, under the drifting

flares. The ultralight banked and turned with a lazy grace that made Turner want to scream. A line of tracers hosed out in a white arc from beyond the site perimeter. Missed.

Get it down. Get it down. He was running, jumping clumps of brush that caught at his ankles, at the hem of his parka.

The flares. The light. Mitchell couldn't use the goggles now, couldn't see the infrared glow of the handwarmers. He was bringing it in wide of the strip. The nose-wheel caught in something and the ultralight cartwheeled, crumpling, torn butterfly, and then lay down in its own white cloud of dust.

The flash of the explosion seemed to reach him an instant before the sound, throwing his shadow before him across the pale brush. The concussion picked him up and threw him down, and as he fell, he saw the broken surgery module in a ball of yellow flame and knew that Webber had used her anti-tank rocket. Then he was up again, moving, running, the gun in his hand.

He reached the wreckage of Mitchell's ultralight as the first flare died. Another one arced out of nowhere and blossomed overhead. The sound of firing was continuous now. He scrambled over a twisted sheet of rusted tin and found the sprawled figure of the pilot, head and face concealed by a makeshift helmet and a clumsy-looking goggle rig. The goggles were fastened to the helmet with dull silver strips of gaffer tape. The twisted limbs were padded in layers of dark clothing.

Turner watched his hands claw at the tape, tear at the infrared goggles; his hands were distant creatures, pale undersea things that lived a life of their own far down at the bottom of some unthinkable Pacific trench, and he watched as they tore frantically at tape, goggles, helmet. Until it all came away, and the long brown hair, limp with sweat, fell across the girl's white face, smearing the thin trickle of dark blood that ran from one nostril, and her eyes opened, revealing empty whites, and he was tugging her up, somehow, into a fireman's carry, and reeling in what he hoped was the direction of the jet.

He felt the second explosion through the soles of his deck shoes, and saw the idiot grin on the lump of plastique that sat on Ramirez's cyberspace deck. There was no flash, only sound and the sting of concussion through the concrete of the lot.

And then he was in the cockpit, breathing the new-car smell of long-chain monomers, the familiar scent of newly minted technology, and the girl was behind him, an awkward doll sprawled in the embrace of the g-web that Conroy had paid a San Diego arms dealer to install behind the pilot's web. The plane was quivering, a live thing, and as he squirmed deeper into his own web, he fumbled for the interface cable, found it, ripped the microsoft from his socket, and slid the cable-jack home.

Knowledge lit him like an arcade game, and he surged forward with the plane-ness of the jet, feeling the flexible airframe reshape itself for jump-off as the canopy whined smoothly down on its servos. The g-web ballooned around him, locking his limbs rigid, the gun still in his hand. 'Go, motherfucker.' But the jet already knew, and g-force crushed him down into the dark.

'You lost consciousness,' the plane said. Its chip-voice sounded vaguely like Conroy.

'How long?'

'Thirty-eight seconds.'

'Where are we?'

'Over Nagos.' The head-up display lit, a dozen constantly altered figures beneath a simplified map of the Arizona-Sonora line.

The sky went white.

'What was that?'

Silence.

'What was that?'

'Sensors indicate an explosion,' the plane said. 'The magnitude suggests a tactical nuclear warhead, but there was no electromagnetic pulse. The locus of destruction was our point of departure.'

The white glow faded and was gone.

'Cancel course,' he said.

'Cancelled. New headings, please.'

'That's a good question,' Turner said. He couldn't turn his head to look at the girl behind him. He wondered if she were dead yet.

15

Box

Marly dreamed of Alain, dusk in a wild flower field, and he cradled her head, then caressed and broke her neck. Lay there unmoving but she knew what he was doing. He kissed her all over. He took her money and the keys to her room. The stars were huge now, fixed above the bright fields, and she could still feel his hands on her neck …

She woke in the coffee-scented morning and saw the squares of sunlight spread across the books on Andrea's table, heard Andrea's comfortingly familiar morning cough as she lit a first cigarette from the stove's front burner. She shook off the dark colours of the dream and sat up on Andrea's couch, hugging the dark red quilt around her knees. After Gnass, after the police and the reporters, she'd never dreamed of him. Or if she did, she'd guessed, she somehow censored the dreams, erased them before she woke. She shivered, although it was already a warm morning, and went into the bathroom. She wanted no more dreams of Alain.

'Paco told me that Alain was armed when we met,' she said, when Andrea handed her the blue enamel mug of coffee.

'Alain armed?' Andrea divided the omelette and slid half onto Marly's plate. 'What a bizarre idea. It would be like … Like arming a penguin.' They both laughed. 'Alain is not the type,' Andrea said. 'He'd shoot his foot off in the middle of some passionate declaration about the state of art and the amount of the dinner bill. He's a big shit, Alain, but that's hardly news. If I were you, I'd expend a bit more worry on this Paco. What reason do you have for accepting that he works for Virek?' She took a bite of omelette and reached for the salt.

'I saw him. He was there in Virek's construct.'

'You saw something – an image only, the image of a child – which only resembled this man.'

Marly watched Andrea eat her half of the omelette, letting her own grow cold on the plate. How could she explain, about the sense she'd had, walking from the Louvre? The conviction that something surrounded her now, monitoring her with relaxed precision; that she had become the focus of at least a part of Virek's empire. 'He's a very wealthy man,' she began.

'Virek?' Andrea put her knife and fork down on the plate and took up her coffee. 'I should say he is. If you believe the journalists, he's the single wealthiest individual, period. As rich as some zaibatsu. But there's the catch, really: *is* he an individual? In the sense that you are, or I am? No. Aren't you going to eat that?'

Marly began to mechanically cut and fork sections of the cooling omelette, while Andrea continued: 'You should look at the manuscript we're working on this month.'

Marly chewed, raised her eyebrows questioningly.

'It's a history of the high-orbit industrial clans. A man at the University of Nice did it. Your Virek's even in it, come to think; he's cited as a counterexample, or rather as a type of parallel evolution. This fellow at Nice is interested in the paradox of individual wealth in a corporate age. In why it should still exist at all. Great wealth, I mean. He sees the high-orbit clans, people like the Tessier-Ashpools, as a very late variant on traditional patterns of aristocracy, late because the corporate mode doesn't really allow for an aristocracy.'

127

She put her cup down on her plate and carried the plate to the sink 'Actually, now that I've started to describe it, it isn't that interesting. There's a great deal of very grey prose about the nature of Mass Man. With caps, Mass Man. He's big on caps. Not much of a stylist.' She spun the taps and water hissed out through the filtration unit.

'But what does he say about Virek?'

'He says, if I remember all this correctly, and I'm not at all certain that I do, that Virek is an even greater fluke than the industrial clans in orbit. The clans are trans-generational, and there's usually a fair bit of medicine involved: cryogenics, genetic manipulation, various ways to combat ageing. The death of a given clan member, even a founding member, usually wouldn't bring the clan, as a business entity, to a crisis point. There's always someone to step in, someone waiting. The difference between a clan and a corporation, however, is that you don't need to literally marry into a corporation ...'

'But they sign indentures ...'

Andrea shrugged. 'That's like a lease. It isn't the same thing. It's job security, really. But when your Herr Virek dies, finally, when they run out of room to enlarge his vat, whatever, his business interests will lack a logical focus. At that point, our man in Nice has it, you'll see Virek and Company either fragment or mutate, the latter giving us the Something Company and a true multinational, yet another home for capital-M Mass Man.' She wiped her plate, rinsed it, dried it. and placed it in the pine rack beside the sink. 'He says that's too bad, in a way, because there are so few people left who can even see the edge ...'

'The edge?'

'The edge of the crowd. We're lost in the middle, you and I. Or I still am, at any rate.' She crossed the kitchen and put her hands on Marly's shoulders. 'You want to take care in this.

A part of you is already much happier, but now I see that I could have brought that about myself, simply by arranging a little lunch for you with your pig of a former lover. The rest of it, I'm not sure ... I think our academic's theory is invalidated by the obvious fact that Virek and his kind are already far from human. I want you to be careful ...' Then she kissed Marly's cheek and went off to her work as an assistant editor in the fashionably archaic business of printed books.

She spent the morning at Andrea's, with the Braun, viewing the holograms of the seven works. Each piece was extraordinary in its own way, but she repeatedly returned to the box Virek had shown her first. *If I had the original here*, she thought, *and removed the glass, and one by one removed the objects inside, what would be left*? Useless things, a frame of space, perhaps a smell like dust.

She sprawled on the couch, the Braun resting on her stomach, and stared into the box. It ached. It seemed to her that the construction evoked something perfectly, but it was an emotion that lacked a name. She ran her hands through the bright illusion, tracing the length of the fluted, avian bone.

She was certain that Virek had already assigned an ornithologist the task of identifying the bird from whose wing that bone had come. And it would be possible to date each object with the greatest precision, she supposed. Each tab of holofiche also housed an extensive report on the known origin of each piece, but something in her had deliberately avoided these. It was sometimes best, when you came to the mystery that was art, to come as a child. The child saw things that were too evident, too obvious for the trained eye.

She put the Braun down on the low table beside the couch and crossed to Andrea's phone, intending to check the time. She was meeting Paco at one, to discuss the mechanics of

Alain's payment. Alain had told her he would phone her at Andrea's at three. When she punched for the time service, an automatic recap of satellite news strobed across the screen: a *JAL* shuttle had disintegrated during re-entry over the Indian Ocean; investigators from the Boston-Atlanta Metropolitan Axis had been called in to examine the site of a brutal and apparently pointless bombing in a drab New Jersey residential suburb; militiamen were supervising the evacuation of the southern quadrant of New Bonn following the discovery, by construction workers, of two undetonated wartime rockets believed to be armed with biological weapons; and official sources in Arizona were denying Mexico's accusation of the detonation of a small-scale atomic or nuclear device near the Sonora border ... As she watched, the recap cycled and the simulation of the shuttle began its fire-death again. She shook her head, tapping the button. It was noon.

Summer had come, the sky hot and blue above Paris, and she smiled at the smell of good bread and black tobacco. Her sense of being observed had receded now, as she walked from the Métro to the address Paco had given her. Faubourg St.-Honoré. The address seemed vaguely familiar. *A gallery*, she thought.

Yes. The Roberts. The owner an American who operated three galleries in New York as well. Expensive, but no longer quite chic. Paco was waiting beside an enormous panel on which were layered, beneath a thick and uneven coat of varnish, hundreds of small square photographs, the kind produced by certain very old-fashioned machines in train stations and bus terminals. All of them seemed to be of young girls. Automatically, she noted the name of the artist and the work's title: *Read Us the Book of the Names of the Dead*.

'I suppose you understand this sort of thing,' the Spaniard

said glumly. He wore an expensive-looking blue suit cut in Parisian business style, a white broadcloth shirt, and a very English-looking tie, probably from Charvet. He didn't look at all like a waiter now. There was an Italian bag of black ribbed rubber slung over his shoulder.

'What do you mean?' she asked.

'Names of the dead,' and he nodded in the direction of the panel. 'You were a dealer in these things.'

'What don't you understand?'

'I sometimes feel as though this, this *culture* is entirely a trick. A ruse. All my life I have served Señor, in one guise or another, you understand? And my work has not been without its satisfactions, moments of triumph. But never, when he involved me with this business of art, have I felt any satisfaction. He is wealth itself. The world is filled with objects of great beauty. And yet Señor pursues ...' He shrugged.

'You know what you like, then.' She smiled at him. 'Why did you choose this gallery for our meeting?'

'Señor's agent purchased one of the boxes here. Haven't you read the histories we provided you with in Brussels?'

'No,' she said. 'It might interfere with my intuition. Herr Virek is paying for my intuition.'

He raised his eyebrows. 'I will introduce you to Picard, the manager. Perhaps he can do something for this intuition of yours.'

He led her across the room and through a doorway. A greying, heavy set Frenchman in a rumpled corduroy suit was speaking into the handset of a phone. On the phone's screen she saw columns of letters and figures. The day's quotations on the New York market.

'Ah,' the man said, 'Estevez. Excuse me. Only a moment.' He smiled apologetically and returned to his conversation. Marly studied the quotations. Pollock was down again. This,

she supposed, was the aspect of art that she had the most difficulty understanding. Picard, if that was the man's name, was
speaking with a broker in New York, arranging the purchase
of a certain number of 'points' of the work of a particular
artist. A 'point' might be defined in any number of ways,
depending on the medium involved, but it was almost certain
that Picard would never see the works he was purchasing.
If the artist enjoyed sufficient status, the originals were very
likely crated away in some vault, where no one saw them at
all. Days or years later, Picard might pick up that same phone
and order the broker to sell.

Marly's gallery had sold originals. There was relatively
little money in it, but it had a certain visceral appeal. And, of
course, there had been the chance that one would get lucky.
She had convinced herself that she'd got very lucky indeed
when Alain had arranged for the forged Cornell to surface
as a wonderful, accidental find. Cornell had his place on the
broker's board, and his 'points' were very expensive.

'Picard,' Paco said, as though he were addressing a servant,
'this is Marly Krushkhova. Señor has brought her into the
matter of the anonymous boxes. She may wish to ask you
questions.'

'Charmed,' Picard said, and smiled warmly, but she
thought she detected a flicker in his brown eyes. Very likely,
he was trying to connect the name to some scandal, relatively
recent ...

'I understand that your gallery handled the transaction,
then?'

'Yes,' Picard said. 'We had displayed the work in our New
York rooms, and it had attracted a number of bids. We decided
to give it its day in Paris, however,' and he beamed, 'and your
employer made our decision most worthwhile. How is Herr
Virek, Estevez? We have not seen him in several weeks ...'

132

Marly glanced quickly at Paco, but his dark face was smooth, utterly controlled.

'Señor is very well, I would think,' he said.

'Excellent,' said Picard, somewhat too enthusiastically. He turned to Marly. 'A marvellous man. A legend. A great patron. A great scholar.'

Marly thought she heard Paco sigh.

'Could you tell me, please, where your New York branch obtained the work in question?'

Picard's face fell. He looked at Paco, then back at Marly. 'You don't know? They haven't told you?'

'Could you tell me, please?'

'No,' Picard said, 'I'm sorry, but I can't. You see, we don't know.'

Marly stared at him. 'I beg your pardon, but I don't quite see how that is possible ...'

'She hasn't read the report, Picard. You tell her. It will be good for her intuition, to hear it from your own lips.'

Picard gave Paco an odd look, then regained his composure.

'Certainly,' he said. 'A pleasure ...'

'Do you think it's true?' she asked Paco, as they stepped out into Faubourg St.-Honoré and summer sunlight. The crowds were thick with Japanese tourists.

'I went to the Sprawl myself,' Paco said, 'and interviewed everyone involved. Roberts left no record of the purchase, although ordinarily he was no more secretive than the next art dealer.'

'And his death was accidental?'

He put on a pair of mirrored Porsche glasses. 'As accidental as that sort of death ever is,' he said. 'We have no way of knowing when or how he obtained the piece. We located it, here, eight months ago, and all' our attempts to work backwards end with Roberts, and Roberts has been dead for a year. Picard neglected to tell you that they very nearly lost the thing. Roberts kept it in his country house, along with a number of other things that his survivors regarded as mere curiosities. The whole lot came close to being sold at public auction. Sometimes I wish it had been.'

'These other things,' she asked, falling into step beside him, 'what were they?'

He smiled. 'You think we haven't tracked them, each one? We have. They were,' and here he frowned, exaggerating the effort of memory, '"a number of rather unremarkable examples of contemporary folk art"...'

'Was Roberts known to be interested in that sort of thing?'

'No,' he said, 'but approximately a year before his death, we know that he made application for membership in the Institut de L'Art Brut, here in Paris, and arranged to become a patron of the Aeschmann Collection in Hamburg.'

Marly nodded. The Aeschmann Collection was restricted to the works of psychotics.

'We are reasonably certain,' Paco continued, taking her elbow and guiding her around a corner, into a side street, 'that he made no attempt to use the resources of either, unless he employed an intermediary, and we regard that as unlikely. Señor, of course, has employed several dozen scholars to sweep the records of both institutions. To no avail ...'

'Tell me,' she said, 'why Picard assumed that he had recently seen Herr Virek. How is that possible?'

'Señor is wealthy. Señor enjoys any number of means of manifestation.'

Now he led her into a chrome-trimmed barn of a place, glittering with mirrors, bottles, and arcade games. The mirrors lied about the depth of the room; at its rear, she could see the reflected pavement, the legs of pedestrians, the flash of sunlight on a hubcap. Paco nodded to a lethargic-looking man behind the bar and took her hand, leading her through the tightly packed shoal of round plastic tables.

'You can take your call from Alain here,' he said. 'We have arranged to reroute it from your friend's apartment.' He drew a chair out for her, an automatic bit of professional courtesy that made her wonder if he might actually once have been a waiter, and placed his bag on the tabletop.

'But he'll see that I'm not there,' she said. 'If I blank the video, he'll become suspicious.'

'But he won't see that. We've generated a digital image of your face and the required background. We'll key that to the image on this phone.' He took an elegant modular unit from the bag and placed it in front of her. A paper-thin polycarbon screen unfurled silently from the top of the unit and immediately grew rigid. She had once watched a butterfly emerge into the world, and seen the transformation of its drying wings.

'How is that done?' she asked, tentatively touching the screen. It was like thin steel.

'One of the new polycarbon variants,' he said, 'one of the Maas products ...'

The phone purred discreetly. He positioned it more carefully in front of her, stepped to the far side of the table, and said, 'Your call. Remember, you are at home!' He reached forward and brushed a titanium-coated stud.

Alain's face and shoulders filled the little screen. The image had the smudged, badly lit look of a public booth. 'Good afternoon, my dear,' he said.

'Hello, Alain.'

'How are you, Marly? I trust you've got the money we discussed?' She could see that he was wearing a jacket of some kind, dark, but she could make out no details. 'Your

135

roommate could do with a lesson in house cleaning,' he said, and seemed to be peering back over her shoulder.

'You've never cleaned a room in your life,' she said.

He shrugged, smiling. 'We each have our talents,' he said. 'Do you have my money, Marly?'

She glanced up at Paco, who nodded. 'Yes,' she said, 'of course.'

'That's wonderful, Marly. Marvellous. We have only one small difficulty ...' He was still smiling.

'And what is that?'

'My informants have doubled their price. Consequently, I must now double mine ...'

Paco nodded. He was smiling, too.

'Very well. I will have to ask, of course ...' He sickened her now. She wanted to be off the phone.

'And they, of course, will agree.'

'Where shall we meet, then?'

'I will phone again, at five,' he said. His image shrank to a single blip of blue-green, and then that was gone as well.

'You look tired,' Paco said, as he collapsed the screen and replaced the phone in his bag. 'You look older when you've talked with him.'

'Do I?' For some reason, now, she saw the panel in the Roberts, all those faces. *Read Us the Book of the Names of the Dead. All the Marlys*, she thought, *all the girls she'd been through the long season of youth.*

16

Legba

'Hey, shithead.' Rhea poked him none too lightly in the ribs. 'Get your ass up.'

He came up fighting with the crocheted comforter, with the half-formed shapes of unknown enemies. With his mother's murderers. He was in a room he didn't know, a room that might have been anywhere. Gold plastic gilt frames on a lot of mirrors. Fuzzy scarlet wallpaper. He'd seen Gothicks decorate rooms that way, when they could afford it, but he'd also seen their parents do whole condos in the same style. Rhea flung a bundle of clothes down on the temperfoam and shoved her hands in the pockets of a black leather jacket.

The pink and black squares of the comforter were bunched around his waist. He looked down and saw the segmented length of the centipede submerged in a finger-wide track of fresh scar tissue. Beauvoir had said that the thing accelerated healing. He touched the bright new tissue with a hesitant fingertip, found it tender but bearable. He looked up at Rhea. 'Get your ass up on *this*,' he said, giving her the finger.

They glared at each other, for a few seconds, over Bobby's upraised middle finger. Then she laughed. 'Okay,' she said, 'you got a point. I'll get off your case. But pick those clothes up and get 'em on. Should be something there that fits. Lucas is due by here soon to pick you up, and Lucas doesn't like to be kept waiting.'

'Yeah? Well, he seems like a pretty relaxed guy to me.' He began to sort through the heap of clothing, discarding a black shirt with a paisley pattern printed on it in laundered-out gold, a red satin number with a fringe of white imitation leather down the sleeves, a black sort of leotard-thing with panels of some translucent material ... 'Hey,' he said, 'where did you get this stuff? I can't wear shit like this ...'

'It's my little brother's,' Rhea said. 'From last season, and you better get your white ass dressed before Lucas gets down here. Hey,' she said, 'that's mine,' snatching up the leotard as though he might be about to steal it.

He pulled the black and gold shirt on and fumbled with domed snaps made of black imitation pearl. He found a pair of black jeans, but they proved to be baggy and elaborately pleated, and didn't seem to have any pockets. 'This all the pants you got?'

'Jesus,' she said. 'I saw the clothes Pye cut off you, man. You aren't anybody's idea of a fashion plate. Just get dressed, okay? I don't want any trouble with Lucas. He may come on all mellow with you, but that just means you got something he wants bad enough to take the trouble. Me, I sure don't, so Lucas got no compunctions, as far as I'm concerned.'

He stood up unsteadily beside the bedslab and tried to zip up the black jeans. 'No zip,' he said, looking at her.

'Buttons. In there somewhere. It's part of the *style*, you know?'

Bobby found the buttons. It was an elaborate arrangement and he wondered what would happen if he had to piss in a hurry. He saw the black nylon thongs beside the slab and shoved his feet into them. 'What about Jackie?' he asked, padding to where he could see himself in the gold-framed mirrors. 'Lucas got any compunctions about her?' He watched her in the mirror, saw something cross her face.

'What's that mean?'

'Beauvoir, he told me she was a horse ...'

'You hush,' she said, her voice gone low and urgent. 'Beauvoir mention anything like that to you, that's his business. Otherwise, it's nothing you talk about, understand? There's things bad enough, you'd wish you were back out there getting your butt carved up.'

He watched her eyes, reflected in the mirror, dark eyes shadowed by the deep brim of the soft felt hat. Now they seemed to show a little more white than they had before.

'Okay,' he said, after a pause, and then added, 'Thanks.' He fiddled with the collar of the shirt, turning it up in the back, down again, trying it different ways.

'You know,' Rhea said, tilting her head to one side, 'you get a few clothes on you, you don't look too bad. 'Cept you got eyes like two pissholes in a snowbank ...'

'Lucas,' Bobby said, when they were in the elevator, 'do you know who it was offed my old lady?' It wasn't a question he'd planned on asking, but somehow it had come rushing up like a bubble of swamp gas.

Lucas regarded him benignly, his long face smooth and black. His black suit, beautifully cut, looked as though it had been freshly pressed. He carried a stout stick of oiled and polished wood, the grain all swirly black and red, topped with a large knob of polished brass. Finger-long splines of brass ran down from the knob, inlaid smoothly in the cane's shaft.

'No, we do not.' His wide lips formed a straight and very serious line. 'That's something we'd very much like to know ...'

Bobby shifted uncomfortably. The elevator made him self-conscious. It was the size of a small bus, and although it wasn't crowded, he was the only white. Black people, he noted, as his eyes shifted restlessly down the thing's length, didn't look half-dead under fluorescent light, the way white people did.

Three times, in their descent, the elevator came to a halt at some floor and remained there, once for nearly fifteen minutes. The first time this happened, Bobby had looked questioningly at Lucas.

'Something in the shaft,' Lucas had said.

'What?'

'Another elevator.'

The elevators were located at the core of the arcology, their shafts bundled together with water mains, sewage lines, huge power cables, and insulated pipes that Bobby assumed were part of the geothermal system that Beauvoir had described. You could see it all whenever the doors opened; everything was exposed, raw, as though the people who built the place had wanted to be able to see exactly how everything worked and what was going where. And everything, every visible surface, was covered with an interlocking net of graffiti, so dense and heavily overlaid that it was almost impossible to pick out any kind of message or symbol.

'You never were up here before, were you, Bobby?' Lucas asked as the doors jolted shut once again and they were on their way down. Bobby shook his head. 'That's too bad,' Lucas said. 'Understandable, certainly, but kind of a shame. Two-a-Day tells me you haven't been too keen on sitting around Barrytown. That true?'

'Sure is,' Bobby agreed.

'I guess that's understandable, too. You seem to me to be a young man of some imagination and initiative. Would you agree?' Lucas spun the cane's bright brass head against his pink palm and looked at Bobby steadily.

'I guess so. I can't stand the place. Lately I've kind of been noticing how, well, nothing ever happens, you know? I mean, things happen, but it's always the same stuff, over and fucking over, like it's all a rerun, every summer like the last one ...' His voice trailed off, uncertain what Lucas would think of him.

'Yes,' Lucas said, 'I know that feeling. It may be a little more true of Barrytown than of some other places, but you can feel the same thing as easily in New York or Tokyo.'

Can't be true, Bobby thought, but nodded anyway, Rhea's warning in the back of his head. Lucas was no more threatening than Beauvoir, but his bulk alone was a caution. And Bobby was working on a new theory of personal deportment; he didn't quite have the whole thing yet, but part of it involved the idea that people who were genuinely dangerous might not need to exhibit the fact at all, and that the ability to conceal a threat made them even more dangerous. This ran directly opposite to the rule around Big Playground, where kids who had no real clout whatever went to great pains to advertise their chrome-studded rabidity. Which probably did them some good, at least in terms of the local action. But Lucas was very clearly nothing to do with local action.

'I see you doubt it,' Lucas said. 'Well, you'll probably find out soon enough, but not for a while. The way your life's going now, things should remain new and exciting for quite a while.'

The elevator door shuddered open, and Lucas was moving, shooing Bobby in front of him like a child. They stepped out into a tiled foyer that seemed to stretch for ever, past kiosks and cloth-draped stalls and people squatting beside blankets with things spread out on them.

'But not to linger,' Lucas said, giving Bobby a very gentle shove with one large hand when Bobby paused in front of stacks of jumbled software. 'You are on your way to the Sprawl, my man, and you are going in a manner that befits a count.'

'How's that?'

'In a limo.'

Lucas's car was an amazing stretch of gold-flecked black bodywork and mirror-finished brass, studded with a collection of baroque gadgets whose purpose Bobby only had time to guess at. One of the things was a dish antenna, he decided, but it looked more like one of those Aztec calendar wheels, and then he was inside, Lucas letting the wide door clunk gently shut behind them. The windows were tinted so dark, it looked like night-time outside, a bustling night-time where the Projects' crowds went about their noonday business. The interior of the vehicle was a single large compartment padded with bright rugs and pale leather cushions, although there seemed to be no particular place to sit. No steering wheel either; the dash was a padded expanse of leather unbroken by controls of any kind.

He looked at Lucas, who was loosening his black tie. 'How do you drive it?'

'Sit down somewhere. You drive it like this: Ahmed, get our asses to New York, lower east.'

The car slid smoothly away from the kerb as Bobby dropped to his knees on a soft pile of rugs.

'Lunch will be served in thirty minutes, sir, unless you'd care for something sooner,' a voice said. It was soft, melodious, and seemed to come from nowhere in particular.

Lucas laughed. 'They really knew how to build 'em in Damascus,' he said.

'Where?'

'Damascus,' Lucas said, as he unbuttoned his suit coat and settled back into a wedge of pale cushions. 'This is a Rolls. Old one. Those Arabs built a good car, while they had the money.'

*

142

'Lucas,' Bobby said, his mouth half full of cold fried chicken, 'how come it's taking us an hour and a half to get to New York? We aren't exactly crawling ...'

'Because,' Lucas said, pausing for another sip of cold white wine, 'that's how long it's taking us. Ahmed has all the factory options, including a first-rate counter-surveillance system. On the road, rolling, Ahmed provides a remarkable degree of privacy, more than I'm ordinarily willing to pay for in New York. Ahmed, you get the feeling anybody's trying to get to us, listen in or anything?'

'No, sir,' the voice said. 'Eight minutes ago our identification panel was infra-scanned by a Tactical helicopter. The helicopter's number was MH-dash-3-dash-848, piloted by Corporal Roberto—'

'Okay, okay,' Lucas said. 'Fine. Never mind. You see? Ahmed got more on those Tacs than they got on us.' He wiped his hands on a thick white linen napkin and took a gold toothpick from his jacket pocket.

'Lucas,' Bobby said, while Lucas probed delicately at the gaps between his big square teeth, 'what would happen if, say, I asked you to take me to Times Square and let me out?'

'Ah,' Lucas said, lowering the toothpick, 'the city's most resonant acre. What's the matter, Bobby, a drug problem?'

'Well, no, but I was wondering.'

'Wondering what? You want to go to Times Square?'

'No, that was just the first place I thought of. What I mean is, I guess, would you let me go?'

'No,' Lucas said, 'not to put too fine a point on it. But you don't have to think of yourself as a prisoner. More like a guest. A *valued* guest.'

Bobby smiled wanly. 'Oh. Okay. Like what they call protective custody, I guess.'

143

'Right,' Lucas said, bringing the gold toothpick into play again. 'And while we are here, securely screened by the good Ahmed, it's time we have a talk. Brother Beauvoir has already told you a little about us, I think. What do *you* think, Bobby, about what he's told you?'

'Well,' Bobby said, 'it's real interesting, but I'm not sure I understand it.'

'What don't you understand?'

'Well, I don't know about this voodoo stuff ...'

Lucas raised his eyebrows.

'I mean, it's your business, what you wanna buy, I mean, *believe*, right? But one minute Beauvoir's talking biz, street tech, like I never heard before, and the next he's talking mambos and ghosts and snakes and – and ...'

'And what?'

'Horses,' Bobby said, his throat tight.

'Bobby, do you know what a metaphor is?'

'A component? Like a capacitor?'

'No. Never mind metaphor, then. When Beauvoir or I talk to you about the loa and their horses, as we call those few the loa choose to ride, you should pretend that we are talking two languages at once. One of them, you already understand. That's the language of street tech, as you call it. We may be using different words, but we're talking tech. Maybe we call something Ougou Feray that you might call an icebreaker, you understand? But at the same time, with the same words, we are talking about other things, and *that* you don't under-stand. You don't need to.' He put his toothpick away.

Bobby took a deep breath. 'Beauvoir said that Jackie's a horse for a snake, a snake called Danbala. You run that by me in street tech?'

'Certainly. Think of Jackie as a deck, Bobby, a cyberspace deck, a very pretty one with nice ankles.' Lucas grinned and

Bobby blushed. 'Think of Danbala, who some people call the snake, as a program. Say as an icebreaker. Danbala slots into the Jackie deck, Jackie cuts ice. That's all.'

'Okay,' Bobby said, getting the hang of it, 'then what's the matrix? If she's a deck, and Danbala's a program, what's cyberspace?'

'The world,' Lucas said.

'Best if we walk from here,' Lucas said.

The Rolls came to a silent, silken halt and Lucas stood, buttoning his suit coat. 'Ahmed attracts too much attention.' He picked up his cane, and the door made a soft clunking sound as it unlocked itself.

Bobby climbed down behind him, into the unmistakable signature smell of the Sprawl, a rich amalgam of stale subway exhalations, ancient soot, and the carcinogenic tang of fresh plastics, all of it shot through with the carbon edge of illicit fossil fuels. High overhead, in the reflected glare of arc lamps, one of the unfinished Fuller domes shut out two-thirds of the salmon-pink evening sky, its ragged edge like broken grey honeycomb. The Sprawl's patchwork of domes tended to generate inadvertent microclimates; there were areas of a few city blocks where a fine drizzle of condensation fell continuously from the soot-stained geodesics, and sections of high dome famous for displays of static-discharge, a peculiarly urban variety of lightning. There was a stiff wind blowing, as Bobby followed Lucas down the street, a warm, gritty breeze that probably had something to do with pressure shifts in the Sprawl-long subway system.

'Remember what I told you,' Lucas said, his eyes narrowed against the grit. 'The man is far more than he seems. Even if he were nothing more than what he seems, you would owe him a degree of respect. If you want to be a cowboy, you're about to meet a landmark in the trade.'

'Yeah, right.' He skipped to avoid a greying length of print-out that tried to wrap itself around his ankle. 'So he's the one you an' Beauvoir bought the—'

'Ha! No! Remember what I told you. You speak in the open street, you may as well put your words up on a bulletin board ...'

Bobby grimaced, then nodded. Shit. He kept blowing it. Here he was with a major operator, up to his neck in some amazing kind of biz, and he kept acting like a wilson. Operator. That was the word for Lucas, and for Beauvoir, too, and that voodoo talk was just some game they ran on people, he'd decided. In the Rolls, Lucas had launched into some strange extended number about Legba, who he said was the loa of communication, 'the master of roads and pathways,' all about how the man he was taking Bobby to meet was a favourite of Legba's. When Bobby asked if the man was another oungan, Lucas said no; he said the man had walked with Legba all his life, so close that he'd never known the loa was there at all, like it was just a part of him, his shadow. And this was the man, Lucas had said, who'd sold them the software that Two-a-Day had rented to Bobby ...

Lucas rounded a corner and stopped, Bobby close behind. They stood in front of a blackened brownstone whose windows had been sealed decades before with sheets of corrugated steel. Part of the ground floor had once been a shop of some kind, its cracked display windows opaque with grime. The door, between the blind windows, had been re-inforced with the same steel that sealed the windows of the upper floors, and Bobby thought he could make out some sort of sign behind the window to his left, discarded neon script tilted diagonally in the gloom. Lucas just stood there, facing the doorway, his face expressionless, the tip of his cane planted neatly on the sidewalk and his large hands one atop the other on the brass knob.

'First thing that you learn,' he said, with the tone of a man reciting a proverb, 'is that you always gotta wait ...'

Bobby thought he heard something scrape, behind the door, and then there was a rattle like chains.

'Amazing,' Lucas said, 'almost as though we were expected.'

The door swung ten centimetres on well-oiled hinges and seemed to catch on something. An eye regarded them, unblinking, suspended there in that crack of dust and dark, and at first it seemed to Bobby that it must be the eye of some large animal, the iris a strange shade of brownish yellow and the whites, mottled and shot through with red, the lower lid gaping redder still below.

'Hoodoo man,' said the invisible face the eye belonged to, then, 'hoodoo man and some little lump of shit. Jesus ...' There was an awful, gurgling sound, as of antique phlegm being drawn up from hidden recesses, and then the man spat. 'Well, move it, Lucas.' There was another grating sound and the door swung inward on the dark. 'I'm a busy man ...' This last from a metre away, receding, as though the eye's owner were scurrying from the light admitted by the open door.

Lucas stepped through, Bobby on his heels, Bobby feeling the door swing smoothly shut behind him. The sudden darkness brought the hairs on his forearms up. It felt alive, that dark, cluttered and dense and somehow sentient.

Then a match flared and some sort of pressure lamp hissed and spat as the gas in its mantle ignited. Bobby could only gape at the face beyond the lantern, where the bloodshot yellow eye waited with its mate in what Bobby would very much have liked to believe was a mask of some kind.

'I don't suppose you were expecting us, were you, Finn?' Lucas asked.

'You wanna know,' the face said, revealing large flat yellow teeth, 'I was on my way out to find something to eat.' He looked to Bobby as though he could survive on a diet of mouldering carpet, or burrow patiently through the brown wood pulp of the damp-swollen books stacked shoulder-high on either side of the tunnel where they stood. 'Who's the little shit, Lucas?'

'You know, Finn, Beauvoir and I are experiencing difficulties with something we acquired from you in good faith.' Lucas extended his cane and prodded delicately at a dangerous-looking overhang of crumbling paperbacks.

'Are you, now?' The Finn pursed his grey lips in mock concern. 'Don't fuck with those first editions, Lucas. You bring 'em down, you pay for 'em.'

Lucas withdrew the cane. Its polished ferrule flashed in the lantern glare.

'So,' the Finn said. 'You got problems. Funny thing, Lucas, funny fucking thing.' His cheeks were greyish, seamed with deep diagonal creases. 'I got some problems, too, three of 'em. I didn't have 'em, this morning. I guess that's just the way life is, sometimes.' He put the hissing lantern down on a gutted steel filing cabinet and fished a bent, unfiltered cigarette from a side pocket of something that might once have been a tweed jacket. 'My three problems, they're upstairs. Maybe you wanna have a look at them ...' He struck a wooden match on the base of the lantern and lit his cigarette. The pungent reek of black Cuban tobacco gathered in the air between them.

'You know,' the Finn said, stepping over the first of the bodies, 'I been at this location a long time. Everybody knows me. They know I'm here. You buy from the Finn, you know who you're buying from. And I stand behind my product, every time ...'

Bobby was staring down at the upturned face of the dead man, at the eyes gone dull. There was something wrong with the shape of the torso, wrong with the way it lay there in the black clothes. Japanese face, no expression, dead eyes ...

'And all that time,' the Finn continued, 'you know how many people ever dumb enough to try to get in here to take me off? None!' Not one, not 'til this morning, and I get fucking *three* already. Well,' he shot Bobby a hostile glance, 'that's not counting the odd little lump of shit, I guess, but ...' He shrugged.

'He looks kind of lopsided,' Bobby said, still staring at the first corpse.

'That's 'cause he's dog food, inside.' The Finn leered. 'All mashed up.'

'The Finn collects exotic weapons,' Lucas said, nudging the wrist of a second body with the tip of his cane. 'Have you scanned them for implants, Finn?'

'Yeah. Pain in the butt. Hadda carry 'em downstairs to the back room. Nothing, other than what you'd expect. They're just a hit team.' He sucked his teeth noisily. 'Why's anybody wanna hit *me*?'

'Maybe you sold them a very expensive product that wouldn't do its job,' Lucas volunteered.

'I hope you aren't sayin' *you* sent 'em, Lucas,' the Finn said levelly, 'unless you wanna see me do the dog food trick.'

'Did I say you'd sold us something that doesn't work?'

'"Experiencing difficulties",' you said. And what else have you guys bought from me recently?'

'Sorry, Finn, but they're not ours. You know it, too.'

'Yeah, I guess I do. So what the fuck's got you down here,

Lucas? You know that stuff you bought wasn't covered by the usual guarantees ...'

'You know,' said the Finn, after listening to the story of Bobby's abortive cyberspace run, 'that's some weird shit out there ...' He slowly shook his narrow, strangely elongated head. 'Didn't used to be this way.' He looked at Lucas. 'You people know, don't you?'

They were seated around a square white table in a white room on the ground floor, behind the junk-clogged store-front. The floor was scuffed hospital tile, moulded in a non-slip pattern, and the walls broad slabs of dingy white plastic concealing dense layers of anti-bugging circuitry. Compared to the storefront, the white room seemed surgically clean. Several alloy tripods bristling with sensors and scanning gear stood around the table like abstract sculpture.

'Know what?' Bobby asked. With each retelling of his story, he felt less like a wilson. Important. It made him feel important.

'Not you, pisshead,' the Finn said wearily. 'Him. Big hoo-doo man. He knows. Knows it's not the same ... Hasn't been, not for a long time. I been in the trade forever. Way back. Before the war, before there was any matrix, or anyway before people *knew* there was one.' He was looking at Bobby now. 'I got a pair of shoes older than you are, so what the fuck should I expect you to know? There were cowboys ever since there were computers. They built the first computers to crack German ice. Right? Codebreakers. So there was ice before computers, you wanna look at it that way.' He lit his fifteenth cigarette of the evening, and smoke began to fill the white room.

'Lucas knows, yeah. The last seven, eight years, there's been funny stuff out there, out on the console cowboy circuit. The

150

new jockeys, *they make deals with things*, don't they, Lucas? Yeah, you bet I know; they still need the hard and the soft, and they still gotta be faster than snakes on ice, but all of 'em, all the ones who really know how to cut it, they got *allies*, don't they, Lucas?'

Lucas took his gold toothpick out of his pocket and began to work on a rear molar, his face dark and serious.

'Thrones and dominions,' the Finn said obscurely. 'Yeah, there's things out there. Ghosts, voices. Why not? Oceans had mermaids, all that shit, and we had a sea of silicon, see? Sure, it's just a tailored hallucination we all agreed to have, cyberspace, but anybody who jacks in knows, fucking *knows* it's a whole universe. And every year it gets a little more crowded, sounds like …'

'For us,' Lucas said, 'the *world* has always worked that way.'

'Yeah' the Finn said, 'so you guys could slot right into it, tell people the things you were cutting deals with were your same old bush-gods …'

'Divine Horsemen …'

'Sure. Maybe you believe it. But I'm old enough to remember when it wasn't like that. Ten years ago, you went in the Gentle-man Loser and tried telling any of the top jocks you talked with ghosts in the matrix, they'd have figured you were crazy.'

'A wilson,' Bobby put in, feeling left out and no longer as important.

The Finn looked at him, blankly. 'A what?'

'A wilson. A fuck-up. It's hotdogger talk, I guess …' Did it again. Shit.

The Finn gave him a very strange look. 'Jesus. That's your word for it, huh? Christ. I *knew* the guy …'

'Who?'

'Bodine Wilson,' he said. 'First guy I ever knew wound up as a figure of speech.'

151

'Was he stupid?' Bobby asked, immediately regretting it

'Stupid? Shit, no, he was smart as hell.' The Finn stubbed his cigarette out in a cracked ceramic Campari ashtray. 'Just a total fuck-up, was all. He worked with the Dixie Flatline once ...' The bloodshot yellow eyes grew distant.

'Finn,' Lucas said, 'where did you get that icebreaker you sold us?'

The Finn regarded him bleakly. 'Forty years in the business, Lucas. You know how many times I've been asked that question? You know how many times I'd be dead if I'd answered it?'

Lucas nodded. 'I take your point. But at the same time, I put one to you.' He held the toothpick out towards the Finn like a toy dagger. 'The real reason you're willing to sit here and bullshit is that you think those three stiffs upstairs have something to do with the icebreaker you sold us. And you sat up and took special notice when Bobby told you about his mother's condo getting wiped, didn't you?'

The Finn showed teeth. 'Maybe.'

'Somebody's got you on their list, Finn. Those three dead ninjas upstairs cost somebody a lot of money. When they don't come back, somebody'll be even more determined, Finn.'

The red-rimmed yellow eyes blinked. 'They were all tooled up,' he said, 'ready for a hit, but one of 'em had some other things. Things for asking questions.' His nicotine-stained fingers, almost the colour of cockroach wings, came up to slowly massage his short upper lip. 'I got it off Wigan Ludgate,' he said, 'the Wig.'

'Never heard of him,' Lucas said.

'Crazy little motherfucker,' the Finn said, 'used to be a cowboy.'

*

How it was, *the Finn began, and to Bobby it was all infinitely absorbing, even better than listening to Beauvoir and Lucas,* Wigan Ludgate had had five years as a top jock, which is a decent run for a cyberspace cowboy. Five years tends to find a cowboy either rich or brain-dead, or else financing a stable of younger cracksmen and strictly into the managerial side. The Wig, in his first heat of youth and glory, had stormed off on an extended pass through the rather sparsely occupied sectors of the matrix representing those geographical areas which had once been known as the Third World.

Silicon doesn't wear out; microchips were effectively immortal. The Wig took notice of the fact. Like every other child of his age, however, he knew that silicon *became obsolete*, which was worse than wearing out; this fact was a grim and accepted constant for the Wig, like death or taxes, and in fact he was usually more worried about his gear falling behind the state of the art than he was about death (he was twenty-two) or taxes (he didn't file, although he paid a Singapore money-laundry a yearly percentage that was roughly equivalent to the income tax he would have been required to pay if he'd declared his gross). The Wig reasoned that all that obsolete silicon had to be going somewhere. Where it was going, he learned, was into any number of very poor places, struggling along with nascent industrial bases. Nations so benighted that the concept of *nation* was still taken seriously. The Wig punched himself through a couple of African backwaters and felt like a shark cruising a swimming pool thick with caviar. Not that any one of those tasty tiny eggs amounted to much, but you could just open wide and *scoop*, and it was easy and filling and it added up. The Wig worked the Africans for a week, incidentally bringing about the collapse of at least three governments and causing untold human suffering. At the end of his week, fat with the cream of several million laughably tiny bank accounts, he retired. As he was going out, the locusts were coming in; other people had got the African idea.

The Wig sat on the beach at Cannes for two years, ingesting only the most expensive designer drugs and periodically flicking on a tiny Hosaka television to study the bloated bodies of dead Africans with a strange and curiously innocent intensity. At some point, no one could quite say where or when or why, it began to be noted that the Wig had become convinced that God lived in cyberspace, or perhaps that cyberspace *was* God, or some new manifestation of same. The Wig's ventures into theology tended to be marked by major paradigm shifts, true leaps of faith. The Finn had some idea of what the Wig was about in those days; shortly after his conversion to his new and singular faith, Wigan Ludgate had returned to the Sprawl and embarked on an epic if somewhat random voyage of cybernetic discovery. Being a former console jockey, he knew where to go for the very best in what the Finn called 'the hard and the soft'. The Finn provided the Wig with all manner of both, as the Wig was still a rich man. The Wig explained to the Finn that his technique of mystical exploration involved projecting his consciousness into blank, unstructured sectors of the matrix and waiting. To the man's credit, the Finn said, he never actually claimed to have met God, although he did maintain that he had on several occasions sensed His presence moving upon the face of the grid. In due course, the Wig ran out of money. His spiritual quest having alienated the few remaining business connections from his pre-African days, he sank without a trace.

'But then he turned up one day,' the Finn said, 'crazy as a shithouse rat. He was a pale little fucker anyway, but now he wore all this African shit, beads and bones and everything.' Bobby let go of the Finn's narrative long enough to wonder how anyone who looked like the Finn could describe somebody as a pale little fucker, then glanced over at Lucas, whose face was dead grim. Then it occurred to Bobby that Lucas might take the Africa stuff personally, sort of. But the Finn was continuing his story.

'He had a lot of stuff he wanted to sell. Decks, peripherals, software. It was all a couple of years old, but it was top gear, so I gave him a price on it. I noticed he'd had a socket implant, and he kept this one sliver of microsoft jacked behind his ear. What's the soft? It's blank, he says. He's sitting right where you are now, kid, and he says to me, it's blank and it's the voice of God, and I live forever in His white hum, or some shit like that. So I think, Christ, the Wig's gone but good now, and there he is counting up the money I'd given him for about the fifth time. Wig, I said, time's money but tell me what you intend to do now? Because I was curious. Known the guy years, in a business way. Finn, he says, I gotta get up the gravity well, God's up there. I mean, he says, He's everywhere but there's too much static down here, it obscures His face. Right, I say, you got it. So I show him the door and that's it. Never saw him again.'

Bobby blinked, waited, squirmed a little on the hard seat of the folding chair.

'Except, about a year later, a guy turns up, high-orbit rigger down the well on a leave, and he's got some good software for sale. Not great, but interesting. He says it's from the Wig. Well, maybe the Wig's a freak, and long out of the game, but he can still spot the good shit. So I buy it. That was maybe ten years ago, right? And every year or so, some guy would turn up with something. "The Wig told me I should offer you this." And usually I'd buy it. It was never anything special, but it was okay. Never the same guy bringing it, either.'

'Was that it, Finn, just software?' Lucas asked.

'Yeah, mainly, except for these weird sculpture things. I'd forgotten that. I figured the Wig made 'em. First time a guy came in with one of those, I bought the 'ware he had, then said what the fuck do you call that? Wig said you might be interested, the guy said. Tell him he's crazy, I said. The guy laughed. Well, you keep it, he says, I'm not carrying the goddam thing back up with me. I mean, it was about the size of a deck, this thing, just a bunch of garbage and shit, stuck together in a box ... So I pushed it behind this Coke crate fulla scrap iron, and forgot it, except old Smith, he's a colleague of mine in those days, dealt mostly art and collectibles, he sees it and wants it. So we do some dipshit deal. Any more of these, Finn, he says, get 'em. There's assholes uptown go for this kind of shit. So the next time a guy turned up from the Wig, I bought the sculpture thing, too, and traded it to Smith. But it was never much money for any of it ...' The Finn shrugged. 'Not until last month, anyway. Some kid came in with what you bought. It was from the Wig. Listen. he says, this is biosoft and it's a breaker. Wig says it's worth a lot. I put a scan on it and it looked right. I thought it looked interesting, you know? Your partner Beauvoir bought it off me. End of story.' The Finn dragged out a cigarette, this one broken, bent double. 'Shit,' he said. He pulled a faded pack of pink cigarette papers from the same pocket and extracted one of the fragile leaves, rolling it tightly around the broken cigarette, a sort of splint. When he licked the glue, Bobby caught a glimpse of a very pointed, grey-pink tongue.

'And where, Finn, does Mr Wig reside?' Lucas asked, his thumbs beneath his chin, his large fingers forming a steeple in front of his face.

'Lucas, I haven't got the slightest fucking clue. In orbit somewhere. And modestly, if the kind of money he was getting out of me meant anything to him. You know, I hear there's places up there where you don't need money, if you fit into the economy, so maybe a little goes a long way. Don't ask me, though, I'm agoraphobic.' He smiled nastily at Bobby, who was trying to get the image of that tongue out of his mind. 'You know,' he said, squinting at Lucas, 'it was about that time that I started hearing about weird shit happening in the matrix.'

'Like what?' Bobby asked.

'Keep the fuck out of this,' the Finn said, still looking at Lucas. 'That was before you guys turned up, the new hoodoo team. I knew this street samurai got a job working for a Special Forces type made the Wig look flat fucking normal. Her and this cowboy they'd scraped up out of Chiba, they were on to something like that. Maybe they found it. Istanbul was the last I saw of 'em. Heard she lived in London, once, a few years ago ... Who the fuck knows? Seven, eight years ...' The Finn suddenly seemed tired, and old, very old. He looked to Bobby like a big, mummified rat animated by springs and hidden wires. He took a wristwatch with a cracked face and a single greasy leather strap from his pocket and consulted it. 'Jesus. Well, that's all you get from me, Lucas. I've got some friends from an organ bank coming by in twenty minutes to talk a little biz ...'

Bobby thought of the bodies upstairs. They'd been there all day ...

'Hey,' the Finn said, reading the expression on his face, 'organ banks are great for getting *rid* of things. I'm paying *them*. Those motherless assholes upstairs, they don't have too much left in the way of organs ...' And the Finn laughed.

'You said he was close to ... Legba? And Legba's the one you and Beauvoir said gave me luck when I hit that black ice?'

Beyond the honeycomb edge of the geodesics, the sky was lightening.

'Yes,' Lucas said. He seemed lost in thought.

'But he doesn't seem to trust that stuff at all ...'

'It doesn't matter,' Lucas said, as the Rolls came into view. 'He's always been close to the spirit of the thing.'

17

The Squirrel Wood

The plane had gone to ground near the sound of running water. Turner could hear it, turning in the g-web in his fever or sleep, water down stone, one of the oldest songs. The plane was smart, smart as any dog, with hardwired instincts of concealment. He felt it sway on its landing gear, somewhere in the sick night, and creep forward, branches brushing and scraping against the dark canopy. The plane crept into deep green shadows and sank down on its knees, its airframe whining and creaking as it flattened itself, belly down, into loam and granite like a manta ray into sand. The mimetic polycarbon coating its wings and fuselage mottled and darkened, taking on the colours and patterns of moon-dappled stone and forest soil. Finally it was silent, and the only sound was the sound of water over a creek bed ...

He came awake like a machine, eyes opening, vision plugged in, empty, remembering the red flash of Lynch's death out beyond the fixed sights of the Smith & Wesson. The arc of the canopy above him was laced with mimetic approximations of leaves and branches. Pale dawn and the sound of running water. He was still wearing Oakey's blue work shirt. It smelled of sour sweat now, and he'd ripped the sleeves out the day before. The gun lay between his legs, pointing at the jet's black joystick. The g-web was a limp tangle around his hips and shoulders. He twisted around and saw the girl, oval face and a brown dried trickle of blood beneath a nostril. She was still out, sweating, her lips slightly parted, like a doll's.

'Where are we?'

'We are fifteen metres south-southeast of the landing co-ordinates you provided,' the plane said. 'You were unconscious again. I opted for concealment.'

He reached back and removed the interface plug from his socket, breaking his link with the plane. He gazed dully around the cockpit until he found the manual controls for the canopy. It sighed up on servos, the lacework of polycarbon leaves shifting as it moved. He got his leg over the side, looked down at his hand flat against the fuselage at the edge of the cockpit. Polycarbon reproduced the grey tones of a nearby boulder; as he watched, it began to paint a hand-sized patch the colour of his palm. He pulled his other leg over, the gun forgotten on the seat, and slid down into earth and long sweet grass, and dreamed of running water.

When he woke, he was crawling forward on his hands and knees, through low branches heavy with dew. Finally he reached a clearing and pitched forward, rolling over, his arms spread in what felt like surrender. High above him, something small and grey launched itself from one branch, caught another, swung there for an instant, then scrambled away, out of his sight.

Lie still, he heard a voice telling him, years away. *Just lay out and relax and pretty soon they'll forget you, forget you in the grey and the dawn and the dew. They're out to feed, feed and play, and their brains can't hold two messages, not for long.* He lay there on his back, beside his brother, the nylon-stocked Winchester across his chest, breathing the smell of new brass and gun oil, the smell of their campfire still in his hair. And his brother was always right, about the squirrels. They came. They forgot the clear glyph of death spelled out below them in patched denim and blue steel; they came, racing along limbs, pausing to sniff the morning, and Turner's .22 cracked, a limp grey body tumbling down. The others scattered, vanishing, and Turner passed the gun to his brother. Again, they waited, waited for the squirrels to forget them.

'You're like me,' Turner said to the squirrels, bobbing up out of his dream. One of them sat up suddenly on a fat limb and looked directly at him. 'I always come back.' The squirrel hopped away. 'I was coming back when I ran from the Dutchman. I was coming back when I flew to Mexico. I was coming back when I killed Lynch.'

He lay there for a long time, watching the squirrels, while the woods woke and the morning warmed around him. A crow swept in, banking, braking with feathers it spread like black mechanical fingers. Checking to see if he were dead.

Turner grinned up at the crow as it flapped away.

Not yet.

He crawled back in, under the overhanging branches, and found her sitting up in the cockpit. She wore a baggy white t-shirt slashed diagonally with the MAAS-NEOTEK logo. There were lozenges of fresh red blood across the front of the shirt. Her nose was bleeding again. Bright blue eyes, dazed and disoriented, in sockets bruised yellow-black, like exotic makeup.

Young, he saw, very young.

'You're Mitchell's daughter,' he said, dragging the name up from the biosoft dossier. 'Angela.'

'Angie,' she said, automatically 'Who're you? I'm bleeding.' She held out a bloody carnation of wadded tissue.

'Turner. I was expecting your father.' Remembering the gun now, her other hand out of sight, below the edge of the cockpit. 'Do you know where he is?'

'In the mesa. He thought he could talk with them, explain it. Because they need him.'

'With who?' He took a step forward.

'Maas. The Board. They can't afford to hurt him. Can they?'

'Why would they?' Another step.

She dabbed at her nose with the red tissue.

'Because he sent me out. Because he knew they were going to hurt me, kill me maybe. Because of the dreams.'

'The dreams?'

'Do you think they'll hurt him?'

'No, no, they wouldn't do that. I'm going to climb up there now. Okay?'

She nodded. He had to run his hands over the side of the fuselage to find the shallow, recessed handholds; the mimetic coating showed him leaf and lichen, twigs ... And then he was up, beside her, and he saw the gun beside her sneakered foot.

'But wasn't he coming himself? I was expecting him, your father ...'

'No. We never planned that. We only had the one plane. Didn't he tell you?' She started to shake. 'Didn't he tell you *anything*?'

'Enough,' he said, putting his hand on her shoulder, 'he told us enough. It'll be all right ...' He swung his legs over, bent, moved the Smith & Wesson away from her foot, and found the interface cable. His hand still on her, he raised it, snapped it into place behind his ear.

'Give me the procedures for erasing anything you stored in the past forty-eight hours,' he said. 'I want to dump that course for Mexico City, your flight from the coast, anything ...'

162

'There was no plan logged for Mexico City,' the voice said, direct neural input on audio.

Turner stared at the girl, rubbed his jaw.

'Where were we going?'

'Bogota,' and the jet reeled out co-ordinates for the landing they hadn't made.

She blinked at him, her lids bruised dark as the surrounding skin. 'Who are you talking to?'

'The plane. Did Mitchell tell you where he thought you'd be going?'

'Japan ...'

'Know anyone in Bogota? Where's your mother?'

'No. Berlin, I think. I don't really know her ...'

He wiped the plane's banks, dumping Conroy's programming, what there was of it: the approach from California; identification data for the site; a flight plan that would have taken them to a strip within three hundred kilometres of Bogota's urban core ...

Someone would find the jet eventually. He thought about the Maas orbital recon system and wondered if the stealth-and-evasion programs he'd ordered the plane to run had done any real good. He could offer the jet to Rudy for salvage, but he doubted Rudy would want to be involved. For that matter, simply showing up at the farm, with Mitchell's daughter in tow, dragged Rudy in right up to his neck. But there was nowhere else to go, not for the things he needed now.

It was a four-hour walk, along half-remembered trails and down a weed-grown, winding stretch of two-lane blacktop. The trees were different, it seemed to him, and then he remembered how much they would have grown over the years since he'd been back. At regular intervals they passed the stumps of wooden poles that had once supported telephone wires, overgrown now with bramble and honeysuckle, the wires pulled down seventy years earlier for copper, the creosote poles chopped down for fuel ... Bees grazed in flowering grass at the roadside ...

'Is there food where we're going?' the girl asked, the soles of her white sneakers scuffing the weathered blacktop.

'Sure,' Turner said, 'all you want.'

'What I want right now's water.' She swiped a lank strand of brown hair back from a tanned cheek. He'd noticed she was developing a limp, and she'd started to wince each time she put her right foot down.

'What's wrong with your leg?'

'Ankle. Something, I think when I decked the 'light.' She grimaced, kept walking.

'We'll rest.'

'No. I want to get there, get anywhere ...'

'Rest,' he said, taking her hand, leading her to the edge of the road. She made a face, but sat down beside him, her right leg stretched carefully in front of her.

'That's a big gun,' she said. It was hot now, too hot for the parka. He'd put the shoulder rig on bareback, with the sleeveless work shirt over it, tails out and flapping. 'Why's the barrel look like that, like a cobra's head, underneath?'

'That's a sighting device, for night fights.' He leaned forward to examine her ankle. It was swelling quickly now. 'I don't know how much longer you'll want to walk on that,' he said.

'You get into a lot of fights, at night? With guns?'

'No.'

'I don't think I understand what it is that you do.'

He looked up at her. 'I don't always understand that myself, not lately. I was expecting your father. He wanted to change companies, work for somebody else. The people he wanted

164

to work for hired me and some other people to make sure he got out of his old contract.'

'But there wasn't any way out of that contract,' she said. 'Not legally.'

'That's right.' Undoing the knot, unlacing the sneaker. 'Not legally.'

'Oh. So that's what you do for a living?'

'Yes.' Sneaker off now, she wore no sock, the ankle swelling badly. 'This is a sprain ...'

'What about the other people, then? You had more people back there, in that ruin? Somebody was shooting, and those flares ...'

'Hard to say who was shooting,' he said, 'but the flares weren't ours. Maybe Maas security team, following you out. Did you think you got out clean?'

'I did what Chris told me,' she said. 'Chris, that's my father.'

'I know. I think I'm going to have to carry you the rest of the way.'

'But what about your friends?'

'What friends?'

'Back there, in Arizona ...'

'Right. Well,' and he wiped sweat from his forehead with the back of his hand, 'can't say. Don't really know.'

Seeing the white-out sky, flare of energy, brighter than the sun. But no pulse of electromagnetics, the plane had said ...

The first of Rudy's augmented dogs picked them up fifteen minutes after they started out again, Angie riding Turner's back, arms around his shoulders, skinny thighs under his armpits, his fingers locked in front of his sternum in a double fist. She smelled like a kid from the up-line 'burbs, some vaguely herbal hint of soap or shampoo. Thinking that, he thought about what he must smell like to her. Rudy had a shower—

'Oh, shit, what's that?' Stiffening on his back. Pointing.

A lean grey hound regarded them from a high clay bank at a turning in the road, its narrow head sheathed and blinkered in a black hood studded with sensors. It panted, tongue lolling, and slowly swung its head from side to side.

'It's okay,' Turner said. 'Watchdog. Belongs to my friend.'

The house had grown, sprouting wings and workshops, but Rudy had never painted the peeling clapboard of the original structure. Rudy had thrown up a taut square of chain-link since Turner's time, fencing away his collection of vehicles, but the gate was open when they arrived, the hinges lost in the morning-glory and rust. The real defences, Turner knew, were elsewhere. Four of the augmented hounds trotted after him as he trudged up the gravel drive, Angie's head limp on his shoulder, her arms still locked around him.

Rudy was waiting on the front porch, in old white shorts and a navy t-shirt, its single pocket displaying at least nine pens of one kind or another. He looked at them and raised a green can of Dutch beer in greeting. Behind him, a blonde in a faded khaki shirt stepped out of the kitchen, a chrome spatula in her hand; her hair was clipped short, swept up and back in a cut that made Turner think of the Korean medic in Hosaka's pod, of the pod burning, of Webber, of the white sky ... He swayed there, in Rudy's gravel driveway, legs wide to support the girl, his bare chest streaked with sweat, with dust from the mall in Arizona, and looked at Rudy and the blonde.

'We got some breakfast for you,' Rudy said. 'When you came up on the dog screens, we figured you'd be hungry ...' His tone was carefully non-committal.

The girl groaned.

'That's good,' Turner said. 'She's got a bum ankle, Rudy.

166

We better look at that. Some other things I have to talk to you about, too.'

'Little young for you, I'd say,' Rudy said, and took another swig of his beer.

'Fuck off, Rudy,' the woman beside him said, 'can't you see she's hurt? Bring her in this way,' she said to Turner, and was gone, back through the kitchen door.

'You look different,' Rudy said, peering at him, and Turner saw that he was drunk. 'The same, but different.'

'It's been a while,' Turner said, starting for the wooden steps.

'You get a face job or something?'

'Reconstruction. They had to build it back from records. He climbed the steps, his lower back stabbed through with pain at every move.

'It's not bad,' Rudy said. 'I almost didn't notice.' He belched. He was shorter than Turner, and going to fat, but they had the same brown hair, very similar features.

Turner paused, on the stair, when their eyes were level. 'You still do a little bit of everything, Rudy? I need this kid scanned. I need a few other things, too.'

'Well,' his brother said, 'we'll see what we can do. We heard something last night. Maybe a sonic boom. Anything to do with you?'

'Yeah. There's a jet up by the squirrel wood, but it's pretty well out of sight.'

Rudy sighed. 'Jesus … Well, bring her in …'

Rudy's years in the house had stripped it of most of the things that Turner might have remembered, and something in him was obscurely grateful for that. He watched the blonde crack eggs into a steel bowl, dark yellow free-range yolks; Rudy kept his own chickens.

'I'm Sally,' she said, whisking the eggs around with a fork.

'Turner.'

'That's all he ever calls you either,' she said. 'He never has talked about you much.'

'We haven't kept all that much in touch. Maybe I should go up now and help him.'

'You sit. Your little girl's okay with Rudy. He's got a good touch.'

'Even when he's pissed?'

'Half pissed. Well, he's not going to operate, just derm her and tape that ankle.' She crushed dry tortilla chips into a black pan, over sizzling butter, and poured the eggs on top. 'What happened to your eyes, Turner? You and her ...' She stirred the mixture with the chrome spatula, slopping in salsa from a plastic tub.

'G-force. Had to take off quick.'

'That how she hurt her ankle?'

'Maybe. Don't know.'

'People after you now? After her?' Busy taking plates from the cabinet above the sink, the cheap brown laminate of the cabinet doors triggering a sudden rush of nostalgia in Turner, seeing her tanned wrists as his mother's ...

'Probably,' he said. 'I don't know what's involved, not yet.'

'Eat some of this.' Transferring the mixture to a white plate, rummaging for a fork. 'Rudy's scared of the kind of people you might get after you.'

Taking the plate, the fork. Steam rising from the eggs. 'So am I.'

'Got some clothes,' Sally said, over the sound of the shower, 'friend of Rudy's left 'em here, ought to fit you ...' The shower was gravity-operated, rainwater from a roof tank, a fat white filtration unit strapped into the pipe above the spray head.

Turner stuck his head out between cloudy sheets of plastic and blinked at her. 'Thanks.'

'Girl's unconscious,' she said. 'Rudy thinks it's shock, exhaustion. He says her crits are high, so he might as well run his scan now.' She left the room then, taking Turner's fatigues and Oakey's shirt with her.

'What is she?' Rudy extending a crumpled scroll of silvery printout.

'I don't know how to read that,' Turner said, looking around the white room, looking for Angie. 'Where is she?'

'Sleeping. Sally's watching her.' Rudy turned and walked back, the length of the room, and Turner remembered it had been the living room once. Rudy began to shut his consoles down, the tiny pilot lights blinking out one by one. 'I don't know, man. I just don't know. What is it, some kind of cancer?'

Turner followed him down the room, past a worktable where a micromanipulator waited beneath its dust cover. Past the dusty rectangular eyes of a bank of aged monitors, one of them with a shattered screen.

'It's all through her head,' Rudy said 'Like long chains of it. It doesn't look like anything I've ever seen, ever. Nothing.'

'How much do you know about biochips, Rudy?'

Rudy grunted. He seemed very sober now, but tense, agitated. He kept running his hands back through his hair. 'That's what I thought. It's some kind of ... Not an implant. Graft.'

'What's it for?'

'For? Christ. Who the fuck knows? Who did it to her? Somebody you work for?'

'Her father, I think.'

'Jesus.' Rudy wiped his hand across his mouth. 'It shadows

like tumour, on the scans, but her crits are high enough, normal. What's she like, ordinarily?'

'Don't know. A kid.' He shrugged.

'Fucking hell,' Rudy said. 'I'm amazed she can walk ...' He opened a little lab freezer and came up with a frosted bottle of Moskovskaya. 'Want it out of the bottle?' he asked.

'Maybe later.'

Rudy sighed, looked at the bottle, then returned it to the fridge. 'So what do you want? Anything as weird as what's in that little girl's head, somebody's going to be after it soon. If they aren't already.'

'They are,' Turner said. 'I don't know if they know she's here.'

'Yet.' Rudy wiped his palms on his grubby white shorts. 'But they probably will, right?'

Turner nodded.

'Where you going to go, then?'

'The Sprawl.'

'Why?'

'Because I've got money there. I've got credit lines in four different names, no way to link 'em back to me. Because I've got a lot of other connections I may be able to use. And because it's always cover, the Sprawl. So damned much *of* it, you know?'

'Okay,' Rudy said. 'When?'

'You that worried about it, you want us right out?'

'No. I mean, I don't know. It's all pretty interesting, what's in your girlfriend's head. I've got a friend in Atlanta could rent me a function analyser, brain-map, one to one; put that on her, I might start to figure out what that thing is ... Might be worth something.'

'Sure. If you knew where to sell it.'

'Aren't you curious? I mean, what the hell *is* she? You pull

170

her out of some military lab?' Rudy opened the white freezer door again, took out the bottle of vodka, opened it, and took a swallow.

Turner took the bottle and tilted it, letting the icy fluid splash against his teeth. He swallowed, shuddered. 'It's corporate. Big. I was supposed to get her father out, but he sent her instead. Then somebody took the whole site out, looked like a baby nuke. We just made it. This far.' He handed Rudy the bottle. 'Stay straight for me, Rudy. You get scared, you drink too much.'

Rudy was staring at him, ignoring the bottle. 'Arizona,' he said. 'It was on the news. Mexico's still kicking about it. But it wasn't a nuke. They've had crews out there, all over it. No nuke.'

'What was it?'

'They think it was a railgun. They think somebody put up a hypervelocity gun in a cargo blimp and blew hell out of some derelict mall out there in the boonies. They know there was a blimp near there, and so far nobody's found it. You can rig a railgun to blow itself to plasma when it discharges. The projectile could have been damn near anything, at those velocities. About a hundred and fifty kilos of ice would do the trick.' He took the bottle, capped it, and put it down on the counter beside him. 'All that land around there, it belongs to Maas, Maas Biolabs, doesn't it? They've been on the news, Maas. Co-operating fully with various authorities. You bet. So that tells us where you got your little honey from, I guess.'

'Sure. But it doesn't tell me who used the railgun. Or why.'

Rudy shrugged.

'You better come see this,' Sally said from the door.

Much later, Turner sat with Sally on the front porch. The girl had lapsed, finally, into something Rudy's EEG called sleep.

171

Rudy was back in one of his workshops, probably with his bottle of vodka. There were fireflies around the honeysuckle vines beside the chain-link gate. Turner found that if he half-closed his eyes, from his seat on the wooden porch-swing, he could almost see an apple tree that was no longer there, a tree that had once supported a length of silvery-grey hemp rope and an ancient automobile tyre. There were fire-flies then as well, and Rudy's heels thumping a bare hard skid of earth as he pumped himself out on the swing's arc, legs kicking, and Turner lay on his back in the grass, watching the stars ...

'Tongues,' Sally said, Rudy's woman, from the creaking rattan chair, her cigarette a red eye in the dark. 'Talking in the tongues.'

'What's that?'

'What your kid was doing, upstairs. You know any French?'

'No, not much. Not without a lexicon.'

'Some of it sounded French to me.' The red amber was a short slash for an instant, when she tapped ash. 'When I was little, my old man took me one time to this stadium, and I saw the testifying and the speaking in tongues. It scared me. I think it scared me more, today, when she started.'

'Rudy taped the end of it, didn't he?'

'Yeah. You know, Rudy hasn't been doing too good. That's mainly why I moved back in here. I told him I wasn't staying unless he straightened himself out, but then it got real bad, so about two weeks ago I moved back in. I was about ready to go when you showed up.' The coal of the cigarette arced out over the railing and fell on the gravel that covered the yard.

'Drinking?'

'That, and the stuff he cooks for himself in the lab. You know, that man knows a little bit of damn near everything. He's still got a lot of friends, around the county; I've heard 'em tell stories about when you and him were kids, before you left.'

172

'He should have left, too,' he said.

'He hates the city,' she said. 'Says it all comes in online anyway, so why do you need to go there?'

'I went because there was nothing happening here. Rudy could always find something to do. Still can, by the look of it.'

'You should've stayed in touch. He wanted you here when your mother was dying.'

'I was in Berlin. Couldn't leave what I was doing.'

'I guess not. I wasn't here then either. I came later. That was a good summer. Rudy just pulled me out of this sleaze-ass club in Memphis; came in there with a bunch of country boys one night, and next day I was back here, didn't really know why. Except he was nice to me, those days, and funny, and he gave my head a chance to slow down. He taught me to cook.' She laughed. 'I liked that, except I was scared of those goddam chickens out back.' She stood up then and stretched, the old chair creaking, and he was aware of the length of her tanned legs, the smell and summer heat of her, close to his face.

She put her hands on his shoulders. His eyes were level with the band of brown belly where her shorts rode low, her navel a soft shadow, and, remembering Allison in the white hollow room, he wanted to press his face there, taste it all ... He thought she swayed slightly, but he wasn't sure.

'Turner,' she said, 'sometimes bein' here with him, it's like bein' here alone ...'

So he stood, rattle of the old swing-chain where the eye-bolts were screwed deep in the tongue-and-groove of the porch roof, bolts his father might have turned forty years before, and kissed her mouth as it opened, cut loose in time by talk and the fireflies and the subliminal triggers of memory, so that it seemed to him, as he ran his palms up the warmth of her bare back, beneath the white t-shirt, that the

173

people in his life weren't beads strung on a wire of sequence, but clustered like quanta, so that he knew her as well as he'd known Rudy, or Allison, or Conroy, as well as he knew the girl who was Mitchell's daughter.

'Hey,' she whispered, working her mouth free, 'you come upstairs now.'

18

Names of the Dead

Alain phoned at five and she verified the availability of the amount he required, fighting to control the sickness she felt at his greed. She copied the address carefully on the back of a card she'd taken from Picard's desk in the Roberts Gallery. Andrea returned from work ten minutes later, and Marly was glad that her friend hadn't been there for Alain's call.

She watched Andrea prop up the kitchen window with a frayed, blue-backed copy of the second volume of the *Shorter Oxford English Dictionary*, sixth edition. Andrea had wedged a kind of plywood shelf there, on the stone ledge, wide enough to support the little hibachi she kept beneath the sink. Now she was arranging the black squares of charcoal neatly on the grate.

'I had a talk about your employer today,' she said, placing the hibachi on the plywood and igniting the greenish firestarter paste with the spark gun from the stove. 'Our academic was in from Nice. He's baffled as to why I'd choose Josef Virek as my focus of interest, but he's also a horny old goat, so he was more than glad to talk.'

Marly stood beside her, watching the nearly invisible flames lick around the coals.

'He kept dragging the Tessier-Ashpools into it,' Andrea continued, 'and Hughes. Hughes was mid to late twentieth-century, and American. He's in the book as well, as a sort of proto-Virek. I hadn't known that Tessier-Ashpool had started to disintegrate ...' She went back to the counter and unwrapped six large tiger prawns.

'They're Franco-Australian? I remember a documentary, I think. They own one of the big spas?'

'Freeside. It's been sold now, my professor tells me. It seems that one of old Ashpool's daughters somehow managed to gain personal control of the entire business entity, became increasingly eccentric, and the clan's interests went to hell. This over the past seven years.'

'I don't see what it has to do with Virek,' Marly said, watching Andrea skewer each prawn on a long needle of bamboo.

'Your guess is as good as mine. My professor maintains that both Virek and the Tessier-Ashpools are fascinating anachronisms, and that things can be learned about corporate evolution by watching them. He's convinced enough of our senior editors, at any rate ...'

'But what did he say about Virek?'

'That Virek's madness would take a different form.'

'Madness?'

'Actually, he avoided calling it that. But Hughes was mad as birds, apparently, and old Ashpool as well, and his daughter totally bizarre. He said that Virek would be forced, by evolutionary pressures, to make some sort of "jump". "Jump" was his word.'

'Evolutionary pressures?'

'Yes,' Andrea said, carrying the skewered prawns to the hibachi, 'he talks about corporations as though they were animals of some kind.'

After dinner, they went out walking. Marly found herself straining, at times, to sense the imagined mechanism of Virek's surveillance, but Andrea filled the evening with her usual warmth and common sense, and Marly was grateful to walk through a city where things were simply themselves. In Virek's world, what could be simple? She remembered the brass knob in the Galerie Duperey, how it had squirmed so indescribably in her fingers as it drew her into Virek's model of the Park Güell. Was he always there, she wondered, in Gaudí's park, in an afternoon that never ended? *Señor is wealthy. Señor enjoys any number of means of manifestation.* She shivered in the warm evening air, moved closer to Andrea.

The sinister thing about a simstim construct, really, was that it carried the suggestion that *any* environment might be unreal, that the windows of the shopfronts she passed now with Andrea might be figments. Mirrors, someone had once said, were in some way essentially unwholesome; constructs were more so, she decided.

Andrea paused at a kiosk to buy her English cigarettes and the new *Elle*. Marly waited on the pavement, the pedestrian traffic parting automatically for her, faces sliding past, students and businessmen and tourists. Some of them, she assumed, were part of Virek's machine, wired into Paco. Paco with his brown eyes, his easy way, his seriousness, muscles moving beneath his broadcloth shirt. Paco, who had worked for Señor all his life ...

'What's wrong? You look as though you've just swallowed something.' Andrea, stripping the cellophane from her twenty Silk Cut.

'No,' Marly said, and shivered, 'but it occurs to me that I very nearly did ...'

And walking home, in spite of Andrea's conversation, her warmth, the shop windows had become boxes, each one, constructions, like the works of Joseph Cornell or the mysterious Boxmaker Virek sought. The books and furs and

Italian cottons arranged to suggest geometries of nameless longing.

And waking, once again, face smudged into Andrea's couch, the red quilt humped around her shoulders, smelling coffee, while Andrea hummed some Tokyo pop song to herself in the next room, dressing, in a grey morning of Paris rain.

'No,' she told Paco, 'I'll go myself. I prefer it.'

'That is a great deal of money.' He looked down at the Italian bag on the cafe table between them. 'It's dangerous, you understand?'

'There's no one to know I'm carrying it, then, is there? Only Alain. Alain and your friends. And I didn't say I'd go alone, only that I don't feel like company.'

'Is something wrong?' The serious deep lines at the corners of his mouth. 'You are upset?'

'I only mean that I wish to be by myself. You and the others, whoever they are, are welcome to follow, to follow and observe. If you should lose me, which I think unlikely, I'm sure you have the address.'

'That is true,' he said. 'But for you to carry several million New Yen, alone, through Paris ...' He shrugged.

'And if I were to lose it? Would Señor register the loss? Or would there be another bag, another four million?' She reached for the shoulder strap and stood.

'There would be another bag, certainly, although it requires some effort on our part to assemble that amount of cash. And, no, Señor would not "register" its loss, in the sense you mean, but I would be disciplined even for the *pointless* loss of a lesser sum. The very rich have the common characteristic of taking care with their money, you will find.'

'None the less, I go by myself. Not alone, but leave me with my thoughts.'

'Your intuition.'

'Yes.'

If they followed, and she was sure they did, they were invisible as ever. For that matter, it seemed most unlikely that they would leave Alain unobserved. Certainly the address he had given her that morning would already be a focus of their attention, whether he were there or not.

She felt a new strength today. She had stood up to Paco. It had had something to do with her abrupt suspicion, the night before, that Paco might be there, in part, for her, with his humour and his manliness and his endearing ignorance of art. She remembered Virek saying that they knew more about her life than she herself did. What easier way, then, for them to pencil in those last few blanks in the grid that was Marly Krushkhova? Paco Estevez. A perfect stranger. Too perfect. She smiled at herself in a wall of blue mirror as the escalator carried her down into the Métro, pleased with the cut of her dark hair and the stylishly austere titanium frames of the black Porshe glasses she'd bought that morning. *Good lips*, she thought, *really not bad lips at all*, and a thin boy in a white shirt and dark leather jacket smiled at her from the escalator, a huge black portfolio case beneath his arm.

I'm in Paris, she thought. For the first time in a very long time, that alone seemed reason to smile. *And today I will give my disgusting fool of a former lover four million New Yen, and he will give me something in return. A name, or an address, perhaps a phone number.* She bought a first-class ticket; the car would be less crowded, and she could pass the time guessing which of her fellow passengers belonged to Virek.

*

179

The address Alain had given her, in a grim northern suburb, was one of twenty concrete towers rising from a plain of the same material, speculative real estate from the middle of the previous century. The rain was falling steadily now, but she felt as though she were somehow in collusion with it; it lent the day something conspiratorial, and beaded on the chic rubber bag stuffed with Alain's fortune. How queer to stroll through this hideous landscape with millions beneath her arm, on her way to reward her utterly faithless former lover with these bales of New Yen.

There was no answer when she buzzed the apartment's numbered speaker-button. Beyond smudged sheet glass, a darkened foyer, entirely bare. The sort of place where you turned the lights on as you entered; they turned themselves off again, automatically, invariably before your elevator had arrived, leaving you to wait there in the smell of disinfectant and tired air. She buzzed again. 'Alain?' Nothing.

She tried the door. It wasn't locked. There was no one in the foyer. The dead eye of a derelict video camera regarded her through a film of dust. The afternoon's watery light seeped in from the concrete plain behind her. Bootheels clicking on brown tile, she crossed to the bank of elevators and pressed button 22. There was a hollow thump, a metallic groan, and one of the elevators began to descend. The plastic indicators above the doors remained unlit. The car arrived with a sigh and a high-pitched, fading whine.

'Cher Alain, you have come down in the world. This place is the shits, truly.'

As the doors slid open on the darkness of the car, she fumbled beneath the Italian bag for the flap of her Brussels purse. She found the flat little green tin flashlight she'd carried since her first walk in Paris, with the lion-headed Pile Wonder trademark embossed on its front, and pulled it out. In the elevators of Paris, you could step into many things: the arms of a mugger, a steaming pile of fresh dog-shit ...

And the weak beam picking out the silver cables, oiled and shining, swaying gently in the vacant shaft, the toe of her right boot already centimetres past the scuffed steel edge of the tile she stood on; her hand automatically jerking the beam down in terror, down to the dusty, littered roof of the car, two levels below. She took in an extraordinary amount of detail in the seconds her flash wavered on the elevator. She thought of a tiny submarine diving the cliffs of some deep seamount, the frail beam wavering on a patch of silt undisturbed for centuries: the soft bed of ancient furry soot; a dried grey thing that was a used condom; the bright reflected eyes of crumpled bits of tinfoil; the frail grey barrel and white plunger of a diabetic syringe ... She held the edge of the door so tightly that her knuckle joints ached. Very slowly, she shifted her weight backwards, away from the pit. Another step and she clicked off her light.

'Damn you,' she said. 'Oh Jesus.'

She found the door to the stairwell. Clicking the little flash back on, she began to climb. Eight floors up, the numbness began to fade, and she was shaking, tears ruining her makeup.

Rapping on the door again. It was pressboard, laminated with a ghastly imitation of rosewood, the lithographed grain just visible in the light from the long corridor's single strip of biofluorescence.

'Damn you, Alain? Alain!' The myopic fisheye of the door's little spyglass, looking through her, blank and vacant. The corridor held a horrible smell, embalmed cooking odours trapped in synthetic carpeting.

Trying the door, knob turning, the cheap brass greasy and cold, and the bag of money suddenly heavy, the strap cutting into her shoulder … The door opening easily. A short stretch of orange carpet flecked with irregular rectangles of salmon-pink, decades of dirt ground into it in a clearly defined track by thousands of tenants and their visitors …

'Alain?' The smell of black French cigarettes, almost comforting …

And finding him there in that same watery light, silver light, the other tower blocks featureless, beyond a rectangle of window, against pale rainy sky, where he lay curled like a child on the hideous orange carpet, his spine a question mark beneath the taut back of his bottle green velour jacket, his left hand spread above his ear, white fingers, faintest bluish tint at the base of his nails.

Kneeling, she touched his neck. Knew. Beyond the window, all the rain sliding down, forever. Cradling his head, legs open, holding him, rocking, swaying, the dumb sad animal keening filling the bare rectangle of the room … And after a time, becoming aware of the sharp thing under her palm, the neat stainless end of a length of very fine, very rigid wire, that protruded from his ear and between the spread cool fingers.

Ugly, ugly, that was no way to die; it got her up, anger, her hands like claws. To survey the silent room where he had died. There was no sense of him there, nothing, only his ragged attaché. Opening that, she found two spiral notebooks, their pages new and clean, an unread but very fashionable novel, a box of wooden matches, and a half-empty blue packet of Gauloise. The leather-bound agenda from Browns was gone. She patted his jacket, slid her fingers through his pockets, but it was gone.

No, she thought, *you wouldn't have written it there, would you? But you could never remember a number or an address, could you?* She looked around the room again, a weird calm overtaking her. You had to write things down, but you were

182

secretive, and you didn't trust my little book from Browns, no; you'd meet a girl in some cafe and write her number in a matchbook or on the back of some scrap, and forget it, so that I found it weeks later, straightening up your things.

She went into the tiny bedroom. There was a bright red folding chair and a slab of cheap yellow foam that served as a bed. The foam was marked with a brown butterfly of menstrual blood. She lifted it, but there was nothing there.

'You'd have been scared,' she said, her voice shaking with a fury she didn't try to understand, her hands cold, colder than Alain's, as she ran them down the red wallpaper, striped with gold, seeking some loose seam, a hiding place. 'You poor stupid shit. Poor stupid dead shit ...'

Nothing. Back into the living room, and amazed, somehow, that he hadn't moved; expecting him to jump up, hello, waving a few centimetres of trick wire. She removed his shoes. They needed resoling, new heels. She looked inside, felt the lining. Nothing. 'Don't do this to me ...' And back into the bedroom. The narrow closet. Brushing aside a clatter of cheap white plastic hangers, a limp shroud of dry-cleaner's plastic. Dragging the stained bedslab over and standing on it, her heels sinking into the foam, to slide her hands the length of a pressboard shelf, and find, in the far corner, a hard little fold of paper, rectangular and blue. Opening it, noticing how the nails she'd done so carefully were chipped, and finding the number he'd written there in green felt pen. It was an empty Gauloise packet.

There was a knock at the door.

And then Paco's voice: 'Marly? Hello? What has happened?'

She thrust the number into the waistband of her jeans and turned to meet his calm, serious eyes.

'It's Alain,' she said, 'he's dead.'

19

Hypermart

He saw Lucas for the last time in front of a big old department store on Madison Avenue. That was how he remembered him, after that, a big black man in a sharp black suit, about to step into his long black car, one black, softly polished shoe already on the lush carpet of Ahmed's interior, the other still on the crumbling concrete of the kerb.

Jackie stood beside Bobby, her face shadowed by the wide brim of her gold-hung fedora, an orange silk headscarf knotted at the back of her neck.

'You take care of our young friend, now,' Lucas said, pointing the knob of his cane at her. 'He's not without his enemies, our Count.'

'Who is?' Jackie asked.

'I'll take care of *myself*,' Bobby said, resenting the idea of Jackie being seen as more capable, yet at the same time knowing that she almost certainly was.

'You do that,' Lucas said, the knob swinging, lined up now with Bobby's eyes. 'Sprawltown's a twisty place, my man. Things are seldom what they seem.' To illustrate his point, he did something to the cane that caused the long brass splines below the ball to open smoothly, for an instant, silently, extended like the ribs of an umbrella, each one glinting sharp as a razor, pointed like needles. Then they were gone, and Ahmed's wide door swung shut with an armour-plated thud.

Jackie laughed. 'Shee-it. Lucas still carryin' that killin' stick. Big time lawyer now, but the street leaves a mark on you. Guess it's a good thing ...'

'Lawyer?'

She looked at him. 'You never mind, honey. You just come with me, do like I tell you, you be okay.'

Ahmed merged with the sparse traffic, a pedicab jockey blaring pointlessly at the receding brass bumper with a hand-held air horn.

Then, one manicured, gold-ringed hand on his shoulder, she led him across the sidewalk, past a sleeping huddle of rag-bundled transients, and into the slowly waking world of Hypermart.

Fourteen floors, Jackie said, and Bobby whistled. 'All like this?' She nodded, spooning brown crystals of rock sugar into the tan foam atop her coffee glass. They sat on scrolly cast iron stools at a marble counter in a little booth, where a girl Bobby's age, her hair dyed and lacquered into a kind of dorsal fin, worked the knobs and levers of a big old machine with brass tanks and domes and burners and eagles with spread chrome wings. The countertop had been something else, originally; Bobby saw where one end was bashed off in a long crooked jag to allow it to fit between two green-painted steel pillars.

'You like it, huh?' She sprinkled the foam with powdered cinnamon from a heavy old glass shaker. ''Bout as far from Barrytown as you been, some ways.'

Bobby nodded, his eyes confused by the thousand colours and textures of the things in the stalls, the stalls themselves. There seemed to be no regularity to anything, no hint of any central planning agency. Crooked corridors twisted off from the area in front of the espresso booth. There seemed to be no central source of lighting either. Red and blue neon glowed beyond the white hiss of a Primus lantern, and one stall, just being opened by a bearded man with leather pants, seemed to be lit with candles, the soft light reflecting off hundreds of polished brass buckles hung against the reds and blacks of old rugs. There was a morning rattle to the place, a coughing and a clearing of throats. A blue Toshiba custodial unit whirred out of a corridor, dragging a battered plastic cart stacked with green plastic bales of garbage. Someone had glued a big plastic doll head to the Toshiba's upper body-segment, above the clustered camera-eyes and sensors, a grinning blue-eyed thing once intended to approximate the features of a leading stimstar without violating Sense/Net copyrights. The pink head, its platinum hair bound up in a length of pale blue plastic pearls, bobbed absurdly as the robot rolled past. Bobby laughed.

'This place is okay,' he said, and gestured to the girl to refill his cup.

'Wait a sec, asshole,' the counter girl said, amiably enough. She was measuring ground coffee into a dented steel hopper on one end of an antique balance. 'You get any sleep last night, Jackie, after the show?'

'Sure,' Jackie said, and sipped at her coffee. 'I danced their second set, then I slept at Jammer's. Hit the couch, you know?'

'Wish I'd got some. Every time Henry sees you dance, he won't let me alone …' She laughed, and refilled Bobby's cup from a black plastic thermos.

'Well,' Bobby said, when the girl was busy again with the espresso machine, 'what's next?'

'Busy man, huh?' Jackie regarded him coolly from beneath the gold-pinned hat brim. 'Got places you need to go, people to see?'

'Well, no. Shit. I just mean, well, is this it?'

'Is what it?'

'This place. We're staying here?'

'Top floor. Friend of mine named Jammer runs a club up there. Very unlikely anyone could find you there, and even if they do, it's a hard place to sneak up on. Fourteen floors of mostly stalls, and a whole lot of these people sell stuff they don't have out in plain view, right? So they're all very sensitive to strangers turning up, anyone asking questions. And most of them are friends of ours, one way or another. Anyway, you'll like it here. Good place for you. Lots to learn, if you remember to keep your mouth shut.'

'How am I gonna learn if I don't ask questions?'

'Well, I mean keep your ears open, more like it. And be polite. Some tough people in here, but you mind your biz, they'll mind theirs. Beauvoir's probably coming by here late this afternoon. Lucas has gone out to the Projects to tell him whatever you learned from the Finn. What *did* you learn from the Finn, hon?'

'That he's got these three dead guys stretched out on his floor. Says they're ninjas.' Bobby looked at her. 'He's pretty weird ...'

'Dead guys aren't part of his usual line of goods. But, yeah, he's weird all right. Why don't you tell me about it? Calmly, and in low, measured tones. Think you can do that?'

Bobby told her what he could remember of his visit to the Finn. Several times she stopped him, asked questions he usually wasn't able to answer. She nodded when he first mentioned Wigan Ludgate.

'Yeah,' she said, 'Jammer talks about him, when he gets going on the old days. Have to ask him ...' At the end of his recitation, she was lounging back against one of the green pillars, the hat very low over her dark eyes.

'Well?' he asked.

'Interesting,' she said, but that was all she'd say.

'I want some new clothes,' Bobby said, when they'd climbed the immobile escalator to the second floor.

'You got any money?' she asked.

'Shit,' he said, his hands in the pockets of the baggy, pleated jeans. '*I* don't have any fucking *money*, but I want some clothes. You and Lucas and Beauvoir are keeping my ass on ice for *something*, aren't you? Well, I'm tired of this god-awful shirt Rhea palmed off on me, and these pants always feel like they're about to fall off my ass. And I'm here because Two-a-Day, who's a low-life fuck, wanted to risk my butt so Lucas and Beauvoir could test their fucking software. So you can fucking well buy me some clothes, okay?'

'Okay,' she said, after a pause, 'I'll tell you what.' She pointed to where a Chinese girl in faded denim was furling the sheets of plastic that had fenced a dozen steel-pipe garment racks hung with clothing. 'You see Lin, there? She's a friend of mine. You pick out what you want, I'll straighten it out between Lucas and her.'

Half an hour later, he emerged from a blanket-draped fitting room and put on a pair of Indo-Javanese mirrored aviator glasses. He grinned at Jackie. 'Real sharp,' he said.

'Oh, yeah.' She did a thing with her hand, a fanning movement, as though something nearby were too hot to touch. 'You didn't like that shirt Rhea loaned you?'

He looked down at the black t-shirt he'd chosen, at the square holodecal of cyberspace on his chest. It was done so you seemed to be punching fast-forward through the matrix, grid lines blurring at the edges of the decal. 'Yeah. It was too tacky ...'

'Right,' Jackie said, taking in the tight black jeans, the heavy leather boots with spacesuit-style accordion folds at

188

the ankles, the black leather garrison belt trimmed with twin lines of pyramidal chrome studs. 'Well, I guess you look more like the Count. Come on, Count, I got a couch for you to sleep on, up in Jammer's place.'

He leered at her, thumbs hooked in the front pockets of the black Levi's.

'Alone,' she added, 'no fear.'

20

Orly Flight

Paco slung the Citröen-Dornier down the Champs, along the north bank of the Seine, then up through Les Halles. Marly sank back into the astonishingly soft leather seat, more beautifully stitched than her Brussels jacket, and willed her mind to blankness, lack of affect. Be eyes, she told herself. Only eyes, your body a weight pressed evenly back by the speed of this obscenely expensive car. Humming past the Square des Innocents, where whores dickered with the drivers of cargo hovers in bleu de travail, Paco steering effortlessly through the narrow streets.

'Why did you say, "Don't do this to me"?' He took his hand from the steering console and tapped his ear-bead into position.

'Why were you listening?'

'Because that is my job. I sent a woman up, up into the tower opposite his, to the twenty-second floor, with a parabolic microphone. The phone in the apartment was dead; otherwise, we could have used that. She went up, broke into a vacant unit on the west face of the tower, and aimed her microphone in time to hear you say, "Don't do this to me". And you were alone?'

'Yes.'

'He was dead?'

'Yes.'

'Why did you say it, then?'

'I don't know.'

'Who did you feel was doing something to you?'

'I don't know. Perhaps Alain.'

'Doing what?'

'Being dead? Complicating matters? You tell me.'

'You are a difficult woman.'

'Let me out.'

'I will take you to your friend's apartment …'

'Stop the car.'

'I will take you to—'

'I'll walk.'

The low silver car slid up to the kerb.

'I will call you, in the—'

'Goodnight.'

'You're certain you wouldn't prefer one of the spas?' asked Mr Paleologos, thin and elegant as a mantis in his white hop-sack jacket. His hair was white as well, brushed back from his forehead with extreme care. 'It would be less expensive, and a great deal more fun. You're a very pretty girl …'

'Pardon?' Jerking her attention back from the street beyond the rain-streaked window. 'A what?' His French was clumsy, enthusiastic, strangely inflected.

'A very pretty girl.' He smiled primly. 'You wouldn't prefer a holiday in a Med cluster? People your own age? Are you Jewish?'

'I beg your pardon?'

'Jewish. Are you?'

'No.'

'Too bad,' he said. 'You have the cheekbones of a certain sort of elegant young Jewess … I've a lovely discount on fifteen days to Jerusalem Prime, a marvellous environment for the price. Includes suit rental, three meals per diem, and direct shuttle from the *JAL* torus.'

'Suit rental?'

'They haven't entirely established atmosphere, in Jerusalem Prime,' Mr Paleologos said, shuffling a stack of pink flimsies from one side of his desk to the other. His office was a tiny cubicle walled with hologram views of Poros and Macao. She'd chosen his agency for its evident obscurity, and because it had been possible to slip in without leaving the little commercial complex in the Métro station nearest Andrea's.

'No,' she said, 'I'm not interested in spas. I want to go here.' She tapped the writing on the wrinkled blue wrapper from a pack of Gauloise.

'Well,' he said, 'it's possible, of course, but I have no listing of accommodation. Will you be visiting friends?'

'A business trip,' she said impatiently. 'I must leave immediately.'

'Very well, very well,' Mr Paleologos said, taking a cheap-looking lap terminal from a shelf behind his desk. 'Can you give me your credit code, please?'

She reached into her black leather bag and took out the thick bundle of New Yen she'd removed from Paco's bag while he'd been busy examining the apartment where Alain had died. The money was fastened with a red band of translucent elastic. 'I wish to pay cash.'

'Oh, dear,' Mr Paleologos said, extending a pink fingertip to touch the top bill, as though he expected the lot of it to vanish. 'I see. Well, you understand, I wouldn't ordinarily do business this way ... But, I suppose, something can be arranged ...'

'Quickly,' she said, 'very quickly ...'

He looked at her. 'I understand. Can you tell me, please,'

his fingers beginning to move over the keys of the lap terminal, 'the name under which you wish to travel?'

21

Highway Time

Turner woke to the silent house, the sound of birds in the apple trees in the overgrown orchard. He'd slept on the broken couch Rudy kept in the kitchen. He drew water for coffee, the plastic pipes from the roof tank chugging as he filled the pot, put the pot on the propane burner, and walked out to the porch.

Rudy's eight vehicles were filmed with dew, arranged in a neat row on the gravel. One of the augmented hounds trotted through the open gate as Turner came down the steps, its black hood clicking softly in the morning quiet. It paused, drooling, swayed its distorted head from side to side, then scrambled across the gravel and out of sight, around the corner of the porch.

Turner paused by the hood of a dull brown Suzuki Jeep, a hydrogen-cell conversion. Rudy would have done the work himself. Four-wheel drive, big tyres with off-road lugs crusted in pale dry river mud. Small, slow, reliable, not much use on the road ...

He passed two rust-flecked Honda sedans, identical, same year and model. Rudy would be ripping one for parts for the other; neither would be running. He grinned absently at the immaculate brown and tan paintwork on the 1949 Chevrolet van, remembering the rusted shell Rudy had hauled home from Arkansas on a rented flatbed. The thing still ran on gasoline, the inner surfaces of its engine likely as spotless as the handrubbed chocolate lacquer of its fenders.

There was half of a Dornier ground-effect plane, under grey plastic tarps, and then a wasp-like black Suzuki racing bike on a homemade trailer. He wondered how long it had been since Rudy had done any serious racing. There was a snowmobile under another tarp, an old one, next to the bike trailer. And then the stained grey hovercraft, surplus from the war, a squat wedge of armoured steel that smelled of the kerosene its turbine burned, its mesh-reinforced apron-bag slack on the gravel. Its windows were narrow slits of thick, high-impact plastic. There were Ohio plates bolted to the thing's ram-like bumpers. They were current.

'I can see what you're thinking,' Sally said, and he turned to see her at the porch-rail with the pot of steaming coffee in her hand. 'Rudy says, if it can't get over something, it can anyway get through it.'

'Is it fast?' Touching the hover's armoured flank.

'Sure, but you'll need a new spine after about an hour.'

'How about the law?'

'Can't much say they like the way it looks, but it's certified street-legal. No law against armour that I know of.'

'Angie's feeling better,' Sally said, as he followed her in through the kitchen door, 'aren't you, honey?'

Mitchell's daughter looked up from the kitchen table. Her bruising, like Turner's, had faded to a pair of fat commas, like painted blue-black tears.

'My friend here's a doctor,' Turner said. 'He checked you out when you were under. He says you're doing okay.'

'Your brother. He's not a doctor.'

'Sorry, Turner,' Sally said, at the stove. 'I'm pretty much straightforward.'

'Well, he's not a doctor,' he said, 'but he's smart. We were worried that Maas might have done something to you, fixed it so you'd get sick if you left Arizona ...'

'Like a cortex bomb?' She spooned cold cereal from a cracked bowl with apple blossoms around the rim, part of a set that Turner remembered.

'Lord,' Sally said, 'what have you got yourself into, Turner?'

'Good question.' He took a seat at the table.

Angie chewed her cereal, staring at him.

'Angie,' he said, 'when Rudy scanned you, he found something in your head.'

She stopped chewing.

'He didn't know what it was. Something someone put there, maybe when you were a lot younger. Do you know what I mean?'

She nodded.

'Do you know who put it there?'

'Yes.'

'Your father?'

'Yes.'

'Do you know why?'

'Because I was sick.'

'How were you sick?'

'I wasn't smart enough.'

He was ready by noon, the hovercraft fuelled and waiting by the chain-link gates. Rudy had given him a rectangular black Ziploc stuffed with New Yen, some of the bills worn almost translucent with use.

'I tried that tape through a French lexicon,' Rudy said, while one of the hounds rubbed its dusty ribs against his legs. 'Doesn't work. I think it's some kind of Creole. Maybe African. You want a copy?'

'No,' Turner said, 'you hang on to it.'

'Thanks,' Rudy said, 'but no thanks. I don't plan on admitting you were ever here, if anybody asks. Sally and I, we're heading in to Memphis this afternoon, stay with a couple of friends. Dogs'll watch the house.' He scratched the animal behind its plastic hood. 'Right, boy?' The dog whined and twitched. 'I had to train 'em off coon hunting when I put their infrareds in,' he said. 'There wouldn't't've been any coons left in the county ...'

Sally and the girl came down the porch steps, Sally carrying a broken-down canvas carryall she'd filled with sandwiches and a thermos of coffee. Turner remembered her in the bed upstairs and smiled. She smiled back. She looked older today, tired. Angie had discarded the bloodstained MAAS-NEOTEK t-shirt in favour of a shapeless black sweatshirt Sally had found for her. It made her look even younger than she was. Sally had also managed to incorporate the remaining bruises into a baroque job of eye makeup that clashed weirdly with her kid's face and baggy shirt.

Rudy handed Turner the key to the hovercraft. 'I had my old Cray cook me a précis of recent corporate news this morning. One thing you should probably know is that Maas Biolabs has announced the accidental death of Dr Christopher Mitchell. Impressive, how vague those people can be.'

'And you just keep the harness on real tight,' Sally was saying, 'or your ass'll be black and blue before you hit that Statesboro bypass ...'

Rudy glanced at the girl, then back at Turner. Turner could see the broken veins at the base of his brother's nose. His eyes were bloodshot and there was a pronounced tic in his left eyelid. 'Well, I guess that's it. Funny, but I'd come to figure I wouldn't see you again. Kind of funny to see you back here ...'

197

'Well,' Turner said, 'you've both done more than I'd any right to expect …' Sally glanced away. 'So thanks. I guess we better go.' He climbed up into the cab of the hover, wanting to be gone. Sally squeezed the girl's wrist, gave her the carry-all, and stood beside her while she climbed up the two hinged footrests. Turner settled into the driver's seat.

'She kept asking for you,' Rudy said. 'After a while it got so bad, the endorphin analogues couldn't really cut the pain, and every two hours or so, she'd ask where you were, when you were coming.'

'I sent you money,' Turner said. 'Enough to take her to Chiba. The clinics there could have tried something new.'

Rudy snorted. 'Chiba? Jesus. She was an old woman. What the hell good would it have done, keeping her alive in Chiba for a few more months? What she mainly wanted was to see you.'

'Didn't work out that way,' Turner said as the girl got into the seat beside his and placed the bag on the floor, between her feet. 'Be seeing you, Rudy.' He nodded. 'Sally.'

'So long,' Sally said, her arm around Rudy.

'Who were you talking about?' Angie asked, as the hatch came down. Turner put the key in the ignition and fired up the turbine, simultaneously inflating the apron-bag. Through the narrow window at his side, he saw Rudy and Sally back quickly away from the hover, the hound cowering and snapping at the noise of the turbine. The pedals and hand-controls were oversized, designed to permit ease of operation for a driver wearing a radiation suit. Turner eased them out through the gates and swung around on a wide patch of gravel drive. Angie was buckling her harness.

'My mother,' he said.

He revved the turbine and they jolted forward.

'I never knew my mother,' she said, and Turner remembered

that her father was dead, and that she didn't know it yet. He hit the throttle and they shot off down the gravel drive, barely missing one of Rudy's hounds.

Sally had been right about the thing's ride; there was constant vibration from the turbine. At ninety kilometres per hour, on the skewed asphalt of the old state highway, it shook their teeth. The armoured apron-bag rode the broken surfaces heavily; the skim effect of a civilian sports model would only be possible on a perfectly smooth, flat surface.

Turner found himself liking it, though. You pointed, eased back the throttle, and you went. Someone had hung a pair of pink, sun-faded foam dice above the forward vision-slit, and the whine of the turbine was a solid thing behind him. The girl seemed to relax, taking in the roadside scenery with an absent, almost contented expression, and Turner was grateful that he wasn't required to make conversation. *You're hot*, he thought, glancing sidelong at her, *you're probably the single most hotly pursued little item on the face of the planet today, and here I am hauling you off to the Sprawl in Rudy's kidstuff war wagon, no fucking idea what I'm going to do with you now … Or who it was zapped the mall …*

Run it through, he told himself, as they swung down into the valley, *run it through again, eventually something'll click.* Mitchell had contacted Hosaka, said he was coming over. Hosaka hired Conroy and assembled a medical crew to check Mitchell for kinks. Conroy had put the teams together, working with Turner's agent. Turner's agent was a voice in Geneva. A telephone number … Hosaka had sent Allison in to vet him in Mexico, then Conroy had pulled him out. Webber, just before the shit hit the fan, had said that she was Conroy's plant at the site … Someone had jumped them, as the girl was coming in, flares and automatic weapons. That

199

felt like Maas, to him; it was the sort of move he'd expect, the sort of thing his hired muscle was there to deal with. Then the white sky ... He thought about what Rudy had said about a railgun ... Who? And the mess in the girl's head, the things Rudy had turned up on his tomograph and his NMR imager. She said her father had never planned on coming out himself.

'No company,' she said, to the window.

'How's that?'

'You don't have a company, do you? I mean, you work for whoever hires you.'

'That's right.'

'Don't you get scared?'

'Sure, but not because of that ...'

'We've always had the company. My father said I'd be all right, that I was just going to another company ...'

'You'll be fine. He was right. I just have to find out what's going on. Then I'll get you where you need to go.'

'To Japan?'

'Wherever.'

'Have you been there?'

'Sure.'

'Would I like it?'

'Why not?'

Then she lapsed into silence again, and Turner concentrated on the road.

'It makes me dream,' she said, as he leaned forward to turn on the headlights, her voice barely audible above the turbine.

'What does?' He pretended to be lost in his driving, careful not to glance her way.

'The thing in my head. Usually it's only when I'm asleep.'

'Yeah?' Remembering the whites of her eyes in Rudy's

200

bedroom, the shuddering, the rush of words in a language he didn't know.

'Sometimes when I'm awake. It's like I'm jacked into a deck, only I'm free of the grid, flying, and I'm not alone there. The other night I dreamed about a boy, and he'd reached out, picked up something, and it was hurting him, and he couldn't see that he was free, that he only needed to let go. So I told him. And for just a second, I could see where he was, and that wasn't like a dream at all, just this ugly little room with a stained carpet, and I could tell he needed a shower, and feel how the insides of his shoes were sticky, because he wasn't wearing socks ... That's not like the dreams ...'

'No?'

'No. The dreams are all big things, and I'm big too, moving, with the others ...'

Turner let his breath out as the hover whined up the concrete ramp to the interstate, suddenly aware that he'd been holding it. 'What others?'

'The bright ones.' Another silence. 'Not people ...'

'You spend much time in cyberspace, Angie? I mean jacked in, with a deck?'

'No. Just school stuff. My father said it wasn't good for me.'

'He say anything about those dreams?'

'Only that they were getting realer. But I never told him about the others ...'

'You want to tell me? Maybe it'll help me understand, figure out what we need to do ...'

'Some of them tell me things. Stories. Once, there was nothing there, nothing moving on its own, just data and people shuffling it around. Then something happened, and it ... It knew itself. There's a whole other story, about that, a girl with mirrors over her eyes and a man who was scared to care about anything. Something the man did helped the

201

whole thing know itself … And after that, it sort of split into different parts of itself, and I think the parts are the others, the bright ones. But it's hard to tell, because *they* don't tell it with words, exactly …'

Turner felt the skin on his neck prickle. Something coming back to him, up out of the drowned undertow of Mitchell's dossier. Hot burning shame in a hallway, dirty cream paint peeling, Cambridge, the graduate dorms … 'Where were you born, Angie?'

'England. Then my father got into Maas, we moved. To Geneva.'

Somewhere in Virginia he eased the hovercraft over onto the gravel shoulder and out into an overgrown pasture, dust from the dry summer swirling out behind them as he swung them left and into a stand of pine. The turbine died as they settled into the apron-bag.

'We might as well eat now.' he said, reaching back for Sally's canvas carryall.

Angie undid her harness and unzipped the black sweatshirt. Under it, she wore something tight and white, a child's smooth tanned flesh showing in the scoop neck above young breasts. She took the bag from him. 'What's wrong with your brother?' she asked, handing him half a sandwich.

'How do you mean?'

'Well, there's something … He drinks all the time, Sally said. Is he unhappy?'

'I don't know,' Turner said, hunching and twisting the aches out of his neck and shoulders. 'I mean, he must be, but I don't know exactly why. People get stuck, sometimes.'

'You mean when they don't have companies to take care of them?' She bit into her sandwich.

He looked at her. 'Are you putting me on?'

She nodded, her mouth full. Swallowed. 'A little bit. I know that a lot of people don't work for Maas. Never have and never will. You're one, your brother's another. But it was a real question. I kind of liked Rudy, you know? But he just seemed so ...'

'Screwed up,' he finished for her, still holding his sandwich. 'Stuck. What it is, I think there's a jump some people have to make, sometimes, and if they don't do it, then they're stuck good ... And Rudy never did it.'

'Like my father wanting to get me out of Maas? Is that a jump?'

'No. Some jumps you have to decide on for yourself. Just figure there's something better waiting for you somewhere ...' He paused, feeling suddenly ridiculous, and bit into the sandwich.

'Is that what you thought?'

He nodded, wondering if it were true.

'So you left, and Rudy stayed?'

'He was smart. Still is, and he'd rolled up a bunch of degrees, did it all on the line. Got a doctorate in biotechnology from Tulane when he was twenty, a bunch of other stuff. Never sent out any résumés, nothing. We'd have recruiters turn up from all over, and he'd bullshit them, pick fights ... I think he thought he could make something on his own. Like those hoods on the dogs. I think he's got a couple of original patents there, but ... Anyway, he stayed there. Got into dealing and doing hardware for people, and he was hot stuff in the county. And our mother got sick, she was sick for a long time, and I was away ...'

'Where were you?'

She opened the thermos and the smell of coffee filled the cabin.

'As far away as I could get,' he said, startled by the anger in his voice. She passed him the plastic mug, filled to the brim with hot black coffee. 'How about you? You said you never knew your mother.'

'I didn't. They split when I was little. She wouldn't come back in on the contract unless he agreed to cut her in on some kind of stock plan. That's what he said, anyway.'

'So what's he like?' He sipped coffee, then passed it back.

She looked at him over the rim of the red plastic mug, her eyes ringed with Sally's makeup. 'You tell me,' she said. 'Or else ask me in twenty years. I'm seventeen, how the hell am I supposed to know?'

He laughed. 'You're starting to feel a little better now?'

'I guess so. Considering the circumstances.'

And suddenly he was aware of her, in a way he hadn't been before, and his hands went anxiously to the controls. 'Good. We still have a long way to go ...'

They slept in the hovercraft that night, parked behind the rusting steel lattice that had once supported a drive-in theatre screen in southern Pennsylvania, Turner's parka spread on the armour-plate floorboards below the turbine's long bulge. She'd sipped the last of the coffee, cold now, as she sat in the square hatch-opening above the passenger seat, watching the lightning bugs pulse across a field of yellowed grass.

Somewhere in his dreams – still coloured with random flashes from her father's dossier – she rolled against him, her breasts soft and warm against his bare back through the thin fabric of her t-shirt, and then her arm came over him to stroke the flat muscles of his stomach, but he lay still, pretending to a deeper sleep, and soon found his way down into the darker passages of Mitchell's biosoft, where strange things came to mingle with his own oldest fears and hurts.

And woke at dawn to hear her singing softly to herself from her perch in the roof-hatch.

> 'My daddy he's a handsome devil
> Got a chain 'bout nine miles long.
> And from every link
> A heart does dangle
> Of another maid
> He's loved and wronged.'

22

Jammer's

Jammer's was up twelve more flights of dead escalator and occupied the rear third of the top floor. Aside from Leon's place, Bobby had never seen a nightclub, and he found Jammer's both impressive and scary. Impressive because of its scale and what he took to be the exceptional quality of the fittings, and scary because a nightclub, by day, is somehow inately unreal. Witchy. He peered around, thumbs snagged in the back pockets of his new jeans, while Jackie conducted a whispered conversation with a long-faced white man in rumpled blue coveralls. The place was fitted out with dark ultrasuede banquettes, round black tables, and dozens of ornate screens of pierced wood. The ceiling was painted black, each table faintly illuminated by its own little recessed flood aimed straight down out of the dark. There was a central stage, brightly lit now with work lights strung on yellow flex, and, in the middle of the stage, a set of cherry red acoustic drums. He wasn't sure why, but it gave him the creeps; some sidelong sense of a half-life, as though something was about to shift, just at the edge of his vision ...

'Bobby,' Jackie said, 'come over here and meet Jammer.'

He crossed the stretch of plain dark carpet with all the cool he could muster and faced the long-faced man, who had dark, thinning hair and wore a white evening shirt under his coveralls. The man's eyes were narrow, the hollows of his cheeks shadowed with a day's growth of beard.

'Well,' the man said, 'you want to be a cowboy?' He was looking at Bobby's t-shirt, and Bobby had the uncomfortable feeling that he might be about to laugh.

'Jammer was a jockey,' Jackie said. 'Hot as they come. Weren't you, Jammer?'

'So they say,' Jammer said, still looking at Bobby. 'Long time ago, Jackie. How many hours you logged, running?' he asked Bobby.

Bobby's face went hot. 'Well, one, I guess.'

Jammer raised his bushy eyebrows. 'Gotta start somewhere.' He smiled, his teeth small and unnaturally even and, Bobby thought, too numerous.

'Bobby,' Jackie said, 'why don't you ask Jammer about this Wig character the Finn was telling you about?'

Jammer glanced at her, then back to Bobby. 'You know the Finn? For a hotdogger you're in pretty deep, aren't you?' He took a blue plastic inhaler from his hip pocket and inserted it in his left nostril, snorted, then put it back in his pocket. 'Ludgate. The Wig. Finn's talking about the Wig? Must be in his dotage.' Bobby didn't know what that meant, but it didn't seem like the time to ask.

'Well,' Bobby ventured, 'this Wig's up in orbit somewhere, and he sells the Finn stuff, sometimes ...'

'No shit? Well, you coulda fooled me. I woulda told you the Wig was either dead or drooling. Crazier than your usual cowboy, you know what I mean? Batshit. Gone. Haven't heard of him in years.'

'Jammer,' Jackie said, 'I think it's maybe best if Bobby just tells you the story. Beauvoir's due here this afternoon, and he'll have some questions for you, so you better know where things stand ...'

Jammer looked at her. 'Well. I see. Mr Beauvoir's calling in that favour, is he?'

'Can't speak for him,' she said, 'but that would be my guess. We need a safe place to store the Count here.'

'What count?'

'Me,' Bobby said, 'that's me.'

'Great,' Jammer said, with a total lack of enthusiasm. 'So come on back into the office.'

Bobby couldn't keep his eyes off the cyberspace deck that took up a third of the surface of Jammer's antique oak desk. It was matte black, a custom job, no trademarks anywhere. He kept craning forward, while he told Jammer about Two-a-Day and his attempted run, about the girl-feeling thing and his mother getting blown up. It was the hottest-looking deck he'd ever seen, and he remembered Jackie saying that Jammer had been such a shit-hot cowboy in his day.

Jammer slumped back in his chair when Bobby was finished. 'You wanna try it?' he asked. He sounded tired.

'Try it?'

'The deck. I think you might wanna try it. It's something about the way you keep rubbing your ass on the chair. Either you wanna try it or you gotta piss bad.'

'Shit yeah. I mean, yeah, thanks, yeah, I would …'

'Why not? No way for anybody to know it's you and not me, right? Why don't you jack in with him, Jackie? Kinda keep track.' He opened a desk drawer and took out two trode-sets. 'But don't *do* anything, right? I mean, just buzz on out and spin. Don't try to run any numbers. I owe Beauvoir and Lucas a favour, and it looks like how I'm paying it back is helping keep you intact …' He handed one set of trodes to Jackie, the other to Bobby. He stood up, grabbed handles on either side of the black console, and spun it around so it faced

Bobby. 'Go on. You'll cream your jeans. Thing's ten years old and it'll still wipe ass on most anything. Guy name of Automatic Jack built it straight from scratch. He was Bobby Quine's hardware artist, once. The two of 'em burnt the Blue Lights together, but that was probably before you were born ...'

Bobby already had his trodes on. Now he looked at Jackie.

'You ever jack tandem before?'

He shook his head.

'Okay. We'll jack, but I'll hang off your left shoulder. I say jack out, jack out. You see anything funny, it'll be because I'm with you, understand?'

He nodded.

She undid a pair of long, silver-headed pins at the rear of her fedora and took it off, putting it down on the desk beside Jammer's deck. She slid the trodes on over the orange silk headscarf and smoothed the contacts against her forehead.

'Let's go,' she said.

Now and ever was, fast-forward, Jammer's deck jacked up so high above the neon hotcores, a topography of data he didn't know. Big stuff, mountain-high, sharp and corporate in the non-place that was cyberspace.

'Slow it down, Bobby.' Jackie's voice low and sweet, beside him in the void.

'Jesus Christ, this thing's slick!'

'Yeah, but damp it down. The rush isn't any good for us. You want to cruise. Keep us up here and slow it down ...'

He eased off on forward until they seemed to coast along. He turned to the left, expecting to see her there, but there was nothing.

'I'm here,' she said, 'don't worry ...'

'Who was Quine?'

'Quine? Some cowboy Jammer knew. He knew 'em all, in his day.'

He took a right-angle left at random, pivoting smoothly at the grid-intersection, testing the deck for response. It was amazing, totally unlike anything he'd felt before in cyberspace. 'Holy shit. This thing makes an Ono-Sendai look like a kid's toy ...'

'It's probably got O-S circuitry in it. That's what they used to use, Jammer says. Take us up a little more ...'

They rose effortlessly through the grid, the data receding below them. 'There isn't a hell of a lot to see up here,' he complained.

'Wrong. You see some interesting stuff, you hang out long enough in the blank parts ...'

The fabric of the matrix seemed to shiver, directly in front of them ...

'Uh, Jackie ...'

'Stop here. Hold it. It's okay. Trust me.'

Somewhere, far away, his hands moving over the unfamiliar keyboard configuration. He held them steady now, while a section of cyberspace blurred, grew milky ... 'What is—'

'Danbala ap monte el,' the voice said, harsh in his head, and in his mouth a taste like blood. *Danbala is riding her.* He knew, somehow, what the words meant, but the voice was iron in his head. The milky fabric divided, seemed to bubble, became two patches of shifting grey.

'Legba,' she said, 'Legba and Ougou Feray, god of war, Papa Ougou! St Jacques Majeur! Viv la Vyèj!'

Iron laughter filled the matrix, sawing through Bobby's head.

'Map kite tout mizé ak tout giyon,' said another voice, fluid and quicksilver and cold. 'See, Papa, she has come here to throw away her bad luck!' And then that one laughed as well, and Bobby fought down a wave of sheer hysteria as the silver laughter rose through him like bubbles.

'Has she bad luck, the horse of Danbala?' boomed the iron voice of Ougou Feray, and for an instant Bobby thought he saw a figure flicker in the grey fog. The voice hooted its terrible laughter. 'Indeed! Indeed! But she knows it not! She is not *my* horse, no, else I would cure her luck!' Bobby wanted to cry, to die, anything to escape the voices, the utterly impossible *wind* that had started to blow out of the grey warps, a hot damp wind that smelled of things he couldn't identify. 'And she calls praise on the Virgin! Hear me, little sister! La Vyèj draws close indeed!'

'Yes,' said the other, 'she moves through *my* province now, I who rule the roads, the highways.'

'But I, Ougou Feray, tell you that your enemies draw near as well! To the gates, sister, and beware!'

And then the grey areas faded, dwindled, shrank ...

'Jack us out,' she said, her voice small and distant. And then she said, 'Lucas is dead.'

Jammer took a bottle of Scotch from his desk drawer and carefully poured six centimetres of the stuff into a plastic highball glass. 'You look like shit,' he said to Jackie, and Bobby was startled by the gentleness in the man's voice. They'd been jacked out for at least ten minutes and nobody had said anything at all. Jackie looked crushed, and kept gnawing at her lower lip. Jammer looked either unhappy or angry, Bobby wasn't sure.

'How come you said Lucas was dead?' Bobby ventured, because it seemed to him that the silence was silting up in Jammer's cramped office like something that could choke you.

Jackie looked at him but didn't seem to focus. 'They

211

wouldn't come to me like that if Lucas were alive,' she said. 'There are pacts, agreements. Legba is always invoked first, but he should have come with Danbala. His personality depends on the loa he manifests with ... Lucas must be dead ...'

Jammer pushed the glass of whisky across the desk, but Jackie shook her head, the trode-set still riding her forehead, chrome and black nylon. He made a disgusted face, pulled the glass back, and downed it himself. 'What a load of shit. Things made a lot more sense before you people started screwing around with them.'

'We didn't bring them here, Jammer,' she said. 'They were just *there*, and they found us because we understood them!'

'Same load of shit,' Jammer said, wearily. 'Whatever they are, wherever they came from, they just shaped themselves to what a bunch of crazed spades wanted to see. You follow me? There's no way in hell there'd be anything out there that you had to talk to in fucking bush Haitian! You and your voodoo cult, they just saw that and they saw a set-up, and Beauvoir and Lucas and the rest, they're businessmen first. And those goddam things know how to make *deals*! It's a natural!' He tightened the cap on his bottle and put it back in the drawer. 'You know, hon, it could just be that somebody very big, with a lot of muscle on the grid, they're just taking you for a ride. Projecting those things, all that shit ... And you *know* it's possible, don't you? Don't you, Jackie?'

'No way,' Jackie said, her voice cold and even. 'But how I know that's not anything I can explain ...'

Jammer took a black slab of plastic from his pocket and began to shave. 'Sure,' he said. The razor hummed as he worked on the line of his jaw. 'I *lived* in cyberspace for eight years, right? Well, I know there wasn't anything out there, not then ... Anyway, you want me to phone Lucas, set your mind at ease one way or the other? You got the phone number for that Rolls of his?'

'No,' Jackie said, 'don't bother. Best we lay low 'til Beauvoir turns up.' She stood, pulling off the trodes and picking up her hat. 'I'm going to lie down, try to sleep. You keep an eye on Bobby ...' She turned and walked to the office door. She looked as though she were sleepwalking, all the energy gone out of her.

'Wonderful,' Jammer said, running the shaver along his upper lip. 'You want a drink?' he asked Bobby.

'Well,' Bobby said, 'it's kind of early ...'

'For you, maybe.' He put the razor back in his pocket. The door closed behind Jackie. Jammer leaned forward slightly. 'What did they look like, kid? You get a make?'

'Just kind of greyish. Fuzzy ...'

Jammer looked disappointed. He slouched back in his chair again. 'I don't think you can get a good look at 'em unless you're part of it.' He drummed his fingers on the chair-arm. 'You think they're for real?'

'Well, I wouldn't wanna try messing one around ...'

Jammer looked at him. 'No? Well, maybe you're smarter than you look, there. I wouldn't wanna try messing one around myself. I got out of the game before they started turning up ...'

'So what do you think they are?'

'Ah, still getting smarter ... Well, I don't know. Like I said, I don't think I can swallow them being a bunch of Haitian voodoo gods, but who knows?' He narrowed his eyes. 'Could be, they're virus programs that have got loose in the matrix and replicated, and got really smart ... That's scary enough, maybe the Turing people want it kept quiet. Or maybe the AIs have found a way to split parts of themselves off into the matrix, which would drive the Turings crazy. I knew this

213

Tibetan guy did hardware mod for jockeys, he said they were tulpas.' Bobby blinked. 'A tulpa's a thought form, kind of. Superstition. Really heavy people can split off a kind of ghost, made of negative energy.' He shrugged. 'More horseshit. Like Jackie's voodoo guys.'

'Well, it looks to me like Lucas and Beauvoir and the others, they sure as hell *play* it like it was all real, and not just like it was an act ...'

Jammer nodded. 'You got it. And they been doing damn well for themselves by it, too, so there's something there ...' He shrugged and yawned. 'I gotta sleep, too. You can do whatever you want, as long as you keep your hands off my deck. And don't try to go outside, or ten kinds of alarms will start screaming. There's juice and cheese and shit in the fridge behind the bar ...'

Bobby decided that the place was still scary, now that he had it to himself, but that it was interesting enough to make the scariness worthwhile. He wandered up and down behind the bar, touching the handles of the beer taps and the chrome drink-nozzles. There was a machine that made ice, and another one that dispensed boiling water. He made himself a cup of Japanese instant coffee and sorted through Jammer's file of audio cassettes. He'd never heard of any of the bands or artists. He wondered whether that meant that Jammer, who was old, liked old stuff, or if this was all really new stuff that wouldn't filter out to Barrytown, probably by way of Leon's, for another two weeks ... He found a gun under the black and silver universal credit console at the end of the bar, a kind of fat little machine gun with a magazine that stuck straight down out of the handle. It was stuck under the bar with a strip of lime green Velcro, and he didn't think it was a good idea to touch it. After a while, he didn't feel frightened any

214

more, just kind of bored and edgy. He took his cooling coffee and walked out into the middle of the seating area. He sat at one of the tables and pretended he was Count Zero, top console artist in the Sprawl, waiting for some dudes to show and talk about a deal, some run they needed done and nobody but the Count was even remotely up for it. 'Sure,' he said, to the empty nightclub, his eyes hooded, 'I'll cut it for you ... *If* you got the money ...' They paled when he named his price.

The place was soundproofed; you couldn't hear the bustle of the fourteenth floor's stalls at all, only the hum of some kind of air conditioner and the occasional gurgles of the hot water machine. Tired of the Count's power plays, Bobby left the coffee cup on the table and crossed to the entranceway, running his hand along an old stuffed velvet rope that was slung between polished brass poles. Careful not to touch the glass doors themselves, he settled himself on a cheap steel stool with a tape-patched leatherette top, beside the coat check window. A dim bulb burned in the coatroom; you could see a couple of dozen old wooden hangers dangling from steel rods, each one hung with a round yellow hand-numbered tag. He guessed Jammer sat here sometimes to check out the clientele. He didn't really see why anybody who'd been a shit-hot cowboy for eight years would want to run a nightclub, but maybe it was sort of a hobby ... He guessed you could get a lot of girls, running a nightclub, but he'd assumed you could get a lot anyway, if you were rich. And if Jammer had been a top jock for eight years, Bobby figured he had to be rich ...

He thought about the scene in the matrix, the grey patches and the voices. He shivered. He still didn't see why it meant Lucas was dead. How could Lucas be dead? Then he remembered that his mother was dead, and somehow that didn't seem too real either. Jesus. It all got on his nerves. He wished he were outside, on the other side of the doors, checking out the stalls and the shoppers and the people who worked there ...

He reached out and drew the velour curtain aside, just wide enough to peer out through the thick old glass, taking in the rainbow jumble of stalls and the characteristic grazing gait of the shoppers. And framed for him, square in the middle of it all, beside a table jammed with surplus analogue VOM's, logic probes, and power conditioners, was the raceless, bone-heavy face of Leon, and the deep-set, hideous eyes seemed to lock into Bobby's with an audible click of recognition. And then Leon did something Bobby couldn't remember ever having seen him do. He smiled.

23

Closer

The *JAL* steward offered her a choice of simstim cassettes: a tour of the Foxton retrospective at the Tate the previous August; a period adventure taped in Ghana (*Ashanti!*); highlights from Bizet's *Carmen* as viewed from a private box at the Tokyo Opera; or thirty minutes of Tally Isham's syndicated talk show *Top People*.

'Your first shuttle flight, Ms Ovski?'

Marly nodded. She'd given Paleologos her mother's maiden name, which had probably been stupid. The steward smiled understandingly. 'A cassette can definitely ease the lift-off. The *Carmen*'s very popular this week. Gorgeous costumes, I understand.' She shook her head, in no mood for opera. She loathed Foxton, and would have preferred to feel the full force of acceleration rather than live through *Ashanti!* She took the Isham tape by default, as the least of four evils.

The steward checked her seat-harness, handed her the cassette and a little throwaway tiara in grey plastic, then moved on. She put the plastic trode-set on, jacked it into the seat-arm, sighed, and slotted the cassette in the opening beside the jack. The interior of the *JAL* shuttle vanished in a burst of Aegean blue, and she watched the words TALLY ISHAM'S TOP PEOPLE expand across the cloudless sky in elegant sans serif capitals.

Tally Isham had been a constant in the stim industry for

as long as Marly remembered, an ageless Golden Girl who'd come in on the first wave of the new medium. Now Marly found herself locked into Tally's tanned, lithe, tremendously *comfortable* sensorium. Tally Isham glowed, breathed deeply and easily, her elegant bones riding in the embrace of a musculature that seemed never to have known tension. Accessing her stim recordings was like falling into a bath of perfect health, feeling the spring in the star's high arches and the jut of her breasts against the silky white Egyptian cotton of her simple blouse. She was leaning against a pocked white balustrade above the tiny harbour of a Greek island town, a cascade of flowering trees falling away below her down a hillside built from whitewashed stone and narrow, twisting stairs. A boat sounded in the harbour.

'The tourists are hurrying back to their cruise ship now,' Tally said, and smiled; when she smiled, Marly could feel the smoothness of the star's white teeth, taste the freshness of her mouth, and the stone of the balustrade was pleasantly rough against her bare forearms. 'But one visitor to our island will be staying with us this afternoon, someone I've longed to meet, and I'm sure that you'll be delighted and surprised, as he's someone who ordinarily shuns major media coverage ...' She straightened, turned, and smiled into the tanned, smiling face of Josef Virek ...

Marly tore the set from her forehead, and the white plastic of the *JAL* shuttle seemed to slam into place all around her. Warning signs were blinking on the console overhead, and she could feel a vibration that seemed to gradually rise in pitch ...

Virek? She looked at the trode-set. 'Well,' she said, 'I suppose you *are* a top person ...'

'I beg your pardon?' The Japanese student beside her bobbed in his harness in a strange little approximation of a bow. 'You are in some difficulty with your stim?'

'No, no,' she said. 'Excuse me.' She slid the set on again and the interior of the shuttle dissolved in a buzz of sensory static, a jarring melange of sensations that abruptly gave way to the calm grace of Tally Isham, who had taken Virek's cool, firm hand and was smiling into his soft blue eyes. Virek smiled back, his teeth very white.

'Delighted to be here, Tally,' he said, and Marly let herself sink into the reality of the tape, accepting Tally's recorded sensory input as her own. Stim was a medium she ordinarily avoided, something in her personality conflicting with the required degree of passivity.

Virek wore a soft white shirt, cotton duck trousers rolled to just below the knee, and very plain brown leather sandals. His hand still in hers, Tally returned to the balustrade. 'I'm sure,' she said, 'that there are many things our audience—'

The sea was gone. An irregular plain covered in a green-black growth like lichen spread out to the horizon, broken by the silhouettes of the Neo-Gothic spires of Gaudí's Church of the Sagrada Familia. The edge of the world was lost in a low bright mist, and a sound like drowned bells tolled in across the plain ...

'You have an audience of one, today,' Virek said, and looked at Tally Isham through his round, rimless glasses. 'Hello, Marly.'

Marly struggled to reach the trodes, but her arms were made of stone. G-force, the shuttle lifting off from its concrete pad ... He'd trapped her here ...

'I understand,' said Tally, smiling, leaning back against the balustrade, her elbows on warm rough stone. 'What a lovely idea. Your Marly, Herr Virek, must be a lucky girl indeed ...'

And it came to her, to Marly, that this wasn't Sense/Net's Tally Isham, but a part of Virek's construct, a programmed point of view worked up from years of *Top People*, and that

219

now there was no choice, no way out, except to accept it, to listen, to give Virek her attention. The fact of his having caught her here, pinned her here this way, told her that her intuition had been correct: the machine, the structure, was there, was real. Virek's money was a sort of universal solvent, dissolving barriers to his will ...

'I'm sorry,' he said, 'to learn that you are upset. Paco tells me that you are fleeing from us, but I prefer to see it as the drive of an artist towards her goal. You have sensed, I think, something of the nature of my gestalt, and it has frightened you. As well it should. This cassette was prepared an hour before your shuttle was scheduled to lift off from Orly. We know your destination, of course, but I have no intention of following you. You are doing your job, Marly. I only regret that we were unable to prevent the death of your friend Alain, but we now know the identity of his killers and their employers ...'

Tally Isham's eyes were Marly's eyes now, and they were locked with Virek's, a blue energy burning there.

'Alain was murdered by the hired agents of Maas Biolabs,' he continued, 'and it was Maas who provided him with the co-ordinates of your current destination, Maas who gave him the hologram you saw. My relationship with Maas Biolabs has been ambivalent, to say the least. Two years ago a subsidiary of mine attempted to buy them out. The sum involved would have affected the entire global economy. They refused. Paco has determined that Alain died because they discovered he was attempting to market the information they had provided, market it to third parties ...' He frowned. 'Exceedingly foolish, because he was utterly ignorant of the nature of the product he was offering ...'

How like Alain, she thought, and felt a wave of pity. Seeing him curled there on the hideous carpet, his spine outlined beneath the green fabric of his jacket ...

'You should know, I think, that my search for our Boxmaker involves more than art, Marly.' He removed his glasses and polished them in a fold of his white shirt; she found something obscene in the calculated humanity of the gesture. 'I have reason to believe that the maker of these artifacts is in some position to offer me freedom, Marly. I am not a well man.' He replaced the glasses, settling the fine gold earpieces carefully. 'When I last requested a remote visual of the vat I inhabit in Stockholm, I was shown a thing like three truck trailers, lashed in a dripping net of support lines ... If I were able to leave that, Marly, or rather, to leave the riot of cells it contains ... Well,' and he smiled his famous smile again, 'what wouldn't I pay?'

And Tally-Marly's eyes swung to take in the expanse of dark lichen and the distant towers of the misplaced cathedral ...

'You lost consciousness,' the steward was saying, his fingers moving across her neck. 'It isn't uncommon, and our onboard medical computers tell us you're in excellent health. However, we've applied a dermadisc to counteract the adaptation syndrome you might experience prior to docking ...' His hand left her neck.

'*Europe After the Rains*,' she said. 'Max Ernst. The lichen ...'

The man stared down at her, his face alert now and expressing professional concern. 'Excuse me? Could you repeat that?'

'I'm sorry,' she said. 'A dream ... Are we there yet, at the terminal?'

'Another hour,' he said.

Japan Air's orbital terminus was a white toroid studded with domes and ringed with the dark-rimmed oval openings of docking bays. The terminal above Marly's g-web – though

221

above had temporarily lost its usual meaning – displayed an exquisitely drafted animation of the torus in rotation, while a series of voices – in seven languages – announced that the passengers on board *JAL*'s Shuttle 580, Orly/Terminus I, would be taxied to the terminal at the earliest opportunity. *JAL* offered apologies for the delay, which was due to routine repairs underway in seven of the twelve bays ...

Marly cringed in her g-web, seeing the invisible hand of Virek in everything now. *No*, she thought, *there must be a way. I want out of it*, she told herself, *I want a few hours as a free agent, and then I'll be done with him ... Goodbye, Herr Virek, I return to the land of the living, as poor Alain never will, Alain who died because I took your job.* She blinked her eyes when the first tear came, then stared wide-eyed as a child at the minute floating spherelet the tear had become ...

And Maas, she wondered, *who were they?* Virek claimed that they had murdered Alain, that Alain had been working for them. She had vague recollections of stories in the media, something to do with the newest generation of computers, some ominous-sounding process in which immortal hybrid cancers spewed out tailored molecules that became units of circuitry. She remembered, now, that Paco had said that the screen of his modular telephone was a Maas product ...

The interior of the *JAL* toroid was so bland, so unremarkable, so utterly like any crowded airport, that she felt like laughing. There was the same scent of perfume, human tension, and heavily conditioned air, and the same background hum of conversation. The point-eight gravity would have made it easier to carry a suitcase, but she only had her black purse. Now she took her tickets from one of its zippered inner pockets and checked the number of her connecting shuttle against the columns of numbers arrayed on the nearest wallscreen.

Two hours to departure. Whatever Virek might say, she was sure that his machine was already busy, infiltrating the shuttle's crew or roster of passengers, the substitutions lubricated by a film of money ... There would be last-minute illnesses, changes in plans, accidents ...

Slinging the purse over her shoulder, she marched off across the concave floor of white ceramic as though she actually knew where she was going, or had some sort of plan. But knowing, with each step she took, that she didn't.

Those soft blue eyes haunted her.

'Damn you.' she said, and a jowly Russian businessman in a dark Ginza suit sniffed and raised his newsfax, blocking her out of his world.

'So I told the bitch, see, you gotta get those optoisolators *and* the breakout boxes out to *Sweet Jane* or I'll glue your ass to the bulkhead with gasket paste ...' Raucous female laughter and Marly glanced up from her sushi tray. The three women sat two empty tables away, their own table thick with beer cans and stacks of styrofoam trays smeared with brown soy sauce. One of them belched loudly and took a long pull at her beer.

'So how'd she take it, Rez?' This was somehow the cue for another, longer burst of laughter, and the woman who'd first attracted Marly's attention put her head down in her arms and laughed until her shoulders shook. Marly stared dully at the trio, wondering what they were. Now the laughter had subsided and the first woman sat up, wiping tears from her eyes. They were all quite drunk, Marly decided, young and loud and rough-looking. The first woman was slight and sharp-faced, with wide grey eyes above a thin straight nose. Her hair was some impossible shade of silver, clipped short like a schoolboy's, and she wore an oversized canvas vest or sleeveless jacket covered entirely in bulging pockets, studs, and rectangular strips of Velcro. The garment hung open, revealing, from Marly's angle, a small round breast sheathed in what seemed to be a bra of fine pink and black mesh. The other two were older and heavier, the muscles of their bare arms defined sharply in the seemingly sourceless light of the terminal cafeteria.

The first woman shrugged, her shoulders moving inside the big vest. 'Not that she'll do it.' she said.

The second woman laughed again, but not as heartily, and consulted a chronometer riveted on a wide leather wristband. 'Me for off,' she said. 'Gotta Zion run, then eight pods of algae for the Swedes.' Then shoved her chair back from the table, stood up, and Marly read the embroidered patch centred across the shoulders of her black leather vest.

O'GRADY – WAJIMA
THE EDITH S.
INTERORBITAL HAULING

Now the woman beside her stood, hitching up the waistband of her baggy jeans. 'I tell you, Rez, you let that cunt short you on those breakouts, it'll be bad for your name.'

'Excuse me,' Marly said, fighting the quaver in her voice.

The woman in the black vest turned and stared at her.

'Yeah?' The woman looked her up and down, unsmiling.

'I saw your vest, the name, *Edith S*, that's a ship, a spaceship?'

'A *spaceship*?' The woman beside her raised thick eyebrows. 'Oh, yeah, honey, a whole mighty *spaceship*!'

'She's a tug,' the woman in the black vest said, and turned to go.

'I want to hire you,' Marly said.

224

'Hire me?' Now they were all staring at her, faces blank and unsmiling. 'What's that mean?'

Marly fumbled deep in the black Brussels purse and came up with the half sheaf of New Yen that Paleologos the travel agent had returned, after taking his fee. 'I'll give you this ...'

The girl with the short silver hair whistled softly. The women glanced at one another. The one in the black vest shrugged. 'Jesus,' she said. 'Where you wanna go? Mars?'

Marly dug into her purse again and produced the folded blue paper from a pack of Gauloise. She handed it to the woman in the black vest, who unfolded it and read the orbital co-ordinates that Alain had written there in green felt pen.

'Well,' the woman said, 'it's a quick enough hop, for that kind of money, but O'Grady and I, we're due in Zion 2300 GMT. Contract job. What about you, Rez?'

She handed the paper to the seated girl, who read it, looked up at Marly, and asked, 'When?'

'Now,' Marly said, 'right now.'

The girl pushed up from the table, the legs of her chair clattering on the ceramic, her vest swinging open to reveal that what Marly had taken for the net of a pink and black bra was a single tattooed rose that entirely covered her left breast. 'You're on, sister, cash up.'

'Means give her the money now,' O'Grady said.

'I don't want anyone to know where we're going,' Marly said.

The three women laughed.

'You come to the right girl,' O'Grady said, and Rez grinned.

24

Run Straight Down

The rain came on when he turned east again, making for the Sprawl's fringe 'burbs and the blasted belt country of the industrial zones. It came down in a solid wall, blinding him until he found the switch for the wipers. Rudy hadn't kept the blades in shape, so he slowed, the turbine's whine lowering to a roar, and edged over the shoulder, the apron-bag nosing past shredded husks of truck tyres.

'What's wrong?'

'I can't see. The wiper blades are rotten.' He tapped the button for the lights, and four tight beams stabbed out from either side of the hover's wedge of hood and lost themselves in the grey wall of the downpour. He shook his head.

'Why don't we stop?'

'We're too close to the Sprawl. They patrol all this. Copters. They'd scan the ID panel on the roof and see we've got Ohio plates and a weird chassis configuration. They might want to check us out. We don't want that.'

'What are you going to do?'

'Keep to the shoulder until I can turn off, then get us under some cover, if I can ...'

He held the hover steady and swung it around in place, the headlights flashing off the dayglo orange diagonals on an upright pole marking a service road. He made for the pole, the bulging lip of the apron-bag bobbling over a thick rectangular crash-guard of concrete. 'This might do it,' he said, as they slid past the pole. The service road was barely wide enough for them; branches and undergrowth scratched against the narrow side windows, scraping along the hover's steel-plate flanks.

'Lights down there,' Angie said, straining forward in her harness to peer through the rain.

Turner made out a watery yellow glow and twin dark up-rights. He laughed. 'Gas station,' he said. 'Left over from the old system, before they put the big road through. Somebody must live there. Too bad we don't run on gasoline ...' He eased the hover down the gravel slope; as he drew nearer, he saw that the yellow glow came from a pair of rectangular windows. He thought he saw a figure move in one of them. 'Country,' he said. 'These boys may not be too happy to see us.' He reached into the parka and slid the Smith & Wesson from its nylon holster, put it on the seat between his thighs. When they were five metres from the rusting gas pumps, he sat the hover down in a broad puddle and killed the turbines. The rain was still pissing down in windblown sheets, and he saw a figure in a flapping khaki poncho duck out of the front door of the station. He slid the side window open ten centimetres and raised his voice above the rain: 'Sorry t' bother you. We had to get off the road. Our wipers are trashed. Didn't know you were down here ...' The man's hands, in the glow from the windows, were hidden beneath the plastic poncho, but it was obvious that he held something.

'Private property,' the man said, his lean face streaked with rain.

'Couldn't stay on the road,' Turner called. 'Sorry to bother you ...'

The man opened his mouth, began to gesture with the thing he held beneath the poncho, and his head exploded. It

227

almost seemed to Turner that it happened before the red line of light scythed down and touched him, pencil-thick beam swinging casually, as though someone were playing with a flashlight. A blossom of red, beaten down by the rain, as the figure went to its knees and tumbled forward, a wire-stocked Savage 410 sliding from beneath the poncho.

Turner hadn't been aware of moving, but he found that he'd stoked the turbines, swung the controls over to Angie, and clawed his way out of his harness. 'I say go, run it through the station ...' Then he was up, yanking at the lever that opened the roof hatch, the heavy revolver in his hand. The roar of the black Honda reached him as soon as the hatch slid back, a lowering shadow overhead, just visible through the driving rain. 'Now!' He pulled the trigger before she could kick them forward and through the wall of the old station, the recoil jarring his elbow numb against the roof of the hover. The bullet exploded somewhere overhead with a gratifying crack; Angie floored the hover and they plunged through the wood frame structure, with barely enough time for Turner to get his head and shoulders back down through the hatch. Something in the house exploded, probably a propane canister, and the hover skewed to the left.

Angie swung them back around as they crashed out through the far wall. 'Where?' she yelled, above the turbine.

As if in answer, the black Honda came corkscrewing down, twenty metres in front of them, and threw up a silver sheet of rain. Turner grabbed the controls and they slid forward, the hover blasting up ten-metre fantails of ground water; they took the little combat copter square in its polycarbon canopy, its alloy fuselage crumpling like paper under the impact. Turner backed off and went in again, faster. This time the broken copter slammed into the trunks of two wet grey pines, lay there like some kind of long-winged fly.

'What happened?' Angie said, her hands to her face. 'What happened?'

Turner tore registration papers and dusty sunglasses from a compartment in the door beside him, found a flashlight, checked its batteries.

'What happened?' Angie said again, like a recording, 'What happened?' He scrambled back up through the hatch, the gun in one hand, the light in the other. The rain had slackened. He jumped down onto the hover's hood, and then over the bumpers and into ankle-deep puddles, splashing towards the bent black rotors of the Honda.

There was a reek of escaping jet fuel. The polycarbon canopy had cracked like an egg. He aimed the Smith & Wesson and thumbed the xenon flash twice, two silent pops of merciless light showing him blood and twisted limbs through the shattered plastic. He waited, then used the flashlight. Two of them. He came closer, holding the flashlight well away from his body, an old habit. Nothing moved. The smell of escaping fuel grew even stronger. Then he was tugging at the bent hatch. It opened. They both wore image-amp goggles. The round blank eye of the laser stared straight up into the night, and he reached down to touch the matted sheepskin collar of the dead man's bomber jacket. The blood that covered the man's beard looked very dark, almost black in the flashlight's beam. It was Oakey. He swung the beam left and saw that the other man, the pilot, was Japanese. He swung the beam back and found a flat black flask beside Oakey's foot. He picked it up, stuffed it into one of the parka's pockets, and dashed back to the hover. In spite of the rain, orange flames were starting to lick up through the wreckage of the gas station. He scrambled up the hover's bumper, across the hood, up again, and down through the hatch.

'What happened?' Angie said, as though he hadn't left. 'What happened?'

He fell into his seat, not bothering with the harness, and revved the turbine. 'That's a Hosaka helicopter,' he said, swinging them around. 'They must have been following us. They had a laser. They waited until we were off the highway. Didn't want to leave us out there for the cops to find. When we pulled in here, they decided to go for us, but they must have figured that that poor fucker was with us. Or maybe they were just taking out a witnesses ...'

'His head,' she said, her voice shaking, 'his head ...'

'That was the laser,' Turner said, steering back up the service road. The rain was thinning, nearly gone. 'Steam. The brain vaporises and the skull blows ...'

Angie doubled over and threw up. Turner steered with one hand, Oakey's flask in the other. He pried the snap-fit lid open with his teeth and gulped back a mouthful of Oakey's Wild Turkey.

As they reached the shoulder of the highway, the Honda's fuel found the flames of the ruined station, and the twisted fireball showed Turner the mall again, the light of the parachute flares, the sky whiting out as the jet streaked for the Sonora border ...

Angie straightened up, wiped her mouth with the back of her hand, and began to shake.

'We've got to get out of here,' he said, driving east again. She said nothing, and he glanced sideways to see her rigid and upright in her seat, her eyes showing white in the faint glow of the instruments, her face blank. He'd seen her that way in Rudy's bedroom, when Sally had called them in, and now that same flood of language, a soft fast rattle of something that might have been patois French. He had no recorder, no time, he had to drive ...

'Hang on,' he said, as they accelerated, 'you'll be okay ...' Sure she couldn't hear him at all. Her teeth were chattering; he could hear it above the turbine. *Stop*, he thought, long enough to get something between her teeth, his wallet or a fold of cloth. Her hands were plucking spastically at the straps of the harness.

'There is a sick child in my house.' The hover nearly left the pavement, when he heard the voice come from her mouth, deep and slow and weirdly glutinous. 'I hear the dice being tossed, for her bloody dress. Many are the hands who dig her grave tonight, and yours as well. Enemies pray for your death, hired man. They pray until they sweat. Their prayers are a river of fever.' And then a sort of croaking that might have been laughter. Turner risked a glance, saw a silver thread of drool descend from her rigid lips. The deep muscles of her face had contorted into a mask he didn't know.

'Who are you?'

'I am the Lord of Roads.'

'What do you want?'

'This child for my horse, that she may move among the towns of men. It is well that you drive east. Carry her to your city. I shall ride her again. And Samedi rides with you, gunman. He is the wind you hold in your hands, but he is fickle, the Lord of Graveyards, no matter that you have served him well ...' He turned in time to see her slump sideways in the harness, her head lolling, mouth slack.

231

25

Kasual/Gothick

'This is the Finn's phone program,' said the speaker below the screen, 'and the Finn, he's not here. You wanna download, you know the access code already. You wanna leave a message, leave it already.' Bobby stared at the image on the screen and slowly shook his head. Most phone programs were equipped with cosmetic video subprograms written to bring the video image of the owner into greater accordance with the more widespread paradigms of personal beauty, erasing blemishes and subtly moulding facial outlines to meet idealised statistical norms. The effect of a cosmetic program on the Finn's grotesque features was definitely the weirdest thing Bobby had ever seen, as though somebody had gone after the face of a dead gopher with a full range of mortician's crayons and paraffin injections.

'That's not natural,' said Jammer, sipping Scotch.

Bobby nodded.

'Finn,' Jammer said, 'is agoraphobic. Gives him the hives to leave that impacted shitpile of a shop. And he's a phone junkie, can't *not* answer a call if he's there. I'm starting to think the bitch is right. Lucas is dead and some heavy shit is going down ...'

'The bitch,' Jackie said, from behind the bar, '*knows* already.'

'She knows,' Jammer said, putting the plastic glass down

232

and fingering his bolo tie, 'she *knows*. Talked to a hoodoo in the matrix, so she knows ...'

'Well, Lucas isn't answering, and Beauvoir isn't answering, so maybe she's right.' Bobby reached out and shut off the phone as the record tone began to squeal.

Jammer was got up in a pleated shirt, white dinner jacket, and black trousers with satin stripes down the leg, and Bobby took this to be his working outfit for the club. 'Nobody's here,' he said now, looking from Bobby to Jackie. 'Where's Bogue and Sharkey? Where's the waitresses?'

'Who's Bogue and Sharkey?' Bobby asked.

'The bartenders. I don't like this.' He got up from his chair, walked to the door, and gently edged one of the curtains aside. 'What the fuck are those dipshits doing out there? Hey, Count, this looks like your speed. Get over here ...'

Bobby got up, full of misgivings – he hadn't felt like telling Jackie or Jammer about letting Leon see him, because he didn't want to look like a wilson – and walked over to where the club owner stood.

'Go on. Take a peek. Don't let 'em see you. They're pretending so hard not to watch us you can almost smell it.'

Bobby moved the curtain, careful to keep the crack no more than a centimetre wide, and looked out. The shopping crowd seemed to have been replaced almost entirely by black-crested Gothick boys in leather and studs, and – amazingly – by an equal proportion of blond Kasuals, the latter decked out in the week's current Shinjuku cottons and gold-buckled white loafers. 'I dunno,' Bobby said, looking up at Jammer, 'but they shouldn't be *together*, Kasuals and Gothicks, you know? They're like natural enemies, it's in the DNA or something ...' He took another look. 'Goddam, there's about a hundred of 'em.'

Jammer stuck his hands deep in his pleated trousers. 'You know any of those guys personally?'

'Gothicks, I know some of 'em to talk to. Except it's hard to tell 'em apart. Kasuals, they'll stomp anything that isn't Kasual. That's mainly what they're about. But I just been cut up by Lobes anyway, and Lobes are supposed to be under treaty with the Gothicks, so who knows?'

Jammer sighed. 'So, I guess you don't feel like strolling out there and asking one what they think they're up to?'

'No,' Bobby said earnestly, 'I don't.'

'Hmmm.' Jammer looked at Bobby in a calculating way, a way that Bobby definitely didn't like.

Something small and hard dropped from the high black ceiling and clicked loudly on one of the round black tables. The thing bounced and hit the carpet, rolling, and landed between the toes of Bobby's new boots. Automatically, he bent and picked it up. An old-fashioned, slot-headed machine screw, its threads brown with rust and its head clotted with dull black latex paint. He looked up as a second one struck the table, and caught a glimpse of an unnervingly agile Jammer vaulting the bar, beside the universal credit unit. Jammer vanished, there was a faint ripping sound – Velcro – and Bobby knew that Jammer had the squat little automatic weapon he'd seen there earlier in the day. He looked around, but Jackie was nowhere in sight.

A third screw ticked explosively on the Formica of the tabletop.

Bobby hesitated, confused, but then followed Jackie's example and got out of sight, moving as quietly as he could. He crouched behind one of the club's wooden screens and watched as the fourth screw came down, followed by a slender cascade of fine dark dust. There was a scraping sound, and then a square steel ceiling grate vanished abruptly, withdrawn into some kind of duct. He glanced quickly at the bar, in time to see the fat recoil-compensator on the barrel of Jammer's gun as it swung up ...

A pair of thin brown legs dangled from the opening now, and a grey sharkskin hem, smudged with dust.

'Hold it,' Bobby said, 'it's Beauvoir!'

'You bet it's Beauvoir,' came the voice from above, big and hollow with the echo of the duct. 'Get that damn table out of the way.' Bobby scrambled out from behind the screen and hauled the table and chairs to the side. 'Catch this,' Beauvoir said, and dangled a bulging olive-drab pack from one of its shoulder-straps, then let it go. The weight of the thing nearly took Bobby to the floor. 'Now get out of my way ...' Beauvoir swung down out of the duct, hung from the opening's edge with both hands, then dropped.

'What happened to the screamer I had up there?' Jammer asked, standing up behind the bar, the little machine gun in his hands.

'Right here,' Beauvoir said, tossing a dull grey bar of phenolic resin to the carpet. It was wrapped with a length of fine black wire. 'No other way I could get in here without a regular army of shitballs knowing about it, as it happens. Somebody's obviously given them the blueprints to the place, but they've missed that one.'

'How'd you get up to the roof?' Jackie asked, stepping from behind a screen.

'I didn't,' Beauvoir said, pushing his big plastic frames back up his nose. 'I shot a line of monomol across from the stack next door, then slid over on a ceramic spindle ...' His short nappy hair was full of furnace dust. He looked at her gravely. 'You know,' he said.

'Yes. Legba and Papa Ougou, in the matrix. I jacked with Bobby, on Jammer's deck ...'

'They blew Ahmed away on the Jersey freeway. Probably used the same launcher they did Bobby's old lady with ...'

'Who?'

'Still not sure,' Beauvoir said, kneeling beside the pack and clicking open the quick-release plastic fasteners, 'but it's starting to shape up ... What I was working on, up until I heard Lucas had been hit, was running down the Lobes who mugged Bobby for his deck. That was probably an accident, just business as usual, but somewhere there's a couple of Lobes with our icebreaker ... That had potential, for sure, because the Lobes are hotdoggers, some of them, and they do a little business with Two-a-Day. So Two-a-Day and I were making the rounds, looking to learn what we could. Which was dick, as it turned out, except that while we were with this dust case called Alix, who's second assistant warlord or something, he gets a call from his opposite number, who Two-a-Day pins as a Barrytown Gothick name of Raymond.' He was unloading the pack as he spoke, laying out weapons, tools, ammunition, coils of wire. 'Raymond wants to talk real bad, but Alix is too cool to do it in front of us. "Sorry, gentlemen, but this is official warlord biz," this dumbshit says, so natch, we excuse our humble selves, shuffle and bow and all, and nip around the corner. Use Two-a-Day's modular phone to ring up our cowboys back in the Sprawl and put them on to Alix's phone, but fast. Those cowboys went into Alix's conversation with Raymond like a wire into cheese.' He pulled a deformed twelve-gauge shotgun, barely longer than his forearm, from the pack, selected a fat drum magazine from the display he'd made on the carpet, and clicked the two together. 'You ever see one of these motherfuckers? South African, pre-war ...' Something in his voice and the set of his jaw made Bobby suddenly aware of his contained fury. 'Seems Raymond has been approached by this guy, and this guy has lots of money, and he wants to hire the Gothicks outright, the whole apparat, to go into the Sprawl and do a number, a real crowd scene. This guy wants it so big, he's gonna hire the Kasuals too. Well, the shit hit the fan then, because Alix, he's kind of conservative. Only good Kasual's a dead one, and then only after *x* number of hours of torture, etc. "Fuck that," Raymond says, ever the diplomat, "we're talking big money here, we're talking *corporate* ..."' He opened a box of fat red plastic shells and began to load the gun, cranking one after another into the magazine. 'Now I could be way off, but I keep seeing these Maas Biolabs PR types on video lately. Something very weird's happened, out on some property of theirs in Arizona. Some people say it was a nuke, some people say it was something else. And now they're claiming their top biosoft man's dead, in what they call an unrelated accident. That's Mitchell, the guy who more or less invented the stuff. So far, nobody else is even pretending to be able to make a biochip, so Lucas and I assumed from the beginning that Maas had made that icebreaker. If it *was* an icebreaker ... But we had no idea who the Finn got it from, or where *they* got it. But if you put all that together, it looks like Maas Biolabs might be out to cook us all. And this is where they plan to do it, because they got us here but good.'

'I dunno,' Jammer said, 'we got a lot of friends in this building ...'

'Had,' Beauvoir put the shotgun down and started loading a Nambu automatic. 'Most of the people on this level and the next one down got bought out this afternoon. Cash. Duffles full of it. There's a few holdouts, but not enough.'

'That doesn't make any sense,' Jackie said, taking the glass of Scotch from Jammer's hand and drinking it straight off. 'What do we have that anybody could want that bad?'

'Hey,' Bobby said, 'don't forget, they probably don't know

those Lobes ripped me for the icebreaker. Maybe that's all they want.'

'No,' Beauvoir said, snapping the magazine into the Nambu, 'because they couldn't have known you hadn't stashed it in your mother's place, right?'

'But maybe they went there and looked ...'

'So how did they know Lucas wasn't carrying it in Ahmed?' Jammer said, walking back to the bar.

'Finn thought someone sent those three ninjas to kill him, too,' Bobby said. 'Said they had stuff to make him answer questions first, though ...'

'Maas again,' Beauvoir said. 'Whoever, here's the deal with the Kasuals and Gothicks. We'd know more, but Alix the Lobe got on his high horse and wouldn't parley with Raymond. No co-employment with the hated Kasuals. Near as our cowboys could make out, the army's outside to keep you people in. And to keep people like *me* out. People with guns and stuff.' He handed the loaded Nambu to Jackie. 'You know how to use a gun?' he asked Bobby.

'Sure,' Bobby lied.

'No,' Jammer said, 'we got enough trouble without arming *him*. Jesus Christ ...'

'What all that suggests to me,' Beauvoir said, 'is that we can expect somebody else to come in after us. Somebody a little more professional ...'

'Unless they just blow Hypermart all to shit and gone,' Jammer said, 'and all those zombies with it ...'

'No,' Bobby said, 'or else they'd already have *done* it.'

They all stared at him.

'Give the boy credit,' Jackie said. 'He's got it right.'

*

Thirty minutes later and Jammer was staring glumly at Beauvoir. 'I gotta hand it to you. That's the most half-assed plan I've heard in a long time.'

'Yeah, Beauvoir,' Bobby cut in, 'why can't we just crawl back up that vent, sneak across the roof, and get over to the next building? Use the line you came over on.'

'There's Kasuals on the roof like flies on shit,' Beauvoir said. 'Some of them might even have brain enough to have found the cap I opened to get down here. I left a couple of baby frag mines on my way in.' He grinned mirthlessly. 'Aside from that, the building next door is taller. I had to go up on that roof and shoot the monomol down to this one. You can't hand-over-hand up monomolecular filament; your fingers fall off.'

'Then how the hell did you expect to get out?' Bobby said.

'Drop it, Bobby,' Jackie said quietly. 'Beauvoir's done what he had to do. Now he's in here with us, and we're armed.'

'Bobby,' Beauvoir said, 'why don't you run the plan back to us, make sure we understand it ...'

Bobby had the uncomfortable feeling that Beauvoir wanted to make sure he understood it, but he leaned back against the bar and began. 'We get ourselves all armed up and we wait, okay? Jammer and I, we go out with his deck and scout around the matrix, maybe we get some idea what's happening ...'

'I think I can handle that by myself,' Jammer said.

'Shit!' Bobby was off the bar. 'Beauvoir *said*! I wanna go, I wanna jack! How am I ever supposed to *learn* anything?'

'Never mind, Bobby,' Jackie said, 'you go on.'

'Okay,' Bobby said, sulkily, 'so, sooner or later, the guys who hired the Gothicks and Kasuals to keep us here, they're gonna come for us. When they do, we take 'em. We get at least one of 'em alive. Same time, we're on our way out, and the Goths 'n' all, they won't expect all the firepower, so we get to the street and head for the Projects ...'

'I think that about covers it,' Jammer said, strolling across the carpet to the locked and curtained door. 'I think that about sums it up.' He pressed his thumb against a coded latch plate and pulled the door half open. 'Hey, you!' he bellowed. 'Not you! You with the hat! Get your ass over here. I want to talk—'

The pencil-thick red beam pierced door and curtain, two of Jammer's fingers, and winked over the bar. A bottle exploded, its contents billowing out as steam and vaporised esters. Jammer let the door swing shut again, stared at his ruined hand, then sat down hard on the carpet. The club slowly filled with the Christmas tree smell of boiled gin. Beauvoir took a silver pressure bottle from the bar counter and hosed the smouldering curtain with seltzer, until the CO_2 cartridge was exhausted and the stream faltered.

'You're in luck, Bobby,' Beauvoir said, tossing the bottle over his shoulder, ''cause brother Jammer, he ain't gonna be punching any deck ...'

Jackie was making clucking sounds over Jammer's hand, kneeling down. Bobby caught a glimpse of cauterised flesh, then quickly looked away.

26

The Wig

'You know,' Rez said, hanging upside down in front of Marly, 'it's strictly no biz of mine, but is somebody maybe expecting you when we get there? I mean, I'm taking you there, for sure, and if you can't get in, I'll take you back to *JAL* Term. But if nobody wants to let you in, I don't know how long I want to hang around. That thing's scrap, and we get some funny people hanging out in the hulks, out here ...' Rez – or Thérèse, Marly gathered, from the laminated pilot's licence clipped to the *Sweet Jane*'s console – had removed her canvas work vest for the trip. Marly, numb with the rainbow of derms Rez had pasted along her wrist to counteract the convulsive nausea of space adaptation syndrome, stared at the rose tattoo. It had been executed in a Japanese style hundreds of years old, and Marly woozily decided that she liked it. That, in fact, she liked Rez, who was at once hard and girlish and concerned for her strange passenger. Rez had admired her leather jacket and purse, before bundling them into a kind of narrow nylon net hammock already stuffed with cassettes, print books, and unwashed clothing.

'I don't know,' Marly managed, 'I'll just have to try to get in ...'

'You know what that thing is, sister?' Rez was adjusting the g-web around Marly's shoulders and armpits.

'What thing?' Marly blinked.

'Where we're going. It's part of the old Tessier-Ashpool cores. Used to be the mainframes for their corporate memory ...'

'I've heard of them,' Marly said, closing her eyes. 'Andrea told me ...'

'Sure, everybody's heard of 'em – they used to own all of Freeside. Built it, even. Then they went tits up and sold out. Had their family place cut off the spindle and towed to another orbit, but they had the cores wiped before they did that, and torched 'em off and sold 'em to a scrapper. The scrapper's never done anything with 'em. I never heard anybody was squatting there, but out here you live where you can ... I guess that's true for anybody. Like they say that Lady 3Jane, old Ashpool's daughter, she's still living in their old place, stone crazy ...' She gave the g-web a last professional tug. 'Okay. You just relax. I'm gonna burn *Jane* hard for twenty minutes, but it'll get us there fast, which I figure is what you're paying for ...'

And Marly slid back into a landscape built all of boxes, vast wooden Cornell constructions where the solid residues of love and memory were displayed behind rain-streaked sheets of dusty glass, and the figure of the mysterious Boxmaker fled before her down avenues paved with mosaics of human teeth, Marly's Paris boots clicking blindly over symbols outlined in dull gold crowns. The Boxmaker was male and wore Alain's green jacket, and feared her above all things. 'I'm sorry,' she cried, running after him, 'I'm sorry ...'

'Yeah. Thérèse Lorenz, the *Sweet Jane*. You want the numbers? What? Yeah, sure we're pirates. I'm Captain fucking Hook already ... Look, Jack, lemme give you the numbers, you can check it out ... I said already. I gotta passenger. Request permission, et goddam cetera ... Marly Something, speaks French in her sleep ...' Marly's lids flickered, opened. Rez was webbed in front of her, each small muscle of her back precisely defined. 'Hey,' Rez said, twisting around in the web, 'I'm sorry. I raised 'em for you, but they sound pretty flaky. You religious?'

'No,' Marly said, baffled.

Rez made a face. 'Well, I hope you can make sense out of this shit, then.' She shrugged out of the web and executed a tight backwards somersault that brought her within centimetres of Marly's face. An optic ribbon trailed from her hand to the console, and for the first time Marly saw the delicate sky-blue socket set flush with the skin of the girl's wrist. She popped a speaker-bead into Marly's right ear and adjusted the transparent microphone-tube that curved down from it.

'You have no right to disturb us here,' a man's voice said. 'Our work is the work of God, and we alone have seen His true face!'

'Hello? Hello, can you hear me? My name is Marly Krushkhova and I have urgent business with you. Or with someone at these co-ordinates. My business concerns a series of boxes, collages. The maker of these boxes may be in terrible danger! I must see him!'

'Danger?' The man coughed. 'God alone decides man's fate! We are entirely without fear ... But neither are we fools ...'

'Please, listen to me. I was hired by Josef Virek to locate the maker of the boxes. But now I have come to warn you. Virek knows you are here, and his agents will follow me ...' Rez was staring at her hard. 'You must let me in! I can tell you more ...'

'Virek?' There was a long, static-filled pause. 'Josef Virek?'

'Yes.' Marly said. 'That one. You've seen his picture all your life, the one with the king of England ... Please, please ...'

'Give me your pilot,' the voice said, and the bluster and

243

hysteria were gone, replaced with something Marly liked even less.

'It's a spare,' Rez said, snapping the mirrored helmet from the red suit. 'I can afford it, you paid me enough ...'

'No,' Marly protested, 'really, you needn't ... I ...' She shook her head. Rez was undoing the fastenings at the spacesuit's waist.

'You don't go into a thing like that without a suit,' she said. 'You don't know what they got for atmosphere. You don't even know they *got* atmosphere! And any kinda bacteria, spores ... What's the matter?' Lowering the silver helmet.

'I'm claustrophobic!'

'Oh ...' Rez stared at her. 'I heard of that ... It means you're scared to be inside things?' She looked genuinely curious.

'Small things, yes ...'

'Like *Sweet Jane*?'

'Yes, but ...' She glanced around at the cramped cabin, fighting her panic. 'I can stand this, but not the helmet ...' She shuddered.

'Well,' Rez said, 'tell you what. We get you into the suit, but we leave the helmet off. I'll teach you how to fasten it. Deal? Otherwise, you don't leave my ship ...' Her mouth was straight and firm.

'Yes,' Marly said, 'yes ...'

'Here's the drill,' Rez said. 'We're lock to lock. This hatch opens, you get in, I close it. Then I open the other side. Then you're in whatever passes for atmosphere, in there. You sure you don't want the helmet on?'

'No,' Marly said, looking down at the helmet she grasped in the suit's red gauntlets, at her pale reflection in the mirrored faceplate.

244

Rez made a little clicking sound with her tongue. 'Your life. If you want to get back, have them put a message through *JAL* Term for the *Sweet Jane*.'

Marly kicked off clumsily and spun forward into the lock, no larger than an upright coffin. The red suit's breastplate clicked hard against the outer hatch, and she heard the inner one hiss shut behind her. A light came on, beside her head, and she thought of the lights in refrigerators. 'Goodbye, Thérèse ...'

Nothing happened. She was alone with the beating of her heart.

Then the *Sweet Jane*'s outer hatch slid open. A slight pressure differential was enough to tumble her out into a darkness that smelled old and sadly human, a smell like a long-abandoned locker room. There was a thickness, an unclean dampness to the air, and, still tumbling, she saw *Sweet Jane*'s hatch slide shut behind her. A beam of light stabbed past her, wavered, swung, and found her spinning.

'Lights,' someone bawled hoarsely. 'Lights for our guest! Jones!' It was the voice she'd heard through the ear-bead. It rang strangely, in the iron vastness of this place, this hollow she fell through, and then there was a grating sound and a distant ring of harsh blue flared up, showing her the far curve of a wall or hull of steel and welded lunar rock. The surface was lined and pitted with precisely carved channels and depressions, where equipment of some kind had once been fitted. Scabrous clumps of brown expansion foam still adhered in some of the deeper cuts, and others were lost in dead black shadow ... 'You'd better get a line on her, Jones, before she cracks her head ...'

Something struck the shoulder of her suit with a damp smack, and she turned her head to see a pink gob of bright plastic trailing a fine pink line, which jerked taut as she watched, flipping her around. The derelict cathedral space filled with the labouring whine of an engine, and, quite slowly, they reeled her in.

'It took you long enough,' the voice said. 'I wondered who would be first, and now it's Virek ... Mammon ...' And then they had her, spinning her around. She almost lost the helmet; it was drifting away, but one of them batted it back into her hands. Her purse, with her boots and jacket folded inside, executed its own arc, on its shoulder strap, and bumped the side of her head.

'Who are you?' she asked.

'Ludgate!' the old man roared. 'Wigan Ludgate, as you well know ... Who else did he send you to deceive?' His seamed, blotched face was clean-shaven, but his grey, untrimmed hair floated free, seaweed on a tide of stale air.

'I'm sorry,' she said. 'I'm not here to deceive you. I no longer work for Virek ... I came here because ... I mean, I'm not at all sure why I came here, to begin with, but on my way I learned that the artist who makes the boxes is in danger. Because there's something else, something Virek thinks he has, something Virek thinks will free him from his cancers ...' Her words ran down to silence, in the face of the almost palpable craziness that radiated from Wigan Ludgate, and she saw that he wore the cracked plastic carapace of an old work suit, with cheap metal crucifixes epoxied like a necklace around the tarnished steel helmet-ring. His face was very close. She could smell his decaying teeth.

'The boxes!' Little balls of spittle curled off his lips, obeying the elegant laws of Newtonian physics. 'You whore! They're of the hand of God!'

'Easy there, Lud,' said a second voice, 'you're scarin' the lady. Easy, lady, 'cause old Lud, he hasn't got too many visitors. Gets him quite worked up, y'see, but he's basically a harmless old bugger ...' She turned her head and met the relaxed gaze of a pair of wide blue eyes in a very young face. 'I'm Jones,' he said. 'I live here, too ...'

Wigan Ludgate threw back his head and howled, and the sound rang wild against the walls of steel and stone.

'Mostly, y'see,' Jones was saying, as Marly pulled her way behind him along a knotted line stretched taut down a corridor that seemed to have no end, 'he's pretty quiet. Listens to his voices, y'know. Talks to himself, or maybe to the voices, I dunno, and then a spell comes on him and he's like this ...' When he stopped speaking, she could still hear faint echoes of Ludgate's howls. 'You may think it's cruel, me leavin' him this way, but it's best, really. He'll tire of it soon. Gets hungry. Then he comes to find me. Wants his tuck, y'see.'

'Are you Australian?' she asked.

'New Melbourne,' he said. 'Or was, before I got up the well ...'

'Do you mind my asking why you're here? I mean, here in this, this ... What is it?'

The boy laughed. 'Mostly, I call it the Place. Lud, he calls it a lot of things, but mostly the Kingdom. Figures he's found God, he does. Suppose he has, if you want to look at it that way. Near as I make it, he was some kind of console crook before he got up the well. Don't know how he came to be here, exactly, other than that it suits the poor bastard ... Me, I came here runnin', understand? Trouble somewhere, not to be too specific, and my arse for out of there. Turn up here – that's a long tale of its own – and here's bloody Ludgate near to starvin'. He'd had him a sort of business, sellin' things he'd scavenge, and those boxes you're after, but he'd got a bit far gone for that. His buyers would come, oh, say, three times a year, but he'd send 'em away. Well, I thought, the hidin' here's as good as any, so I took to helpin' him. That's it, I guess.'

'Can you take me to the artist? Is he here? It's extremely urgent ...'

'I'll take you, no fear. But this place, it was never really built for people, not to get around in, I mean, so it's a bit of a journey ... It isn't likely to be going anywhere, though. Can't guarantee it'll make a box for you. Do you really work for Virek? Fabulous rich old shit on the telly? Kraut, isn't he?'

'I did,' she said, 'for a number of days. As for nationality, I would guess Herr Virek is the sole citizen of a nation consisting of Herr Virek ...'

'See what you mean,' Jones said, cheerily. 'It's all the same, with these rich old fucks, I suppose, though it's more fun than watching a bloody zaibatsu ... You won't see a zaibatsu come to a messy end, will you? Take old Ashpool – countryman of mine, he was – who built all this; they say his own daughter slit his throat, and now she's bad as old Lud, holed up in the family castle somewhere. The Place being a former part of all that, y'see ...'

'Rez ... I mean, my pilot, said something like that ... And a friend of mine, in Paris, mentioned the Tessier-Ashpools recently ... The clan is in eclipse?'

'Eclipse? Lord! Down the bloody tube's more like it ... Think about it: we're crawlin', you an' me, through what used to be their corporate data cores. Some contractor in Pakistan bought the thing; hull's fine, and there's a fair bit of gold in the circuitry, but not as cheap to recover as some might like ... It's been hangin' up here ever since, with only old Lud to keep it company, and it him. 'Til I come along, that is. Guess one day the crews'll come up from Pakistan and get cuttin' ... Funny, though, how much of it still seems to work,

248

at least part of the time. Story I heard, one got me here in the first place, said T-As wiped the cores dead, before they cut it loose ...'

'But you think they are still operative?'

'Lord, yes. About the way Lud is, if you call that operative. What do you think your Boxmaker is?'

'What do you know about Maas Biolabs?'

'Moss what?'

'Maas. They make biochips ...'

'Oh. Them. Well, that's all I do know about 'em ...'

'Ludgate speaks of them?'

'He might. Can't say as I listen all that close. Lud, he does speak a fair bit ...'

27

Stations of the Breath

He brought them in through avenues lined with rusting slopes of dead vehicles, with wrecker's cranes and the black towers of smelters. He kept to the back streets as they eased into the western flank of the Sprawl, and eventually gunned the hover down a brick canyon, armoured sides scraping sparks, and drove it hard into a wall of soot-blown, compacted garbage. An avalanche of refuse slid down, almost covering the vehicle, and he released the controls, watching the foam dice swing back and forth, side to side. The kerosene gauge had been riding on empty for the last twelve blocks.

'What happened back there?' she said, her cheekbones green in the glow of the instruments.

'I shot down a helicopter. Mostly by accident. We were lucky.'

'No, I mean after that. I was ... I had a dream.'

'What did you dream?'

'The big things, moving ...'

'You had some kind of seizure.'

'Am I sick? Do you think I'm sick? Why did the company want to kill me?'

'I don't think you're sick.'

She undid her harness and scrambled back over the seat, to crouch where they had slept. 'It was a bad dream ...' She began to tremble. He climbed out of his harness and went to her, held her head against him, stroking her hair, smoothing it back against the delicate skull, stroking it back behind her ears. Her face in the green glow like something hauled from dreams and abandoned, the skin smooth and thin across the bones. The black sweatshirt half unzipped, he traced the fragile line of her collarbone with a fingertip. Her skin was cool, moist with a film of sweat. She clung to him.

He closed his eyes and saw his body in a sun-striped bed, beneath a slow fan with blades of brown hardwood. His body pumping, jerking like an amputated limb, Allison's head thrown back, mouth open, lips taut across her teeth.

Angie pressed her face into the hollow of his neck.

She groaned, stiffened, rocked back. 'Hired man,' the voice said. And he was back against the driver's seat, the Smith & Wesson's barrel reflecting a single line of green instrument-glow, the luminous bead on its front sight eclipsing her left pupil.

'No,' the voice said.

He lowered the gun. 'You're back.'

'No. Legba spoke to you. I am Samedi.'

'Saturday?'

'Baron Saturday, hired man. You met me once on a hillside. The blood lay on you like dew. I drank of your full heart that day.' Her body jerked violently. 'You know this town well …'

'Yes.' He watched as muscles tensed and relaxed in her face, moulding her features into a new mask …

'Very well. Leave the vehicle here, as you intended. But follow the stations north. To New York. Tonight. I will guide you with Legba's horse then, and you will kill for me …'

'Kill who?'

'The one you most wish to kill, hired man.'

Angie moaned, shuddered, and began to sob.

'It's okay,' he said. 'We're halfway home.' *It was a*

meaningless thing to say, he thought, helping her out of the seat; neither of them had homes at all. He found the case of cartridges in the parka and replaced the one he'd used on the Honda. He found a paint-spattered razor-knife in the dash toolkit and sliced the ripstop lining out of the parka, a million microtubes of poly insulation whirling up as he cut. When he'd stripped it out, he put the Smith & Wesson in the holster and put the parka on. It hung around him in folds, like an oversized raincoat, and didn't show the bulge of the big gun at all.

'Why did you do that?' she asked, running the back of her hand across her mouth.

'Because it's hot out there and I need to cover the gun.' He stuffed the Ziploc full of used New Yen into a pocket. 'Come on,' he said, 'we got subways to catch ...'

Condensation dripped steadily from the old Georgetown dome, built forty years after the ailing Federals decamped for the lower reaches of McLean. Washington was a Southern city, always had been, and you felt the tone of the Sprawl shift here, if you rode the trains down the stations from Boston. The trees in the District were lush and green, and their leaves shaled the arc-lights as Turner and Angela Mitchell made their way along the broken sidewalks to Dupont Circle and the station. There were drums in the circle, and someone had lit a trash fire in the giant's marble goblet at the centre. Silent figures sat beside spread blankets as they passed, the blankets arrayed with surreal assortments of merchandise: the damp-swollen cardboard covers of black plastic audio discs beside battered prosthetic limbs trailing crude nerve-jacks, a dusty glass fishbowl filled with oblong steel dog tags; rubber-banded stacks of faded postcards; cheap Indo trodes still sealed in wholesaler's plastic; mismatched ceramic salt-and-pepper sets; a golf club with a peeling leather grip; Swiss army knives with missing blades; a dented tin waste-basket lithographed with the face of a president whose name Turner could almost remember (Carter? Grosvenor?); fuzzy holograms of the Monument ...

In the shadows near the station's entrance, Turner haggled quietly with a Chinese boy in white jeans, exchanging the smallest of Rudy's bills for nine alloy tokens stamped with the ornate BAMA Transit logo.

Two of the tokens admitted them to the station. Three of them went into vending machines for bad coffee and stale pastries. The remaining four carried them north, the train rushing silently along on its magnetic cushion. He sat back with his arm around her, and pretended to close his eyes; he watched their reflections in the opposite window. A tall man, gaunt now and unshaven, hunched back in defeat with a hollow-eyed girl curled beside him. She hadn't spoken since they'd left the alley where he'd abandoned the hover.

For the second time in an hour he considered phoning his agent. If you had to trust someone, the rule ran, then trust your agent. But Conroy had said he'd hired Oakey and the others through Turner's agent, and the connection made Turner dubious ... Where was Conroy tonight? Turner was fairly certain that it would have been Conroy who ordered Oakey after them with the laser. Would Hosaka have arranged the railgun, in Arizona, to erase evidence of a botched defection attempt? But if they had, why order Webber to destroy the medics, their neurosurgery, and the Maas-Neotek deck? And there was Maas again ... Had Maas killed Mitchell? Was there any reason to believe that Mitchell was really dead? *Yes*, he thought, as the girl stirred beside him in uneasy sleep, *there was Angie*. Mitchell had feared they'd kill her; he'd arranged the defection in order to get her out, get her to Hosaka, with no plan for his own escape. Or that was Angie's version, anyway.

He closed his eyes, shut out the reflections. Something stirred, deep in the silt of Mitchell's recorded memories. Shame. He couldn't quite reach it ... He opened his eyes suddenly. What had she said, at Rudy's? That her father had put the thing into her head because she wasn't smart enough? Careful not to disturb her, he worked his arm from behind her neck and slid two fingers into the waist pocket of his pants, came up with Conroy's little black nylon envelope on its neck-cord. He undid the Velcro and shook the swollen, asymmetrical grey biosoft out onto his open palm. Machine dreams. Rollercoaster. Too fast, too alien to grasp. But if you wanted something, something specific, you should be able to pull it out ...

He dug his thumbnail under the socket's dust cover, pried it out, and put it down on the plastic seat beside him. The train was nearly empty, and none of the other passengers seemed to be paying any attention to him. He took a deep breath, set his teeth, and inserted the biosoft ...

Twenty seconds later, he had it, the thing he'd gone for. The strangeness hadn't touched him, this time, and he decided that that was because he'd gone after this one specific thing, this fact, exactly the sort of data you'd expect to find in the dossier of a top research man: his daughter's IQ, as reflected by annual batteries of tests.

Angela Mitchell was well above the norm. Had been, all along.

He took the biosoft out of his socket and rolled it absently between thumb and forefinger. The shame. Mitchell and the shame and grad school ... *Grades*, he thought. *I want the bastard's grades. I want his transcripts.*

He jacked the dossier again.

Nothing. He'd got it, but there was nothing ...

No. Again.

Again ...

'God damn,' he said, seeing it.

A teenager with a shaved head glanced at him from a seat across the aisle, then turned back to the stream of his friend's monologue: 'They're gonna run the games again, up on the hill, midnight. We're goin', but we're just gonna hang, we're not gonna make it, just kick back and let 'em thump each other's butts, and we're gonna laugh, see who gets thumped, 'cause last week Susan got her arm busted, you there for that? An' it was funny, 'cause Cal was tryin' t' takem to the hospital but he was dusted 'n' he ran that shitty Yamaha over a speedbump ...'

Turner snapped the biosoft back into his socket.

This time, when it was over, he said nothing at all. He put his arm back around Angie and smiled, seeing the smile in the window. It was a foetal smile; it belonged to the edge.

Mitchell's academic record was good, extremely good. Excellent. But the arc wasn't there. The arc was something Turner had learned to look for in the dossiers of research people, that certain signal curve of brilliance. He could spot the arc the way a master machinist could identify metals by observing the spark-plume off a grinding wheel. And Mitchell hadn't had it.

The shame. The graduate dorms. Mitchell had known, known he wasn't going to make it. And then, somehow, he had. How? It wouldn't be in the dossier. Mitchell, somehow, had known how to edit what he gave the Maas security machine. Otherwise, they would have been on to him ... Someone, something, had found Mitchell in his postgraduate slump and had started feeding him things. Clues, directions.

And Mitchell had gone to the top, his arc hard and bright and perfect then, and it had carried him to the top ...

Who? What?

He watched Angie's sleeping face in the shudder of subway light.

Faust.

Mitchell had cut a deal. Turner might never know the details of the agreement, or Mitchell's price, but he knew he understood the other side of it. What Mitchell had been required to do in return.

Legba, Samedi, spittle curling from the girl's contorted lips.

And the train swept into old Union in a black blast of midnight air.

'Cab, sir?' The man's eyes were moving behind glasses with a polychrome tint that swirled like oil slicks. There were flat, silvery sores across the backs of his hands. Turner stepped in close and caught his upper arm, without breaking stride, forcing him back against a wall of scratched white tile, between grey ranks of luggage lockers.

'Cash,' Turner said. 'I'm paying New Yen. I want my cab. *No* trouble with the driver. Understand? I'm not a mark.' He tightened his grip. 'Fuck up on me, I'll come back here and kill you, or make you wish I had.'

'Got it. Yessir. Got it. We can do that, sir, yessir. Where d'you wanna go to, sir?' The man's wasted features contorted in pain.

'Hired man.' The voice came from Angie, a hoarse whisper. And then an address. Turner saw the tout's eyes dart nervously behind the swirls of colours. 'That's Madison?' he croaked. 'Yessir. Get you a good cab, real good cab ...'

*

'What is this place,' Turner asked the cabby, leaning forward to thumb the SPEAK button beside the steel speaker grid, 'the address we gave you?'

There was a crackle of static. 'Hypermart. Not much open there this time of night. Looking for anything in particular?'

'No,' Turner said. He didn't know the place. He tried to remember that stretch of Madison. Residential, mostly. Uncounted living-spaces carved out of the shells of commercial buildings that dated from a day when commerce had required clerical workers to be present physically at a central location. Some of the buildings were tall enough to penetrate a dome …

'Where are we going?' Angie asked, her hand on his arm.

'It's okay,' he said. 'Don't worry.'

'God,' she said, leaning against his shoulder, looking up at the pink neon HYPERMART sign that slashed the granite face of the old building, 'I used to dream about New York, back on the mesa. I had a graphics program that would take me through all the streets, into museums and things. I wanted to come here more than anything in the world …'

'Well, you made it. You're here.'

She started to sob, hugged him, her face against his bare chest, shaking. 'I'm scared. I'm so scared …'

'It'll be okay,' he said, stroking her hair, his eyes on the main entrance. He had no reason to believe anything would ever be okay for either of them. She seemed to have no idea that the words that had brought them here had come from her mouth. *But then*, he thought, *she hadn't spoken them …* There were bag people huddled on either side of Hypermart's entranceway, prone hummocks of rag gone the exact shade of the sidewalk; they looked to Turner as though they were

257

being slowly extruded from the dark concrete, to become mobile extensions of the city.

'Jammer's,' the voice said, muffled by his chest, and he felt a cold revulsion, 'a club. Find Danbala's horse.' And then she was crying again. He took her hand and walked past the sleeping transients, in under the tarnished gilt scrollwork and through the glass doors. He saw an espresso machine down an aisle of tents and shuttered stalls, a girl with a black crest of hair swabbing a counter.

'Coffee.' he said. 'Food. Come on. You need to eat.'

He smiled at the girl while Angie settled herself on a stool. 'How about cash?' he said. 'You ever take cash?'

She stared at him, shrugged. He took a twenty from Rudy's Ziploc and showed it to her. 'What do you want?'

'Coffees. Some food.'

'That all you got? Nothing smaller?'

He shook his head.

'Sorry. Can't make the change.'

'You don't have to.'

'You crazy?'

'No, but I want coffee.'

'That's some tip, mister. I don't make that in a week.'

'It's yours.'

Anger crossed her face. 'You're with those shitheads upstairs. Keep your money. I'm closing.'

'We aren't with anybody,' he said, leaning across the counter slightly, so that the parka fell open and she could see the Smith & Wesson. 'We're looking for a club. A place called Jammer's.'

The girl glanced at Angie, back to Turner. 'She sick? Dusted? What is this?'

'Here's the money,' Turner said. 'Give us our coffee. You want to earn the change, tell me how to find Jammer's place It's worth it to me. Understand?'

She slid the worn bill out of sight and moved to the espresso machine. 'I don't think I understand anything any more.' She rattled cups and milk-filmed glasses out of the way. 'What is it with Jammer's? You a friend of his? You know Jackie?'

'Sure,' Turner said.

'She came by early this morning with this little wilson from the 'burbs. I guess they went up there ...'

'Where?'

'Jammer's. Then the weirdness started.'

'Yeah?'

'All these creeps from Barrytown, greaseballs and white-shoes, walking in like they owned the place. And now they damn well do, the top two floors. Started buying people out of their stalls. A lot of people on the lower floors just packed and left. Too weird ...'

'How many came?'

Steam roared out of the machine. 'Maybe a hundred. I been scared shit all day, but I can't reach my boss. I close up in thirty minutes anyway. The day girl never showed, or else she came in, caught the trouble smell, and walked ...' She took the little steaming cup and put it in front of Angie. 'You okay, honey?'

Angie nodded.

'You have any idea what these people are up to?' Turner asked.

The girl had returned to the machine. It roared again. 'I think they're waiting for someone,' she said quietly, and brought Turner an espresso. 'Either for someone to try to leave Jammer's or for someone to try to get in ...'

Turner looked down at the swirls of brown foam on his coffee. 'And nobody here called the police?'

'The police? Mister, this is Hypermart. People here don't call the police ...'

Angie's cup shattered on the marble counter.

'Short and straight, hired man,' the voice whispered. 'You know the way. Walk in.'

The counter girl's mouth was open. 'Jesus,' she said, 'she's gotta be dusted bad ...' She looked at Turner coldly. 'You give it to her?'

'No,' Turner said, 'but she's sick. It'll be okay.' He drank off the black bitter coffee. It seemed to him, just for a second, that he could feel the whole Sprawl breathing, and its breath was old and sick and tired, all up and down the stations from Boston to Atlanta ...

28

Jaylene Slide

'Jesus,' Bobby said to Jackie, 'can't you wrap it up or something?' Jammer's burn filled the office with a smell, like overdone pork, that turned Bobby's stomach.

'You don't bandage a burn,' she said, helping Jammer sit down in his chair. She began to open his desk drawers, one after another. 'You got any painkillers? Derms? Anything?'

Jammer shook his head, his long face slack and pale. 'Maybe. Behind the bar, there's a kit ...'

'Get it!' Jackie snapped. 'Go on!'

'What are you so worried about him for?' Bobby began, hurt by her tone. 'He tried to let those Gothicks in here ...'

'Get the box, asshole! He just got weak for a second, is all. He got scared. Get me that box or you'll need it yourself.'

He darted out into the club and found Beauvoir wiring pink hot dogs of plastic explosive to a yellow plastic box like the control unit for a kid's toy truck. The hot dogs were mashed around the hinges of the doors and on either side of the lock.

'What's that for?' Bobby asked, scrambling over the bar.

'Somebody might want in,' Beauvoir said. 'They do, we'll open it for them.'

Bobby paused to admire the arrangement. 'Why don't you just mash it up against the glass, so it'll blow straight out?'

'Too obvious,' Beauvoir said, straightening up, the yellow detonator in his hands. 'But I'm glad you think about these things. If we try to blow it straight out, some of it blows back in. This way is ... neater.'

Bobby shrugged and ducked behind the bar. There were wire racks filled with plastic sacks of krill wafers, an assortment of abandoned umbrellas, an unabridged dictionary, a woman's blue shoe, a white plastic case with a runny-looking red cross painted on it with nail polish ... He grabbed the case and climbed back over the bar.

'Hey, Jackie ...' he said, putting the first aid kit down beside Jammer's deck.

'Forget it.' She popped the case open and rummaged through its contents. 'Jammer, there's more poppers in here than anything else ...' Jammer smiled weakly. 'Here. These'll do you.' She unrolled a sheet of red derms and began to peel them off the backing, smoothing three across the back of the burnt hand. 'What you need's a local, though.'

'I was thinking,' Jammer said, staring up at Bobby. 'Maybe now's when you can earn yourself a little running time ...'

'How's that?' Bobby asked, eyeing the deck.

'Stands to reason,' Jammer said, 'that whoever's got those jerks outside, they've also got the phones tapped.' Bobby nodded. Beauvoir had said the same thing, when he'd run his plan down to them. 'Well, when Beauvoir and I decided you and I might hit the matrix for a little look-see, I actually had something else in mind.' Jammer showed Bobby his expanse of small white teeth. 'See, I'm in this because I owed Beauvoir and Lucas a favour. But there are people who owe me favours, too, favours that go way back. Favours I never needed to call in.'

'Jammer,' Jackie said, 'you gotta relax. Just sit back. You could go into shock.'

'How's your memory, Bobby? I'm going to run a sequence by you. You practise it on my deck. No power, not jacked.

Okay?' Bobby nodded. 'So dry run this a couple of times. Entrance code. Let you in the back door ...'

'Whose back door?' Bobby spun the black deck around and poised his fingers above the keyboard.

'The Yakuza,' Jammer said.

Jackie was staring at him. 'Hey, what do you—'

'Like I said. It's an old favour. But you know what they say, the Yakuza never forget. Cuts both ways ...' A whiff of singed flesh reached Bobby and he winced.

'How come you didn't mention this to Beauvoir?' Jackie was folding things back into the white case.

'Honey,' Jammer said, 'you'll learn. Some things you teach yourself to remember to forget.'

'Now look,' Bobby said, fixing Jackie with what he hoped was his heaviest look, 'I'm running this. So I don't need your loas, okay, they get on my nerves ...'

'She doesn't call them up,' Beauvoir said, crouching by the office door, the detonator in one hand and the South African riot gun in the other, 'they just *come*. They want to come, they're *there*. Anyway, they like you ...'

Jackie settled the trodes across her forehead. 'Bobby,' she said, 'you'll be fine. Don't worry, just jack.' She'd removed her headscarf. Her hair was cornrowed between neat furrows of shiny brown skin, with antique resistors woven in at random intervals, little cylinders of brown phenolic resin ringed with colour-coded bands of paint.

'When you punch out past the Basketball,' Jammer said to Bobby, 'you wanna dive right three clicks and go for the floor, I mean straight down ...'

'Past the what?'

'Basketball. That's the Dallas–Fort Worth Sunbelt Co-Prosperity Sphere, you wanna get your ass down fast, all the

263

way, then you run how I told you, for about twenty clicks. It's all used car lots and tax accountants down there, but just stand on that mother, okay?' Bobby nodded, grinning. 'Anybody sees you going by, well, that's their lookout. People who jack down there are used to seeing some weird shit anyway ...'

'Man,' Beauvoir said to Bobby, 'get it *on*. I gotta get back to the door ...'

Bobby jacked.

He followed Jammer's instructions, secretly grateful that he could feel Jackie beside him as they plunged down into the workaday depths of cyberspace, the glowing Basketball dwindling above them. The deck was quick, super-slick, and it made him feel fast and strong. He wondered how Jammer had come to have the Yakuza owing him a favour, one he'd never bothered to collect, and a part of him was busily constructing scenarios when they hit the ice.

'Jesus ...' And Jackie was gone. Something had come down between them, something he felt as cold and silence goddam it!' He was frozen, somehow, locked steady. He could still see the matrix, but he couldn't feel his hands.

'Why the hell anybody plug the likes of you into a deck like that? Thing ought to be in a museum, *you* ought to be in grade school.'

'Jackie!' The cry was reflex.

'Man,' said the voice, 'I dunno. It's been a long few days I haven't slept, but you sure don't look like what I was set to catch when you came out of there ... How old are you?'

'Fuck off!' Bobby said. It was all he could think of to say.

The voice began to laugh. 'Ramirez would split his sides at this, you know? He had him a fine sense of the ridiculous. That's one of the things I miss.'

'Who's Ramirez?'

'My partner. Ex. Dead. Very. I was thinking maybe you could tell me how he got that way.'

'Never heard of him,' Bobby said. 'Where's Jackie?'

'Sittin' coldcocked in cyberspace while you answer my questions, wilson. What's your name?'

'B— Count Zero.'

'Sure. Your name!'

'Bobby. Bobby Newmark ...'

Silence. Then: 'Well. Hey. Does make a little sense, then. That was your mother's place I watched those Maas spooks use the rocket on, wasn't it? But I guess you weren't there, or you wouldn't be here. Hold on a sec ...'

A square of cyberspace directly in front of him flipped sickeningly and he found himself in a pale blue graphic that seemed to represent a very spacious apartment, low shapes of furniture sketched in hair-fine lines of blue neon. A woman stood in front of him, a sort of glowing cartoon squiggle of a woman, the face a brown smudge.

'I'm Slide,' the figure said, hands on its hips. 'Jaylene. You don't fuck with me. Nobody in LA,' and she gestured, a window suddenly snapped into existence behind her, 'fucks with me. You got that?'

'Right,' Bobby said. 'What *is* this? I mean, if you could sort of explain ...' He still couldn't move. The 'window' showed a blue-grey video view of palm trees and old buildings.

'How do you mean?'

'This sort of drawing. And you. And that old picture ...'

'Hey, man, I paid a designer an arm and a leg to punch this up for me. This is my space, my construct. This is LA, boy. People here don't do *anything* without jacking. This is where I *entertain!*'

'Oh,' Bobby said, still baffled.

'Your turn. Who's back there, in that sleaze-ass dance hall?'

'Jammer's? Me, Jackie, Beauvoir, Jammer.'

'And where were you headed when I grabbed you?'

Bobby hesitated. 'The Yakuza. Jammer has a code ...'

'What for?' The figure moved forward, an animated sensuous brush-sketch.

'Help.'

'Shit. You're probably telling the truth ...'

'I am, I am, swear to God ...'

'Well, you ain't what I need, Bobby Zero. I been out cruising cyberspace, all up and down, trying to find out who killed my man. I thought it was Maas, because we were taking one of theirs for Hosaka, so I hunted up a spook-team of theirs. First thing I saw was what they did to your momma's condo. Then I saw three of them drop in on a man they call the Finn, but those three never came back out ...'

'Finn killed 'em,' Bobby said. 'I saw 'em. Dead.'

'You did? Well, then, could be we do have things to talk about. After that, I watched the other three use that same launcher on a pimpmobile ...'

'That was Lucas,' he said.

'But no sooner had they done it than a copter overflew 'em and fried all three with a laser. You know anything about that?'

'No.'

'You think you can tell me your story, Bobby Zero? Make it quick!'

'I was gonna do this run, see? And I'd got this icebreaker off Two-a-Day, from up the Projects, and I ...'

When he finished, she was silent. The slinky cartoon figure stood by the window, as though she were studying the television trees.

'I got an idea,' he ventured. 'Maybe you can help us ...'

266

'No,' she said.

'But maybe it'll help you find out what you want ...'

'No. I just want to kill the motherfucker who killed Ramirez.'

'But we're trapped in there, they're gonna kill us. It's Maas, the people you were following around in the matrix! They hired a bunch of Kasuals and Gothicks ...'

'That's not Maas,' she said. 'That's a bunch of Euros over on Park Avenue. Ice on 'em a mile deep.'

Bobby took that in. 'They the ones in the copter, the ones killed the other Maas guys?'

'No. I couldn't get a fix on that copter, and they flew south. Lost 'em. I have a hunch, though ... Anyway, I'm sending you back. You want to try that Yak code, go ahead.'

'But, lady, we need *help* ...'

'No percentage in help, Bobby Zero,' she said, and then he was sitting in front of Jammer's deck, the muscles in his neck and back aching. It took him a while before he could get his eyes to focus, so it was nearly a minute before he saw that there were strangers in the room.

The man was tall, maybe taller than Lucas, but rangier, narrower at the hips. He wore a kind of baggy combat jacket that hung around him in folds, with giant pockets, and his chest was bare except for a horizontal black strap. His eyes looked bruised and feverish, and he held the biggest handgun Bobby had ever seen, a kind of distended revolver with some weird fixture moulded under the barrel, a thing like a cobra's head. Beside him, swaying, stood a girl who might have been Bobby's age, with the same bruised eyes – though hers were dark – and lank brown hair that needed to be washed. She wore a black sweatshirt, several sizes too large, and jeans. The man reached out with his left hand and steadied her.

Bobby stared, then gaped as the memory hit him.

Girl voice, brown hair, dark eyes, the ice eating into him, his teeth burring, her voice, the big thing leaning in ...

'Viv la Vyèj,' Jackie said, beside him, rapt, her hand gripping his shoulder hard, 'the Virgin of Miracles. She's come, Bobby. Danbala has sent her!'

'You were under a while, kid,' the tall man said to Bobby. 'What happened?'

Bobby blinked, glanced frantically around, found Jammer's eyes, glazed with drugs and pain. 'Tell him,' Jammer said.

'I couldn't get to the Yak. Somebody grabbed me, I don't know how ...'

'Who?' The tall man had his arm around the girl now.

'She said her name was Slide. From Los Angeles.'

'Jaylene,' the man said.

The phone on Jammer's desk began to chime.

'Answer it,' the man said.

Bobby turned as Jackie reached over and tapped the callbar below the square screen. The screen lit, flickered, and showed them a man's face, broad and very pale, the eyes hooded and sleepy-looking. His hair was bleached nearly white, and brushed straight back. He had the meanest mouth Bobby had ever seen.

'Turner,' the man said, 'we'd better talk now. You haven't got a lot of time left. I think you should get those people out of the room, for starts ...'

268

29

Boxmaker

The knotted line stretched on and on. At times they came to angles, forks of the tunnel. Here the line would be wrapped around a strut or secured with a fat transparent gob of epoxy. The air was as stale, but colder. When they stopped to rest in a cylindrical chamber, where the shaft widened before a triple branching, Marly asked Jones for the flat little work light he wore across his forehead on a grey elastic strap. Holding it in one of the red suit's gauntlets, she played it over the chamber's wall. The surface was etched with patterns, microscopically fine lines ...

'Put your helmet on,' Jones advised, 'you've got a better light than mine ...'

Marly shuddered. 'No.' She passed him the light. 'Can you help me out of this, please?' She tapped a gauntlet against the suit's hard chest. The mirror-domed helmet was fastened to the suit's waist with a chrome snap-hook.

'You'd best keep it,' Jones said. 'It's the only one in the Place. I've got one, where I sleep, but no air for it. Wig's bottles won't fit my transpirator, and his suit's all holes ...' He shrugged.

'No, please,' she said, struggling with the catch at the suit's waist, where she'd seen Rez twist something. 'I can't stand it ...'

Jones pulled himself half over the line and did something

she couldn't see. There was a click. 'Stretch your arms, over your head,' he said. It was awkward, but finally she floated free, still in the black jeans and white silk blouse she'd worn to that final encounter with Alain. Jones fastened the empty red suit to the line with another of the snap-rings mounted around its waist, and then undid her bulging purse. 'You want this? To take with you, I mean? We could leave it here, get it on our way back ...'

'No,' she said, 'I'll take it. Give it to me ...' She hooked an elbow around the line and fumbled the purse open. Her jacket came out, but so did one of her boots. She managed to get the boot back into the purse, then twisted herself into the jacket.

'That's a nice piece of hide,' Jones said.

'Please,' she said, 'let's hurry.'

'Not far now,' he said, his work light swinging to show her where the line vanished through one of three openings arranged in an equilateral triangle.

'End of the line,' he said. 'Literal, that is.' He tapped the chromed eyebolt where the line was tied in a sailor's knot. His voice caught and echoed, somewhere ahead of them, until she imagined she heard other voices whispering behind the round of echo. 'We'll want a bit of light for this,' he said, kicking himself across the shaft and catching a grey metal coffin-thing that protruded there. He opened it. She watched his hands move in the bright circle of the work light; his fingers were thin and delicate, but the nails were small and blunt, outlined with black, impacted grime. The letters CJ were tattooed in crude blue across the back of his right hand. The sort of tattoo one did oneself, in jail ... Now he'd fished out a length of heavy, insulated wire. He squinted into the box, then wedged the wire behind a copper D-connector.

The dark ahead vanished in a white flood of light.

'Got more power than we need, really,' he said, with something akin to a homeowner's pride. 'The solar banks are all still workin', and they were meant to power the mainframes ... Come on, then, lady, we'll meet the artist you come so far to see ...' He kicked off and out, gliding smoothly through the opening, like a swimmer, into the light. Into the thousand drifting things. She saw that the red plastic soles of his frayed shoes had been patched with smears of white silicon caulking.

And then she'd followed, forgetting her fears, forgetting the nausea and constant vertigo, and she was there. And she understood.

'My God,' she said.

'Not likely,' Jones called. 'Maybe old Wig's, though. Too bad it's not doing it now, though. That's even more of a sight ...'

Something slid past, ten centimetres from her face. An ornate silver spoon, sawn precisely in half, from end to end.

She had no idea how long she'd been there, when the screen lit and began to flicker. Hours, minutes ... She'd already learned to negotiate the chamber, after a fashion, kicking off like Jones from the dome's concavity. Like Jones, she caught herself on the thing's folded, jointed arms, pivoted and clung there, watching the swirl of debris. There were dozens of the arms, manipulators, tipped with pliers, hexdrivers, knives, a subminiature circular saw, a dentist's drill ... They bristled from the alloy thorax of what must once have been a construction remote, the sort of unmanned, semi-autonomous device she knew from childhood videos of the high frontier. But this one was welded into the apex of the dome, its sides fused with the fabric of the Place, and hundreds of cables and optic lines snaked across the geodesics to enter it. Two of

271

the arms, tipped with delicate force-feedback devices, were extended; the soft pads cradled an unfinished box.

Eyes wide, Marly watched the uncounted things swing past. A yellowing kid glove, the faceted crystal stopper from some vial of vanished perfume, an armless doll with a face of French porcelain, a fat, gold-fitted black fountain pen, rectangular segments of perf board, the crumpled red and green snake of a silk cravat ... Endless, the slow swarm, the spinning things ...

Jones tumbled up through the silent storm, laughing, grabbing an arm tipped with a glue gun. 'Always makes me want to laugh, to see it. But the boxes always make me sad ...'

'Yes,' she said, 'they make me sad, too. But there are sadnesses and sadnesses ...'

'Quite right ...' He grinned. 'No way to make it go, though. Guess the spirit has to move it, or anyway that's how old Wig has it. He used to come out here a lot. I think the voices are stronger for him here. But lately they've been talking to him wherever, it seems like ...'

She looked at him through the thicket of manipulators. He was very dirty, very young, with his wide blue eyes under a tangle of brown curls. He wore a stained grey zipsuit, its collar shiny with grime. 'You must be mad,' she said, with something like admiration in her voice, 'you must be totally mad, to stay here ...'

He laughed. 'Wigan's madder than a sack of bugs. Not me.

She smiled. 'No, you're crazy. I'm crazy, too ...'

'Hello then,' he said, looking past her. 'What's this? One of Wig's sermons, looks like, and no way we can shut it off without me cutting the power ...'

She turned her head and saw diagonals of colour strobe across the rectangular face of a large screen glued crookedly to the curve of the dome. The screen was occluded, for a second, by the passage of a dressmaker's dummy, and then the face of Josef Virek filled it, his soft blue eyes glittering behind round lenses.

'Hello, Marly,' he said. 'I can't see you, but I'm sure I know where you are.'

'That's one of Wig's sermon screens,' Jones said, rubbing his face. 'Put 'em up all over the Place, 'cause he figured one day he'd have people up here to preach to. This geezer's linked in through Wig's communication gear, I guess. Who is he?'

'Virek,' she said.

'Thought he was older …'

'It's a generated image,' she said. 'Ray tracing, texture mapping …' She stared as the face smiled out at her from the curve of the dome, beyond the slow-motion hurricane of lost things, minor artifacts of countless lives, tools and toys and gilded buttons.

'I want you to know,' the image said, 'that you have fulfilled your contract. My psychoprofile of Marly Krushkhova predicted your response to my gestalt. Broader profiles indicated that your presence in Paris would force Maas to play their hand. Soon, Marly, I will know exactly what it is that you have found. For four years I've known something that Maas didn't know. I've known that Mitchell, the man Maas and the world regards as the inventor of the new biochip processes, was being fed the concepts that resulted in his breakthroughs. I added you to an intricate array of factors, Marly, and things came to a most satisfying head. Maas, without understanding what they were doing, surrendered the location of the conceptual source. And you have reached it. Paco will be arriving shortly …'

'You said you wouldn't follow,' she said. 'I knew you lied …'

'And now, Marly, at last I think I shall be free. Free of the four hundred kilograms of rioting cells they wall away behind

273

surgical steel in a Stockholm industrial park. Free, eventually, to inhabit any number of real bodies, Marly. Forever.'

'Shit,' Jones said, 'this one's as bad as Wig. What's he think he's talking about?'

'About his jump,' she said, remembering her talk with Andrea, the smell of cooking prawns in the cramped little kitchen. 'The next stage of his evolution ...'

'You understand it?'

'No,' she said, 'but I know that it will be bad, very bad ...' She shook her head.

'Convince the inhabitants of the cores to admit Paco and his crew, Marly,' Virek said. 'I purchased the cores an hour before you departed Orly, from a contractor in Pakistan. A bargain, Marly, a great bargain. Paco will oversee my interests, as usual.'

And then the screen was dark.

'Here now,' Jones said, pivoting around a folded manipulator and taking her hand, 'what's so bad about all that? He owns it now, and he said you'd done your bit ... I don't know what old Wig's good for, except to listen to the voices, but he's not long for this side anyway. Me, I'm as easy for out as not ...'

'You don't understand,' she said. 'You can't. He's found his way to something, something he's sought for years. But nothing he wants can be good. For anyone ... I've seen him, I've felt it ...' And then the steel arm she held vibrated and began to move, the whole turret rotating with a muted hum of servos.

30

Hired Man

Turner stared at Conroy's face on the screen of the office phone.

'Go on,' he said to Angie. 'You go with her.' The tall black girl with the resistors woven into her hair stepped forward and gently put her arm around Mitchell's daughter, crooning something in that same click-infested Creole. The kid in the t-shirt was still gaping at her, his jaw slack.

'Come on, Bobby,' the black girl said. Turner glanced across the desk at the man with the wounded hand, who wore a wrinkled white evening jacket and a bolo tie with thongs of braided black leather. Jammer, Turner decided, the club owner. Jammer cradled his hand in his lap, on a blue-striped towel from the bar. He had a long face, the kind of beard that needed constant shaving, and the hard, narrow eyes of a stone professional. As their eyes met, Turner realised that the man sat well out of the line of the phone's camera, his swivel chair pushed back into a corner.

The kid in the t-shirt, Bobby, shuffled out behind Angie and the black girl, his mouth still open.

'You could've saved us both a lot of hassle, Turner,' Conroy said. 'You could've called me. You could've called your agent in Geneva.'

'How about Hosaka,' Turner said, 'could I have called them?'

Conroy shook his head, slowly.

'Who are you working for, Conroy? You went double on this one, didn't you?'

'But not on you, Turner. If it had gone down the way I planned it, you'd have been in Bogota, with Mitchell. The railgun couldn't fire until the jet was out, and if we cut it right, Hosaka would have figured Maas took the whole sector out to stop Mitchell. But Mitchell didn't make it, did he, Turner?'

'He never planned to,' Turner said.

Conroy nodded. 'Yeah. And the security on the mesa picked up the girl, going out. That's her, isn't it, Mitchell's daughter ...'

Turner was silent.

'Sure,' Conroy said, 'figures ...'

'I killed Lynch,' Turner said, to steer the subject away from Angie. 'But just before the hammer came down, Webber told me she was working for you ...'

'They both were,' Conroy said, 'but neither one knew about the other.' He shrugged.

'What for?'

Conroy smiled. 'Because you'd have missed 'em if they weren't there, wouldn't you? Because you know my style, and if I hadn't been flying all my usual colours, you'd have started to wonder. And I knew you'd never sell out. Mr Instant Loyalty, right? Mr Bushido. You were bankable, Turner. Hosaka knew that. That's why they insisted I bring you in ...'

'You haven't answered my first question, Conroy. Who did you go double for?'

'A man named Virek,' Conroy said. 'The money man. That's right, same one. He'd been trying to buy Mitchell for years. For that matter, he'd been trying to buy Maas. No go. They're getting so rich, he couldn't touch them. There was a standing offer for Mitchell making the rounds. A blind offer. When

Hosaka heard from Mitchell and called me in, I decided to check that offer out. Just out of curiosity. But before I could, Virek's team was on me. It wasn't a hard deal to cut, Turner, believe me.'

'I believe you.'

'But Mitchell fucked us all over, didn't he, Turner? Good and solid.'

'So they killed him.'

'He killed himself,' Conroy said, 'according to Virek's moles on the mesa. As soon as he saw the kid off in that ultralight. Cut his throat with a scalpel ...'

'Lot of dead people around, Conroy,' Turner said. 'Oakey's dead, and the Jap who was flying that copter for you.'

'Figured that when they didn't come back,' Conroy shrugged.

'They were trying to kill us,' Turner said.

'No, man, they just wanted to *talk* ... Anyway, we didn't know about the girl then. We just knew you were gone and that the damn jet hadn't made it to the strip in Bogota. We didn't start thinking about the girl until we took a look at your brother's farm and found the jet. Your brother wouldn't tell Oakey anything. Pissed off 'cause Oakey burned his dogs. Oakey said it looked like a woman had been living there, too, but she didn't turn up ...'

'What about Rudy?'

Conroy's face was a perfect blank. Then he said, 'Oakey got what he needed off the monitors. Then we knew about the girl.'

Turner's back was aching. The holster-strap was cutting into his chest. *I don't feel anything*, he thought, *I don't feel anything at all ...*

'I've got a question for you, Turner. I've got a couple. But the main one is, what the fuck are you doing in there?'

'Heard it was a hot club, Conroy.'

'Yeah. Real exclusive. So exclusive, you had to break up two of my doormen to get in. They knew you were coming, Turner, the spades and that punk. Why else would they let you in?'

'You'll have to work that one out, Connie. You seem to have a lot of access, these days ...'

Conroy leaned closer to his phone's camera. 'You bet your ass. Virek's had people all over the Sprawl for months, feeling out a rumour, cowboy gossip that there was an experimental biosoft floating around. Finally his people focused on the Finn, but another team, a Maas team, turned up, obviously after the same thing. So Virek's team just kicked back and watched the Maas boys, and the Maas boys started blowing people away. So Virek's team picked up on the spades and little Bobby and the whole thing. They laid it all out for me when I told 'em I figured you'd headed this way from Rudy's. When I saw where they were headed, I hired some muscle to ice 'em in there, until I could get somebody I could trust to go in after them ...'

'Those dusters out there?' Turner smiled. 'You just dropped the ball, Conroy. You can't go anywhere for professional help, can you? Somebody's twigged that you doubled, and a lot of pros died, out there. So you're hiring shitheads with funny haircuts ... The pros have all heard you've got Hosaka after your ass, haven't they, Conroy? And they all know what you did.' Turner was grinning now; out of the corner of his eye, he saw that the man in the dinner jacket was smiling, too, a thin smile with lots of neat small teeth, like white grains of corn ...

'It's that bitch Slide,' Conroy said. 'I could've taken her out on the rig ... She punched her way in somewhere and started asking questions. I don't even think she's really on to it, yet, but she's been making sounds in certain circles ... Anyway, yeah, you got the picture. But it doesn't help your ass any, not now. Virek wants the girl. He's pulled his people off the other thing and now I'm running things for him. Money, Turner, money like a zaibatsu ...'

Turner stared at the face, remembering Conroy in the bar of a jungle hotel. Remembering him later, in Los Angeles, making his pass, explaining the covert economics of corporate defection ... 'Hi, Connie,' Turner said, 'I know you, don't I?'

Conroy smiled. 'Sure, baby.'

'And I know the offer. Already. You want the girl.'

'That's right.'

'And the split, Connie. You know I only work fifty-fifty, right?'

'Hey,' Conroy said, 'this is the big one. I wouldn't have it any other way ...'

Turner stared at the man's image.

'Well,' Conroy said, still smiling, 'what do you say?'

And Jammer reached out and pulled the phone's line from the wall-plug. 'Timing,' he said. 'Timing's always important.' He let the plug drop. 'If you'd told him, he'd have moved right away. This way buys us time. He'll try to get back, try to figure what happened.'

'How do you know what I was going to say?'

'Because I seen people. I seen a lot of them, too fucking many. Particularly I seen a lot like you. You got it written across your face, mister, and you were gonna tell him he could eat shit and die.' Jammer hunched his way up in the office chair, grimacing as his hand moved inside the bar towel. 'Who's this Slide he was talking about? A jockey?'

'Jaylene Slide. Los Angeles. Top gun.'

'She was the one hijacked Bobby,' Jammer said. 'So she's damn close to your pal on the phone ...'

'She probably doesn't know it, though.'

'Let's see what we can do about that. Get the boy back in here.'

31

Voices

'I'd better find old Wig,' he said.

She was watching the manipulators, hypnotised by the way they moved; as they picked through the swirl of things, they also caused it, grasping and rejecting, the rejected objects whirling away, striking others, drifting into new alignments. The process stirred them gently, slowly, perpetually.

'I'd better,' he said.

'What?'

'Go find Wig. He might get up to something, if your boss man's people turn up. Don't want him to hurt himself, y'know.' He looked sheepish, vaguely embarrassed.

'Fine,' she said. 'I'm fine, I'll watch.' She remembered the Wig's mad eyes, the craziness she'd felt roll off him in waves; she remembered the ugly cunning she'd sensed in his voice, over the *Sweet Jane*'s radio. Why would Jones show this kind of concern? But then she thought about what it would be like, living in the Place, the dead cores of Tessier-Ashpool. Anything human, anything alive, might come to seem quite precious, here ... 'You're right,' she said. 'Go and find him.' The boy smiled nervously and kicked off, tumbling for the opening where the line was anchored.

'I'll come back for you,' he said. 'Remember where we left your suit ...'

The turret swung back and forth, humming, the manipulators darting, finishing the new poem ...

She was never certain, afterwards, that the voices were real, but eventually she came to feel that they had been a part of one of those situations in which *real* becomes merely another concept.

She'd taken off her jacket, because the air in the dome seemed to have grown warmer, as though the ceaseless movement of the arms generated heat. She'd anchored the jacket and her purse on a strut beside the sermon screen. *The box was nearly finished now*, she thought, although it moved so quickly, in the padded claws, that it was difficult to see ... Abruptly, it floated free, tumbling end over end, and she sprang for it instinctively, caught it, and went tumbling past the flashing arms, her treasure in her arms. Unable to slow herself, she struck the far side of the dome, bruising her shoulder and tearing her blouse. Drifting, stunned, she cradled the box, staring through the rectangle of glass at an arrangement of brown old maps and tarnished mirror. The seas of the cartographers had been cut away, exposing the flaking mirrors, landmasses afloat on dirty silver ... She looked up in time to see a glittering arm snag the floating sleeve of her Brussels jacket. Her purse, half a metre behind it and tumbling gracefully, went next, hooked by a manipulator tipped with an optic sensor and a simple claw.

She watched as her things were drawn into the ceaseless dance of the arms. Minutes later, the jacket came whirling out again. Neat squares and rectangles seemed to have been cut away, and she found herself laughing. She released the box she held. 'Go ahead,' she said. 'I am honoured.' The arms whirled and flashed, and she heard the whine of a tiny saw.

I am honoured I am honoured I am honoured – Echo of

282

her voice in the dome setting up a shifting forest of smaller, partial sounds, and behind them, very faint . . . Voices . . .

'You're here, aren't you?' she called, adding to the ring of sound, ripples and reflections of her fragmented voice.

– Yes, I am here.

'Wigan would say you've always been here, wouldn't he?'

– Yes, but it isn't true. I came to be, here. Once I was not. Once, for a brilliant time, time without duration, I was everywhere as well . . . But the bright time broke. The mirror was flawed. Now I am only one . . . But I have my song, and you have heard it. I sing with these things that float around me, fragments of the family that funded my birth. There are others, but they will not speak to me. Vain, the scattered fragments of myself, like children. Like men. They send me new things, but I prefer the old things. Perhaps I do their bidding. They plot with men, my other selves, and men imagine they are gods . . .

'You are the thing that Virek seeks, aren't you?'

– No. He imagines that he can translate himself, code his personality into my fabric. He yearns to be what I once was. What he might become most resembles the least of my broken selves . . .

'Are you . . . Are you sad?'

– No.

'But your . . . Your songs are sad . . .'

– My songs are of time and distance. The sadness is in you. Watch my arms. There is only the dance. These things you treasure are shells.

'I . . . I knew that. Once.'

But now the sounds were sounds only, no forest of voices behind them to speak as one voice, and she watched the perfect globes of her tears spin out to join forgotten human memories in the dome of the Boxmaker.

'I understand,' she said, some time later, knowing that she spoke now for the comfort of hearing her own voice. She spoke quietly, unwilling to wake that bounce and ripple of sound. 'You are someone else's collage. Your maker is the true artist. Was it the mad daughter? It doesn't matter. Some-one brought the machine here, welded it to the dome, and wired it to the traces of memory. And spilled, somehow, all the worn sad evidence of a family's humanity, and left it all to be stirred, to be sorted by a poet. To be sealed away in boxes. I know of no more extraordinary work than this. No more complex gesture ...' A silver-fitted tortoise shell comb with broken teeth drifted past. She caught it like a fish and dragged the teeth through her hair.

Across the dome, the screen lit, pulsed, and filled with Paco's face. 'The old man refuses to admit us, Marly,' the Spaniard said. 'The other, the vagabond, has hidden him. Señor is most anxious that we enter the cores and secure his property. If you can't convince Ludgate and the other to open their lock, we will be forced to open it ourselves, depressurising the entire structure.' He glanced away from the camera, as though consulting an instrument or a member of his crew. 'You have one hour.'

32

Count Zero

Bobby followed Jackie and the brown-haired girl out of the office. It felt like he'd been in Jammer's for a month, and he'd never get the taste of the place out of his mouth. The stupid little recessed spots staring down from the black ceiling, the fat ultrasuede seats, the round black tables, the carved wooden screens ... Beauvoir was sitting on the bar with the detonator beside him and the South African gun across his grey sharkskin lap.

'How come you let 'em in?' Bobby asked, when Jackie had led the girl to a table.

'Jackie,' Beauvoir said. 'She tranced while you were iced. Legba. Told us the Virgin was on her way up with this guy.'

'Who is he?'

Beauvoir shrugged. 'A merc, he looks like. Soldier for the zaibatsus. Jumped-up street samurai. What happened to you when you were iced?'

He told him about Jaylene Slide.

'LA,' Beauvoir said. 'She'll drill through diamond to get the man who fried her daddy, but a brother needs help, forget it.'

'I'm not a brother.'

'I think you got something there.'

'So I don't get to try to get to the Yakuza?'

'What's Jammer say?'

'Dick. He's in there now, watchin' your merc take a call.'

'A call? Who?'

'Some white guy with a bleach job. Mean-looking.'

Beauvoir looked at Bobby, looked at the door, looked back. 'Legba says sit tight and watch. This is getting random enough already, the Sons of the Neon Chrysanthemum aside ...'

'Beauvoir,' Bobby said, keeping his voice down, 'that girl, she's the one, the one in the matrix, when I tried to run that—'

He nodded, his plastic frames sliding down his nose. 'The Virgin.'

'But what's happening? I mean ...'

'Bobby, my advice to you is just take it like it comes. She's one thing to me, maybe something different to Jackie. To you, she's just a scared kid. Go easy. Don't upset her. She's a long way from home, and we're still a long way from getting out of here.'

'Okay ...' Bobby looked at the floor. 'I'm sorry about Lucas, man. He was ... He was a dude.'

'Go talk to Jackie and the girl,' Beauvoir said. 'I'm watching the door.'

'Okay ...'

He crossed the nightclub carpet to where Jackie sat with the girl. She didn't look like much, and there was only a small part of him that said she was the one. She didn't look up, and he could see that she'd been crying.

'I got grabbed,' he said to Jackie. 'You were flat gone.'

'So were you,' the dancer said. 'Then Legba came to me ...'

'Newmark,' the man called Turner said, from the door to Jammer's office, 'we want to talk to you.'

'Gotta go,' he said, wishing the girl would look up, see the big dude asking for him. 'They want me.'

Jackie squeezed his wrist.

*

286

'Forget the Yakuza,' Jammer said. 'This is more complicated. You're going into the LA grid and locking into a top jock's deck. When Slide grabbed you, she didn't know my deck sussed her number ...'

'She said your deck oughta be in a museum.'

'Shit she knows,' Jammer said. 'I know where she lives, don't I?' He took a hit from his inhaler and put it back on the desk. 'Your problem is, she's written you off. She doesn't wanna hear from you. You gotta get into her and tell her what she wants to know ...'

'What's that?'

'That it was a man named Conroy got her boyfriend offed,' the tall man said, sprawled back in one of Jammer's office chairs with the huge pistol on his lap. 'Conroy. Tell her it was Conroy. Conroy hired those bighairs outside.'

'I'd rather try the Yak,' Bobby said.

'No,' Jammer said, 'this Slide, she'll be on his ass first. The Yak'll measure my favour, check the whole thing out first ... Besides, I thought you were all hot to learn deck ...'

'I'll go with him,' Jackie said, from the door.

They jacked.

She died almost immediately, in the first eight seconds.

He felt it, rode it out to the edge and almost knew it for what it was. He was screaming, spinning, sucked up through the glacial white funnel that had been waiting for them ...

The scale of the thing was impossible, too vast, as though the kind of cybernetic megastructure that represented the whole of a multinational had brought its entire weight to bear on Bobby Newmark and a dancer called Jackie. Impossible ...

But somewhere, on the fringe of consciousness, just as he lost it, there was something ... Something plucking at his sleeve ...

*

He lay on his face on something rough. Opened his eyes. A walk made of round stones, wet with rain. He scrambled up, reeling, and saw the hazy panorama of a strange city, with the sea beyond it. Spires there, a sort of church, mad ribs and spirals of dressed stone ... He turned and saw a huge lizard slithering down an incline, towards him, its jaws wide. He blinked. The lizard's teeth were green-stained ceramic, a slow drool of water lapping over its blue mosaic china lip. The thing was a fountain, its flanks plastered with thousands of fragments of shattered china. He spun around, crazy with the nearness of her death. Ice, ice, and a part of him knew then exactly how close he'd really come, in his mother's living room ...

There were weird curving benches, covered with the same giddy patchwork of broken china, and trees, grass ... A park.

'Extraordinary,' someone said. A man, rising from his seat on one of the serpentine benches. He had a neat brush of grey hair, a tanned face, and round, rimless glasses that magnified his blue eyes. 'You came straight through, didn't you?'

'What is this? Where am I?'

'Park Güell, after a fashion. Barcelona, if you like.'

'You killed Jackie.'

The man frowned. 'I see. I think I see. Still, you shouldn't be here. An accident.'

'Accident? *You killed Jackie!*'

'My systems are overextended today,' the man said, his hands in the pockets of a loose tan overcoat. 'This is really quite extraordinary ...'

'You can't do that shit,' Bobby said, his vision swimming in tears. 'You can't. You can't kill somebody who was just there ...'

'Just where?' The man took off his glasses and began to

288

polish them with a spotless white handkerchief he took from the pocket of his coat.

'Just alive,' Bobby said, taking a step forward.

The man put his glasses back on. 'This has never happened before.'

'You can't.' Closer now.

'This is becoming tedious. Paco!'

'Señor.' Bobby turned at the sound of the child's voice and saw a little boy in a strange stiff suit, with black leather boots that fastened with buttons.

'Remove him.'

'Señor,' the boy said, and bowed stiffly, taking a tiny blue Browning automatic from his dark suit coat. Bobby looked into the dark eyes beneath the glossy forelock and saw a look no child had ever worn. The boy extended the gun, aiming it at Bobby.

'Who are you?' Bobby ignored the gun, but didn't try to get any closer to the man in the overcoat.

The man peered at him. 'Virek. Josef Virek. Most people, I gather, are familiar with my face.'

'Are you on *People of Importance* or something?'

The man blinked, frowning. 'I don't know what you're talking about. Paco, what is this person doing here?'

'An accidental spillover,' the child said, his voice light and beautiful. 'We've engaged the bulk of our system via New York, in an attempt to prevent Angela Mitchell's escape. This one tried to enter the matrix, along with another operator, and encountered our system. We're still attempting to determine how he breached our defences. You are in no danger.' The muzzle of the little Browning was absolutely steady.

And then the sensation of something plucking at his sleeve. Not his sleeve, exactly, but part of his mind, something …

'Señor,' the child said, 'we are experiencing anomalous

289

phenomena in the matrix, possibly as a result of our own current overextension. We strongly suggest that you allow us to sever your links with the construct until we are able to determine the nature of the anomaly.'

The sensation was stronger now. A scratching, at the back of his mind ...

'What?' Virek said. 'And return to the tanks? It hardly seems to warrant that ...'

'There is the possibility of real danger,' the boy said, and now there was an edge in his voice. He moved the barrel of the Browning slightly. 'You,' he said to Bobby, 'lie down upon the cobbles and spread your arms and legs ...'

But Bobby was looking past him, to a bed of flowers, watching as they withered and died, the grass going grey and powdery as he watched, the air above the bed writhing and twisting. The sense of the thing scratching in his head was stronger still, more urgent.

Virek had turned to stare at the dying flowers. 'What is it?'

Bobby closed his eyes and thought of Jackie. There was a sound, and he knew that he was making it. He reached down into himself, the sound still coming, and touched Jammer's deck. *Come!* he screamed, inside himself, neither knowing nor caring what it was that he addressed. *Come now!* He felt something give, a barrier of some kind, and the scratching sensation was gone.

When he opened his eyes, there was something in the bed of dead flowers. He blinked. It seemed to be a cross of plain, white-painted wood; someone had fitted the sleeves of an ancient naval tunic over the horizontal arms, a kind of mould-spotted tailcoat with heavy, fringed epaulettes of tarnished gold braid, rusting buttons, more braid at the cuffs ... A rusted cutlass was propped, hilt up, against the white upright, and beside it was a bottle half filled with clear fluid.

290

The child spun, the little pistol blurring ... And crumpled, folded into himself like a deflating balloon, a balloon sucked away into nothing at all, the Browning clattering to the stone path like a forgotten toy.

'My name,' a voice said, and Bobby wanted to scream when he realised that it came from his own mouth, 'is Samedi, and you have slain my cousin's horse ...'

And Virek was running, the big coat flapping out behind him, down the curving path with its serpentine benches, and Bobby saw that another of the white crosses waited there, just where the path curved to vanish. Then Virek must have seen it, too; he screamed, and Baron Samedi, Lord of Graveyards, the loa whose kingdom was death, leaned in across Barcelona like a cold dark rain.

'What the hell do you want? Who are you?' The voice was familiar, a woman's. Not Jackie's.

'Bobby,' he said, waves of darkness pulsing through him. 'Bobby ...'

'How did you get here?'

'Jammer. He knew. His deck pegged you when you iced me before.' He'd just seen something, something huge ... He couldn't remember ... 'Turner sent me. Conroy. He said tell you Conroy did it. You want Conroy ...' Hearing his own voice as though it were someone else's. He'd been somewhere, and returned, and now he was here, in Jaylene Slide's skeletal neon sketch. On the way back, he'd seen the big thing, the thing that had sucked them up, start to alter and shift, gargantuan blocks of it rotating, merging, taking on new alignments, the entire outline changing ...

'Conroy,' she said. The sexy scrawl leaned by the video window, something in its line expressing a kind of exhaustion, even boredom. 'I thought so.' The video image whited

291

out, formed again as a shot of some ancient stone building. 'Park Avenue. He's up there with all those Euros, clicking away at some new scam.' She sighed. 'Thinks he's safe, see? Wiped Ramirez like a fly, lied to my face, flew off to New York and his new job, and now he thinks he's safe ...' The figure moved, and the image changed again. Now the face of the white-haired man, the man Bobby had seen talking to the big guy, on Jammer's phone, filled the screen. *She's tapped into his line*, Bobby thought ...

'Or not,' Conroy said, the audio cutting in. 'Either way, we've got her. No problem.' *The man looked tired*, Bobby thought, *but on top of it. Tough. Like Turner.*

'I've been watching you, Conroy,' Slide said softly. 'My good friend Bunny, he's been watching you for me. You ain't the only one awake on Park Avenue tonight ...'

'No,' Conroy was saying, 'we can have her in Stockholm for you tomorrow. Absolutely.' He smiled into the camera.

'Kill him, Bunny,' she said. 'Kill 'em all. Punch out the whole goddam floor and the one under it. Now.'

'That's right,' Conroy said, and then something happened, something that shook the camera, blurring his image. 'What is that?' he asked, in a very different voice, and then the screen was blank.

'Burn, motherfucker,' she said.

And Bobby was yanked back into the dark ...

33

Wrack and Whirl

Marly passed the hour adrift in the slow storm, watching the Boxmaker's dance. Paco's threat didn't frighten her, although she had no doubt of his willingness to carry it out. He would carry it out, she was certain. She had no idea what would happen if the lock were breached. They would die. She would die, and Jones, and Wigan Ludgate. Perhaps the contents of the dome would spill out into space, a blossoming cloud of lace and tarnished sterling, marbles and bits of string, brown leaves of old books, to orbit the cores forever. That had the right tone, somehow; the artist who had set the Boxmaker in motion would be pleased ...

The new box gyrated through a round of foam-tipped claws. Discarded rectangular fragments of wood and glass tumbled from the focus of creation, to join the thousand things, and she was lost in it, enchanted, when Jones, wild-eyed, his face filmed with sweat and dirt, heaved up into the dome, trailing the red suit on a lanyard.

'I can't get the Wig into a place I can seal,' he said, 'so this is for you ...' The suit spun up below him and he grabbed for it, frantic.

'I don't want it,' she said, watching the dance.

'Get into it! Now! No time!' His mouth worked, but no sound came. He tried to take her arm.

'No,' she said, evading his hand. 'What about you?'

'Put the goddam suit on!' he roared, waking the deeper range of echo.

'No.'

Behind his head, she saw the screen strobe itself into life, fill with Paco's features.

'Señor is dead,' Paco said, his smooth face expressionless, 'and his various interests are undergoing reorganisation. In the interim, I am required in Stockholm. I am authorised to inform Marly Krushkhova that she is no longer in the employ of the late Josef Virek, nor is she an employee of his estate. Her salary in full is available at any branch of the Bank of France, upon submission of valid identification. The proper tax declarations are on file with the revenue authorities of France and Belgium. Lines of working credit have been invalidated. The former corporate cores of Tessier-Ashpool SA are the property of one of the late Herr Virek's subsidiary entities, and anyone on the premises will be charged with trespass.'

Jones was frozen there, his arm cocked, his hand tensed open to harden the striking edge of his palm.

Paco vanished.

'Are you going to hit me?' she asked.

He relaxed his arm. 'I was about to. Coldcock you and stuff you into this bleeding suit ...' He started to laugh. 'But I'm glad I don't have to now ... Here, look, it's done a new one.'

The new box came tumbling out of the shifting litter of arms. She caught it easily.

The interior, behind the rectangle of glass, was smoothly lined with the sections of leather cut from her jacket. Seven numbered tabs of holofiche stood up from the box's black leather floor like miniature tombstones. The crumpled wrapper from a packet of Gauloise was mounted against black leather at the back, and beside it a black-striped grey matchbook from a brasserie in Napoleon Court.

And that was all.

Later, as she was helping him hunt for Wigan Ludgate in the maze of corridors at the far end of the cores, he paused, gripping a welded handhold, and said, 'You know, the queer thing about those boxes ...'

'Yes?'

'Is that Wig got a damn good price on them, somewhere in New York. Money, I mean. But sometimes other things as well, things that came back up ...'

'What sort of things?'

'Software, I guess it was. He's a secretive old fuck when it comes to what he thinks his voices are telling him to do ... Once, it was something he swore was biosoft, that new stuff ...'

'What did he do with it?'

'He'd download it all into the cores.' Jones shrugged.

'Did he keep it, then?'

'No,' Jones said, 'he'd just toss it into whatever pile of stuff we'd managed to scrounge for our next shipment out. Just jacked it into the cores and then resold it for whatever he could get.'

'Do you know why? What it was about?'

'No,' Jones said, losing interest in his story, 'he'd just say that the Lord moved in strange ways ...' He shrugged. 'He said God likes to talk to Himself ...'

34

A Chain 'Bout Nine Miles Long

He helped Beauvoir carry Jackie out to the stage, where they laid her down in front of a cherry red acoustic drum kit and covered her with an old black topcoat they found in the checkroom, with a velvet collar and years of dust on the shoulders, it had been hanging there so long.

'Map fè jubile mnan,' Beauvoir said, touching the dead girl's forehead with his thumb. He looked up at Turner. 'It is a self-sacrifice,' he translated, and then drew the black coat gently up, covering her face.

'It was fast,' Turner said. He couldn't think of anything else to say.

Beauvoir took a pack of menthol cigarettes from a pocket in his grey robe and lit one with a gold Dunhill. He offered Turner the pack, but Turner shook his head. 'There's a saying in Creole,' Beauvoir said.

'What's that?'

'Evil exists.'

'Hey,' said Bobby Newmark, dully, from where he crouched by the glass doors, eye to the edge of the curtain. 'Musta worked, one way or another ... The Gothicks are starting to leave, looks like most of the Kasuals are already gone ...'

'That's good,' Beauvoir said, gently. 'That's down to you, Count. You did good. Earned your handle.'

Turner looked at the boy. He was still moving through the fog of Jackie's death, he decided. He'd come out from under the trodes screaming, and Beauvoir had slapped him three times, hard, across the face, to stop it. But all he'd said to them, about his run, the run that had cost Jackie her life, was that he'd given Turner's message to Jaylene Slide. Turner watched as Bobby got up stiffly and walked to the bar; he saw the care the boy took not to look at the stage. Had the two been lovers? Partners? Neither seemed likely.

He got up from where he sat, on the edge of the stage, and went back into Jammer's office, pausing to check on the sleeping Angie, who was curled into his gutted parka on the carpet, beneath a table. Jammer was asleep, too, in his chair, his burned hand still on his lap, loosely enveloped in the striped towel. *Tough old mother*, Turner thought, *an old jockey*. The man had plugged his phone back in as soon as Bobby had come off his run, but Conroy had never called back. He wouldn't now, and Turner knew that that meant that Jammer had been right about the speed with which Jaylene would strike, to revenge Ramirez, and that Conroy was almost certainly dead. And now his hired army of suburban bighairs was decamping, according to Bobby ...

Turner went to the phone and punched up the news recap, and settled into a chair to watch. A hydrofoil ferry had collided with a miniature submarine in Macao; the hydrofoil's life-jackets had proven to be substandard, and at least fifteen people were assumed drowned, while the sub, a pleasure craft registered in Dublin, had not yet been located ... Someone had apparently used a recoilless rifle to pump a barrage of incendiary shells into two floors of a Park Avenue coop building, and Fire and Tactical teams were still on the scene; the names of the occupants had not yet been released, and so far no one had taken credit for the act ... (Turner punched

297

this item up a second time ...) Fission Authority research teams at the site of the alleged nuclear explosion in Arizona were insisting that minor levels of radioactivity detected there were far too low to be the result of any known form of tactical warhead ... In Stockholm, the death of Josef Virek, the enormously wealthy art-patron, had been announced, the announcement surfacing amid a flurry of bizarre rumours that Virek had been ill for decades and that his death was the result of some cataclysmic failure in the life-support systems in a heavily guarded private clinic in a Stockholm suburb ... (Turner punched this item past again, and then a third time, frowned, and then shrugged.) For the morning's human interest note, police in a New Jersey suburb said that—

'Turner ...'

He shut the recap off and turned to find Angie in the doorway.

'How you doing, Angie?'

'Okay. I didn't dream.' She hugged the black sweatshirt around her, peered up at him from beneath limp brown bangs. 'Bobby showed me where there's a shower. Sort of a dressing room. I'm going back there soon. My hair's horrible.'

He went over to her and put his hands on her shoulders. 'You've handled this all pretty well. You'll be out of here, soon.'

She shrugged out of his touch. 'Out of here? Where to? Japan?'

'Well, maybe not Japan. Maybe not Hosaka ...'

'She'll go with us,' Beauvoir said, behind her.

'Why would I want to?'

'Because,' Beauvoir said, 'we know who you are. Those dreams of yours are real. You met Bobby in one, and saved his life, cut him loose from black ice. You said, "Why are they doing that to you?" ...'

298

Angie's eyes widened, darted to Turner and back to Beauvoir.

'It's a whole long story,' Beauvoir said, 'and it's open to interpretation. But if you come with me, come back to the Projects, our people can teach you things. We can teach you things we don't understand, but maybe you can ...'

'Why?'

'Because of what's in your head.' Beauvoir nodded solemnly, then shoved the plastic eyeglass frames back up his nose. 'You don't have to stay with us, if you don't want to. In fact, we're only there to serve you ...'

'Serve me?'

'Like I said, it's a long story ... How about it, Mr Turner?'

Turner shrugged. He couldn't think where else she might go, and Maas would certainly pay to either have her back or dead, and Hosaka as well. 'That might be the best way,' he said.

'I want to stay with you,' she said to Turner. 'I liked Jackie, but then she ...'

'Never mind,' Turner said. 'I know.' *I don't know anything*, he screamed silently. 'I'll keep in touch ...' *I'll never see you again*. 'But there's something I'd better tell you, now. Your father's dead.' *He killed himself*. 'The Maas security people killed him; he held them off while you got the ultralight off the mesa.'

'Is that true? That he held them off? I mean, I could feel it, that he was dead, but ...'

'Yes,' Turner said. He took Conroy's black wallet from his pocket, hung the loop around her neck. 'There's a biosoft dossier in there. For when you're older. It doesn't tell the whole story. Remember that. Nothing ever does ...'

*

Bobby was standing by the bar when the big guy walked out of Jammer's office. The big guy crossed to where the girl had been sleeping and picked up his grungy army coat, put it on, then walked to the edge of the stage, where Jackie lay – looking so small – beneath the black coat. The man reached into his own coat and drew out the gun, the huge Smith & Wesson Tactical. He opened the cylinder and extracted the shells, put the shells into his coat pocket, then lay the gun down beside Jackie's body, quiet, so it didn't make a sound at all.

'You did good, Count,' he said, turning to face Bobby, his hands deep in the pockets of his coat.

'Thanks, man.' Bobby felt a surge of pride through his numbness.

'So long, Bobby.' The man crossed to the door and began to try the various locks.

'You want out?' He hurried to the door. 'Here. Jammer showed me. You goin', dude? Where you gonna go?' And then the door was open and Turner was walking away through the deserted stalls.

'I don't know,' he called back to Bobby. 'I've got to buy eighty litres of kerosene first, then I'll think about it …'

Bobby watched until he was gone, down the dead escalator it looked like, then closed the door and relocked it. Looking away from the stage, he crossed Jammer's to the office door and looked in. Angie was crying, her face pressed into Beauvoir's shoulder, and Bobby felt a stab of jealousy that startled him. The phone was cycling, behind Beauvoir, and Bobby saw that it was the news recap.

'Bobby,' Beauvoir said, 'Angela's coming to live with us, up the Projects, for a while. You want to come, too?'

Behind Beauvoir, on the phone screen, the face of Marsha Newmark appeared, Marsha-momma, his mother.

'—ning's human interest note, police in a New Jersey

suburb said that a local woman whose condo was the target of a recent bombing was startled when she returned last night and disco—'

'Yeah,' Bobby said, quickly, 'sure, man.'

35

Tally Isham

'She's good,' the unit director said, two years later, dabbing a crust of brown village bread into the pool of oil at the bottom of his salad bowl. 'Really, she's very good. A quick study. You have to give her that, don't you?'

The star laughed and picked up her glass of chilled retsina. 'You hate her, don't you, Roberts? She's too lucky for you, isn't she? Hasn't made a wrong move yet …' They were leaning on the rough stone balcony, watching the evening boat set out for Athens. Two rooftops below, towards the harbour, the girl lay sprawled on a sun-warmed waterbed, naked, her arms spread out, as though she were embracing whatever was left of the sun.

He popped the oil-soaked crust into his mouth and licked his thin lips. 'Not at all,' he said. 'I don't hate her. Don't think it for a minute.'

'Her boyfriend,' Tally said, as a second figure, male, appeared on the rooftop below. The boy had dark hair and wore loose, casually expensive French sports clothes. As they watched, he crossed to the waterbed and crouched beside the girl, reaching out to touch her. 'She's beautiful, Roberts, isn't she?'

'Well,' the unit director said, 'I've seen her "befores". It's surgery.' He shrugged, his eyes still on the boy.

'If you've seen my "befores",' she said, 'someone will hang for it. But she does have something. Good bones …' She sipped her wine. 'Is she the one? "The new Tally Isham"?'

He shrugged again. 'Look at that little prick,' he said. 'Do you know he's drawing a salary nearly the size of mine, now? And what exactly does he do to earn it? A bodyguard …' His mouth set, thin and sour.

'He keeps her happy.' Tally smiled. 'We got them as a package. It's a rider in her contract. You know that.'

'I loathe that little bastard. He's right off the street and he knows it and he doesn't care. He's trash. Do you know what he carries around in his luggage? A cyberspace deck! We were held up for three hours yesterday, Turkish customs, when they found the damned thing …' He shook his head. The boy stood now, turned, and walked to the edge of the roof. The girl sat up, watching him, brushing her hair back from her eyes. He stood there a long time, staring after the wake of the Athens boats, neither Tally Isham nor the unit director nor Angie knowing that he was seeing a grey sweep of Barrytown condos cresting up into the dark towers of the Projects.

The girl stood, crossed the roof to join him, taking his hand.

'What do we have tomorrow?' Tally asked finally.

'Paris,' he said, taking up his Hermès clipboard from the stone balustrade and flipping automatically through a thin sheaf of yellow printouts. 'The Krushkhova woman.'

'Do I know her?'

'No,' he said. 'It's an art spot. She runs one of their two most fashionable galleries. Not much of a backgrounder, though we do have an interesting hint of scandal, earlier in her career …'

Tally Isham nodded, ignoring him, and watched her understudy put her arm around the boy with the dark hair.

36

The Squirrel Wood

When the boy was seven, Turner took Rudy's old nylon-stocked Winchester and they hiked together along the old road, back up into the clearing.

The clearing was already a special place, because his mother had taken him there the year before and shown him a plane, a real plane, back in the trees. It was settling slowly into the loam there, but you could sit in the cockpit and pretend to fly it. It was secret, his mother said, and he could only tell his father about it and nobody else. If you put your hand on the plane's plastic skin, the skin would eventually change colour, leaving a handprint there, just the colour of your palm ... But his mother had got all funny then, and cried, and wanted to talk about his uncle Rudy, who he didn't remember. Uncle Rudy was one of the things he didn't understand, like some of his father's jokes. Once he'd asked his father why he had red hair, where he'd got it, and his father had just laughed and said he'd got it from the Dutchman. Then his mother threw a pillow at his father, and he never did find out who the Dutchman was.

In the clearing, his father taught him to shoot, setting up lengths of pine against the trunk of a tree. When the boy tired of it, they lay on their backs, watching the squirrels. 'I promised Sally we wouldn't kill anything,' he said, and then explained the basic principles of squirrel hunting. The boy listened, but part of him was daydreaming about the plane. It was hot, and you could hear bees buzzing somewhere close, and water over rocks. When his mother had cried, she'd said that Rudy had been a good man, that he'd saved her life, saved her once from being young and stupid, and once from a real bad man ...

'Is that true?' he asked his father, when his father was through explaining about the squirrels. 'They're just so dumb they'll come back over and over and get shot?'

'Yes,' Turner said, 'it is.' Then he smiled. 'Well, almost always ...'

NEUROMANCER

William Gibson

The novel that launched the cyberpunk generation, inspired the Hollywood blockbuster franchise *The Matrix*, heralded the coming of the internet, and won the Hugo, Nebula and Philip K. Dick awards

The Matrix. A world within a world. A global hallucination experienced daily by billions. It is the graphic representation of every byte of data in cyberspace.

Case was the sharpest data-thief in the business, until his nervous system was crippled by a client he double-crossed. Japanese experts in nerve-splicing and microbionics have left him broke and close to dead.

But at last Case has found a cure. He's going back into the system. Not for the bliss of cyberspace but to steal again. This time from the big boys – the almighty megacorps. The target – an unthinkably powerful artificial intelligence orbiting Earth in service of the sinister Tessier-Ashpool business clan. In return Case will stay cured. But first he needs to survive.

• • •

'A masterpiece that moves faster than the speed of thought and is chilling in its implications' *New York Times*

'"Neuromancer" has inspired technologists from Silicon Valley to Wall Street' *The Sunday Times*

'Gibson is the Raymond Chandler of SF' *Observer*

MONA LISA OVERDRIVE

William Gibson

Book Three in the seminal *Neuromancer* trilogy

The AIs of *Neuromancer* have suffered a traumatic, cataclysmic self-awakening, and now haunt cyberspace. Into this world comes Mona, a young girl with a murky past and an uncertain future. Her life is on a collision course with famous Hollywood stim star, Angie Mitchell. Since childhood, Angie has been able to tap into cyberspace without a computer. The efforts of the studio bosses have kept her in ignorance, forced her to forget. But now she's starting to remember again.

From inside cyberspace, a kidnapping plot is masterminded by a phantom entity who has planes for Mona, Angie and all humanity. Behind the intrigue lurks the shadowy Yakuza. And an impossibly tall and powerful skyscraper of data has appeared on the landscape of the Matrix, attracting the attention of those greedy for money and power.

• • •

'Gibson's most accomplished book to date' *Time Out*

'Another brilliant, gritty, densely textured novel' *Kirkus Reviews*

'A big-budget widescreen diorama of urban decadence and technological anarchy that only the imagination could do justice' *SF Reviews*

BURNING CHROME

William Gibson

A collection of masterful short fiction from the Hugo, Nebula, and Philip K. Dick Award-winning author of *Neuromancer*

Tautly-written and suspenseful, *Burning Chrome* showcases ten of Gibson's best short stories, and features a preface from Bruce Sterling, co-Cyberpunk and editor of the seminal anthology *Mirrorshades*.

These brilliant, high-resolution stories show Gibson's characters and intensely-realised worlds at his absolute best. Lowlife characters, ghosts and hallucinations haunt the malls and plazas of a holographic world of name-branded society, cloned Ninja bodyguards and retro fashions.

• • •

'A fistful of fast, challenging, hot-wired short stories'
New Musical Express

'Furiously inventive, brilliantly written, the cutting edge of SF'
Guardian

'Some subversives are still at work proving that SF can pack its strongest blows into its shortest works . . . He's at his best dealing with the victims of the new, the people burnt out by drugs, computers, huge corporations or the strangeness of space' *Fiction Magazine*

'At once a lament and a critique, these stories show the way SF is being rewired. Gibson, his finger jitteringly on the fast-forward button, shows the direction in which our literature might be headed' *The Times*

ABOUT GOLLANCZ

Gollancz is the oldest SF publishing imprint in the world. Since being founded in 1927 Gollancz has continued to publish a focused selection of bestselling and award-winning authors. The front-list includes **Ben Aaronovitch**, **Joe Abercrombie**, **Charlaine Harris**, **Joanne Harris**, **Joe Hill**, **Alastair Reynolds**, **Patrick Rothfuss**, **Nalini Singh** and **Brandon Sanderson**.

As one of the largest Science Fiction and Fantasy imprints in the UK it is no surprise we have one of the most extensive backlists in the world. Find high quality SF on Gateway written by such authors as **Philip K. Dick**, **Ursula Le Guin**, **Connie Willis**, **Sir Arthur C. Clarke**, **Pat Cadigan**, **Michael Moorcock** and **George R.R. Martin**.

We also have a strand of publishing in translation, which includes French, Polish and Russian authors. Gollancz is home to more award-winning authors than any other imprint, with names including **Aliette de Bodard**, **M. John Harrison**, **Paul McAuley**, **Sarah Pinborough**, **Pierre Pevel**, **Justina Robson** and many more.

The SF Gateway
More than 3,000 classic, rare and previously out-of-print SF novels at your fingertips.
www.sfgateway.com

The Gollancz Blog
Bringing you news from our worlds to yours. Stories, interviews, articles and exclusive extracts just for you!
www.gollancz.co.uk

GOLLANCZ
LONDON